Imperial Smuggler

Decline and Fall of the Galactic Empire

Book 2

Andrew Moriarty

This is a work of fiction.

Names, characters, businesses, places, events and incidents are either the products of the author's imagination or used in a fictitious manner. Any resemblance to actual persons, living or dead, or actual events is purely coincidental.

Special thanks to my dedicated team of beta readers – Michael R, Peter B, Greg D, Dave W, Christopher G, Jolayne W, Haydn H, Skip C, Michael G, Bryan, Scott, Tigui R, Vince, and Alex, and to my editor Samantha Pico.

ISBN: 978-1-956556-14-8

CHAPTER ONE

Gavin punched the Intercom button above the engine room console. "Abort the landing, Skipper. I've got all sorts of failures here. Abort, abort." He held onto the shaking ship with one hand and tapped his flashing red-and-yellow control screens with the other. The intercom speaker hissed and snapped, but no coherent speech emerged.

"Another thing on the fix-it list." He pulled himself up with a grab bar and unlatched the engine room air lock. He ducked sideways as the inner hatch swung open and banged into the stops. Inside the air lock, he pulled the line closed. It took two tries before the hatch seated until he could spin it closed and pop the outer hatch.

"Anybody awake up in the control room?" Gavin radioed, climbing up the ladder in the central tunnel.

The engine room smelled of burned plastic, and hot metal. The smell dissipated as he approached the ship's main living quarters.

First Centurion Anastasios answered, "Is this important, Punk? We're kind of busy up here."

"Why are you answering the comm, Old Man? Where's Dirk? Where's Lee?"

"He's drunk, as is usual during landings. She's doing some navigator thing. We don't have a position, just landmarks. She's looking at pictures of rivers right now."

"Listen, Old Man, external temperature is in the red, the ship feels like we're shaking to bits, and according to the sensors, the landing legs have fallen off."

"Pretty typical landing for Navy, then. And you're not supposed to call me Old Man. Commander Navy's orders, remember?"

"You're not supposed to call me Punk, either."

"Pshaww. Temperature should drop soon as we go lower and slower," Ana said. "And you can suck up the vibration. Why, I remember in the legion—"

"To the Imperial hells with your legion," Gavin said, cutting the connection. He reached the top of the ladder and climbed through the open hatch into the lounge.

Dena, a slim blond woman, sat at the table, pale-faced and sweating.

"Keep the connecting hatch closed during landings," Gavin said, holding onto a table.

The room smelled like twice-microwaved potatoes with a side of vomit.

"I hate spaceships. And you," Dena said. She licked her lips and clutched a bag.

"If we have a hull breach while landing, and the hatch is open, we could all die."

"I already feel like I'm dying. It's just not happening fast enough." After a repulsive gulp, Dena spewed vomit into the bag.

"Make sure you put that in the biological recycling," Gavin said.

Dena cursed him between retches. Gavin couldn't make it out, but it didn't sound complimentary. She wiped vomit off her chin.

"Not your best look," Gavin said. "Bet you miss that miserable planet you grew up on now."

"I'm miserable right now, but this will be over in a few minutes. But boring dead-end planets last forever. If I stayed there, I might as well be dead."

"Might be able to help you with that, if we keep on with this landing," Gavin said.

He resumed his climb. With the main engines firing, downward was toward the ship's rear, so he had to pull himself up against the acceleration. He reached the control room hatch—the open control room hatch—and pulled himself through. Sweat and hot electronics replaced the food-vomit stench.

Scruggs, the youngest of their crew members, sat at a smaller console in front of him. "Recruit Scruggs, you forgot to dog the hatches shut again."

Scruggs didn't look up. "It's Private Scruggs now, Engineer. And that's on Dena's checklist, not mine. I'm responsible for making sure that the sensors, landing gear, and thrusters are pulled back in their bays. She has internal controls." She pointed at her course plot. "Centurion, why did we change course here?"

"Navy there"—Senior Centurion Ana pointed at the sweating pilot seated at the front left console—"saw those mountains coming closer and realized that somebody could put a missile there, so he swung away to stay out of range. Really, he didn't think it, he just reacted. He may be a drunk, but the Imperial Navy trained him well."

"Pilot Dirk is not a drunk," Lee, the navigator and fourth member of the control room crew, said. "He just needs something to relax him before he lands."

"Isn't that his girlfriend back there, Ms. Sexy Pant's job to do that?" Ana said.

"She is not his girlfriend. They're just space friends," Lee said.

Ana laughed. "Space friends? Is that what the kids are calling it now? I like that."

"I've located the river," Lee said. "Pilot Dirk, turn twenty-two degrees spinward, and we'll be lined up on it."

The ship tilted, turned, then settled on its new course.

"Does nobody care that all the sensors say that we're going to crash when we land, shake to bits, and burn up in the atmosphere?" Gavin asked.

"I thought that's why we crank those Empire-dammed covers over the trusses and containers," Ana said, "To make everything streamlined."

"Landing legs aren't in," Gavin said," We're going to crash."

"Absolutely no chance of that happening," Ana said. "No way we'll crash when we land."

"They teach you all about landings in the Army, Centurion?" Gavin asked.

"Not a thing. But I'm not worried about crashing," Ana said.

"Why not, Centurion?" Scruggs asked.

Ana tapped his console, which mirrored onto hers, and pointed to a red warning message. "Because, on this course, we'll burn up in a fiery explosion long before we land."

The vote against a fiery explosion was brief and unanimous. To drop speed, Lee instructed Dirk to temporarily cut the main engines, and the ship would glide into the ground.

"The landing gear might not deploy when we land," Gavin said.

"Another maintenance failure on your part," Ana said. "I have to say, the engineering department isn't keeping up to speed here. Perhaps we should acquire a more experienced engineer."

"Good idea, Centurion," Gavin said. "We'll just head up to the nearest Imperial recruiting station and post an ad for one. Think the fake personal IDs you provided will hold there?"

"Probably as well as your fake ship ID will," Ana said. "Why won't the landing gear deploy?"

"The shield over it might have retracted while we were in reentry. If it's open to space, the heat might damage it or cause it to freeze."

"By 'retracted,' do you mean, 'broke open'?" Ana said. "Are the landing legs deployed?"

"They could be," Gavin said.

"I checked on the board, like you showed me," Scruggs said. "It showed the landing legs cranked in. And I went down and manually gave each one three cranks. Just like the list said."

"She did. I double-checked it," Ana said. "As wearying as I find the lot of you sometimes, I have no plans to die in a bizarre reentry accident. When I die, I'm going to die with a weapon in my hand. Preferably a bayonet."

Scruggs beamed. "Sounds romantic."

"It sounds like you'll be trying to push your own intestines back in after somebody cuts your stomach open. That's what it sounds like," Gavin said. "Stop listening to Dena or reading any of her novels."

"I like her novels," Scruggs said. "I don't trust her, but her novels are good."

"Great sex scenes in them," Ana said. "Ms. Sexy Pants knows how to pick them."

Scruggs blushed, and Gavin blinked. "Centurion?"

"I'm old, not dead," Ana said. "That girl's a grade-A opportunistic, self-absorbed narcissist in my opinion, but if those books are any indication, she knows her way around a bedroom."

"I'm right here, you Imperial anuses," Dena called over from the lounge. "I can hear you."

"Good," Ana said. "I won't have to shout, then." He looked at Gavin. "Sensors show the gear is locked up. What do you want us to do?"

"For about five minutes, the sensors showed the loss of the heat shield over the starboard forward-landing legs," Gavin said.

Ana wiped sweat from his face. "For about five minutes? What does it show now?"

"The, uh . . . the whole array is down. None of my port side external sensors are reporting. Everything is down."

"Everything can't be down. It's the monitoring program, isn't it?"

"That stupid software upgrade in port reset everything. Things keep going offline all the time for no reason and saying they're broken when they're not, but . . ."

"But we can't just assume that the heat shield is there or that the landing legs will deploy." Ana nodded, leaning toward the navigator. "Lee, can you put us down gently when we land?"

"No."

"No? Just no?"

"We've only got landmarks, not a course, and not all of them." She gestured to the screen. Dark green jungles cloaked Planet Postatis, bisected by river systems that drained into shallow seas. "I'm in contact with the ground. We're given a landmark like a river fork, then told to overfly it. Then we get a new course and another landmark. I can't predict how fast or how hard we'll be going when they tell us to drop."

"Professional smugglers, then," Ana said. "They have agents to watch us as we go over, make sure we are who we say we are, and all the turns will force any customs ship shadowing us to be evident. Makes sure we're all alone at the rendezvous."

Gavin clutched a grab bar as the ship rolled left, then back, and wiped sweat from his forehead with his free hand. "Good thing that we have a professional smuggler along on our first trip."

"Professional smuggler chaser," Ana said. "And since it's your contacts that got us this cargo, I think you're the professional smuggler. But professional doesn't necessarily mean competent."

"Think what you like, but I got us a good price on our goods," Gavin said.

"But silk?"

"The planetary government tariffs luxuries at the spaceport."

"Good thing we're not landing in the spaceport, then," Ana said. He unbuckled his harness and clung to a grab bar as Dirk swung the ship along another tight curve. "Private, you're with me."

"What are we doing, Centurion?" Scruggs asked.

"Going to hand-crank some landing gear down. Solve the engineer's problem. Save the ship and crew."

"Outstanding," Scruggs said.

"Main engine's back on in ten," Lee said over the intercom.

"We're going to manually crank the landing gear down," Ana said. "I've seen a half dozen rivers on the displays. They must want us down soon."

"Deploying the struts will increase the turbulence," Lee said. "It will get bumpy."

The ship pivoted right before swaying.

"How will we tell the difference?" Ana asked.

"Get more bumpy," Lee said.

***

Gavin unbolted a panel on the starboard side of the main air lock. He flipped it up, exposing a set of gears with a handle on them. "Specs say three hundred turns to deploy the struts. I'll open the port panel. Then I'll go and check the displays in engineering." He moved to the starboard side and loosened another set of bolts.

"Private, give fifty, then let me take over," Ana said.

Scruggs crouched and sat in the open hatch, using one hand to grasp the handle and the other to steady herself. The ship swayed as she cranked the struts out.

"Forty-eight, forty-nine, fifty," Ana said. "My turn. You count."

They switched till he hit one hundred, then switched again as necessary. It was tight, and the cranking resistance increased as they pushed the struts into the airstream. His hand slipped as sweat dripped on the handle. Gavin flipped the starboard panel open and slid back to engineering. The ship continued swaying as the extended landing gear heightened the drag.

After two hundred fifty cranks, they swapped again, and Ana got in twenty more before the handle locked. He strained, but it didn't move.

Scruggs punched the bonging intercom. "Scruggs."

"Starboard landing gear shows green now."

"Centurion can't turn the crank any farther."

"Go to port now," Gavin said.

Scruggs and Ana switched sides and repeated their turning and counting. Scruggs took over after two hundred, then got up to two forty when the crank held.

"Centurion?" Scruggs asked.

"Give it a push," Ana said.

Scruggs leaned into the crank before it snapped forward and spun freely.

"Either the gear is down or something just broke," Ana said. He reached for the intercom. "Gavin, we got to two forty, and now, it's just spinning. What's your status?"

"No report on those sensors," Gavin said. "I can't tell."

Lee's voice broke into the intercom. "Got our final checkpoint. We're landing in less than a minute."

"As slow as you can," Ana said. "The gear might not be down."

"I can see it in the cameras," Lee said. "It looks down."

"It might not be locked," Ana said.

"Well, lock it, then. We need to land."

"Emperor's testicles. What do you think we were doing back here, Praetorian?" Ana asked. "Jacking up a ground car?"

"I'm not a Praetorian right now. I'm on leave. Landing in twenty seconds."

"Private, crank that as fast as you can to three hundred fifty, then strap in. Go go go." Scruggs whirled the handle, counting out loud. Ana crawled forward and strapped into his console.

"Centurion, the panels," Scruggs yelled.

"Emperor's testicles to the panels. Get up here and strap in."

Lee had put the forward cameras on the main screens. Green-bordered rivers flashed below. A homing signal beeped as they approached. The ship approached a hill the river forked around. One-third of the way up, the trees ended, and vines shrouded the hill. The audio changed to the constant tone of a landing beacon.

Dirk pushed the ship down. They cleared the last trees, crashed through sparse vegetation, then touched down.

"Too fast, too fast," Lee yelled as the skids hit the vines.

The ship slid along the greenery and up the hill, nearly halting as it crested the top.

"Well," Ana said, "that was another outstanding Navy landing, brought to us by the—whoa—"

The ship finally crested the hill, slid to the other side, and accelerated.

"Hang on," Lee said.

"We're down," Dirk said, speaking his first words since leaving orbit.

"We're sliding," Lee said as they tilted forward and skidded down.

They ripped through the vines and rolled toward a soft, sandy beach. The river widened into a green algae-covered lake.

"Going into that lake," Ana said.

"Are we down?" Gavin asked over the intercom. "Why are we moving?"

"We're dirtside," Ana said. "Just sliding."

"Lake coming up," Lee said.

The ship slid farther and faster down the slope but slowed as they dug into the sand before continuing out into the water. An alarm flashed on the screens.

"Rocks, rocks under the water," Lee said. "Pilot Dirk, watch out."

Dirk folded his hands on his lap and regarded her. "What would you have me do, Navigator? Take off into the rocks?"

They slid into the water and scraped up and over the first rock. The ship tilted sideways, then upright, then slapped back down with a crash and a surge of vaporized water. Then they smacked to a halt as the struts impacted another rock.

Everybody slammed forward, whiplashed by their harness belts.

"Foofh," Ana said, regaining his breath. "As I was saying, another fine Navy landing."

"Are we done?" Gavin asked again.

"Look out the window, Engineer? Do you see space out there?"

"I see a lake. A big green lake covering the side hatches."

"But not the dorsal one," Ana said. "Private, get our weapons up here. We'll go up top and check things out."

"Be careful, please, Centurion," Lee said. "They'll be armed, but this group doesn't have a reputation for violence."

"According to the engineer, they don't," Ana said.

Lee frowned at him. "Don't start anything. We need this money."

"Too true," Ana agreed. "I won't start anything." Scruggs arrived with a rifle and a shotgun, then took the rifle. "But if anything starts, we'll finish it."

Gavin called over the intercom. "Looks like landing struts are holding. Dorsal hatch will be clear of the water. All the others could be partially under."

"What about the goods?" Ana asked.

"As long as the containers kept integrity, they'll be fine. The important one, the one full of the silk, should be just above water level."

"Good," Ana said.

Metal ground in the background, and the ship tilted left.

"What's that sound?" Lee asked.

"Sounds like metal bending," Ana said.

The grinding turned into a screech, and the ship dropped eight feet on the left side, throwing everybody into the bulkheads. They pulled themselves upright, and water gurgled.

"Now what's that sound?" Lee said.

"Water filling a container, fast," Ana said.

They held onto the wall and waited. The gurgling reached a crescendo, then died out, shifting focus to the waves slapping the hull.

Scruggs looked around. "Is water bad for silk?"

"Only if we want to sell it," Ana said.

CHAPTER TWO

Devin, the Lord Lyon and Imperial Tribune, slashed at the armored figure in front of him. His gladius sliced in, then slid off. He stepped forward, but his foot slipped on the waxed floor. He dropped to one knee, recovered, and rolled to the side. After jumping to his feet, he stepped back and screamed his war cry. "God and the Emperor!" He pushed forward and hacked at the shoulder—the armor splintered. He hacked again and again. Another hack at the bare shoulder. The sword stuck, and he drew it back in a long cut. The figure remained upright, so he rocked onto his back foot, extended his right arm back, and swung forward at the neck with all his strength.

He cut the head cleanly off. It popped up, bounced off the roof, then smashed into the floor, breaking up into a shower of splinters.

He dropped his sword hand and struggled to catch his breath. The wooden exercise dummy ahead of him tipped over and fell. The head was snapped off, one arm was missing, and chunks of wood were stripped from the torso.

Devin sheathed his sword and placed his hands on his knees. He stood until he wasn't gasping. A uniformed figure stamped to attention in front of him.

"Can I help you, Bosun McSanchez?" Devin said.

"Do you need another training dummy, sir?" the bosun said, glancing around. "You appear to have used this one up."

Devin eyed the piles of splintered wood. "Sorry about the mess. Can you have someone clean this up?"

"I'll take care of it myself, Tribune."

"Bosuns don't clean up piles of trash," Devin said.

"With respect, sir, when the trash is planet-grown solid hardwood, they do. I keep all those shavings for my carvings. Myself and some of the others. We have a carving group."

"You carve, Bosun?" Devin wiped his forehead with his wrist.

"For years, sir."

"What do you do with them—the carvings, I mean—when you're done."

"Sell 'em on planet, sir."

"Oh, well, I suppose that's acceptable," Devin said. "It's scrap wood, after all." He frowned. "Kind of commercial, isn't it?"

McSanchez smiled. "Nothing dishonorable, sir. Our carving's not all that great. The value is in that it's made of wood. We get good money for wood. After materials and tools, all the profits go to the NCO's hardship account, the one we use for helping the troops with issues. Family problems, disasters, that sort of thing."

Devin nodded. "Of course you're not profiting by this. It was wrong of me to suggest that." He mopped his brow with his sleeve again. "When we're done here, go to my clerk. From now on, when one of you sells a carving, I'll match the selling price with a donation to the fund."

"Could be substantial, sir. Some of the folks are good carvers. Spacer Witsend, hers sell for hundreds of credits, and she carves a lot."

"I can afford it. See to it."

"Sir," McSanchez said.

Devin looked around. The training room was packed, as it usually was on the Pollux. Devin insisted all of his crew, not just the Marines, train with hand weapons three times a week. They could pick whatever weapon they wanted, but they had to practice.

Everyone in the room stared at him, and when his gaze swept them, they returned to their sparring and slashing and smacking. Devin rounded on the nearest lieutenant. "Training going well, Lieutenant?"

The lieutenant stiffened. "Very well. Thank you, sir."

"And yet, you felt it necessary to stop to watch a lazy, overweight, senior officer hack at a standing target."

The lieutenant saluted across his chest, remaining silent.

"They weren't looking at you, sir," McSanchez said. "They were all looking at the sword. You don't normally bring it out, and they're curious."

Devin unsheathed the sword and twirled it in his hand. He raised his eyebrows at the silent lieutenant, who nodded once. Devin twirled the sword again until it was hilt forward and offered it to him. "Try it out."

"Are you sure, sir?" The lieutenant reached for it. "Is it real?"

"We believe so. The family has a provenience for it. The pattern and the composition match all historical records."

The lieutenant grasped the hilt and held the sword up. The blade was two feet long, a shade over two inches wide, straight edged, with the last three inches running to a point. The hilt was small, the guard tiny. "It's a real Roman Gladius? From Old Earth?"

"Mainz pattern," Devin said. "Found near a place called Trier. The sword is original. The hilt and wrapping is a more recent addition. The original would have been leather or wood and rotted away long ago."

The lieutenant twisted it. The overhead lights shone on the edge and reflected on his face. "How old is it, sir?"

"Hard to say. Thousands of years, at least. You can't carbon date metal, so we can't be exact. But it's been in my family since before the founding of the Empire. I've been told it's one of the three oldest in the Empire, which makes sense because my great-great-great-great-great-grandfather was wearing it during the very first Imperial senate meeting."

"This sword could have been held by one of Julius Caesar's centurions at the battle of Alesia," the lieutenant said.

"More likely it was held by a fussy, middle-aged headquarters optio, named Corruptus Maximus, who lurked around the fort at Trier, cheating on his accounts and selling army equipment at a discount out the back door."

The lieutenant gave back the sword. "Thank you for letting me hold it, sir. It's an honor."

"You'd think it was less of an honor if you had to oil it every day like I must," Devin said. "But you are welcome. Return to your training."

The lieutenant saluted and stepped back. Devin turned to the bosun, who had somehow acquired a gym towel without Devin noticing. He accepted it with a thanks.

"I don't think the ell-tee would mind oiling that sword every day if you asked, Tribune."

"If I didn't use it so often, I wouldn't have to oil it so often."

"Practice is good for the troops, sir."

"Even for fat, older Tribunes?"

"Especially Tribunes, sir. They need it the most."

Devin laughed. "But you didn't come here to watch a lazy, overweight officer's unskilled slashes, either, did you, Bosun?"

"You're not lazy, sir."

"Not lazy? What about my weight?"

"It's well known that the tribune employs an exceptionally skilled cook, sir. It would be an Imperial shame to not take advantage of it. But, yes, sir, your visitors are here. They say they've come all the way from the capital."

"Long trip."

"They also said, and I quote, 'Please tell the captain that it would be a mistake to keep Internal Security waiting.'"

"They say that, do they? Well, in that case"—Devin tossed his damp towel in the cleaning bin—"in that case, I'll make them wait even longer."

After a cool-down stretch and a shower, Devin returned to his office. At the touch of the entry button, the door dragged open. Two figures sat in chairs in front of his desk, then stood and faced him as he walked in. The woman was tall, had curly hair and a muscular build. She wore a cropped jacket made of what looked like real leather, with matching ankle boots over a fitted skin suit. The effect was both stylish and sexy. The man was a male version—form fitting skin suit, a day-old scruffy beard, and his own leather jacket.

"Lieutenant Weeks," the man said. "And this is Lieutenant Hernandez." He extended his hand.

Devin walked around them and sat. "Normally, junior officers salute their seniors."

"We discourage that in Internal Security," Weeks said. "Too easy to fall into the habit and mess up undercover. And we're not in uniform, either."

"Next time you're here, then, make sure you're in uniform," Devin said. "And render proper respect."

"We come direct from Internal Security," Hernandez said. "We have orders for you."

"I don't care where you come from," Devin said, extending his hand. "You hand-carried orders? Give them to me."

Hernandez scanned the office. "Is it just us?"

"Just us," Devin said.

"Where's your security?" she asked. "Imperial Nobles always have security."

"I keep none in my office."

"We could be killers. Assassins."

Devin leaned back and rubbed his head. "I am armed. I can defend myself. Admittedly not well, given how tired I am, when all I have is my sword."

"You'd stop an assassination with a sword?" Weeks said.

Devin pulled his gladius out and laid it on the desk. "I've probably killed more people with this sword than this ship has with its main batteries. And, yes, I'll defend myself with it."

"You think you could take us?" Hernandez asked. "With a sword. Both of us? We're armed."

Devin looked her up and down, noting her allure. "It would be interesting to try."

"Want to?" She smiled and cocked a hip.

Devin grinned back. "If I were younger, I'd ask you out to dinner on the strength of just that comment."

"Your security is hopeless," Weeks said. "We weren't even searched or scanned. We brought our sidearms right in without being challenged."

"My security is wonderful. You've been scanned multiple times since arriving. You both have standard officers' sidearms in shoulder holsters but loaded with special armored slugs designed to penetrate regular walls but not pressure bulkheads. You, young lady, have a knife in your left boot, and Officer Scruff has what looks like a garrote in his right pocket. Try the access door."

Hernandez got up and pulled the door handle. She yanked it, then thumped it. "Not a regular door. Armored?"

"Just steel but four centimeters of it."

She stomped. "No vibrations. Steel decks?"

"Walls, too. You're inside an armored box. You'll need heavy weapons to get out. And there are no crew-served weapons in these quarters. Just what you brought in."

"We could still kill you," Weeks said.

"Of course you could. But you'll never get out alive."

"What if we didn't want to?"

Devin got up and walked to his sideboard, then poured himself a drink. "You'd be surprised how little I care about what you want." He took a slug of his drink. "It's almost impossible to stop a fanatic who doesn't care if they live or die.

But regular killers pause when they realize they can't escape."

"But you'd still be dead." He waved at Devin's glass. "Drinking in front of guests and not offering them something is rude."

"You're not guests. You're just jumped-up security guards."

"Even security guards can kill you."

"I serve the Empire. There are lots of ways that I could die. That's just another one. Give me my orders." Devin extended his hand again.

Weeks crossed his arms. "We come directly from Internal Security."

"You said that before. It's boring, and why do I care?"

"You should be nervous. You're not nervous enough."

"To the Imperial hells with Internal Security," Devin said. "They're just a bunch of tabbo-sucking time servers."

"You've taken an Imperial frigate and been lollygagging around the edge of the Empire for the last few months, on some sort of private vendetta. And now Internal Security is here to speak to you. You should be petrified," Weeks said.

"I have nothing to hide. I serve the Empire."

"The Empire, in the person of Naval Intelligence, is recalling you. Personally."

"Naval Intelligence, in the person of the two of you, can kiss my hairy Imperial anus."

Hernandez and Weeks looked at each other. Hernandez grinned. "You're not what we expected, Tribune."

"What did you expect?"

"Somebody more . . . accommodating."

"Go back to the core, then. I hear they're more accommodating there."

Weeks produced an order chip and extended his hand. "Tribune, you're being recalled. You're to accompany us immediately coreward on board the first official transport."

"No." Devin stood. "You've done your job. I have my orders. You can go now."

"Not without you." Weeks put the order chip on Devin's desk.

Devin stepped back to the desk and pocketed the chip. After walking around the desk and leaning against the wall, he stirred his drink with his finger. "Let me explain things to you. To both of you, Officer Scruff and Officer Tight-Jacket. First, you can try to kill me. You may well succeed. I'm older and slower than I used to be. But you won't get out of here alive. My staff monitors the video feed, and they have strict orders to let nobody leave without my permission. They've stopped people before. You lack the weapons to force your departure. So, if you want to kill me, get on with it, but know it's a suicide mission." Devin pulled the order chip out of his pocket and tossed it within his hand. "Second, the only way I'm going back to the core systems is if the Emperor himself drops into that chair, gives me a bottle of good whiskey, and personally orders me back. And I know that will never happen."

"You don't think the Emperor will ever order you home?"

"No, I think he has horrible taste in whiskey. He's only ever offered me something lousy, and if I'm going to go all that distance, I demand something decent to drink." Devin finished his drink and put the cup on the sideboard. "Your move."

Weeks extended his hand.

"What?" Devin asked.

"May I have that chip, Tribune, if you aren't going to follow those orders?"

Devin tossed it to him. Weeks reached into his other pocket and produced a different chip, which he tossed on the desk. "We were briefed on a number of possibilities. Here is an alternate one."

"And where am I supposed to accompany you for this one?" Devin asked.

Hernandez and Weeks stood. "Nowhere," Hernandez said. "You are released from regular duties and assigned to assist Naval Intelligence. They have a number of special missions for you, detailed there. Very specific special missions. They won't take long, but after, you'll have to loiter near the frontier for the next few months—possibly longer—until they play out. Other than those specific missions assigned by Naval Intelligence, you'll be free to pursue any . . . private issues in your spare time."

"Private issues?"

"The name Dirk Friedel was mentioned to us. We understand you're supposed to kill him."

"Who told you that?"

"Lady Crystal Belt."

"She would say that."

"She did say that. Repeatedly."

"Is that part of my orders?" Devin asked.

"You'll have to read them and see," Hernandez said. "We'll be leaving now."

"Always glad to be of service to Internal Security," Devin said.

"But you may be seeing us later, just not in the guise you think. It's all in there. Good luck, Tribune."

They walked to the door. Weeks pushed the button, but the door didn't move. The two officers turned to Devin. Devin turned to the ceiling and made a hand gesture. The doors ground open.

Weeks and Hernandez faced the open door. Six armored Marines stood, pointing weapons at them. Two more were prone on the floor. One hovered behind them with a black tube.

Hernandez peeked around to see it. "Grenade launcher?"

"If the hand gestures weren't correct, he fires it in as the door slides. Kills everybody in here," Devin said. "No mess outside my quarters, no external fires, no risk for my troops."

Hernandez nodded. "Well done." She smiled at Devin again. "We're on station for another two days. Perhaps you would reconsider that dinner invitation?"

Andrew Moriarty

CHAPTER THREE

"This water is colder than it looks," Lee said. "The air is so hot here, you'd expect the river to be warmer." She splashed back from the half-submerged bent container and swung her hammer. It broke the pin holding a locking chain. "That's one."

"And one more to go." Gavin kicked the river water, bent over, cupped a handful of it, and tasted it. He spat it out. "It's not a river, it's an ocean. A bay, maybe. This is salt water." He coughed, then retched it out. "Very foul-tasting salt water."

The ship had slid down the hill and rested in the shallows. The water was twenty meters wide and perhaps two meters deep in the middle, shallower near the banks. Off in the distance, it widened, perhaps to become a bay. The Heart's Desire sat in the shallows but had tipped over to the side far enough that the hatches and bottom containers on that side were underwater. River rocks had cracked the front container of silks, and the waves lapped in and out. The bottom and sides were stained green, and water dripped off.

"Ouch," Lee said. She reached into the muddy water and lifted a sharp rock. "Stupid river rocks. Don't drink any more. All this algae can't be good for you." She stripped the tangled vines from the bottom of the container, then swung her hammer at the last chain. The pin moved, then the chain dropped off. "What's holding it now?"

"No idea. It's jammed in there. We'll have to rock the ship or something."

"Company coming," Ana yelled from the top of the ship.

"Dangerous?" Gavin yelled.

"Doesn't look like it. Just two people on a raft. I'm sending Scruggs down."

"Why not you?"

"First, I'm better with the rifle than she is, and I can see quite a distance here. Second, she's got the shotgun, and that's better at close range. Third, she's a pretty woman in a tight skin suit, and that will be distracting."

"I'm not good enough?" Lee yelled.

"Jovians aren't to everyone's taste."

"What if they were women?" Lee yelled. "What, then?"

"I'm right here," Gavin said. "I'd charm the women."

"I'd send Navy out," Ana yelled. "He's a pretty boy."

Lee laughed. Gavin scowled. Scruggs climbed down the shipside ladder and dropped into the river. She sank to her knees but kept the shotgun pointed across her chest. "Centurion says I'm to watch, and if I see any weapons come out, point

17

the shotgun at them. If they point any at you, I'm supposed to start shooting."

"He would say that," Gavin said. "I don't suppose you'd be willing to try to talk our way out of things."

"I'm not part of the talking group," Scruggs said. "I'm part of the shooting group."

"And it doesn't bother you, shooting people?" Gavin asked.

Scruggs looked at him. "Should it?"

"Never mind, Sister Scruggs," Lee said. "Who's the more attractive man—Engineer three Gavin or Pilot Dirk?"

Scruggs blushed and stuttered.

"No problem shooting strangers, but ask her about men, and she clams up," Gavin said.

"That's different," Scruggs said.

"How?" Lee asked. "Sleeping together is natural."

"Speaking of sleeping together," Gavin said, "how is your project going? The one where you have to sleep with ten men before you marry?"

"You need to sleep with ten men? Why?" Scruggs asked.

"I am making progress, but perhaps not as fast as I should," Lee said.

"Why do you—" Scruggs said.

"Heads up down there," Ana yelled. "Inbound."

The three crew members turned toward a barge that had been put-putting around the river bend from upstream. It was a flat metal raft with about a foot of freeboard and no bulwarks. A five meter-long tug pushed it from behind. Greasy woodsmoke poured from the stack. The bows were raised and reinforced for pushing, a bridge high enough to see over any containers piled on the raft, and a folded crane in the back. It motored over to and stopped next to the submerged ship. One man was in the tug wheelhouse and two others stood on barge.

"Morning," the first barge man said, looking at the ship. "We're expecting a delivery here. Should be you."

"That's us," Gavin said. "I'm Gavin."

The three men looked at the debris trail running from the hilltop.

"Good landing," the first speaker said. "You must have a great pilot."

"The best," Gavin said. "You ready for transfer?"

"Which container is ours?"

Gavin pointed at the submerged silks.

"You know you're supposed to put it up top, keep it out of the water?"

"We—we didn't get that memo," Gavin said.

"Looks like it's busted."

"It does, yes."

"Saltwater ruins silk."

"Didn't know that."

"Now you do."

"Maybe it's not all soaked up?" Gavin said.

The metal container screeched, then it dropped into the river with a splash. The spectators ducked as the waves and spray washed over them. When they stood back up, the container floated downstream from the two ships.

"Your goods are floating away," Gavin said.

"Not for long," the man said.

As the container floated farther out into the river, water gurgled into it, sinking it lower. When the corner grounded downstream, it settled lower and rocked on the river bottom, with the current running through it. A bubble of air burped up, and the container sank lower.

"Sunk now," the man said. "And soaked. We paid good money for dry, non-sunk silks. Not wet algae."

"We had problems on landing. It could happen to anybody," Gavin said.

"You need to speak to your cargo master on that," the man said. "Who is it?"

"That's me," Gavin said.

The bent landing strut screeched, and the ship dropped an inch.

"That so," the man said.

The strut snapped with a twang, and the ship dropped another meter into the river. Ana yelled from the top, lost his footing, and slid down to land next to them with a splash. He came up cursing.

"And your engineering department doesn't seem to understand how landing struts work. Who's your engineer?"

Gavin looked around at the sunken silks, the wrecked ship, and his waterlogged crew mates. "That would also be me."

***

"Well, at least they paid us something," Scruggs said.

The crew was eating in the lounge, and she was slurping through a food tray. She stopped to season it with a red sauce from a bottle.

"Not nearly enough," Gavin said. "Five percent."

"Better than we would have done trying to sell waterlogged silks," Ana said. "Private, your taste in food is outstandingly bad. What type of spice are you putting on those potatoes?"

"Thank you, Centurion," Scruggs said. "It's called Tabasco. I've never had it before. I love it."

"And you have questionable music tastes." Ana tilted his head to listen to the sounds coming through the speakers. "What do you call that?"

"Lindy hop, Centurion," Scruggs said.

"I knew a Lindy once," Ana said. "Hated her. Could we change it?"

"It's her day to pick," Gavin said. "Wait your turn, Old Man."

"You like this?" Ana said.

"Nope. I want more guitars. Electric guitars." Gavin listened. "But all those brass instruments are kind of . . . happy."

"It's fun music," Scruggs said.

"Of course, we wouldn't have this problem if Dirk here hadn't crashed us," Dena said.

"I got us down in one piece. That's all I ever promise," Dirk said. "You should be happy with that. Let me try some of that Tabasco." Scruggs handed him the bottle.

"You're a worthless pilot," Dena said. "A selfish lover, and now you're going to stink of that sauce."

"And you get sick every time you get onto a ship and have no useful space skills, and you only slept with me to get off that stupid planet." Dirk picked up his glass of basic and drank.

"Unhappy with your boyfriend, are you Ms. Sexy Pants?" Ana said.

"Friend Dena, remember," Dena said.

"Friend Dena," Ana agreed. "But you are right. The pilot could have done better."

"On the ship or in bed?" Dena asked.

Dirk slammed his empty glass on the table, startling everyone. "You want to try landing next time? Go for it. I've managed to take this worn-out rust bucket, bring it down on more than one uncharted planet—in the middle of hurricanes, rainstorms, floods, fires, life support failures, power failures, drive failures, and camera shorts. I've landed with no gravity, no thrusters, no main engine, broken struts, no fuel. Nobody, not you five, certainly, and not ninety percent of merchant skippers could have done as much. If I wasn't the one flying, you'd all be either a damp patch on the side of a mountain or a frozen patch next to a docking ring somewhere. You're all Empire-damned lucky that you've got a pilot like me who lands, whatever the situation is. And even if you don't think that you're lucky, think about this—I'm the only pilot you've got. And anyone who isn't happy with that can hop out of that hatch at the next station and ask the nearest Imperial warship for a ride somewhere. How about that." He held up his cup in the silence. "Can somebody pour me more basic, please?"

Lee filled it and extended it back. Dirk gulped another drink. "The real problem was that the engineer can't seem to keep things running properly, even with all the maintenance budget we give him."

"Maintenance budget?" Gavin said. "My budget won't buy a bowl of tabbo droppings. I've got refurbished parts, twice-refurbished parts, and plain old broken parts to choose from. If you could stop crashing into things, maybe I could get ahead of all our problems."

"He doesn't crash much. And to be fair to Pilot Dirk, they are difficult landings to perform."

"They're only difficult," Gavin said, "because you keep steering us into disaster. Who plots a landing site in a rock-covered river?"

"I didn't have a choice."

"You didn't see those big rocks?"

"We don't have the sensors to see big rocks. Or if we do, they're either broken because of poor maintenance, or sheared off because Pilot Dirk smashed them against an ore barge." Lee stood. "Paterfather Zeus, give me strength. I'm going to my quarters till we're at the station." She stalked off.

"I need a nap," Dirk said, getting up. "Landings are stressful."

"Take a bottle with you," Gavin said. "That's your usual way of dealing with stress." Dirk glared. He cleaned his tray and tossed it in the recycling before heading into his cabin.

Dena and Gavin watched him go, then Dena turned to Gavin. "So, since the pilot's out for the count, and the navigator is mad at you, the two of us—"

"Not a chance. You're not interested in me. You're just trying to manipulate me or make Dirk angry. Go away." Gavin tossed his tray at the recycling container, missed, and watched it clatter to the deck. "I'm going to engineering to fix everything that you folks break. Again." He walked to the hatch and climbed in.

"Men," Dena said. "Can't live with them. Can't shoot them 'cause of those stupid laws." She looked at her plate. "This is disgusting. Who eats this?"

Scruggs finished spooning her potatoes into her mouth. She turned bright red again.

Dena glared at her. "What are you looking at?" She left her tray on the table and stomped off to her quarters.

Scruggs was quiet. Ana finished eating from his tray, slid it aside, and pulled Dena's over. He spooned up the rest of her vegetables. "Nothing wrong with this food. I don't know what they are talking about."

Scruggs sat silently and looked at the centurion.

"So, read any good books lately, Private?" Ana said.

***

"Harder," Ana said, extending his arms. "Slap them away."

Scruggs slammed her palm into the extended arms, forcing one, then the other to the side.

"Good, very good. Now faster, faster."

Scruggs slapped left, right, left. Ana matched her. Their tempo increased till both hands were a blur.

Dena slouched on a weight bench beside her comm and fiddled with free weights. "Harder? Faster? Harder? Do the two of you want some privacy?"

Ana smirked. "Privacy won't help. But you're right, harder, faster, Private."

"That is all a waste of time," Dena said. "You're not going to make that little girl into a fighting machine."

Scruggs stepped back from Ana and glared at Dena. "Want to try a round?"

"Too busy doing weights, little girl," Dena said. She scooped up a hand bar with round weights on either end. The bar tilted, and the right weight slid off,

21

crashed into the floor, and rolled in a circle to land at Ana's feet.

"Is that how you do weights on that rockhole planet?" Ana said. "Never seen that technique before. What's it called? Lift and drop?"

"Empress's vagina," Dena said. "Is this defective?"

"Something's defective," Scruggs said.

She picked up the five kilo weight, stepped to Dena, and yanked the bar out of her hand. She slid the weight back onto the bar, twisted the locking knobs on the end, pivoted the weight in her hands, then tossed it onto Dena's stomach.

Dena intercepted it with both hands, but the momentum crashed her off the bench, knocking her comm underneath. She flipped backward and rolled right over and back onto her feet. She flexed her knees, stamped her left leg forward, and drew the weight to throw.

"STOP," Ana yelled. Dena froze but flicked her eyes to Ana. "Stay out of this, Old Man. It's between her and me."

"You're strong enough," Ana said. "Young and healthy and vicious. But you have no technique whatsoever. Where did you learn to fight? Who taught you?"

"Not a who, a what. Losing taught me. Don't start a fight. Win a fight."

"I thought that's what I was teaching here," Ana said. "But you appear to disagree. Stand down, Private. I want to hear this."

Scruggs stepped back, eyeing Dena.

Ana folded his arms. "Why won't she win a fight? And put that weight down."

Dena hefted the weight bar, then stepped over and slid it in the rack. "She's half your size, half the size of any man. She'll never beat a man in hand-to-hand combat."

"How would you do it?" Ana asked.

"Hit him from behind before he knows he's in a fight. Knock him down and kick him. Bring friends. Friends with steel-toed boots."

"An excellent idea."

"I can take you," Scruggs said to Dena. "Just say the word."

"We're the same size," Dena said. "Anybody bigger—like the engineer or Dirk—would kick you around the room. And no you can't."

"I hit hard."

"Hit them hard, and you'll probably break your hand," Dena said. "Why do you think the old man there is teaching you to slap hands away, rather than punch back? If you try to just block a punch, it'll break your arm and knock you over."

"That's the truth, Private." Ana smiled. "Then you'll be on the floor when Dena's friends come to kick you to death. An excellent point. So, Ms. Sexy Pants—"

"Don't call me that," Dena said.

"Thus demonstrating my point," Ana said. "Sometimes, a fight is forced on you, when you don't want it. What do you do then?"

"Fight," Scruggs said.

"Run," Dena said. "Why stand and get yourself beaten up?"

"Because there's more than just you involved in this. What if you're protecting your friends?" Ana asked.

"I don't see any friends here," Dena said. "Not-enemies. Is that the word?"

"Too busy chopping wood to learn how to speak properly?" Scruggs said.

"Actually, yeah, I was," Dena said. "I chopped a lot of wood. We had to. Space travel isn't what I expected, but at least I haven't seen an ax since I've been here."

"There's one in the ship's locker. We'll contact you if we need any trees cut."

"Thanks," Dena said. "I'm glad to be useful."

"But you're not . . . useful, I mean," Ana said. "You can't fly or navigate, you freak out outside, you get space sick, and you can't fight. What do you do on the ship?"

"Other than sleeping with the captain," Scruggs said.

"Private," Ana said.

"Wish you were me, scraggly girl? Grind your teeth when you think of me in there with him?"

"He can do better," Scruggs said. "Way better."

"You mean you?"

"I mean anybody. Anybody who doesn't stink of skank."

Dena bounced forward and threw a right fist. Scruggs slapped it aside with the move she had just been practicing. Dena punched left, and Scruggs slapped it aside, too. Dena stepped forward and smashed her forehead into Scruggs's nose. Scruggs reached up and throttled her. The two surged around the gym area. Ana stepped back, and Dirk climbed down the ladder from the lounge.

"What's going on?"

"The girls are playing," Ana said. "Leave them be. This has been a long time coming."

"Shouldn't we separate them?"

"I'll take care of this," Ana said.

"They'll kill each other."

"Not hardly."

"I want it to stop."

"Scruggs will if I tell her to. Want me to tell her to stop fighting with Dena 'cause she's your girlfriend?"

Dirk looked at Ana. "Even I know that's a bad idea. No permanent damage?"

"None," Ana agreed. "This will be over shortly."

Dirk slid back and kept his eyes on the fight.

Dena had her fingers under Scruggs's hands, giving her enough air to breathe but not enough to renew her head-smashing move. Scruggs had tucked her chin to protect her nose and gripped Dena's throat for dear life. They staggered across the gym, with Dena rotating the pair and pushing Scruggs back over the weight bench. They tripped over the bench, and Dena crashed onto Scruggs, breaking her hold. Scruggs lay still, stunned, while Dena rolled away, gasping.

Ana slow clapped as the two women sat up. "A good start. Ms. Sexy Pants, now you see why close quarter practice is useful. Private, consider Ms. Sexy Pants's point. How different would this fight have been if you'd had even one friend with steel-toed shoes around? And good use of your hands and that ducking motion, well done. Would you girls like round two?"

Dena hauled herself up onto the bench, then sat. She gasped and massaged her neck. "To the Imperial hells with both of you." She stood and stalked to the ladder. Partway, she tripped over a loose dumbbell, causing her to sprawl face-first. Dirk leaned down to help her, but she slapped his hands away and climbed up to the hab module.

Dirk bit his lip and looked at Ana. Ana pointed at the hatch leading to the lounge. Dirk ducked into it and made himself scarce.

"I habe herb," Scruggs said.

"Pinch your nostrils and lean forward." Ana lifted Scruggs up to sit on the bench and tilted her head forward.

"I hate her," Scruggs said.

"I can see that," Ana said. "Why?"

"Why?"

"Why do you hate her? She's never done anything to you."

"How come you didn't stop us, Centurion?"

"It's good practice for you to fight somebody who really, really wants to hurt you. Keeps you sharp. For her, I wanted to see how well she would do in a fight. Like it or not, we're on the same ship, so if we get in a brawl, I need to know what she's capable of. And besides"—Ana grinned—"I like violence."

Scruggs grinned back. "It is kind of fun."

"That's the evil secret, Private. Violence is hard-wired into people. It feels good when you win. Practice means you can make sure you win."

"Yes, Centurion."

"But you didn't answer. Why do you hate her?"

"Do I need a reason?"

"Are you saying you don't have a reason?"

"I didn't at the start. She's just, so, so . . ."

Ana sat on the bench next to her and raised his eyebrows.

"Lucky," Scruggs said. "She got to do all these woodsy things, outdoor things. Use axes. Chop wood. Hunt animals. Be a trader on those sailing ships. Things I never got to do. It all sounds so exciting."

"Being on a dead-end, low-tech planet and living in a wooden hut is exciting to you?"

"It just sounds like fun. Exciting. Romantic."

"Romantic? Having to live with bugs and inbred backwoods losers is exciting?"

Scruggs removed her fingers from her nostrils and wiped blood from her mouth. "You know, Centurion, you can die of boredom. Not physically, but if you never do anything or risk anything, the joy just drains out of you till you're an empty shell, with nothing left inside."

Ana grinned. "That sounds very philosophical, Private. I don't disagree—I can't disagree. I don't have any basis for comparison. My life has been many things but not boring."

"This ship isn't boring," Scruggs said. "This ship is an adventure."

"An adventure is other people being miserable far away," Ana said. "I'm not fond of adventures."

"Maybe now, but what were you like when you were my age, Centurion?"

Ana laughed and slapped her shoulder. "You've got me there, Private. I was quite a handful when I was your age. Well, if it's adventure you want, this is the place. This ship seems doomed to be full of adventure. So, that's why you hate her?"

"That's why I hate her," Scruggs said.

"You're bleeding again. Not much. Pinch your nostrils for another minute."

Scruggs complied.

"But in fact," Ana said, "to me, it seems more like it's more jealousy than hatred."

Scruggs's eyes clouded. Then she nodded. "She can do all those things. She can even fight, and she didn't have to learn them."

"She can fight. She just proved that. And she did learn them, just not the same way you are, looks like."

Scruggs rubbed her nose. "No more blood."

"Go to the medic. She'll give you some gauze for the nose. Have her check if your nose is broken. If it is, we'll reset it. That will hurt. You'll want drugs."

"Yes, Centurion," Scruggs said. She rubbed the dried blood from her hands.

"Dena can fight," Ana said. "And she's not shy about it. Those are things you need to learn more of."

"Yes, Centurion."

"The men find her attractive, too. The young men," Ana said. He stood and picked up the dumbbell rolling on the ground. "Do you agree, Private?"

Scruggs's face turned bright red, and she dropped her eyes to the ground. "I guess so. I think so."

"It does seem that way." Ana put the dumbbell back on the rack. "Not sure how she does it, but it's interesting, isn't it, that it works for her? She seems very practiced at it. And that move with her head was good, too."

Scruggs muttered something unintelligible.

"You should learn that." He flipped the comm on and glanced at the screen. "She'll want this. Why don't you take it to her, and while you're there, ask her how she did it?"

Scruggs's eyes widened. "Centurion?"

"Go and ask her how she did it."

"How she . . . how she . . ."

"How she broke your nose," Ana said. "It's a useful skill."

"Yes, Centurion."

Ana waited a beat. "Now would be good, Private."

"Of course, Centurion. Yes, Centurion." She stood and limped to the ladder.

"And, Scruggs?"

"Centurion?"

"She's an interesting young woman, about your age. You could probably learn other things from her, if you pay attention."

***

Dirk sat on the bunk in his cube. It wasn't really a bunk but an actual accel couch that pivoted depending on where gravity was. Right then, they were going ballistic, gliding into Winsome Station, but Lee had spun the ship, so out was down, and he was pressed into the covers.

His intercom crackled.

"Pilot, can you come up here?" Lee asked.

"I'm not drunk, so I won't be much help, according to the lot of you," Dirk said. "But I've got a bottle down here. I could start."

"I just want you to look at something, Pilot. It's unusual."

"What's unusual?"

"Traffic patterns."

"Should I take the drink first?"

Lee didn't answer, so Dirk cursed but got up. He was wearing his skin suit and station shoes. He stepped to his cabin door and thought for a moment. Then he reached back, clipped his helmet to its holder, stepped out of his cabin, and climbed up to the lounge.

Ana and Scruggs had pivoted the lounge table to account for the changed gravity, and they were examining something on their comm screens.

"Going for a walk outside, Navy?" Ana asked.

"Why do you say that?"

"You've got your helmet."

"It's prudent to carry my helmet."

"You're too lazy, and you never bother. This is the first time I've seen you with one when you're not going outside."

"Regs say that the pilot should always have their helmet in reach when on shift."

"The Regs also say you should wash your clothes once a week, but by the smell, you don't do that, either." Ana spun his comm. "Look at this."

Dirk peered at the comm. "This is a targeting program."

"Great education you got in the Navy. I've got Scruggs learning how to use the sensors for targeting other ships."

"We don't have any weapons."

"She's younger than either of us, and someday, she'll be on a ship with weapons, and it will be helpful for her to know how to target them. I've had her running simulations on any ships in sensor distance. It will help her get a better rating, more money, and might save her life."

"Good long-term plan, Centurion."

"It might save your life, too, but that's just an unfortunate byproduct. Notice anything unusual?"

"I'm just a drunken pilot."

"True. But you were correct. You are the only pilot we have. And you fly surprisingly well for a drunk."

"So, I'm a competent drunken pilot?"

"Competent? Let's not get ahead of ourselves here. We'll stick with adequate. Private, cycle through those targeting solutions you set up and explain them to the adequate pilot here."

"Yes, Centurion. Captain, I do a wide-range radar scan. Anything that I see, I request a beacon call and then I look the beacon up in the database. Once I read the type of ship, if it's not military, I track it with the radar. Then I put a telescope on it and confirm it's as identified."

"Confirm it's as identified?" Dirk asked.

"I compare the visuals to the standard plans for the type the beacon reports. Total length as measured by the radar if possible, then compare that to how long that class of ship should be. Hello, Nature Girl."

Dena had stepped out of her cabin to get a glass of basic. She ignored the group and poured a glass from the faucet.

"Why not warships?" Dirk asked.

"Warships can tell we're scanning them. They might come and investigate why we're doing that."

"Good point. That's not something we want. But our sensors aren't that good. How do you determine the target's aspect?"

"I use the infrared telescope. It gives less detail, but it tells me exactly what the drive plume is, and I can use that to figure out aspect. The centurion has me doing math to figure out how long it should look by the angle I see."

"That's actually quite clever," Dirk said.

"Suck-up," Dena said, stepping over. "Anything for attention."

Scruggs narrowed her eyes.

"Going to blush at me again, little girl?" Dena asked.

"When we're at the station," Scruggs said to Dena. "Perhaps the pilot can arrange a meeting, like the engineer and the centurion had. We have a few things to talk about."

"Anytime," Dena said.

"What you say to a little wager, Navy?" Ana said. "I'll back my girl against yours any time."

"The relationships aren't exactly comparable, Centurion."

"Too true. I'll bet Friend Dena here never learned a new unarmed throw from you."

"No. But she learned some other things, I imagine," Dirk said.

Dena laughed. "Hardly any. But I have a question." She pointed at the screen. "Two questions, actually. One, Ms. Suck-Up here can tell if the scanned ships match their actual registry just by checking the length, correct?"

"Not one hundred percent," Ana said. "But we can come close. If it's only a few meters difference, then it's probably a scan error. But if our math says a ship is twice as long as its broadcast specs are, then that's a problem."

"What type of problem?"

"A ship broadcasting a false ID problem."

"Like us?"

"Like us. But also like smugglers, pirates pretending to be merchant ships, and customs or military ships pretending to not be customs or military ships."

"Can other people do that to us?" Dena asked.

"Not if we match our broadcast specs. Do we match our broadcast specs?" Dirk said. He reached over and punched the intercom. "Gavin?"

"I'm busy," Gavin said. "What do you want, Pilot?"

"We're looking at some scans here. How close are we to our fake specifications? Can somebody determine we're not who we say we are because our measurements aren't right?"

"I'm coming up," Gavin said. "Stand by."

Three minutes later, Gavin was looking at Scruggs's comm. She had described how she tested ships against their broadcast specifications. "That's a neat idea. We'd fail if somebody paid attention. Our ID is bigger than us by ten percent."

"That could be a problem," Dirk said.

"Not really, Pilot. A merchant won't scan us, and a sloppy customs ship won't notice. A warship might. An Imperial warship probably would. Their scans are great, and they auto link to their databases."

"So, it's pilot now, not skipper?" Dirk asked.

"Yep."

"How do you know Imperial warships auto link to databases?" Ana asked. "Spent time on one?"

Gavin reached down to manipulate the screen.

"Can we fix that?" Dirk asked. "Or at least determine if we're being scanned?"

"I have a radar detector in storage," Gavin said. "Just not enough time to fix it. You know, with me fixing landing struts and all."

"Right," Dirk said.

"But that's not the issue right now," Gavin said. "The traffic pattern is." He punched the intercom. "Lee, I'm looking at the traffic in this system. It isn't right. What's going on?"

"I saw it, too," Lee said. "Not right away. Scruggs saw it first."

"It is strange," Ana said. "Could it be a random coincidence?"

"Lee, any notifications or indications as to what's going on?" Gavin asked.

Dena looked at Scruggs's comm. "I see it now. Is this unusual, all the ships moving like this?"

"Very," Lee said over the intercom. "I've never seen anything like it before. And no notices to shipping."

Dirk grunted. "Well, apparently, the pilot is the last to know. I don't see anything strange in this traffic pattern."

"Look at the ships, Navy," Ana said.

"Twenty ships on the screen. Not an extremely high number. Looks like merchant ships, small and large. That one there"—he tapped the screen—"could be an armed customs cutter. Heading in different directions—that group is going to the jump limit, so is that one. Those three are going to scoop gas from that gas giant. What's strange about that?"

"Look at the direction, Navy, the direction. Just watch the updates."

Dirk furrowed his brow at the screen. It refreshed periodically. After two refreshes, he was sure. "Everyone is outbound. All of them."

Ana nodded. "They're all going away from the station. All of them."

"Except us," Dirk said.

"Yup," Gavin said. "We're the only one going to a station that everyone is fleeing."

CHAPTER FOUR

"Winsome Station, this is Heavyweight Items, inbound. Sending identification and request docking clearance and lock assignment," Lee said. The ship was registered in the Empire as the Heart's Desire, but when communicating, they used the name on the fake registry Gavin had provided, Heavyweight Items.

She sat to Dirk's right in the control room's front row. Dirk had the pilot's screen loaded. Ana and Scruggs sat in the second row, Ana watching as Scruggs ran her simulated attacks.

"Heavyweight Items, pick any open lock," the station said.

Dirk and Lee looked at each other. "Strange," Dirk said.

Lee keyed the radio. "Understand any open lock? We can pick?"

"Any lock."

Lee tapped her screen and highlighted the nearest freighter lock. Dirk fired the maneuvering jets, then pulsed the main engines once to head to the station. A bong sounded an alert, and the ship spun. Dirk cursed and tapped screens.

"What's happening?" Scruggs asked.

"Starboard thrusters failed," Lee said. "Pilot is trying to compensate."

"Probably not the thrusters, probably the software," Dirk said.

"Engineer," Lee said over the intercom.

"I know. I have the alert here. I'm rebooting the software now."

"We need better software."

"I want a better computer."

"I want to be the Emperor's personal starship driver," Gavin said over the intercom. "But given how little money we have right now, that will probably happen before we get a new computer and software."

Dirk stopped the spin, then corrected their heading to intersect the station's orbit.

"And we need fuel," Gavin said. "We dumped a full tank into that swamp back there. And I want station power while I fix the sensors."

"How much will that cost?" Ana asked.

"Less than running out of air mid-jump because the pumps failed," Gavin said.

Dirk keyed the mic off, let out a long string of curses about thrusters, then yawed the ship before resuming the docking.

"Hey, Navy," Ana said. "That spin up and around, is that a normal docking maneuver?"

"As you are well aware, it's not," Dirk said. "If that is a comment on my flying, you're wasting your breath. I did the best I could with what I had."

Ana laughed. "Touchy today. No, I'm not commenting on your flying, but shouldn't somebody?"

"Which somebody?"

"Why didn't the station call us on it? They should have been watching the approach and noticed our shenanigans. At least called you up and asked what you were doing."

Dirk nodded. "They should have, shouldn't they?"

"They should have waved us off," Lee said. "Suggested a tug or putting a stationmaster on board. Or at least asked about a malfunction."

Dirk tapped his screen again. "We're set. Lee, call them up."

"About what?"

"Status check. Something, just see what they say."

Lee keyed her mic again. "Station, Heavyweight Items. Did our ID clear for billing? We need to schedule fuel and station power services."

"Heavyweight Items, station. We're not checking IDs anymore. Power is free—pull as much as you need. We're out of fuel. Other station services are mostly shut down or will be shut down soon. But if it's working, you can have it. No charge."

"No fuel available, Station?" Lee said.

"None, Heavyweight Items. We're fresh out. You need to find your own. Some of the private suppliers have some, but the station-owned tanks are empty."

"Station, we need fuel to depart," Lee said.

"Don't we all, Heavyweight Items?" the station said. "Don't we all. Good luck to you. Make your approach as you prefer. We're closing comms now. Station out."

"Closing comms?" Lee said. "By the Paterfather's nostril, I've never heard that."

"Why no fuel?" Scruggs asked.

"Somebody will sell us fuel," Dirk said. "Somebody always will."

"Wonder what it will cost?" Ana said.

***

Ana and Scruggs were standing by the air lock as they locked on.

"What are we looking for, Centurion?" Scruggs said. She wore a holster with a revolver and held a shotgun across her chest. Ana had the same.

"Anything unusual," Ana said. "Strange activities, strange actions, strange people."

"How will I know it?" Scruggs said.

"Follow my lead."

Dena appeared at the lock, wearing tight leather pants, boots, a fabric shirt, and a leather jacket. She had discarded the borrowed skin suit from before.

"You look like you just came out of the backwoods," Ana said.

"And you look like you want to shoot anybody who looks at you," Dena said. "Dirk told me to find out what's going on."

"You think people will talk to you?"

"People are more likely to talk to somebody who they think won't shoot them," Dena said.

The intercom cracked. "Hard seal," Lee said.

They flipped the inner air lock open, and Ana spun the locking wheel on the outer lock and stepped through. They were on a standard cargo lock. Two-story ceiling, enough room to drop pallets of random cargo, and a track-based system farther inside to move it from lock to lock. Winsome Station was equipped for trans-shipment and break bulk. Freighters moved up and dropped or picked up cargo out in the dark. Smaller cargos and supplies came on board via the lock.

About twenty people were wandering around the lock. As the door swung open, they surged forward, yelling.

Ana pointed his shotgun up and fired. The first round impacted the ceiling and dropped in a shower of dust. "First one's frangible," he said. "Next ones are station-safe slugs."

The crowd surged back as fast as they had surged forward.

"Do you call this unusual, Old Man?" Dena asked.

"Shut up, Ms. Sexy Pants," Ana said, raising his voice. "Everybody stay clear of our lock or you get shot. Now, what's going on?"

"When are you leaving?" a man yelled. "I'll pay to come with you."

"I'll pay, too. How many places do you have?" another said.

Ana kept his eyes and shotgun on the crowd. "Private?"

"Next to you, Centurion."

"Watch right, I'll watch left."

"What's going on? Why do you all want to leave?" Dena asked. She poked her head forward but didn't advance past the two guards.

The crowd erupted in bedlam, but one word stood out.

"What war?" Ana asked. "Whose war?"

"You don't know?" the man in front said.

"We just got here," Ana said. "You, tell us what's going on."

"The Confeds and the Nationalists are mobilizing," the man said. "They've had clashes on the outer rim. They're going to go at it, and we're right between them."

"This is a private corporate station," Ana said. "They don't attack independents."

"Not anymore. The local corp pulled out four days ago. They sold everything to a Confed company. They brought in twenty chartered freighters, loaded all their staff and supplies on their ships, and booted it for the Empire. All that's left is people who couldn't or wouldn't go. The Confeds will be here anytime."

"Who's running things?" Ana asked.

"The local merchants, the small guys. They formed a council. They armed some people, and they're running basic services. Word is they're just waiting for whoever gets here first to surrender to and hope they don't get blown up. The rest of us just want to get out of the way. When are you leaving?"

"Soon."

"Do you have fuel?" the man asked.

"Why do you ask that?" Ana said.

A murmur ran through the crowd. "You don't, do you? Three other ships here that can't get out. The station's out of fuel. You're stuck here. Stuck like the rest of us," the man said.

**

The whole crew had gathered at the lock. Leaving it unguarded was a bad idea. Scruggs had to see off three groups trying to get on board. One group looked like they were going to rush the ship, but Ana and Scruggs had faced them off. The meeting was just inboard of the door. Scruggs was facing out, with her shotgun in evidence.

"Right," Gavin said. "I checked the station news, and I made some calls. It's true, the Confeds and the Nats are going to go at it. There's been border skirmishes for the past months, and things are heating up."

"We don't want to be in the middle of this," Lee said. "We need to get out of here."

"We need fuel," Gavin said. "But I can't find any for sale."

"Did you check . . . unofficial sales areas?" Dirk asked.

"I started there. Not even stolen fuel for sale."

"No stolen fuel?" Dirk asked. "There's always some stolen fuel."

"I got offered ten crates of black-market whiskey, three different types of stolen personal electronics, a fake gold bracelet, two sexual encounters, and all the hallucinogens I can eat. No fuel."

"We need to go somewhere other than here," Lee said.

"Where would we go?" Dena asked.

"Two jumps in any direction," Dirk said. "A fleet can't operate with uncontrolled planets in its rear—they need supplies, food, that stuff. So, they attack a border system, maybe raid the next one over, but if you're two jumps away, you're pretty safe."

"Warships can jump farther than a freighter like ours, can't they?" Dena asked.

"Imperial warships can. And so can the fleet train logistic ships," Dirk said. "But the lesser Empires' ships can't jump as far, and their logistics trains are worthless. They mostly use re-purposed freighters. They have to carry enough fuel with them to be able to jump back, in case the battle goes against them. If they jump into an opposed system, and they're outnumbered, they can't retreat, and they'll be destroyed."

"Best not to jump into an opposed system, then," Dena said. "Even a rustic like me can see that. But how do you know if there're enemy ships in a system?"

"Only way is to send a scout," Dirk said. "But that takes a couple weeks in Jump, out and back, and the enemy could have moved ships in by then."

"How does anyone ever win a war, then?" Dena asked.

"Overwhelming force or good intelligence of enemy fleet movements," Dirk said.

"You learn all that in command college, Navy?" Ana asked.

"Actually, yes, I was quite studious when I attended."

The crew shook their heads.

Dirk grimaced. "Fine, I was trying to sleep with one of the instructors, so I paid special attention to her lessons."

Everyone nodded.

Another group approached the air lock, and Scruggs raised her shotgun, then lowered it. "Can I help you, Elder?"

The crew looked past her. A family group was approaching. A short man with a big smile and wavy hair led a group of women. One was clearly his wife, and the next seven were miniature copies of the couple. A thirteen-year-old girl, her five younger sisters, and a boy about five years old. The women wore caps with their hair bound under it and long dresses. The boy wore shiny black shoes, short pants, and a white shirt. His father wore a heavy white shirt with a high-starched collar embroidered with symbols.

"The blessings of the one spirit on you," the man said.

"And to you, Elder," Scruggs said.

"What do you want, mister?" Ana asked.

"You should address him as Elder, Centurion," Scruggs said.

Ana looked at her. "Pardon?"

"Call him Elder, Centurion," Scruggs said. "It's polite."

Ana pursed his lips, then turned back to the man. "How can I help you, Elder?"

"The blessings of the one spirit on you, brother," the man said. "She called you Centurion, is that correct?"

"It will do."

"When you say come, do they come? And when you say go, do they go?"

Ana pursed his lips again. "Sometimes. What do you want?"

Scruggs glared. Ana pursed his lips again. "What do you want, Elder?"

"Centurion, myself and my family seek passage off this station. We wish to return to the Empire."

"What makes you think we can help you?"

"Are you not a centurion in the Imperial forces? You look like such."

"Before. Not now. Now I'm just nobody."

"None of us are nobody in God's eyes." The man turned to them. "You have the look of Imperials about you. Are any of you officers?"

The group shuffled, and everyone stared at Dirk.

"Not anymore," Dirk said.

"But once?"

"What do you want?"

"To leave, as we said. Will you help us?"

"We're kind of busy right now, preacher," Dirk said.

"Elder," Scruggs said.

"We're kind of busy, Elder," Dirk said.

"But you will be leaving?"

Ana interrupted. "It's not really any concern of yours, Elder."

"It is a sad day, when officers of the Imperium overlook their sworn duty," the elder said. He glowered at Scruggs.

Scruggs shuffled and looked at the ground. "Something wrong, Elder?"

"Have we met before, sister?" he asked.

"No, Elder, I would have remembered."

Ana leaned forward. "We've got work to do here, Elder."

The elder's smile reappeared. "Thank you for your time, sister. Blessings upon you. Come, children. We need to seek others who have not forgotten their allegiance."

The family filed away in silence.

Ana turned to Scruggs. "Elder? What's that about?"

"It's respectful," Scruggs said. "He's an elder of the one church. You always told me that, if I knew somebody's title, I should use it. Respect others, and they will respect you. Isn't that what you said?"

"Sounds like the kind of annoying army-speak that he'd say," Gavin agreed.

"I did say that. Elder it is, then."

"We should have helped him," Scruggs said. "This will come back on us."

"Could be. But we're in no place to help anyone right now. We need fuel," Ana said.

"And parts," Gavin said. "We need sensors, some standard electrical plugs, wiring harness, and we need something for the software. And I have to fix the struts."

"We don't have time to bang metal," Ana said. "Just get us the fuel."

"No landing groundside till we fix the struts," Gavin said.

"If we approach a real station," Lee said, "and if the software fails like that, they'll put a crew on board to bring us in."

"At least somebody will fix something," Dena said.

"If they put a half competent crew on board, they'll see we don't match the ID we're broadcasting and turn us in," Gavin said. "Anything wrong with this ship, we have to fix for ourselves."

"Let's summarize," Dena said. "We can't land on planets or stations, we have no fuel, our computer isn't working right, we're in the middle of a war, we have tons of things to fix, but we can't let experts help us because they'll turn us into the authorities, and that doesn't matter because we don't have enough parts anyway, and we spent all our money on an ill-fated, silk-smuggling venture." She looked around. "Have I got it right?"

"Well, when you put it that way," Dirk said. "It sounds a bit . . . negative."

"Negative? That's all you have to say?" Dena said.

"I've been in worse," Ana said. "Work with what we have. Engineer, go see what parts are on this station. Take somebody with you. Somebody armed, maybe Navy—no, take Scruggs, she's looking more and more the grim warrior these days."

Scruggs beamed at the unexpected compliment. "Thank you, Centurion."

"Don't grin like that, Private. It makes you look too young and harmless. Think of somebody you hate, that will make you glower."

Scruggs looked at Dena with a darkened expression. Ana nodded. "Like that. Navy, you and Ms. Sexy Pants here get out there. Find a bar. Be sociable. Buy some drinks—or let people buy you drinks. Ask around. We need fuel. Spread the word. Somebody has it. They're just waiting for the chance to make a deal on it. We can make a deal. The navigator can find us the closest places to hop to when we get fuel and monitor the news. She's good at that."

"Remember our talk about you not being in charge?" Gavin said.

"I have no recollection of that," Ana said. "What I do know is that this station is insecure, and I'm in charge of security. And as Navy recently pointed out about his piloting, I may not be the security person you want, but I'm the one you got."

"He's good at this," Dirk said. "He's mean, suspicious, ruthless, and violent."

Ana bowed from the waist. "Why thank you, Navy. That's the nicest thing you've said about me in ages."

"And what will you do while we're running around the station?" Gavin asked.

"I'll have a nice breakfast and then take a nap. After, I'll see if any of the spas are open and maybe get a shave. What do you think I'm going to do? I'll be standing at that door with my shotgun, and if anything happens, I'll shoot first and ask questions not at all."

"I can truthfully say that, if the centurion is here, the ship will be here and safe, when we return," Dirk said. "I have no doubt of that. He's a man of integrity."

"Plus, he can't work the pilot or engineering boards," Gavin said.

"Another true point," Dirk said.

"Action stations," Ana said. "Move out."

"Should we say hoorah?" Gavin said.

"Only if you want me to slap you," Ana said.

The crew was gone almost a full shift. Ana stayed at the lock, pointing the shotgun at anybody who came close. Gavin and Scruggs made two trips, returning with a pallet of parts each time.

"Everything's on sale," Gavin said. "Big time on sale. They figure the Confeds will take everything, so they're dumping stuff. If we had more cash, I could have bought everything I needed."

"Did you get anything useful?" Ana asked.

"Lots of minor stuff on the list. Sensors. Intercom speaker. More computer memory is a big thing. Computer won't go faster, but we'll probably stress it less."

"What about the struts? Didn't you say that we need that fixed first?"

"I did. I got the exact thing I need to fix them. I have it right here. Want to see?"

"Sure," Ana said.

Gavin held up a hammer. "Four-pound sledge. I just need this, and ten thousand hammer strikes, and we should be fine. I'm starting now."

Dirk and Dena were not so successful.

"One marriage proposal, two suggested threesomes, six offers of dates, and unlimited drinks with fake fruit in them," a tipsy Dena said.

"A marriage proposal? Even I think that's impressive," Ana said.

"Oh, it wasn't for me, it was for him. An older lady took quite a liking to our dashing captain here," Dena said. "I got the free drinks. I think I'm going to go nap now." She toddled off.

Lee had tracked all the nearby systems that had stations or water they could convert to fuel after they landed, ranking them by desirability, distance, cost, and ease of landing. None of them were reachable without more fuel.

Ana sent everybody to bed—by then, it was mid-first shift, and the station was mostly asleep. He had his usual insomnia. He wandered the cargo lock, cradling his shotgun. Surveilling the control room cameras was an option, but he liked to be on the move. A twinge of the day's efforts caught up with him, and he slipped a pill out of his pocket and dry-swallowed it. Just before the beginning of second shift, a man approached the ship.

Ana swung his shotgun up. "Go away."

The man wore a brightly patterned shirt, bright cuffs, and ankle ruffles in clashing colors.

"Hiya, sport, is this here the Heavyweight Items?"

"I said go away," Ana said.

"Listen, sport-o, you departing the station anytime?"

"Go away, or I'll kill you," Ana said.

"I didn't think so. See, I hear you're stuck here because you need fuel."

Ana pointed the shotgun lower. "Not only will I kill you, but I'll do it slowly, starting with your knees."

"Whoa, whoa," the man said, backing off. "You're a little tense. I understand. None of my business, sport-o, I'm going. I'm going. But I just wanted to get a look at the ship. A ship whose people were asking around for fuel in the bar a few hours ago."

Ana lowered his gun. "You got any fuel?"

The man stopped retreating. "You look like former military. Were you in the Imperial Marines?"

"Who wants to know?" Ana asked.

"Name's Cheong."

"Never heard of you. What do you want?"

"I'm just a guy who needs some work done, work that's well within the competence of a former Imperial Marine. You were an Imperial Marine, weren't you?"

"What type of work?"

"Because that captain guy—he's Imperial Navy, no matter what he says. Him and his daughter there."

"His daughter?"

"The girl with him at the bar. Looked like his daughter. They acted that way, too. He introduced her around. She was very popular with the boys. Good-looking girl."

Navy is smarter than I believed, Ana thought. "You looking for a date?"

"Just some help with a little problem. Your captain, you, even the girl look like they could be helpful to me."

"And what do we get if we help you?"

"All the fuel you can load," the man said. "And a way off this station."

CHAPTER FIVE

"Do you understand my orders, Captain?" Devin said. He lounged in his chair on the Pollux's bridge, staring at the screen, which showed the captain of the nearby fast freighter. Her blue-and-yellow uniform matched her ship's paint scheme.

"This is a Union of Nations-registered ship," she said, "and I'm a National citizen, and this is a member nations aerospace. I don't take orders from any Imperials. Not here."

"You are being well-paid to do this, so you mind your tongue, you colonial dog, and show an Imperial noble the proper respect, or I'll blast you and your ill-mannered ship into space dust."

"You wouldn't dare. You're too far from the Imperial border."

"I agree. I'm eight or nine parsecs from the nearest Imperial base, yet there doesn't appear to be any National warships nearby. Or cargo ships. Or any ships. Just you, me, and all my lasers. Our party will be there shortly. Do as you're told." Devin shut off the screen. Subprefect Lionel hovered nearby. "What?"

"How can a ship be ill-mannered?" Subprefect Lionel asked. "Does the drive system burp insults in code?"

"I detest speaking with those freighter types. Especially when they're under my lasers."

"Colonial dog? You've got to stop watching those adventure vids."

"It seemed appropriate. Better I embarrass myself with stilted insults than fail to have them understand. Then I'll have to destroy them."

"Well, you won't be shooting him with your lasers, whatever you say."

"Why ever not?"

"We don't have any, remember? They replaced them all with positron beams last refit. The only lasers we have now are targeting and communication."

"I still call them lasers," Devin said.

"Can't live in the past forever, Tribune," Lionel said.

"I prefer the past. Things were simpler then."

"Prefect, the last container is latching right now," the comm officer said.

Devin and Lionel looked at the main screen. The Pollux's utility tug was pushing a container into the freighter's chains.

"Zoom in on our container, please," Devin said. "And put the one next to it up on screen as well."

The comm officer obliged, and the screens displayed two images side by side, all of which looked like standard shipping containers.

"They got the colors right," Lionel said. "The blue and yellow looks good."

"Yes," Devin agreed. "But something still stands out."

"Too new. You can tell one is newer than the other."

"That's it." Devin looked closely. "Ours looks brand new, right from the store."

"Nothing to be done about it. And ships do get new containers from time to time."

"Not backwoods freighters, but it doesn't stand out unless you're looking for it."

Hernandez and Weeks entered the bridge. They were in skin suits and had small courier packages belted to their waists. "We're ready to go, Tribune."

"Very well. My pilot will shuttle you over. I'll send some Marines with you to make sure that captain understands the gravity of his situation."

"That's not necessary, Tribune. She's being well-paid."

"You can be the carrot. I will represent the stick. The stick will be in the form of Marines." He looked at the pouches on their belts. "I thought those would be bigger. Are they secure?"

"Wrong person tries to open them, there's enough explosives to vaporize all the contents. And the hand of the person opening them."

"Very well. Do you need anything else from me? Weapons? Communication gear?"

Hernandez smiled. "We're very well-equipped, Tribune, but thank you for the offer. And thank you for the dinner last night. It was exciting."

Lionel raised an eyebrow. "The tribune provided an exciting dinner last night, Lieutenant Hernandez? For you and Lieutenant Weeks?"

"Oh, I didn't go, sir," Weeks said. "Wasn't invited."

Devin's face reddened.

"He certainly did," Hernandez said. "Not only was the food amazing, but we ended up in a brawl."

"Brawl? Is that what it's called now?" the helm officer muttered.

Devin glared at him. "Watch our spacing, helm, pay attention to keeping us on station, not bridge gossip."

"Sir," the helm officer said.

Lionel grinned. "Brawling? Hand-to-hand combat."

"Swords. The tribune showed me his beautiful sword. I got to handle it."

"Did you?" Lionel said, looking at Devin. "You handled his sword?"

"Yes and then we fought over it."

"Who won?" Lionel asked.

"It was a draw, but I think we both enjoyed it," Hernandez said.

The helmsman repressed a snigger.

"Enough of this," Devin said. "Are you ready to depart?"

"I could have used more rest after our dinner, but certainly."

Devin let the comment pass. "Well, I would rather not linger so far from the

Empire."

"Scared, Tribune?" Weeks asked.

"Cautious."

"You can destroy half of the Nationalist Fleet with this one ship," Weeks said.

"Yes," Devin said. "But I'm worried that the other half might show up as well. We're only one parsec from their largest fleet base. Best we move on." He stood, faced the two Internal Security agents, and cross-chest saluted. "Currant ad bellum."

The two intelligence officers exchanged glances, saluted, and walked to the lift.

Lionel waited till the door shut. "Jackals."

"Internal Security performs a distasteful but necessary role within the Empire," Devin said.

"They did before, but not now. They wanted to arrest you."

"Arrest me? Why?"

"They don't need a reason, not anymore."

"They wouldn't do that."

"Not out here, this far from the core. Not on your own ship. But if we were closer in? They'd take you out of your own office in cuffs, and nobody would do a thing about it."

"You believe that?" Devin asked.

"It's not the same Empire it was, Tribune."

"Perhaps. But my duty is the same."

"She reminds me of someone."

"My late wife."

"I thought so. Attractive lady."

"She spent the whole dinner trying to worm information out of me."

"Did she succeed?"

"Absolutely. I told stories for hours and told her everything I know about everything."

"That's not wise, Tribune."

"Those types are so crooked that, when presented with complete honesty, they turn themselves into knots, trying to figure out the hidden game behind them. Confuses them to no end."

"Will this scheme of theirs work?"

"I haven't told you anything of their scheme. It's above your pay grade."

"Then that's a no. Why did you let them leave? We could have just dumped them here."

"My new orders say I have to wait for them to communicate to us, and that gives us another reason to linger in this area."

"You can't hunt Dirk forever."

"I'm not hunting Dirk, I'm assisting Internal Security."

"Good story. Make sure you stick to it."

The bridge was silent for the next few minutes. Devin brooded in his chair.

Lionel looked up as an officer signaled to him. "Shuttle's on its way back, Tribune. We need to get out of here."

"Helm?" Devin said.

"Course to the jump limit laid in, Tribune. Two jumps, both to empty systems where we can refuel, then a short hop back to the Empire."

"Very well. As soon as the shuttle is secured, get us out of here."

"Understood, Tribune—"

A screen bonged.

"Status change. Jump signature."

"Warship?"

"Unknown," the sensor operator said. "Processing. Designate Target-1."

"Set course for Target-1. Half speed."

"Our shuttle, sir?"

"Leave it. We'll come back. General quarters."

Lights flashed, and bells bonged. In a few minutes, the Pollux was vectoring out to Target-1.

"Sensors say it's a freighter. Minimal drives, no shields or weapons."

"What class?" Lionel asked.

"No class designation, sir. It's just a tramp freighter. Probably a one off from some frontier planet, made of spare parts."

"Beacon broadcast," the comm officer announced. "Captain Hector Dixey, tramp freighter. Full load of animal feed pellets. En route to Davis's world."

"Crew?" Lionel asked.

"Seven."

"Registry?"

The comm officer glanced at the tribune, who sat silently in his chair. "Target-1 is Confederation-registered."

Devin sat up straight. "Any other traffic in this system?"

"Our shuttle and the National freighter, sir."

"Can Target-1 see us?"

"Possibly. We're far in system, we've got our ECM on, and their sensors are lousy. But we are accelerating and giving off a thermal plume."

"What if we go dark?" Devin asked.

"We should be okay, sir," the sensor operator said.

"Never mind us," Lionel said. "Can it see our shuttle and the freighter?"

"If they look in the right direction, absolutely, sir. Freighter is bigger, not shielded, and the shuttle has a thermal plume like nobody's business right now."

Lionel looked at Devin. "Could be they're not looking in the right direction."

"Or they are and not saying anything about it. Why are we hearing the beacon? Did we hail them?"

"Automatic beacon, sir. They probably never turn it off."

"All stop," Devin said. "Go silent. If they don't see us, we'll just let them go."

"Take our chances with the freighter?" Lionel asked.

"Yes," Devin said.

"All stop, sir. Dead in space. ECM off," the sensor operator said.

"Very well," Lionel said. He looked at Devin, but the catatonic tribune just stared into the distance.

They sat still for almost two minutes, then the comm officer's panel bonged. He took his time, tapping his panel. He put his finger to his ear, listening to something, then turned to Lionel. "Target-1 has just hailed the National freighter, sir. A friendly greeting, a request for system information." He stopped and continued listening.

The bridge waited.

"And?" Lionel said.

The comm officer grimaced. "And a question as to why an Imperial shuttle is maneuvering near them?"

Devin stirred in his seat. "Helm, resume course to Target-1. Flank speed."

"Aye, sir."

"Tactical?"

"Sir?"

"As soon as you have a good targeting solution," Devin said, "a very good targeting solution, destroy that freighter."

"Understood, sir."

"Don't mess this up, tactical. Make it clean. One shot. Complete destruction. I don't want anybody going by inches in a suit or an escape pod."

"Understood, sir," the tactical officer said.

Devin looked at the screen. "No need to make them suffer unnecessarily."

The bridge was silent. Devin looked around. "We serve the Empire."

"The Empire," everyone answered.

Devin left the bridge.

An hour later, they watched the Nationalist freighter jump to the next system.

"Set course for jump limit," Devin said.

Lionel came over to the chair. "Wasn't your fault. It had to be done. Bad luck on their part."

"Very bad luck," Devin agreed. "I hope our Internal Security friends take advantage of what we've bought them."

Devin slumped in his chair.

"You liked her," Lionel said.

"Very much. Young. Vibrant. Full of energy. And brave. Very brave. Like Shelia. If Shelia had lived, she might have had duty much like this."

"She's a fanatic. They're dangerous."

"Fanatics are annoying. Nothing to worry about." Devin watched the screen for a moment. "Brave people are the ones I worry about."

CHAPTER SIX

"Seriously, you're not going to buy me a drink?" Cheong asked Dirk and Ana. "After all I've done for you?"

"You haven't done anything at all for me," Ana said. "Yet. You've just told us to meet you here. And this isn't a bar."

"Great place, though, isn't it? You should get the combo special, the shave, the manicure, and the foot massage," Cheong said. He rubbed his freshly barbered chin, smiling at the young woman putting his feet in a bucket of warm water. "Ahh, that feels good."

Dirk sniffed. "Ah, the sweet smell of acetone and lubricating oil. I haven't had a station manicure in a while, but I'm not in the mood right now."

Ana sat in the chair next to Cheong, gesturing the therapist over. With his palms down, he extended his hands to her. She took them, peered at them, then nodded. He spoke to her in a tonal-based language, and she answered, then dropped his hands and went to get her kit.

"Your friend speaks Cantonese," Cheong said to Dirk.

"Was that Cantonese? I wouldn't know," Dirk said.

"Sounds like it," Cheong said.

"Don't you speak it?" Dirk asked.

"Nope. Where'd you learn Cantonese?" Cheong asked Ana.

"Canton," Ana said.

"What were you doing there?" Cheong asked.

"Minding my own business," Ana said. "Like you should."

"Well, excuse me," Cheong said.

"I don't really speak it, just a few words," Ana said.

As the manicurist approached, he conversed with her and made her giggle. Shaking her head and coming down from the laughter, she filed his nails.

"Sounds like more than a few," Cheong said.

"We're here now," Ana said. "Start talking."

"Such hostility. Is that any way to treat the guy who's going to get you out of here?"

"Unless I miss my guess, you're going with us, so you need us as much as we need you," Dirk said.

"Untrue, sport-o," Cheong said. "I'll be staying here."

"There's supposed to be a Confederation destroyer on the way here, with a company of Naval Landing Infantry to occupy this station," Dirk said. "And all non-Confed citizens will be taken to an internment camp in Confederation space."

"Is that the latest rumor?" Cheong asked. "I've heard everything from a task force to just a governor and customs staff. And non-Confeds aren't going to be transported. There're going to be shot or spaced or evacuated in an Imperial cruise liner that's on the way."

"Do you believe any of that?" Dirk asked.

"None of it, and I don't care."

"Whatever happens, it's going to be difficult for Imperial citizens," Dirk said.

"Good thing that I'm a Confederation citizen, then," Cheong said. "And that I work for a Confed headquartered company. I'm staying."

Dirk and Ana looked at each other. The manicurist stopped and said something to Ana. He spoke a sentence and shook his head. She continued filing.

"Well," Dirk said, "that's pretty interesting. If you're staying, and you're in no danger, what do you need us for?"

"Welllll," Cheong said, "I may have a little office problem. I work for Consolidated Shipping and Storage. Know them?"

"Insurance company, right?" Dirk said.

"Big one. I'm the branch manager here. It's a small office, so I pretty much run my own thing here. They leave me alone. We show a small profit. Most of the time."

Dirk shrugged. "So, you're an unsuccessful insurance agent?"

"I'm normally ignored because I'm basically in Nationalist space, and it's just a courtesy for the captains who come through. They file departure surveys, declare minor problems as they arrive, that sort of thing. I'm not expected to actually sell much."

"Again, so what?"

"The thing is, sport-o, if a task force or even a single ship comes down here and says this is a Confederation space, then this will become a kind of a Confederation station, then head office will send out more staff. If we're actually in the Confederation, they'll expect more sales."

"Then, you'll be an unsuccessful office with more staff—oh, I see," Dirk said. "You've been cooking the books."

"I've performed a few non-standard transactions, yes," Cheong said. "I'd rather they'd not come out."

"So, you're a crooked insurance agent," Dirk said. "We're not exactly forensic accountants. Or anti-forensic accountants. And you must know some people on station who you can deal with."

"I know, I know," Cheong said. "But you do want to leave, don't you?"

"Just like everybody else," Dirk said.

"So, if I have you do a little favor for me and give you some fuel, you would leave right away, won't you?"

"I don't see why not."

Ana swapped hands with the manicurist. "You can't use your local contacts because they'll still be here. You need strangers who can do whatever this is, then leave, and you can blame it on them."

"You got it, sport-o," Cheong said.

"Tell me about the fuel," Ana said. "You're an insurance company, not a shipyard. Where do you get fuel?"

"Consolidated, Shipping and Storage, remember?" Cheong said. "We've got a few locks leased to us, places where we store stuff. And we help passing ships store items temporarily. I know of at least three containers with fuel bladders in them. Plenty of fuel, even for a ship your size."

"It's not even your fuel?" Dirk said.

"Not exactly. But nobody else is using it right now, and the real owners won't be back for months, if ever."

"And what else?" Ana said.

"What else? What do you mean?"

"Money," Ana said. "Credits. We need some working cash."

"I'm giving you all the fuel you can load."

"Five thousand."

"You don't even know what the job is," Cheong said.

"Still want money."

"I don't have five thousand credits. But if you do this job, I'll give you all the fuel you can carry and something worth way more than five thousand credits."

"Tell us," Dirk said.

Cheong told them.

***

"Centurion speaks Cantonese?" Scruggs said.

"Apparently," Lee said.

She and Scruggs were sitting at a table in Central Station, the closest bar to the docking station. The food was greasy, the beer watery, but it was close enough to the station's commercial sector to connect to Consolidated Shipping and Storage's wireless network. Lee logged in, and Scruggs was security. Having the two of them allowed them to talk to the others over the radio and not look crazy.

"That's pretty funny," Scruggs said.

"Not nearly as funny as the fact that he made Cheong call over some sort of soothsayer that worked in the manicurists' shop and predict the future. They threw these funny-shaped coins, then they agreed the future held 'good fortune for new business endeavors.' He made Cheong pay for the whole thing."

"That's the centurion." She blinked as her ear bud crackled. "What is it, Dena?"

"We're nearly at that office. What's your status?"

"Navigator is working on getting you in," Scruggs said before looking at Lee. "How's it going?"

"I'm connected, but the door system isn't taking the passwords I was given. I'm trying again."

"You think this Cheong guy screwed us?" Scruggs asked.

"I'm almost certain of it," Lee said.

***

Dena sauntered along the corridor between Gavin and Ana. The two men loomed large over her. She wore her "nature girl" outfit, as Ana had taken to calling it—leather pants, jacket, a tight top, and a pack on her back. He and Gavin were in skin suits with coveralls and wore soft spacer caps. Both carried tool kits in their right hands. Ana had a spacer's wrench in his left hand, and Gavin held a prybar. Dena leaned up against the wall on the cross corridor, pulled out her comm, and displayed a map. She appeared to be searching for a listing. Gavin and Ana proceeded down the cross corridor, examining signs as they went by.

"I'm not so sure about this breaking into an office. What do you think, Old Man?" Gavin said.

"Funny that, coming from you, Punk," Ana said. He sized up the next door, which was blank, and shook his head. "Not far enough down."

"You know you're not supposed to call me Punk anymore."

"And you're not supposed to call me Old Man."

"It doesn't bother you," Gavin said. "Coming from me. Not anymore."

"You know that for a fact?" Ana said.

"Yeah," Gavin said. "Punk doesn't bother me, either." He smiled at Ana.

"Really? I'll stop saying it, then. Find something you don't like."

"I think you're starting to like me."

"Now you're just being mean."

"You suggested we work together on this break-in."

"That's because I know that you've done break-ins before. And I want to keep an eye on you."

"How do you know I've done break-ins before?"

"Because you're a disreputable, lying con man," Ana said, "who isn't telling the truth about his history."

"That's harsh, Old Man."

"Truth hurts. Where is this place?"

"Here it is," Gavin said. "Consolidated Shipping and Insurance."

"In place," Ana said into his mic. "Lee, get this door open."

"I'm trying," Lee said over the radio. "But these passwords aren't working. I'm trying a cracking program."

"How long will that take?"

"Not long. Fifteen minutes."

"We can't stay here for fifteen minutes," Ana said. "Not standing in the hallway looking like drunken sailors."

"Have you got a better idea?" Lee asked.

Ana looked down the empty corridor. He set down his tool kit, transferred the wrench to his right hand, stepped back, and swung the wrench in a vicious smack to the handle. The handle dropped with a clang. Then he reversed the wrench, gripped it in both hands, and used the handle end to stab into the lock mechanism. Once, and it twisted, twice, and it bent. The third time, the mechanism popped out.

"Yeah, I do. We're in," he said over the radio.

"Company," Dena said over the radio channel. "Two guys in uniform with stun sticks, walking down the hall."

Ana pulled the door open and gestured Gavin inside. The office was dark and shadowed. The lights from a temperature control system illuminated the room enough to avoid furniture. "Dena, we'll hide in the office."

"They're checking doors," Dena said.

"Don't let them check ours."

"How?"

"Think of something. Unbutton your blouse another button."

"Seriously? That's your go-to suggestion? Show my boobs?"

"It's not like you're going to engage them in a scintillating discussion on the merits of early Imperial deconstructionism art," Ana said.

"I don't have any idea what that means," Dena said.

"Just keep 'em away from this office somehow. Talk to them. Flatter them. Entice them with your knowledge of art history."

"So, I don't have to show my boobs?"

"If you have a better idea, use it," Ana said. "But turn down the volume on your ear bud."

Dena used her comm to fix her ear bud, then looked at the two men walking down the hall. "Emperor's anus, I hate all of you." She undid one button from her blouse, thought for a moment, then undid a second button. She leaned back against the wall and tapped her console.

Two men in matching gray uniforms approached her, both carrying stun sticks. "Lost, Miss?"

Dena jerked her head up, as if startled. "Not anymore. I thought I was in the wrong place, but it looks like I was in the right place but at the wrong time."

"Wrong time?" the first man asked.

"I had to go thumb some papers at Consolidated Storage. They said I had to come by in person for some reason. But I got the time wrong. They were closed when I got there. I called them and rattled the door. Nobody was there. I even tried the places next door, but they were all closed."

"Consolidated," the second said. "That's Cheong's place."

"Why you going to see an insurance company in person?" the first asked. "Why not remote?"

"He said I could do it remotely, but I had other errands to do," Dena said.

"That's how you dress when you see your insurance agent?"

"Well, the thing is," Dena leaned over to flaunt her cleavage. "This Cheong guy, he was giving me these looks over the vids. He looked kind of . . ."

"Greasy," the first guard said.

"Sleazy," the second said.

"I was going to say creepy," Dena said. "But those work, too. So, because of that, I figured he would give me some sort of discount if I came by in person and was friendly. He doesn't look like the type who gets much attention from women."

"You've got that right," the first one said. "A bigger lying scumbag you'll never meet."

"He's always got some stupid scam going. Can't be trusted."

Dena groaned. "That's bad news. I just messaged him, and he said he'll come back to the office if I wait here. So, I'm going to stay and wait for him."

"Stay here, huh? Think he'll show?"

"It's worth the wait, I think," Dena said. "After all, if I get a serious discount, I have enough money to get out of here. This deal with Cheong could be a good deal for me. So, I'm going to wait till he gets here."

"That's the first time I ever heard 'Cheong' and 'good deal' in the same sentence," the first man said. "Couldn't you meet him somewhere public? Might be safer."

Dena stepped away and leaned over, making sure to stretch in all the right ways, then pulled the knife out of her boot. "I think I can take care of myself. And I really need that discount."

The second man laughed. "I bet you give him a surprise. How long did he say he'd be?"

"He said he'd be here in thirty minutes, but I wouldn't be surprised if he makes me wait."

"Well, good luck, then, but be careful."

"Yeah, this time of day, all sorts of shady characters in the corridors," the second one said.

"Don't worry," Dena said. "They won't bother me. Some of my best friends are shady characters."

CHAPTER SEVEN

"Search the whole place," Ana said after Dena confirmed the guards departure. "Start with the desks. Every drawer, every shelf. Everywhere. I'll do the cabinets."

Once through the outer office door, two metal chairs lined the wall to the right, followed by four small cubes. A shoulder-high set of cabinets lined the walls on the left. At the back was a larger office with glass walls, set with a kitchen and bathroom area.

"I know how to toss a place." Gavin pointed to the nearest desk. "I'll start over here."

"Funny that," Ana said. "You knowing how to toss a place. An unusual skill."

Gavin pulled out a drawer and dumped the contents on the floor. He smiled. "Gotta do what you love, Old Man."

Ana furrowed his brows. "Are you enjoying this?"

"What's wrong with that?"

"Do you realize how many things can go wrong here? How many already went wrong? How many can still go wrong?"

"But that's part of the fun," Gavin said. "The not knowing. Take it as it comes. Life is full of surprises. There's plenty of bad ones, but there're good ones, too."

"I don't like surprises," Ana said.

"Said the guy who spent the last twenty or maybe forty years having strangers try to kill him. You can't tell me that you weren't excited by that. Otherwise, why join up?"

Ana pulled a flashlight out of his tool case and shone it into the cupboards on the left side of the outer room. The first two were empty. "I enjoyed the excitement when I was younger, but that faded fast. But that wasn't really the main reason I joined up."

"Imperial anus," Gavin said, jumping back.

"What you got?" Ana asked.

Gavin waved. "Half-eaten sandwich. And yogurt or some milky-white thing. Covered in mold."

"Pigs."

"Seriously, it's all over the inside of this drawer. And it stinks."

"Add it to the pile," Ana said. Gavin dumped the contents on the floor and moved to the next desk.

The third cupboard contained large data packs. Ana checked a note on his comm and ran through them, selecting two of them and putting them into his toolbox. "Got two." The rest, he dumped on the floor.

"Nothing here yet," Gavin said, opening another drawer. "So, why did you join up? The Army or the militia or the Marines, whatever."

"Why'd you leave home?" Ana asked. "Since we're sharing."

Gavin kicked the pile. "Because an Imperial cruiser bombed it into glass, and there was nothing left to stay for. That's why."

Ana closed the latest door carefully. "Huh. Good reason." He pulled the next one open and rooted through the data packs. "A woman."

"What?"

"I joined up to impress a woman."

"And it didn't work out?"

"Worked out great. She was very impressed. We got married."

Gavin stood and cracked his back. "Still married?"

"Nope."

"Didn't think so. What happened?"

"I was a stepping stone to something better. She used me to get off planet, and as soon as we got to sector headquarters, she dumped me for a better offer."

"Let me guess, a better Navy offer?" Gavin said. "Some sort of dashing, Dirk-like officer?"

"Pretty astute there, Punk."

"I'm smarter than I look," Gavin said.

"You'd almost have to be," Ana said.

Gavin slid another drawer open. "Pay dirt, this one's full of data packs."

"Check the list."

Gavin referenced his comm. "Why data packs? Why don't they just update electronically?"

"Proprietary information. Look at the desks."

Each cube had a tiny desk and chair that faced a single chair for customers. Two computers occupied each desk. One was a standard office-style. The second was a smaller yellow one and had a thumbprint entry pad. Cables ran from the yellow computers to the ceiling-mounted trays, across the roof, and down into the cupboards on the far side.

"Two computers," Ana said. "One for regular station work, one with their insurance database and client information. Air-gapped system. That way, no possibility of somebody hacking in."

"Unless they go in like we do," Gavin said.

"Right. Is the other pack there?"

"I'm checking. So, what happened after she dumped you?"

"I got really, really angry at everything and everybody, and took it out in random violence."

"Went to jail?"

"Promoted. Empire can always use people who want to rage-kill. I got better—it became my specialty. Took courses. Eventually taught some."

Light flooded the room. Ana dropped his flashlight and grabbed his wrench. Gavin flipped his arm, and a knife appeared in his hand.

"Really, boys?" Dena stood in the door.

Gavin lowered his knife, and Ana dropped his wrench.

"Good way to get yourself killed, Friend Dena," Gavin said.

"Kill the light," Ana said. "We don't want to be seen from outside."

"The corridor lights are bright, and anybody who looks close enough at the door to see if the light is on will be more interested in why the lock is smashed off."

Ana grunted and turned back to searching the cupboards. "Scruggs and Lee?"

"On their way back to the ship. Pilot is switching locks soon."

"Pilot? Are you calling him that in bed now?"

"We don't do that anymore," Dena said. "We agreed."

"You got what you wanted, and you're just dumping him?" Ana asked.

"Or he got what he wanted, and he's just dumping me," Dena said. "You need any help?"

"No," Ana said. He pulled another cupboard open, one full of coffee cups. He rattled between them. Just cups.

Gavin returned to the desk. "We've got it covered."

Dena slid by them. "The stuff on the floor is icky." She stopped to examine the office door.

"Don't step in it, then," Ana said.

"We're not supposed to look in the office," Gavin said.

"And it's locked," Ana said.

"Let's see," Dena rattled the handle, then walked back to Ana's tool kit, picked up the wrench, and returned to the office. Two swings, and she knocked the lock mechanism off. The door slid open with a push. "Tell Cheong it was open when we got here."

Ana shrugged, then dumped the contents of another cupboard on the floor.

***

Dirk flicked a switch forward. Then back. Then forward again. Keep it together, hotshot, he thought. The air lock light lit.

"Onboard, Pilot," Lee said over the intercom. "Dropping the chains now."

"Understood," Dirk said. He was sweating, and his hands were shaking. He took a deep breath and closed his eyes. Then another.

Lee bustled up into the control room, sat, then pulled up displays on her screen. "Once you drop the magnets, we can go. Scruggs is on the fuel system."

"Understood," Dirk said again.

He breathed deep and thumbed his screen, disengaging the magnets with a click. Dirk backed the ship out, pivoted, and moved along the station at a sedate pace. He didn't try anything flashy, just an agonizing slowness as he moved around the perimeter.

"Pilot, are you okay?" Lee asked.

"Why? What's wrong."

"You're just so . . . controlled."

"That's unusual?"

Lee sniffed the air. The usual alcohol scent was missing. "You know it is. There. Storage truss six, level thirty-five." She pointed at a hexagonal metal truss sticking out from the station. At each of the forty levels, six containers were locked end-on onto the truss. Approximately one in four containers had a red power cable connector plugged in.

Dirk maneuvered up to level thirty-five and pivoted the ship sideways until he saw the first of the three containers that had been described to them. "That's the first one there," he said.

"No good for us. No power. If it's water, it's frozen."

"Why would Cheong send us to a frozen container? He knows we can't use it."

"Because he's an Imperial turd," Lee said.

"Can't be that simple," Dirk said. He tapped his console. "Scruggs?"

"Here, Pilot," Scruggs said over the intercom. "I've got the lock open. I see the container."

Dirk flinched. He hadn't noticed the lock opening. The light was on his display, but he hadn't been paying attention. Focus. "Can you chain us on?"

"I'm not sure how," she said.

"Why bother? We can't use frozen water," Lee said.

"What if it's not water?" Dirk said.

***

"Got it," Gavin said. He held up a data pack from the fourth cubicle's desk drawer. "Main backup. There're three in the drawer here."

"With the other two I have, that's it," Ana said. "We've got all five. Come out, Nature Girl."

Dena didn't move, so Ana waved to catch her attention.

Dena stepped out of the office. "I can't hear you from in there."

"We've got the backups," Ana said. "The system ones and the private one that Cheong's people make. Did you find anything?"

"Two credit chips with six point three credits total between them, a coupon for a year's supply of water from any of Cheong's corporate refueling stations, lots of ship registration information, and a portable vid player with some mildly disturbing pornography."

"You're in the big city now, Nature Girl," Ana said. "Gotta get used to that sort of thing."

"You want to see it?"

"Not particularly," Ana said. "But I'm sure it wouldn't upset me."

"You might be surprised," Dena said. "You're in it."

"What?" Ana shook his head. "I would have remembered if I did that sort of thing."

"You didn't. Cheong did. He must have taken your picture. He's pasted it in place for some of the actors."

The three of them contemplated that in silence.

"Disturbing," Gavin said.

Ana shrugged. "As long as I get a good part. Hang on." His comm bonged. "We're using the station network, Navy. That wasn't the plan."

"I need Gavin," Dirk said. "We're at the first fuel dump."

"And?" Gavin said.

"It's not heated."

"Frozen water's no good."

"I know that. I'm chained up right now. I'm getting Scruggs to look at it. What should we look for when she pops a valve?"

"A-ha," Gavin said. "Got it. It should out-gas right away."

"I don't understand," Dena said. "What's the problem?"

"We usually split water to H and O to make fuel for our engines," Gavin said. "We use the fusion plant for that. It's safer that way—less risk of fire and explosion. But we can take the raw elements if they are loaded separately. But the fueling stations usually load them both at once. Or at least have them colocated."

"Scruggs is going across now," Dirk said.

"If it comes out as a gas," Gavin said, "a white gas, it's hydrogen. If it's a blue liquid, it's oxygen."

"White gas, she says."

"Load up the H tank."

"This will take twice as long as we thought. You guys have to wait."

"Navy," Ana said. "I don't really feel like we should linger in a place we broke into."

"Do you trust Cheong?" Dirk asked. "This was supposed to be water. We'd fill up and be ready to go. It's H. We can use that, but we still need the O content. If the next place isn't O . . ."

"Then, we've got no leverage," Ana said. "Right, we'll wait." He looked at Dena and Gavin. "Did either of you bring a deck of cards?"

Lee's voice broke into the channel. "We've got another problem."

"What's that?" Ana asked.

"A Confederation ship just jumped into the system. They're broadcasting that they're taking possession of the station, as per an agreement with the corp. They've ordered all traffic to halt and be inspected."

"Scruggs, is there any way you can hurry this up?" Dirk asked her over the radio.

"Pump is running at optimal speed, like the engineer showed me, Pilot."

"It's just that I really, really don't want to be interrogated by the Confeds."

"On account of you're an Imperial Duke and a crimes-against-humanity person?" Scruggs asked.

"We agreed not to talk about all that," Dirk said. "Remember?"

"I understand, Pilot," Scruggs said. "As you requested. But there's nothing else we can do. Just wait."

"How long to pump all that H?" Dirk asked.

"Another thirty minutes."

"And ten to get locked onto the other container. And pump that. Maybe another thirty, forty."

"And a half hour at least to get back to the lock and pick up the others," Lee said.

"How long till that Confed ship docks?"

"Two hours, max. Less till it's close enough to cause problems."

"We need a new plan," Dirk said, drumming his fingers and keying the comm screen. "Centurion, Engineer, listen up."

Ana and Gavin looked at each other as Dirk relayed his instructions over the comm.

Dena was digging through a desk. "Now I have six used credit chips, a total of fourteen point six credits."

"Do you have your skin suit on under that?" Gavin asked.

Dena turned toward him, cocked a hip, and slapped her butt. "Does it look like I'm wearing anything under this?" She shook her head. "It's in my pack there."

"You need to put it on," Gavin said.

"I'm not going outside. I don't like it there."

"We have to. Otherwise, we won't make the ship."

"Space freaks me out. I get sick."

"Everybody gets sick the first few times," Ana said. "You just have to get over it."

"I don't want to."

"Doesn't matter what you want. Do you want us to leave you here, then?"

"No."

"So, suit up," Gavin said.

"Right here?"

The cubes were open as the office walls were glass.

"You see anywhere else?"

Dena looked around, then smiled. "Well, get ready for a show."

***

Dirk was still in the control room, and Lee had come down to the airlock to speed things up.

Lee knocked helmets with Scruggs as she climbed into the air lock. "Everything working, Sister Scruggs?"

"Yes. Pump's working like the engineer showed me before. We're seventy-two percent full. According to the engineer, I'm to pump till the flow rate drops below twenty-five percent or when we fill up, whichever comes first."

"And you're set for the oxygen?"

"Right here—" Scruggs identified another set of hoses lying in the air lock. It was ready to be hauled out and connected.

"Good," Lee said. "Pilot, I'm trying for the other container. You can follow me on the camera." She stepped to the edge of the air lock, glanced at the tower of containers, and pushed herself out into space.

Scruggs watched as she floated away and keyed a private channel to Dirk. "She's so graceful. It's like she's flying. I wish I could float like that."

"It's not flying, really," Dirk said. "It's more like dancing. But it's easy to be graceful in space, if you practice. Enough practice, and you'll get expert at anything."

"Not dancing. I can dance, but I'll never be good enough at it to be an expert."

"You need to practice more."

"That sounds like my mother talking. But not everything is possible, even with lots of practice."

"I disagree. Enough practice, and you master everything."

"Even landings?"

Dirk's sigh echoed over the channel. "Stay in the lock, Private. We'll need you there shortly."

Lee sailed on, oblivious to their private conversation, counting each level as she passed. "Thirty-six, thirty-seven, firing." She fired the magnetic harpoon above her head. The recoil slowed her down, the harpoon impacted on the steel container, and the magnet stuck. She slowed as the coiled spring in the harpoon engaged. "Thirty-eight, thirty-nine."

Lee remotely disengaged the magnet. The line coiled back into the hand harpoon, then she reached for the container. A quick pivot, and her boots stuck on. She walked around the container and saw the next one. After a hop, she was across. She checked her comm on her wrist. She had one more rank to go. She leaped, landed, locked, then examined the container.

"Good news, Pilot," she said, "this one has power."

"Pop the inspection valve," Dirk said.

"There isn't one," Lee said.

"There isn't one?"

"It's not a liquid container, it's a solid. But it's got power. It should be heated."

"That doesn't help."

"Let me get the door open," Lee said.

She clomped down the side and yanked the door handle. It wasn't locked, so she pulled the lever, ensuring her boots were magnetized.

A gush of atmosphere flooded over her, condensing to ice crystals. She waved them away as she looked inside. Rather than a specially constructed liquid tank container, it was a standard cargo container filled with a bladder.

"There's a bladder inside. I'll check if it's still liquid."

She stepped forward and grasped the panel on the bladder. The bladder was plastic, with a metal panel of readouts, a plug for a heating unit, a hose coupling, and an inspection valve.

She cracked the inspection valve, and a blue liquid pulsed out, sticking to her glove.

"It's O," she said. "Come on up, Pilot."

"I'm getting Scruggs to decouple now," Dirk said. "We'll be there in a jiff."

Lee examined the hose connections. It wasn't a standard fuel bladder or station fuel cell but rather a bag with hose connections. Non-standard hose connections.

"I wonder how we'll get this on the ship," Lee mused. "Could take a while."

"We don't have a while," Dirk said. "Hang on, Scruggs. Maneuvering."

CHAPTER EIGHT

"Wasn't much of a show," Gavin said as Dena slipped her jacket over her skin suit.

"In this world, you get what you pay for," she said. "And you paid . . . nothing, so—"

"We don't have time for mating rituals," Ana said. "Computers first. Smash everything."

"You call that a mating ritual? We didn't even—"

"Less talking, more hitting," Ana said, handing her a spare wrench from his toolbox.

Gavin used his prybar to pop the top of the computers and hammered the inside. "It's not a mating ritual if we don't actually mate."

Dena surveyed him. "I'm certainly not going to mate with you dressed like that."

"So, I still have a chance," Gavin said, prying the top off another computer.

Ana used his wrench to hammer the memory modules to bits. "Somewhere between zero and a snowball's chance inside a neutron star, I would guess. Get the faceplates off those servers in the cabinets."

Gavin dropped his wrench and pulled out a screwdriver. "Can do. But I think I have a better chance than that."

"What about the screens?" Dena asked. "And your chances aren't improving by talking about them."

"Smash the screens," Ana said. "Everything. Before we go, dump the desk drawers as well."

"What happens if I get you a drink?" Gavin asked. His screwdriver torqued out of the screws on the last server, and he cursed.

"Then, I have a drink." Dena smashed a screen and jumped as the power arced at her. "What did you expect? Kiss on the cheek?"

"Unplug 'em first," Ana said. "We don't need a fire. Can't have anybody find this before we're gone."

"We're leaving DNA all over the place," Dena said.

"Doesn't matter if they know who did it." Ana smashed a server. "As long as they don't know why. Gavin, what's the holdup?"

"This last one, the faceplate's stuck." Gavin pried at the case. "I can't budge it."

"Grab a sledge from your kit," Ana said.

Gavin pulled one out and hammered the last server case, only bending it. Ana and Gavin alternated hammering the case. The metal twisted enough to hammer the faceplate off. Ana used the handle of his wrench to beat the insides. Then the power supply blew up, showering it in sparks and puffing acrid smoke.

"So much for unplugging things," Gavin said.

Dena stepped back from the billowing smoke. "Well done, expert burglars. You might as well just have pulled the fire alarm."

Ana waved the smoke away and coughed. "Better hope we don't set anything off missy, or you'll be most unhappy."

"Why is that?" Dena asked.

"Because we're supposed to go spinward, then to the outer ring, and climb a tower to get to the Heart's Desire. But if the alarm goes off, we're out the first walk we see, and it's a long hop outside to that tower. Think you'll like that?"

"The Empress's hairy armpits," Dena said. "Let's not do that."

"Didn't think so." Ana surveyed the debris. "Looks like a herd of drunken tabbos came through. Collect our tools and let's go."

***

"Flow rates dropping, Pilot," Scruggs said over the comm.

"How much?" Dirk said.

"Down below fifty percent, but we're only at eighty-seven percent full—"

"Cut us loose. Turn the valve off at the tank and decouple."

"Understood."

Dirk checked his screens while waiting for Scruggs. The inbound Confederation ship was broadcasting a beacon, repeating the "Stay Put" message. One other ship had undocked and was heading for the jump limit. Dirk checked its course. The inbound Confed ship could still alter course and catch it, but it made no move to intercept.

"Pilot, I'm as ready as can be up here," Lee said.

"Scruggs?"

"I'm closing the air lock now," she said.

Dirk waited till the air lock door winked green, then gently thrust Heart's Desire away from the station. It pitched up. He pulsed the main engine to move up, parallel to the truss. The top row of containers came into view. This time, Dirk used the thrusters to stop, rolled till the truss was above the control room, and circled around till Lee came to the door of an open container.

"Get ready to lock on, Scruggs," Dirk said.

"She can't," Lee said over the radio. "With the doors opened, there's no room, and we need them open to pump. You'll have to hover."

"Hover the whole time?" Dirk said.

"Yes. I need Scruggs to help me with the hose, figure out if we can fit it."

"What do you mean, if?"

"I called the engineer. He's on his way," Lee said. "We'll need his help to get

59

this set up."

"Can I open the air lock yet?" Scruggs said.

"Yes, hand me the hose as soon as it's open."

Dirk rolled till the air lock faced the container, then monitored the cursing and muttering on the channel. Scruggs and Lee were talking with a lot of "over there" and "push that one" that Dirk couldn't fully make out.

He wiped sweat from his forehead. "What's going on down there?"

"We're busy, Pilot. Just try to keep us close and don't jerk the ship so much."

"If I can't see, I'm jerking all over the place."

"Use the cameras," Lee said. "The docking ones."

"Right," Dirk said. He'd forgotten those. A rookie mistake. Try to calm down.

He brought the cameras up. Lee and Scruggs were holding a hose over a fitting on the bladder. The fitting would roll on, but they couldn't get it locked. As he watched, the ship drifted away, and the hose stretched. They fiddled for a moment, then dropped it to float free.

"Pilot," Lee yelled.

"I see, I see," Dirk said. He eased the ship back. "We need a chain."

"Ours aren't long enough to hold us. And the hose won't lock."

"Where's the engineer?" Scruggs asked.

"What happens if you can't lock?" Dirk asked.

"We're stuck here. Stuck like everyone else."

***

"Stop playing with your tools and get moving," Ana said.

They had climbed a level, went anti-spinward, then crowded into an air lock. Once inside, Gavin had dumped the contents of both tool cases onto the floor and sorted them, throwing a selection into the smallest cases.

"Lee is having problems getting the second hose in. I need some tools."

"I can carry one case," Ana said.

"What about her?"

"What about me?" Dena said.

Ana looked at her. "Where's your tether? And your mag boots?"

"Tether?" Dena looked at Ana and Gavin.

She had on a leather jacket and high-heeled boots over her skin suit, leather studs with metal rings incising her belt. The two men had work boots with magnetic bottoms, and each had a four-meter tether strapped to their tool belt.

"Ooops," she said.

"Outstanding," Ana said. "Right, adapt, improvise, overcome. Engineer, take the tools you need—one case—and climb up that tower as fast as you can. Dena, come over here and climb onto my lap."

"Pardon?"

"Climb onto my lap. Wrap your legs around my waist and put your arms around my shoulder."

"Shouldn't you at least buy me a drink first?"

"Given the way this is going to play out, you should buy one for me."

"That's not the way this male-female thing works, Centurion. If you want me to do a deep-space lap dance, I get the money up front."

"I need my hands free in front of me to work with my tether." Ana unclipped the tether from his belt. "My feet have to be clear, so I can lock on, and if you're in front of me, I can see how far your head sticks up and I won't kill you by banging it against a metal beam." Ana paused. "Much as I'd like to."

"Ready to dump the air," Gavin said. "Check me."

Ana stepped over and ran his hands over values, readouts, and checked the seals around his boots, gloves, and helmet. "Good to go."

Gavin did the same for him. Then Ana ran his hands over Dena while Gavin waited by the controls.

"I'm sure this is just an excuse for you to feel my boobs," Dena said.

"If there's a seam there, I'm all over them. But otherwise, we don't have time for that. She's good, Gavin."

Gavin punched the button, and the colors in the lock sharpened as the air pulled out.

"Stand back against the wall and let him go first," Ana said over the radio.

Dena complied, and Gavin slid between them, dropping his toolbox. As soon as the light flashed, he spun the locking wheel, pulled it in, then stepped outside, disappearing from view.

Dena leaned over and grasped the hatch frame. The blackness extended ahead of her, the stars pinpricks in the distance, and even the primary was half the size and brightness of Earth's moon.

"Ohh. Ohh." She grabbed the door frame. "Things are swimming."

"Look at me," Ana said. He sailed over to the door and extended his left arm to stop his drift, using his right to turn Dena to face him.

"All aboard. Climb on." He pulled her into him. She locked her legs around his waist, wrapping her arms around his chest.

The outer ring spun at half Earth-normal, so Ana grabbed her with one hand and used the other to maneuver out the door. He spun them around till the bottom of the tower was six meters away.

Gavin was already pulling out of sight as he climbed.

"We'll just walk over there and start climbing. Only a few minutes to the ship."

"Right," Dena said. "There's so many stars."

Ana stepped gingerly, ensuring he locked each foot down as he stepped across the station.

"Centurion?"

"What is it?"

"I think I'm going to be sick. All those stars . . ."

"Close your eyes," Ana said. "Don't think about stars. Concentrate on relaxing. Pretend you're in bed with a beautiful man."

"Like you?"

"No, not like me, you young idiot. Somebody more age-appropriate."

"Huh." Dena shifted. "That works. I feel better. Does your hand have to be there?"

Ana realized that, with gripping her tight, his hands had dropped lower than he intended. "Sorry, old habits." He removed his hand.

"Been a while since you've had a sexy woman sitting on you?"

"Given that you're about to vomit and wearing a skin suit, I don't have one sitting on me right now. But, yes, it has been a while. We're at the tower. This is the hard part. I'm going to be using feet to push us up, hands just for guidance, but there's lots of beams and flanges, so hold tight."

Ana clanked one boot onto a cross beam and pushed up. He and Dena rose. He used his free hands to stop short of a beam, but Dena kept rising, and her head slammed into the crossbeam.

"Emperor's anus," she said. "That hurt."

"Hold on tight."

It didn't help. She hit two of five cross beams.

"Centurion?"

"What? I'm doing the best I can."

"I can't believe I'm saying this, but . . ."

"What?"

"Can you grab my ass, please? And hold tight?"

***

Gavin arrived at the top container to find Lee and Scruggs wrestling with the hose. His breath rasped over the channel. "Status?" he asked.

"Hose won't lock, Engineer," Scruggs said. "And the ship swinging so much we can't even get an emergency seal around it."

"Pilot, hold us steady."

"I'm trying," Dirk said, then cursed as the ship flipped away again.

"Drunken Imperial idiot," Gavin said. "Keep us close."

The ship swung back, and Dirk overcompensated. "Look out, get away."

Gavin dove off the container as the ship slammed into the side. Scruggs dove into the air lock, and Lee retreated into the container. The Heart's Desire slammed onto the doors, bending them out of shape.

"Emperor's hairy testicles," Gavin yelled. "You nearly killed me. Incompetent, upper-class twit. This is why everybody hates the Empire."

"Not everybody hates the Empire," Dirk said.

"Everybody with sense. Hold about four meters away."

"I don't think—"

"Shut up. Hold off. Scruggs, pull that locking chain out."

"They're too short, Engineer, they don't reach."

"I know. Pull that one out—unspool it as far as you can."

Scruggs did so. Gavin grabbed a chisel and hammer from his tool case. He pushed off from the container, pivoted midair, and landed feetfirst next to Scruggs. "Hold the chain against the ship. Keep your hands about a foot apart."

"That Confed ship is closing," Dirk said. "They'll be docking in a few—"

"Be quiet," Gavin said. "Scruggs, ready?"

"Yes, Engineer." Scruggs held the chain.

"Hold it taut on the ship."

Gavin waited till she was positioned, then put the chisel's edge against a link near the ship and swung his hammer. The hammer smacked the chisel, cutting the link, and Gavin banged off into space but rolled and grabbed the truss as he flew away.

"Well, congratulations, Engineer," Dirk said over the radio. "I can see that you've provided us with a nice length of broken chain."

Gavin ignored him. "Scruggs, peel that busted link apart. Give the end with the locking nuts to Lee. Lee, lock that chain to the container's portside chain plate."

"It won't reach the ship, Gavin," Lee said.

"Not yet. Scruggs?"

Scruggs heaved the chain to Lee, who caught the snaking chain and hooked it to the container.

"Ready, Engineer."

"Now we do it again on the other chain."

This time, Gavin cut it twice, so he had an extra length of chain without the locking mechanism. He threw the spare end-pieces into the air lock and pushed back to his tool kit. He removed two locking carabiner loops—open chain links—with snap fittings. He pulled out the docking chain from the ship, snapped the new length on, added another snap fitting on the end, then heaved it to Lee. Lee snapped them together.

"Right, Pilot, drift us out to the end of the chain. Just enough to stretch it. Scruggs, help me wind this hose over."

Dirk puffed the ship. "Low fuel warning. No more fuel till we mix the tanks."

"There's still a hundred kilograms left when the low fuel light goes on," Gavin said.

"The low fuel light's been on for an hour," Dirk said. "I ignored it. This is the no-fuel light."

"Well, we're locked on," Gavin said.

He and Scruggs wound the fuel hose around the chain twice, pulled more slack, then pushed it over to Lee. She fitted it around the nozzle, rotated it a quarter turn clockwise, and pulled the lever that locked the collar.

"It's not pulling loose now," Lee said. "But it's not sealed, either."

"There's a can of sealant in my kit," Gavin said. "Dig it out."

Lee dug in his kit and pulled out a can. "Got it."

Gavin jumped and hit next to her with an oof. He locked his boots, grabbed the hose, and shoved it farther into the fitting. "Spray it around with the sealant. Start at the bottom." Lee obeyed, running the spray can around the hose.

Gavin released the hose and let it hang loose. "Again." Lee ran the can around again.

"Scruggs, start the pumps," Gavin said. "Like I showed you, but just ten percent."

The hose fitting was just outside the air lock. Scruggs pulled a locking lever, and the internal valve released. She ducked back inside, pulled a lever on the pump panel, then turned the flow knob.

"Ten percent," she said over the radio.

"Go to twenty," Gavin said.

Scruggs turned the knob. "Twenty."

"Thirty. Now forty."

"Steady at forty."

Gavin examined the hose. It flexed but didn't leak. Yet.

"Try fifty."

"Going for fifty," Scruggs said.

Gavin yelled, "Back. Back."

A mist of liquid oxygen burped out of the fitting, staining Lee's suit. The spray slowed down but didn't stop entirely.

"Back to forty," Scruggs said.

Gavin tapped the hose. It was leaking at the fitting but only drops. It would have to do.

"Forty it is," Gavin said. "How much in the tank?"

"Three percent. Three and a half." She paused. "Nearly four."

"Pilot, we're pumping," Gavin said. "But less than half the normal flow rate."

"How long till we're full of O?" Dirk asked.

"A while. An hour, maybe."

"We don't have that type of time."

"The Confed ship will dock and deal with the station first," Gavin said. "We can get away from them."

"We can get away from the ship, yes," Dirk said. "But they just launched a shuttle, and it's vectored toward us."

CHAPTER NINE

"You don't have to enjoy it so much, you know," Dena said. "The ass-grabbing, I mean."

She clung to Ana as he steadily mounted the truss toward the Heart's Desire. She was like a space limpet, and his hand was firmly in place on her left cheek.

"What's life if you can't take pleasure in the little things?" Ana asked. "A baby's smile, a pretty flower, a firm female behind."

"I can't really see you taking pleasure in a pretty flower, Centurion. You don't seem the type."

"I'll have you know that I won an award for my flower arrangements," Ana said.

"There's no way I'll believe that."

"Get me a selection of them sometime, and I'll show you," Ana said. "Don't forget the base greens. You need a green background—ferns are good. Everybody always forgets the ferns."

"I won't forget the ferns," Dena said before pausing. "My eyes are still closed."

"That's good."

"I'm very afraid."

"I know. The dark is scary. It's hard to get used to."

"You aren't scared."

"No."

"None of the others are scared."

"No."

"It's just me, isn't it? This is embarrassing."

"That's natural. People didn't evolve in space. Takes some getting used to." Ana shook his head as sweat dripped down his face.

"I'll bet the others didn't. I'll bet Scruggs didn't."

"She doesn't seem bothered by it."

"There's not much she's afraid of, is there?"

"Not that I can see. Useful characteristic for a budding space-Marine."

"Unlike me. I'm afraid all the time," Dena said.

"What's there to be afraid of?" Ana asked.

"I'm afraid of you."

"Good point. I'm dangerous."

"I think you'd space me without a second's thought," Dena said.

"Why are you telling me this?" Ana asked. He paused in the crossbeam. His pulse throbbed in his temples. "I just need a rest here."

"I'm afraid of space. I'm afraid of being left behind. I'm afraid of you. And I'm useless. I'm the only crew member who can't do anything on the ship."

"Well, you have other skills."

"You mean my willingness to sleep with the captain?"

"I was referring to the fact that you pack a mean slingshot, but that's a skill, too."

"What do I do now that we're not together? Dirk and me?"

"Find someone else?"

"Who? You? The engineer?"

"I wouldn't try me. Maybe the engineer."

"Lee would stab me in my sleep."

"Probably." Ana resumed climbing.

"I'm lucky Scruggs doesn't shoot me for sport. She has a crush on the captain."

"Yes. That's the plan."

Dena opened her eyes. "Really?"

"I'm the bad guy. The captain is the good guy. She wants to please us both. Troop morale one-oh-one. That's how we motivate them." Ana's breath rasped over the radio, and he stopped again.

"This was planned?"

"Yes. I think everything through."

"I don't think things through," Dena said.

Ana resumed climbing. "That's evident. I figured that out from the beginning."

"You did?"

"Sure. You wanted to get away from something. Your past. Bad relationship. Lousy family. Congrats, it worked. You got away. And now . . ."

"Now I'm stuck on a spaceship. I have no useful space skills, except the ability to flirt with men, some skill with a slingshot, and good fashion sense."

"Hard to find, good fashion sense."

"I've been reading a lot, from the ship's database. There's so much to know. And so much to read."

"How did you learn things in the past?"

"Flirting came natural."

"Other things."

"We just did stuff. Worked on the ranch, in the woods. Traveled to trade. I learned things by doing. That doesn't work now. There's so much to read."

Ana stretched his neck back. "Only a little farther to climb. What have you been reading about?"

"I started with ship and small craft specifications. Figured that would be the first thing I needed to know."

"Did you happen to read about a Confederation model Alpha-five shuttle?"

"I think so. Why?"

"One's coming at us right now."

***

"Everything is clear of the hatches, Engineer," Scruggs said. Standing in the air lock by Gavin, she was surrounded by tools, hoses, and pipes near the pump control board. "Tools and everything. But we're not pumping very fast."

"I'm ready as well, Engineer," Lee said.

She was on the ship's hull next to the manual shut-off valves and chain connections.

Gavin stood in the container door and tapped the connecting chain. "How much oxygen in the tank?"

"Forty percent and climbing. Another thirty minutes to fill."

"We don't have thirty minutes. Where's the centurion?"

"Just below you," Ana said over the radio.

"Move yourself," Gavin said. "There's a shuttle inbound."

"I see it. And it's not inbound, it's here."

"Get onboard, now," Gavin said. "Where are you?"

"As soon as I climb around this hose contraption you've got here," Ana said. "I've got this girl grabbing my chest, causing problems."

"Scruggs, get ready to shut off the pump," Gavin said. "But not till I'm ready. We need it running to the last second to drain the hose. Lee, you'll have to unclip the chains on the connectors. Once the chains are loose, I'll pull the hose off. We need the shut-off valve on the shipside closed, so we don't vent our tank back into space—careful that we don't let O spew around. It's explosive, even in vacuum. Soon as Ana and Dena are aboard, we go."

"The air lock is full of tools and stuff," Scruggs said. "Not a lot of room."

"Gavin," Dirk said over the radio. "That shuttle is hovering off our port bow. They're opening an air lock."

"That model doesn't have any weapons, Navy," Ana said.

"How do you know?" Dirk asked.

"Dena told me."

"She's an expert on shuttles now?" Lee asked.

"She's been studying," Ana said.

"I don't see any ship weapons," Dirk said. "But I do see a suited Marine type in an air lock."

"Is he armed?" Ana asked.

"He's got something," Dirk said. "A boarding shotgun, maybe."

Ana appeared around the hose. "Well, don't let him board, then. Scruggs, we need to get past you."

Gavin stepped onto the hull so Ana could pass. "Get in, cycle, and clear out for Scruggs. As soon as you're clear, Scruggs will hop in, and we'll disconnect and go. Scruggs, clear the air lock."

Scruggs stepped onto the hull. Ana waddled past into the air lock, still holding Dena.

Lee watched the air lock door close. "Was he holding her ass?"

"Seems like," Scruggs said.

"Not now, you two," Gavin said. He pushed off the hull and landed on the container next to the hose fittings. "Stand by, Pilot."

Scruggs tethered to the side of the ship, waiting to reenter the lock. Lee was below her, standing next to the docking chains, ready to pull the chains with a wrench.

"Soon as the air lock light goes green, back in," Gavin said.

All three watched the air lock light flash green.

"Go," Gavin said.

Scruggs spun the locking wheel and stepped inside to reach the pump controls. Lee unscrewed the carabiner, holding the chains together. Gavin waited.

"Pump's off," Scruggs said.

"Chain's coming lose," Lee said. "Next pivot in, I'll have it off." She reeled the chain in. "I don't have a hand to close the valve."

"Scruggs, get that shut-off valve closed," Gavin said.

"Doing that now, Engineer." She clambered out back onto the hull and boot-locked next to the valves.

"Uncoupling," Gavin said.

He leaned into the locking lever on the hose. He had to lock his foot magnets to the container wall to get enough leverage. The collar opened up, and the hose was supposed to release.

Except it didn't. The sealant had hardened, and the hose became stuck, leaving the Heart's Desire still attached to the station, at the end of a hose full of explosive liquid oxygen.

"Fuel light's on," Dirk said over the radio. "I am completely out of fuel. I can't maneuver. You need to mix the tanks or something."

"We're stuck here." Gavin kicked the hose's fitting. "That Empire-damned hose is holding us."

Scruggs tried to pull the handle on the outer valve, but it was stuck. She repositioned her boots and pulled harder. It didn't budge.

Heart's Desire swung at the end of the hose and pitched forward.

"Engineer," Dirk said. "Gavin—Emperor's balls. We're spinning. I'm going to hit something. Give me more fuel."

"Engineer, the shut-off valve is locked open," Scruggs said. "I can't move it."

Gavin jiggered the hose locking lever closed, open, closed, then open again. The hose remained stuck.

"Gavin—" Dirk said.

"Not now, Pilot. We've got problems out here," Gavin said.

"We've got problems in here, too. That Confed raider is docking on the main ring," Dirk said. "They're calling us to stand by for boarding."

"Where's the shuttle?" Gavin asked.

"Standing off from us. They're calling, too. They don't want to get near us while we're spinning, in case we explode or something."

"There's fuel in those lines. We need to drain them before we leave."

"We don't have time."

"Scruggs, get inside and turn the pump up to max," Gavin said.

"I'll help," Lee said.

She shouldered the makeshift chains and followed Scruggs back into the air lock. They pushed the controls to max flow.

The seal around the hose shrunk as the suction came on, then expanded. Liquid oxygen burped out and sprayed the inside of the container.

Gavin stepped back from the spray and rocked the hose clamp open again. The hose flexed. He grabbed the radio. "I need somebody to open the main tanks so Dirk can maneuver. We'll keep the hose sucking till the last minute. That will keep our tanks from draining out to space."

"I'll do it," Ana said over the radio. "Where am I going?"

"There's six valves on the bulkhead just below the lock," Gavin said. "One says main tank cross flow, another says external fuel."

"Stand by," Ana said. After forty seconds of silence, his voice came back. "I'm there."

"Close external fuel. Clockwise is closed."

"External fuel closed," Ana said.

"Open the main tank cross flow," Gavin said. "Counter-clockwise is open."

"Ya think? You mean like every other valve in the Imperium? Punk."

"Shut up and open the valve, Old Man."

"Engineer, the pump is sucking," Scruggs said.

"Turn it off. Totally off."

"I've got fuel. Maneuvering," Dirk said. The ship stopped spinning, then pivoted up and away from the station. "I'm getting us out of here. Everybody, hang on."

"Wait for me," Gavin yelled. He braced his feet and dove at the Heart's Desire, clearing the air lock door and diving in.

"Engineer's on board," Lee said from the air lock frame. "I'm closing the air lock."

Dirk's voice came over the radio. "Main engines in five, four, three—"

Everybody grabbed something and held on.

Dirk pulsed the main engines, and the Heart's Desire strained. The hose held for just a moment, then the seals cracked, and the ship snapped forward.

The open container bladder belched ice as liquid oxygen seeped out and froze. The trailing fuel hose spat oxygen out, then whiplashed back and forth. Inside the air lock, Lee lost her hold on the locking wheel and smashed forward. She flew past Scruggs and slammed into Gavin. They lay inside the air lock, stunned.

"They're in," Scruggs said. "But they look hurt. I'm closing the outer door."

Scruggs pushed it shut and spun the wheel. The air lock lights flashed green, and Scruggs pushed the button to air up the lock.

"Ana, get up here and track that shuttle and those Confeds," Dirk said over the radio.

Ana arrived in the bridge and took over his station. "What am I looking for?"

"Pursuit," Dirk said. "Communications."

"Can they come in now?" Dena asked over the radio.

"Keep 'em in the air lock for now," Ana said to Dena.

"Why? They're hurt."

"Something, somebody said, I don't know. Just stand by." Ana tapped through bridge screens. "The communication board is completely lit up, and I'm going to ignore that for now."

"Find me the Confed frigate," Dirk said.

Ana ran through his sensors. "It's docked. They've got crew on the station."

"Where's the shuttle?"

"It's behind us, following. I can see its drive plume."

"The Emperor's hairy anus," Dirk said. "Just our luck."

"Wait, the drive plume just got brighter."

"Chasing us?"

"Nope." Ana smiled. "They pivoted. They're heading back. We're on our way."

Dirk let out his breath with a whoosh. "How is everybody?"

"Dena's onboard. Scruggs is in the lock with Lee and Gavin. They were banged up a bit after our unscheduled departure. We need to get them in and take a look at them."

"That was the worst fueling experience I've ever had," Dirk said.

"Me, too," Ana said, blinking. "Fueling experience. How cold is the air in the air lock?"

"Very cold," Dirk said. "We don't bother to heat it, we just need to be able to pressurize, then breathe. It would mess up the off gassing if we warmed things up."

"Off gassing," Ana said. "Liquid oxygen. Does liquid oxygen freeze in the dark?"

Dirk nodded. "Sometimes." He looked at Ana and punched the intercom. "Don't open the lock!"

***

"Let us in," Scruggs said from inside the lock.

"Centurion said to wait," Dena said.

"Okay," Scruggs said. "Then, we wait."

Dena looked at Scruggs through the view port. "This is stupid. Stand back.

I'm opening up."

"But—"

"Stand back," Dena said.

Dena had finished spinning the locking wheel open when Dirk yelled.

"Too late," she said. "I've only just opened it. Why?"

She looked at Scruggs, who was standing in her suit.

"What?" Scruggs said.

Warm air had flowed in, melting the oxygen. Hydrogen had melted and vaporized as well, creating an explosive mixture. A microscopic spark from the pump mechanism provided the catalyst. The hydrogen exploded with a boom and rocked the air lock.

CHAPTER TEN

Devin hadn't seen so much activity on the targeting board since his first fleet battle. The main display had been switched to a targeting screen, and it blazed with color. Red for numbered mass driver shots. Red-blue for missile tracks. Yellow circles for different energy weapons, encompassing nearby ships. Two dozen ships had been targeted, and the tactical officer used every single weapon system the Pollux had.

"General quarters," he said, hopping into his chair.

The operations officer didn't even pause but pushed the alert button on her console. "General quarters, aye."

The alert bonged throughout the ship, and lights flashed red. The bridge crew was locking onto acceleration couches and donning helmets.

"Stations for space combat," Devin said. "Tactical, what is our threat status?"

After a startled look at him, the tactical officer turned to his board, double-checked, and reported, "Board is clear, sir. No threats."

"What? No threats?"

"No armed ships detected in system," he said.

Devin pointed at the main display. "What are all of those, then? Asteroids?"

The tactical officer swiveled his head to see the board, then turned back. "Merchant ships, sir, shuttles, ore barges. Nothing unfriendly—well, not unfriendly now—and even if they weren't, they're not armed."

"No threats?"

"None at all, Tribune. Board is clear."

Devin looked up at the board, then called to the ops officer. "Secure from general quarters."

"Secured from general quarters, aye."

The lights and noises stopped, and she made a short announcement, returning everyone to their duties.

Devin stared at the main display. "Somebody explain these targets to me."

The tactical officer coughed. "The subprefect had us set it up, sir. I've got the main mass driver pointed here"—he highlighted a group of ships—"they're all running ballistic. If we fire a long burst with a spread first, we should get all of them. These ones over here are close enough to the laser batteries—"

"We don't have laser batteries," Devin said.

"No, sir, not for a long time. They're positron beams. But you kept calling them lasers, so we all just kept—"

"Solving my problems for me. Thank you. But I don't want to know how you'd destroy all the ships in this system. I want to know why."

"Subprefect told us to simulate sweeping the system, sir," the tactical officer said.

"I see. Well, I will ask the subprefect when he arrives."

The bridge door slid open, and the subprefect walked in.

"Subprefect, just in time. Did you order a simulation drill of destroying all the ships in the system?"

"I did, sir. How did they do? Put it on the screen, please, tactical."

The main screen lit up to reveal the targeting solutions.

"This is outrageous," Devin said.

"I'll say," Lionel said. "Tactical, you used eight missiles? Do you know what those things cost?"

The tactical officer hung his head. "Yes, sir. Sorry, sir."

"You could have got most of them with the mass driver if you just were more aggressive with the ship positioning," Lionel said.

"Yes, sir, but wouldn't it be better for all departments to participate?"

"We need the missiles for warships. Do it again. Don't use any missiles this time."

"Understood, sir."

Devin got up from his chair and paced the bridge. "Why are we wasting our time expending munitions on harmless civilian ships? Or planning on how to expend munitions."

"We just wanted to anticipate the tribune's needs," the subprefect said.

"I need to destroy unarmed ships?"

"Sir."

"We don't do that," Devin said. The bridge crew looked at him. "Well, we do. But just that once."

The bridge crew's expressions didn't budge.

"Because Internal Security said so," Devin said.

"Understood, sir," Lionel said. "As Internal Security says. Does Internal Security have any other orders you'd like to pass on?"

"Internal Security does not run this ship. I do," Devin said.

"As you say, sir."

Devin rubbed his forehead. "Will you join me in my cabin, Subprefect?"

"Of course, sir," the subprefect said, stepping back. "Lead on."

Devin strode to his door.

"Tribune, a Marine assault carrier has just jumped into the system. Pegasus class," the comm officer said.

"An assault carrier? Here? From Where?"

"Headquartered at Bishop's world, sir. Under the command of Brigadier Santana. They say they are conducting unscheduled exercises."

"Of course they are," Devin said. "Subprefect, do you know anything about this?"

"Marines are a mystery to me, Tribune."

"Brigadier Santana wants to know if he can come aboard," the comm officer said.

"Of course he does," Devin said. "Signal him to come aboard as soon as he rendezvouses. I'm sure"—Devin glared at Lionel—"that he intends to rendezvous."

Lionel shrugged. "Marines. Who knows why they do anything?"

"Carry on, comm. Subprefect, my room, please."

Devin waited till the bridge door closed. "I am not going to rebel and try to take the core systems by force."

"I didn't think you would for a second," Lionel said.

"Good."

"Certainly not with just a frigate and single Marine assault carrier. Not nearly enough troops for a core world."

"Subprefect!"

"Now a provincial capital. That might work. One with a shipyard. Have you looked at the sub-sector capital here? Big spaceport. Can repair jump drives. Probably can make them, too."

"We are not going to capture a provincial capital." Devin sat, holding his head in his hands. "But you know that, so what is this about? You know I'd never do that."

"Those Internal Security people were a surprise."

"They're gone now."

"Yes, but they tried to recall you."

"It didn't work."

"Next time, they won't be alone. They'll come with a ship. With a Marine contingent," Lionel said.

"You think they'll use Marines to capture me?"

"I think they'll use Marines to kill you. If you're recalled to the palace, and you disappear en route, who's to know what happened to you?"

"That's crazy."

"Things are getting a little crazy."

"I serve the Empire. As long as the Emperor wants me out here, I'll stay out here," Devin said.

"Yes, but what if the Emperor's dead?"

"That's treasonous talk."

"Oh, I'm not planning on killing him, nor is anybody on this ship."

"Thank you so much, Subprefect. Good to know."

"Nor the Empress, nor you. Well, probably not. Both of you do have tempers."

"I'm an Imperial Tribune. What gives you the right to talk to me like this?"

Lionel held up his left hand, his middle and ring fingers missing at the first joint. "Remember this?"

"Why don't you get that fixed? They can get a graft or a prosthesis, at least."

Lionel waggled his remaining fingers and examined the stubs. "I could, but it's much more effective as a way of making you feel guilty."

"They gave you a medal."

"For saving the ship. I got nothing for dragging rash young officers out of burning compartments."

"What about my lifelong gratitude?"

"Not enough. But back to our point. What now?"

"We have to support Imperial policies. Even on the verge. Without the Empire, there is nothing. Without the Emperor, there is no Empire. We do our duty."

"Of course we do," Lionel said. "But in the meantime, it's good to make contingency plans, isn't it?"

***

"So, I told them, 'Fine, if that's the case, then I want four chickens, not two,'" Brigadier Santana said.

Lionel and Devin laughed at the off-color joke. The tribune's excellent cook had produced a feast, and Santana enjoyed every minute of it.

"Well, that joke notwithstanding, we're glad you're here," Lionel said.

"We are?" Devin said. "Since when is the Navy glad to have Marines around. All they do is drop onto worthless planets and make us stooge around until we have to come to their inevitable rescue."

"Our view is that, if the Navy just let us get on with our job and got us to the right place at the right time, we wouldn't be left having to solve things with one hand tied behind our backs."

"I spent a year seconded to the purchasing and budgetary directorate earlier in my career," Devin said. "At the time, I was taught to refer to the Confeds and the Nats as our opponents. We reserved the use of the word 'enemy' for the Marine budgetary team."

"First thing we do, let's kill all the naval officers. Isn't that what that Old Earth play guy said?"

"Something like that," Devin agreed. "How long will you be with us, Brigadier?"

"As long as you want, if you keep feeding me like this," Santana said. "But currently, our plan is to conduct joint drills with you as you traverse various systems."

"There's a lot of systems out here that we might traverse," Devin said.

"Then, we'll do a lot of joint drills."

Devin regarded him for a moment. "Why are you really here?"

"We thought, we all thought," Santana said, "that a squad or a company of Marines sent all the way from the core—if they were told the right things—might be willing to fight a ship's company, or the Marines attached to a particular ship. But they wouldn't be willing to go against a Marine unit on a Marine ship commanded by a Marine. They'd back off."

"Who is this we?"

"Myself and some others," Santana said. "I'm not going to name them at this time."

"Do you think that there's an arrest order on the way?"

Santana looked at Lionel. "I understand there's already been one."

"Just a misunderstanding," Devin said, "I'll clear it up with the Emperor next time I see him."

"Have you spoken with him recently?" Santana asked.

"That's none of your business," Devin said. "And in any event, it would be about private and family matters, not military."

"Perhaps you should try to speak to him," Santana said. "Just to make sure, that he's taking your calls. Or anyone's calls."

Devin looked at him. "How did you find us?"

"We took a guess at which systems you'd be in and tried them one at a time till we found you."

"You knew the contents of my orders?" Devin said.

"Not at all. But we had some idea where Dirk Friedel might be, and we figured you'd be looking to talk to him."

Devin grimaced at Santana. "I would like to talk to Dirk, yes."

"So would we," Santana said. "Maybe all three of us can have a chat with him if you find him?"

CHAPTER ELEVEN

"You're lucky that you're not dead," Lee said to Dena as she wrapped a bandage around her burned arm, then taped the ends together.

"Not so tight. That hurts," Dena said.

Scruggs came back up the ladder from stowing the tools in the lockers below. "Pull it tighter, then."

"Bite me, kiddo. This is no joke," Dena said. She held up her arm. The flash explosion had burned it an angry red. "Could have burnt my skin off."

"Then you shouldn't have opened the air lock till you were told, shouldn't you?"

"Bite me," Dena said again. She rubbed her chin. "Feels like I got a right cross."

"That's what happens when you get hit by a swinging air lock hatch. It should have broken your jaw. Lucky."

"A sprained wrist, a cracked rib, and a burnt arm, and all that you can say is how lucky I am? What a bunch."

"A safe bunch." Ana scrubbed soot off a wrench. "Normally. Gotta pay attention in space."

"I am paying attention. Who knew that would explode?"

"Anybody who knows the meaning of the word 'fire,'" Ana said, "which is oxygen plus a fuel—in this case random, combustible gases."

"Are you going to tell me how lucky I was—"

"Yes, that the engineer keeps trace gases low and because everybody was still wearing a sealed skin suit when that flashed."

"My favorite tool belt is melted," Scruggs said.

"I'll buy you another," Dena said.

"With what? You haven't earned any money lately."

"Neither have you, neither have any of you, and for a big bunch of space renegades, you seem to spend a lot of time just going around stealing water. Big career criminals we are." Dena stood, swayed for a moment, then walked to the hatch. "I'll be in my bunk."

"We should put her back in her cage," Scruggs said.

"No cages," Ana said. "She's in the crew now."

"This could be a problem," Lee said. "She's not got a lot of experience in space. Even Scruggs had more when she started."

Scruggs smiled. "Thank you, Sister Lee."

"And you, Sister Scruggs."

Dirk came back from the cockpit. "Who doesn't have experience?"

"Dena," Ana said. "She blew them up."

"Could have happened to anybody," Dirk said. "We're in space. It's dangerous."

"I told her not to open the hatch," Ana said. "But she did anyway."

"And you're more upset about that than the accident, aren't you?" Dirk asked. "You're not really used to people not taking your orders. Especially younger people."

Ana leaned back. "You know, Navy, sometimes I forget that you're more than just a pompous, unskilled pilot and a lazy, skirt-chasing, degenerate upper-class twit."

"Thanks," Dirk said.

"You're also a self-righteous, condescending Imperial turd."

"It pays to have skills. But I think the fact that Scruggs here was willing to take direction makes her more sympathetic to you. You're more willing to overlook her faults."

"She's young. Youngsters make mistakes. They need to learn."

"I'm right here, you know," Scruggs said. "You don't need to talk about me like I'm not here." She turned to Lee. "They know I can hear them, right?"

"It's a male-of-the-species thing," Lee said. "This conversation isn't about you, it's about which of them is in charge."

Ana and Dirk looked at Lee then turned away.

"Why Dena makes more mistakes," Ana said, "is because she doesn't listen."

"The reason we're all here," Dirk said, "all of us, is that we didn't listen to somebody about something. It's just by random chance that some of us listen to each other and not to others."

"That's a very convoluted sentence, Navy," Ana said. "Care to elaborate? Or just dig yourself a deeper hole."

"My feeling is that doing what people told her up to now in life has made Dena pretty unhappy. Just because people act the way they're expected to doesn't mean that they like it. When you make your own decisions, even bad ones, you're more yourself, and you feel better because of it."

"And if you're making your own decisions, you can't blame others for your failures anymore. It's all on you. That's hard for some people," Lee said.

"Aren't we a bunch of armchair psychologists?" Ana said. "We should open a clinic. But this Dena thing, one way or another," Ana said, "needs to be dealt with."

"Can you handle it?" Dirk asked. "Since you like to call yourself the executive officer."

"Actually," Ana said, "no. I'm not the right person for this. Somebody else has to step up."

Scruggs crossed her arms. Lee raised her eyebrows.

"Don't all jump at once," Ana said. "But everyone think about this. We need to make her a functioning part of the crew. The space-based crew. Or we need to get rid of her. Drop her on some other planet."

"Don't want to space her?" Dirk asked.

"I'm mellowing in my old age," Ana said. "Marooning her is sufficient."

"We'll table that for now," Dirk said. "How's the engineer?"

"In bed," Lee said. "He was more shook up than me. I gave him painkillers, lots of fluid, and sleeping pills. He's down for a shift, and he'll hurt afterwards but no permanent damage."

"Which leads to something that Dena mentioned," Dirk said. "We're not exactly master criminals. Our ventures up to now haven't gone well. We need a new start. Or at least we need to take this smuggling thing more seriously."

"Pretty risky," Ana said.

"Risk is our business," Dirk said.

Ana laughed. "Pompous twit. No, staying quiet and avoiding Imperial notice is our business. The risk is an unfortunate byproduct. As is the poverty."

"There is a chance we can make enough from Cheong's idea to keep us going for a long time."

"What's the date?" Ana asked. "Scruggs, when were we supposed to . . . deliver this ship to the owners?"

Scruggs glanced at her comm. "It was a week ago."

"So, what does that make us now, Private? Renegades? Pirates? Smugglers."

"We've just borrowed the ship," Lee said. "We'll return it."

"When?" Ana asked.

"Well, when—when we're done with it."

Ana sniffed twice.

"What is it?" Lee asked.

"You smell that?"

"No."

"That's the sweet smell of justification," Ana said. "It has a distinct tang."

He turned to Dirk. "On to practical matters. Think you can avoid flying us into a swamp this time?" Ana asked.

"No swamps. Ice. And other ships."

"What's going on?" Scruggs said. "We got the fuel we were promised. Sort of. Was there more?"

"Indeed, a chance of more," Dirk said. "And some money. Navigator, do we have fuel for the jump?"

"Two jumps," Lee said. "We'll be at the jump limit in a half shift."

"Where's that Confed cruiser?"

"Still docked at the station. In theory, they could catch us, but they seem busy. There's a lot of video from the station. Troops moving around, taking over offices. No violence but a lot of motion."

"Soon as we clear the jump limit, I'll give you a destination."

***

"The planet has no name, just a catalog number. 967-11-11," Lee said to the group in the control room. She, Dirk, Ana, and Scruggs were at the consoles. Dena hovered behind. Gavin was patched in over the intercom. "Very small, very cold, very far from the primary. Noon sunlight is less than ten percent Earth standard. Mostly ice caps. Water ice caps. Frozen oceans. But also volcanoes."

She tapped a control, and the displays on the others mirrored her screen. "The volcanoes create local hot spots, so the ice is thinner. Two different space lanes cross here. Cheong's company has a trans-shipment facility here and a starport."

"A starport?" Gavin commed. "Like with repair facilities, parts stores, skilled labor?"

"And different food?" Scruggs asked.

"No," Lee said. "A starport, as in, a flat piece of ice shelf with lots of containers piled up, small office, fusion reactor, a bunch of heated pumps that sell seawater for a fee, frozen rock. And a carbon dioxide atmosphere."

"So, we can't breathe."

"Almost. You need to keep a filter mask on but not a full helmet. You still might want to keep the helmet. It's pretty cold. Below freezing all the time. We come in for a landing, pick any spot, and settle. We're going to be on ice, either with water or rock underneath. They'll deliver water cheap, and most ships drop off or pick up containers. Large corporate ships that go there, not independents."

"Once we're on the ground, we have to move fast," Dirk said. "Most ships only spend two or three shifts there. We need to land, pickup water, and we've got Cheong to thank for that. He actually gave us a credit chip for free water there, so we'll load up."

"He gave that for free?" Gavin said.

"Dena stole it out the office when we were trashing it," Dirk said. "We've got a year's supply of discount codes."

"Seems like I'm not useless, after all," Dena said.

"Free water. Whoop-de-do," Scruggs said. "All bow to the brave warrior."

"Private," Ana scowled.

"Shutting up, Centurion," Scruggs said.

"In any event," Dirk said, "I'm going to land us as close to that container farm as I can. We'll get the water and load up. Engineer, I need you to go out and do some sort of maintenance. That's our excuse for going there, that and picking up a container."

"That won't be hard," Gavin said, "I have so much to do. Pilot, you do know that our landing strut is only good for a gentle landing until I reinforce it?"

"Right. I'll do my best," Dirk said.

"Going to have to do better than your best, at least from what I've seen so far," Gavin said. "We need to touch down gently, very gently. Otherwise, it will snap."

"Can't you reinforce it?" Ana asked.

"Ever tried to weld on a ship traveling through jump space with crappy welding gear, Old Man?"

"All right. What about regular space? When we come out?"

"No time," Dirk said. "This planet is small and far out. The jump limit isn't far away, and everybody exits right on the mark."

"Traders make mistakes all the time and come out too far," Ana said.

"Good to know that you're an expert on space navigation," Gavin said.

"There is regular traffic there," Lee said. "It's steady but not busy. Two or so ships a day. It's all corporate lines that drop there all the time. They hit their mark, sail down, fuel up, swap containers, and leave. We'll be attracting enough attention by not being a corporate ship. But we won't have that attention till after we've landed. If we go in quietly, there's a good chance we won't get a second look. But if we come in looking like kooky navigators, people will be watching us all the time. We need to be nondescript, boring, mundane."

"But what's the point?" Scruggs said. "I mean, yay on Dena's water and all—I know we need fuel—but what's the point of going to a frozen planet on the edge of nowhere, with nothing, and try to escape notice? If we need to hide, why not find a nice warm planet with lots of free water and a breathable atmo, land there, and spend a few weeks doing maintenance and whatever?"

"Well, we want the rest of the payment that Cheong promised us," Dirk said.

"And it's there?"

"It is."

"How do we get it?"

"We steal it."

CHAPTER TWELVE

"Okay, Pilot, you take over now," Lee said.

They had exited jump space an hour prior, and had since moved into planetary orbit.

Gavin had gone outside with a hammer and some equipment to shore up their landing struts, at least enough for one landing. He climbed back in.

Dirk didn't move. His eyes were closed, and he was breathing slowly. Lee looked at him. "Pilot?"

"Hmm?" he said, eyes closed.

"Time to land us. Please."

"Got it," Dirk said. He opened his eyes and tapped his screen.

Lee watched him, then keyed the intercom. "Starting landing."

"All buckled and locked in back here," Gavin said.

"And I'm hanging out, strapped in my bunk, if anyone cares," Dena said.

"Nobody does," Scruggs muttered.

"Private, did you say something?" Ana asked.

"Just confirming the pilot will overfly the container field so that we can get a good look as we land."

Everybody looked at Dirk, whose eyes were closed again.

"Pilot?" Lee said.

"I heard you," Dirk said. "I'll overfly the field."

"Will you be landing with your eyes closed, Pilot?" Lee asked.

"Do you think it will make a difference in the quality of my landing?"

"Not much," Ana said. He sniffed the air. "Pilot, have you been drinking?"

"No," Dirk said, eyes still closed.

"And why not?"

"I'm trying to land sober this time."

Ana, Scruggs, and Lee exchanged glances. As one, they all tightened their restraints.

"Inbound ship, this is Planetary Control," a voice said over the radio.

"Planetary Control, this is Heavyweight Items, inbound for refueling and minor maintenance," Lee said.

"Heavyweight Items, control. We don't have you on the schedule."

"We're a charter with Consolidated Freight and Shipping," Lee said. "You're going to give us a free tank of water."

The voice laughed. "Are we? That will be a first."

"Consolidated gave us a code. Transmitting now," Lee said.

"Received," the voice said. "I've heard of these, but I have to look up the procedure."

"You send us a challenge—" Lee said.

"Got it. Sending challenge, and your software replied already. Congrats, Heavyweight Items, load up with as much water as you want. Be advised we do not staff full time. One shift lockdown starting in two hours. We'll assign you a landing spot. Stand by."

"That's a problem," Ana said. "We need to be close to that container field. We can't be on the far side, or they'll see us loading."

"We can land at the wrong spot," Lee said.

They looked at Dirk, who was performing deep breathing exercises.

"I don't think the extra stress will be good for the pilot," Ana said. "And we're trying to not attract extra notice. Can we force them to put us somewhere?"

"This map says the fueling stations are different," Scruggs said. "Does that help?" She highlighted a series of notes on her console and mirrored it on the others.

Lee looked at the display, then keyed the radio. "Control, can you put us somewhere with a standard fifteen-centimeter pump? We see some over by the container farms."

"Heavyweight, we can, but those are a long way from the office. We won't be able to get staff out before shutdown. You'll have to wait till start of next shift."

"Control, if it's a standard pump, we can just attach ourselves. It's not like we've never pumped water before. That way, you won't have to send anybody out. I don't want to have to wait for your next shift to start."

"Heavyweight, there are different charge rates for different pumps."

"We're not paying, remember? Doesn't matter to us. If you put us out there, we'll be done and gone before you're back up tomorrow. Less work for you," Lee said.

The control room held their breath. Cheong had given them full stats for the station. Only two pumping stations had hoses that small, with one closer to the container farm than the other.

"Landing station F3. Suck all you want. We're offline at midnight local, no staffing till start of first shift."

"We'll be gone by then," Lee said.

"Safe travels, then. Cleared to Landing station F3 for pumping operations. Planetary control out."

"We're in," Lee said. "Now we just need to get down in one piece."

The ship shuddered as it felt the atmosphere's effects.

Dirk came alive, adjusting the throttles, and the turbulence eased. He looked around. "Everybody, stop staring at me like that. We'll be down in two ticks of a tabbo's claws."

Scruggs looked up. "Do tabbos actually have claws?"

"Quiet, Private," Ana said. "Don't confuse the pilot."

Dirk took them on two complete orbits before beginning the final descent. The ship shook the whole way down. Gavin and Dena were talking over the intercom.

"This part always makes me sick," Dena said.

"You'll get over it," Gavin said.

"Really?"

"Sure, we either land or die. Either way, it ends."

"Why is this landing taking so long?"

"We're pretending to be a simple corporate trader. This is standard corporate trading—don't stress the equipment. Slide down slowly."

"But the shaking. Won't something come loose?"

"It has every other time," Gavin said.

"Important things? Things we need to fly?"

"Pretty much."

***

"I see the container field," Scruggs said as the ship coasted down to the landing spot.

"Do you see those ice mountains ringing the field as well?" Ana asked. "Pilot, I'm talking to you."

"Never mind the field, can you read the ID numbers on the containers?" Lee asked.

"Some of them—the angle's bad. Working on it now," Scruggs said. "We're saving the videos."

"Ground forty meters, Pilot," Lee said. "Dropping faster than profile."

Dirk tilted the controls.

"Thirty meters," Lee said. "Still out of profile."

Dirk tweaked the throttle.

"Twenty meters," Lee said.

The proximity alarm bonged. "Warning. Terrain. Terrain."

"Ten meters, Pilot," Lee said. "Too fast, too fast."

The ship dropped lower and lower. A second alarm joined the first. "Velocity. Velocity."

Lee keyed the intercom. "Hang on."

Dirk pushed the thrusters to max. Steam and ice particles billowed around them. The ship slowed, stalled, then lifted.

The cabin crew exhaled.

Dirk pulled the shut-off valve, and the ship stopped in midair.

"The Emperor's testicles," Ana said in the silence. "Brace. Brace. Brace."

The ship fell three meters and crunched into the ice. The crew slammed into their restraints, then bounced. Fog and ice exploded out in all directions, shutting down every light, external monitor, and console.

They sat in the dark for three seconds. Then the emergency lights came back on. A fan started up, then another. The consoles rebooted.

"Everybody okay?" Ana asked.

"Yes, Centurion," Scruggs said.

"I'm fine. Navigation board is done," Lee said.

Dirk closed his eyes.

"The Empress's hairy vagina," Dena said over the radio. "What was that? I think I prefer the ones that make me sick."

"Engineer?" Ana said. "How is it back there?"

"Controls still restarting," Gavin said. "But nothing looks broken."

"Thank Paterfather Zeus that nothing broke," Lee said.

The ship sagged to the left with a bang.

"Well, almost nothing," Gavin said.

"It's really cold out here—and dark," Gavin said over the radio. He had popped the ventral hatch in the air lock and climbed down. "I think full helmets are going to be necessary, just for the wind. But at least full atmo pressure."

"Full pressure if you can breathe carbon dioxide," Lee said. "Remember, not much oxygen. What's the status of our landing struts?"

"Surprisingly good," Gavin said. "Only one support strut gave way. A small one, and it had been damaged before, but I had just hammered it into shape rather than replacing it."

"So, the rough landing was down to poor maintenance habits, then?" Ana asked.

"The pilot dropping us like a barge of iron ore pellets also contributed," Gavin said. "And the fact I didn't have a spare strut to replace that one with when I welded the others into place. You found our target yet?"

"Scruggs found three containers on Cheong's list," Ana said. "Pump components, electric motors, and wine."

"I vote for the rare wines," Gavin said.

Dena had come up to the control room to see what was happening. "What rare wines? Why are we getting wines?"

"Because Cheong only gave us a short list of the most valuable containers he was insuring," Ana said. "And just the ones that he thought would be here. Those are the only three that he gave us inventories for that we can find. And it's not rare wines. It just says, wine, red, bottles."

"Hundreds, perhaps thousands of containers here," Dena said, "and we're stealing cheap wine?"

"And maybe pump parts and electric motors," Ana said. "If we have space."

"We've got space for two containers," Lee said. "So, pick two."

"There're hundreds of containers here," Dena said. "There must be things way more valuable that pump parts. Computers. Drive components. Drugs."

"I'm sure there's all of that and more," Ana said. "But the only ones we know the content on are the ones that he gave us inventories for. The ones he insured."

"We could pick one at random," Dena said.

"And maybe get a container of aluminum ore pellets for industrial furnaces?"

"Better move along," Gavin said. "We've got one shift to steal things. And can somebody help me connect these pumps? I need a second set of hands."

"Scruggs," Ana said. "You help with the pumps. Navigator and I will go grab two containers. Which two are nearest?"

"Wine and pump parts," Lee said.

"Right. We need to get one of those electric crane things to get the one we need."

"And who's going to drive it?" Lee asked.

Ana cursed. "Engineer?"

"What?"

"Can you drive those self-propelled cranes?"

"You know I can."

"I'll get my helmet. Think Scruggs and I can load the fuel?"

"Same as you've done before. Call me if you have questions."

"Let's keep the calls to a minimum," Ana said. "In fact, I think we all need to stay off the radio. They might have an alarm triggered to radio action at that office. For emergencies. We don't want them to wake up and ask what we need."

"That would be standard in these small stations," Gavin said. "With the one shift shutdown."

"So, no radios," Lee said. "That's not a problem."

"Everybody suit up," Ana said. "Scruggs and I will fuel up. Navigator will find those containers. Engineer will steal them."

"You're not in charge, Old Man," Gavin said. "This isn't a military operation. It's commercial."

"Your point, Punk?" Ana said.

"Stop pushing us around," Gavin said. "We know what we're doing."

"Do we need to have another private discussion? You and me?" Ana asked.

Gavin stood. "We didn't quite finish things last time, did we? But no, I'm not saying that you don't have good ideas. You just have to remember that you're not in charge."

Ana's forehead tightened. Then he nodded. "You're right. You two should be in charge here."

"I bet you hate saying that," Gavin said.

"Very, very much," Ana said. "But I'm a realist. What do you want me to do?"

"When Lee and I bring back the first container, they need to be chained up. Can you do that?"

"I've seen it done enough. I can do that while the fuel is flowing. Scruggs can help."

"And what do I do?" Dena asked.

"Keep an eye on things here. See how the pilot is doing."

"He's passed out in the lounge."

"Easy to keep an eye on, then."

"I can help."

"First, you're hurt," Ana said, pointing to her bandaged arm. "Second, the reason you're hurt is because you don't pay attention. Third, your help also got other people hurt, so just stay out of the way."

Dena glared, then stomped away.

"Harsh, Centurion," Gavin said over the radio.

"Necessary," Ana said. "We need to get this done."

Lee broke in. "That's a Nationalist warship over there, on the other edge of the field."

"A warship?" Gavin said. "At a container farm? Can't be."

"Sorry," Lee said. "Auxiliary warship. Registered as a freighter but with guns. Two lasers."

"Not much of a warship," Gavin said.

"Some warship beats no warship," Ana said. "What's it doing here?"

"Loading and fueling like us, looks like," Lee said. "They've got hoses out, can't tell if they're pumping. And they've got space for more containers. I see one has been dropped off next to them. Probably waiting for next shift and the base to pick it up and swap it."

"Can they see us?" Ana asked.

"We're sitting in the middle of a field."

"Technically, it's a glacier. And it's dark."

"Whatever. Everybody here can see us if they point a telescope or the right sensors at us, but we're not visible to casual looks, no," Lee said.

"We told the station we're going to fuel up." Ana got up. "Let's get going on that. Then you two scope out the two containers we're taking, and as soon as the shift changes and things go dark, we'll load up."

"I've never stolen anything before," Scruggs said.

"It's easier than you think," Ana said. "And kind of fun but a bad habit to get into."

"I think I could probably use a few bad habits," Scruggs said.

Lee and Ana looked at her.

"Well," Lee said. "If it's bad habits you want, this crew is probably the right place to be."

The lights in the office complex went out at the end of the shift, and activity ceased.

Ana and Scruggs were outside, connecting the pumps. Gavin inspected the connections and pronounced them good. The water tanks filled, and he allowed them to run the cracking mechanism concurrently to fill the secondary oxygen and hydrogen tanks. Given a shift, they would be bursting with fuel, drinking water, oxygen, and hydrogen.

"You two are both awarded pump technician level one," Gavin said. "Just keep an eye on the valves."

"Sounds difficult," Ana said. "What do the F and E on this gauge mean?" He shook his head. "Kids. You need anything else from us?"

"Lee found both the closest containers. We're going to get the first one."

"We'll stand by," Ana said.

Ana and Scruggs were able to step inside, eat, drink, and defecate while waiting for Gavin, Lee, and the electric tug to bring back the first container. Dirk was useless for a shift or two after the landing, and they wanted him rested to get them off planet. Dena was nowhere to be seen.

The weather deteriorated as it got colder. Frost formed on the ship, and carbon dioxide ice clouds blanketed the ships and containers nearby.

It was almost shift midpoint before Gavin and Lee arrived back. The electric tug trundled along the ice, and a blue-and-yellow-colored container stood on the cradle.

They'd stopped using suit radios to minimize the chance of anyone catching a signal and asking what they were doing. Scruggs had seen them on the external monitors, and she and Ana suited up and ran outside.

Ana locked helmets with Gavin. "Well?"

"Harder than we thought. We had to move two other containers to get this one. The interface is kind of tricky. And it's hard to see."

"Can we get the other one before we leave?"

"We have to move three containers to get to that one."

"Not good. Should we just grab a random one?"

"And get a load of empty drink containers, maybe?"

"Right. Can you pull this off before dawn?"

"I think so. More containers to move, but my old skills are coming back to me. I'm moving things faster now."

"So, you used to work at a cargo site?" Ana asked.

Gavin leaned back so the centurion could see his face. He wagged his eyebrows, shook his head, then leaned back in to touch helmets. "Good try, Centurion. I'll lift it up. Think you and Scruggs can chain it on?"

"Yes, you'll have to inspect, though."

Gavin lifted the container to the upper position. Scruggs and Ana connected chains and winched them in. Gavin climbed up and checked their connections as Lee folded the crane back. Gavin made only minor adjustments, then told them to lock the magnets and check up on the fuel.

Lee and Gavin trundled off. Scruggs and Ana waited. After an hour, the cracker had filled the oxygen and hydrogen, and they closed them up. No Gavin or Lee. Another hour, and the water tanks topped off. They turned off the pumps and disconnected the hoses. Still no Gavin and Lee.

They coiled and stowed the hoses, then woke Dirk to ready him for lift-off. The next shift's start coincided with planetary dawn, and the primary peeked over the horizon.

Dirk was in the control room. Scruggs and Ana were waiting outside. Ana had found a wired connection so that he and Scruggs could plug into the intercom and could talk without the radio.

"Are you sure that we shouldn't go in there to find them?" Dirk asked.

"Go in where? It's a maze in there. We can't see in with this windstorm. We know where they're supposed to be, but getting there is a bit of a trick. And if we do go in, what can we do? I don't know how to work cargo-loading equipment. Do you?"

"We should help them," Dirk said.

"You should sit there and get us ready to lift," Ana said. "As soon as they get back, we lock it on and bounce."

"What about the office over there? It's getting light out."

"What about it, Navy? Nobody there. They're closed till first shift. We've got nothing to worry about till those lights come on and we see people in the offices."

"I don't think—wait, there they come," Dirk said. "On the left."

Ana and Scruggs turned from their spot at the bottom of the ventral hatch. The electric container tug was trundling out from the far left with another blue-and-yellow container on its bed.

"Up we go," Ana said to Scruggs. "Stand by the chains." They disconnected the intercom, climbed up the outside of the ship, and stood on the hull.

Scruggs touched helmets. "Centurion," she said. "One of those door lights just lit up."

"This will just take a few minutes," Ana said. "We have nothing to worry about till the main lights come on."

The tug trundled over. Lee hopped out of the cab and climbed up the ladder to Ana and Scruggs. Gavin was in the cab, controlling the container's lift.

"Sorry," Lee said, pushing her helmet to Ana. "We couldn't get out. In one of the aisles, the containers were packed too close. We couldn't get around them. We had to backtrack, then move another."

"Well, let's get going. We're almost out of time."

The lights on the main compound blazed on, and the perimeter lights clicked on one at a time. Ana and Lee shielded their faces as the nearest light flared right into their faceplate, illuminating the three figures on the top of the ship.

"Strike that," Ana said. "We're actually out of time."

CHAPTER THIRTEEN

"Up, up, up," Ana said over the radio.

With daylight and the lights turning on, they had abandoned the no-radio rule. Their voice traffic would be lost in that of other ships.

Gavin was using the crane on the tug to lift the stolen container. Ana and Scruggs stood by to chain the container, and Lee climbed back inside to help with the launch.

"Steady, steady," Gavin said. He thunked the container into place. "Hit the grapples." The container jerked as the magnets engaged.

"Right, Centurion, you two chain up. I'll get this lifter out of the way."

"Just dump it," Ana said.

"I've got to move it back away from the blast," Gavin said. "If I put it back where it was, nobody will know that we took it."

"Centurion," Lee said over the radio, "that National auxiliary is calling us."

"Ignore it. Scruggs, over here. We need to winch this in." Scruggs clambered over to the centurion, and they took turns on the winch, attaching the container's bow end.

"Centurion," Lee said, "what color are those containers?"

"Color? We're in the middle of a heist, and you want to do some decorating?"

"I've got a camera on that Confed ship that's calling us. It's first ring has loaded six containers," Lee said. "All bright blue with yellow markings. And there are three empty spots on the second ring."

Ana stepped back and looked up. "Yup. Bright blue with yellow markings. Both of them."

"We appear to have stolen their load-up," Lee said.

"Too bad for them," Ana said. "What are they going to do about it?"

Lee started to respond, but the ionized particles drowned out her transmission when the Confed ship fired her dorsal laser turret.

"Empress's fat ankles. They're firing at us?" Scruggs said. "In atmosphere? Even I know that's stupid."

Ana grabbed Scruggs and dragged her forward. "Inside, inside, now. Where's the engineer?"

"Coming," Gavin said on the radio. Ana caught a glimpse of a figure running under the ship. He spun the top hatch and shoved Scruggs into it, then dropped in himself, pulling it closed behind him. The two of them met Gavin, who was climbing in from the bottom, and banged together in a heap. The bottom hatch dropped open, and Gavin cursed until they pulled it up.

"Scruggs, check the side hatch," Ana said. "Everybody, lock the wheels hard, then hang on." He took a deep breath, then another. He climbed up and double-checked the dorsal hatch. Gavin stepped back from the ventral hatch and snapped the cover over the ventral pit back into place. Ana grabbed the ladder rings and held on for dear life. Scruggs and Gavin copied him. They all stood there, staring at each other, grasping holds and not moving.

"Centurion," Scruggs said, "why aren't we moving?"

"Military-trained pilots always blast up and out as fast as possible when under fire," Ana said. "First thing they learn. I don't want to be paste on the wall when Navy fires up." He took another breath.

They stood there. The radio channel crackled, and the ship shook. It still didn't move. The radio crackled again.

"Another laser shot," Gavin said.

"Why doesn't he scramble?" Ana said.

"Does the laser mess up the systems?" Scruggs asked.

"Radio and wireless but nothing in the ship, it's all shielded against cosmic rays and suchlike," Gavin said.

"He should have scrambled." Ana punched the intercom. "Pilot? Pilot? What's going on?"

The channel was silent.

***

"We should launch, Pilot," Lee said. The laser interfered with her radio link, so she had popped her helmet.

"I need to know what's going on," Dirk said. "Are they on board?"

"What's going on is they're shooting at us."

"Do you want to leave the engineer?"

"No, but I don't want to get blown up, either."

The main lock door boomed open behind them, and cold fog rolled into the control room.

"In the Emperor's name," Dirk said.

"Sorry," Ana said, climbing into his seat. "Didn't have time to drain the air lock. Good old-fashioned icy carbon dioxide."

"Is it poisonous?" Scruggs asked, slipping into her console next to Ana.

"No," Lee said. "Well, not much. Not right away."

"Fix it later." Ana gasped. He was having problems talking. "Pilot, why didn't you scramble?"

"Scramble?"

"Later."

Sweat soaked Ana, and his face was red. Scruggs looked over at him, then reached into her skin suit pocket. She pulled a small vial out and shook a pill into her hand before extending it to Ana.

Ana looked at the pill in her hand, then at her face. She bobbed her head. He grabbed it and put it in his mouth. His face relaxed, and his breathing settled.

Gavin came over the intercom. "Fusion plants spooled up. Engines are ready to go. What's the holdup?"

"Why aren't we dead?" Dirk asked. "Why haven't they shot us."

"No angle," Ana said. "Turret is on top of the ship, doesn't depress. Probably can't bear on us. And the atmo dissipates the beam."

"They can fix that by lifting," Lee said. "And tilting."

"Or clearing the ventral turret," Ana said. "Scruggs, try to model their fields of fire like I showed you. Pilot, can we blast straight out to sea, as fast as possible and then lift?"

Dirk looked at his screen and nodded. "I can lift, but where will we be going—"

"I'll have a course by the time you're up," Lee said. "Somewhere close."

"Engineer," Ana said over the radio. "Strap in. This will be violent, even by Navy's standards."

"Where's Dena?" Dirk asked.

"Not my day to watch her," Ana said. "Quarters, probably. Hopefully, she's learned enough to be strapped in. Scruggs, have you got that visual?"

Scruggs mirrored her console to the others. It showed a red circle with bites taken out of it centered on the Confed ship. Piles of ice, other ships, and the office building created safe zones with their shadows.

"Well, that's pretty evident," Lee said. "Stay low till you pass that pile of ice, slip behind it, then start climbing. Once we're over the horizon, we can climb."

"Range on that laser isn't that far in atmo," Ana said. "Soon as we're a klick away, you can climb. They'll never get us."

"They're clearing the hoses," Lee said, looking through the cameras. "They can launch soon. We need to go now."

They all looked at Dirk. He closed his eyes, took several deep breaths, then shoved a lever forward.

The ship powered off the ground like a bullet from a revolver. No warning, no slow accel, just banged forward at full speed, only meters above the ground. They were all pushed back into their seats as Heart's Desire surged forward. It spun along, creating a cloud of ice smoke, then whipped a right, then a left as it pulled behind a rock-ice outcrop.

Ana gritted his teeth. "New technique for takeoff, Navy? First, give them a free shot at us, then try to hit things as we go?"

"Don't like being shot at."

"Isn't that why you drink before you do these?" Ana asked.

A laser flashed by above them.

"Ignore it," Ana said. "We're out of effective range already."

Dirk changed their angle of attack and boosted their climb. The view changed from the green-blue of atmosphere to the dark blue of near space, then the black of the orbit.

Dena came over the intercom. "What in the name of twenty dead Emperors was that?"

"Just another patented Navy takeoff," Ana said. "Get used to it."

Dirk set them up to race for the nearest jump limit. Lee had picked the third-closest system within jump range.

"We'll be gone when we hit the jump limit. Destination is a dead-end system, no listed population," Lee said. "But water and air so we can recoup and fix some things."

"Like landing struts?" Ana asked.

"Among other things," Lee said.

"Anything you want to say about engineering, say it to my face," Gavin said.

"I don't feel like walking back there, so the radio is fine. But it would be nice if we weren't always stopping to fix things," Ana said.

"Would be nice too if we weren't always running away from people shooting at us," Gavin said.

"I had nothing to do with that," Ana said.

"You helped set it up. You and Dirk," Gavin said.

"And since we're on the topic of what would be nice," Ana slapped Dirk on the shoulder. "What was that all about, Navy, sitting there on the ground?"

Dirk's dropped his hand to his hip. "Hit me again. You'll find out."

"Find out what? That you don't know how to fly?" Ana shook his head. "And, by the way, you're not wearing a gun belt, so I don't know what you're reaching for."

Dirk looked down. "Odd, I thought I was."

"I can't believe it," Lee said.

"That Navy here forgot to wear a belt? We're lucky that he remembers to wear pants," Ana said.

"No, that Nat ship is following us."

"They launched already?" Dirk said.

"And they're running their engines at max by their drive plume," Lee said. "Why?"

"They're mad about us stealing their containers?" Scruggs said. "They want them back?"

"That's not how it works," Gavin said over the radio. "They're merchants. There's no money in chasing somebody who stole cargo. It's not even their cargo, and they've got witnesses that it was stolen. They'll just call their insurance company and get reimbursed. It's no loss at all to them. From their point of view, it's a victimless crime."

"This doesn't cost them anything?" Scruggs asked.

"Not a thing, insurance takes care of it. They might even make something on the deal."

"What if they don't have insurance?"

"That's the thing, youngster," Dirk said. "We know they have insurance. That's why we arranged this, er . . . borrowing."

"Theft," Gavin said. "It's a theft. But we had the keys, sort of. Cheong didn't have money to pay us, so he gave us a list of the nearest spots with high-value cargo that we could steal. That's why we came here. We had a list of containers that we could pick up, and this was an easy spot to lift things."

"I don't understand," Scruggs said.

"It was all arranged," Gavin said. "Look, stealing containers is easy. Most places aren't well guarded, so you can break into them or take them relatively easy. It's not simple, but it's not that hard. The problem isn't stealing the containers, it's which one to steal. You have to know the contents, and normally, only the shipping line does. Or their insurance company."

"Cheong was broke,," Dirk said. "But he knew which containers had the highest insurance premiums. That's how he paid us, telling us which ones to steal."

"So, if they're not going to lose any money, why are they chasing us so hard? And why did they shoot at us?" Gavin asked.

"What's in the containers?" Scruggs asked.

"Pump parts and cheap wine," Ana said.

"Unless it isn't," Dirk said.

"What?" Ana said.

"That's what we were told was in them. What's actually in them?" Dirk asked.

"Lee, how long till we get somewhere?"

"Jump limit in ten minutes," Lee said. "Then short jump. About thirty hours."

"Can they follow us?"

"There's only one planet in this direction that's within Jump range, so they can guess, and they'll guess right."

"Right," Ana unbuckled his belt. "Engineer, I'll take the top one, and you take the bottom one. Let's see what's really in there."

Ana and Scruggs took one stolen container, Lee and Gavin the other.

"Sensors?" Ana asked Scruggs.

She tapped the readouts by the container inspection hatch. "Nothing, Centurion. Shows as not connected."

"Right, we had a hasty departure."

"Engineer showed me how to connect them, but I didn't have time—"

"Because they were firing on us. Understood, Private. No blame."

"I can fix it, but I'd have to go outside . . ."

"Not a good idea in jump space. I hope they don't need power, either."

"We didn't have time to connect anything, Centurion. There should be an access lock, though."

"Pop the hatch then," Ana said.

Scruggs pulled the lever and rotated the access door away. The container's door was smooth, unmarked metal.

"No inspection hatch?" Ana said. "That's odd."

"I thought all containers had them," Scruggs said.

"They do. Those numbers are upside down."

Scruggs tilted her head. "Yeah, the container is upside down."

"It's not upside down, it's backward. Wrong end in." He keyed the intercom near the door.

"What is it, Old Man," Gavin said. "This one is locked. I'm working on the lock."

"Get Nature Girl to do it. We need your help," Ana said. "You and your welder-cutter thing."

The steel was tough, resisting the torch. Gavin scribed a circle big enough for Scruggs to crawl through and began to cut. The metal bubbled, and a stream of vapor whistled out.

"Leak." Gavin jumped back. "What is it?"

"Everybody out," Lee said.

They all jumped back into the central walkway and pulled the door shut. Lee punched a recessed red button, and an alarm bonged.

"Control room," Dirk's said from the intercom. "What's happening?"

"Pilot, we might have a blowout," Lee said. "What's our status?"

"Blowout?" Dirk said. "Where? What?"

"Second row containers access space," Lee said. "Some sort of noxious gas."

"I've got no readings. Everything is nominal."

"Are you sure, Pilot? There's something gassing into that compartment."

"Sensors say . . . nothing. Just normal."

Lee peered through the view port in the hatch. "There's smoke all over the place in there."

"Nothing here," Dirk said. "Just a slight drop in temperature and more water vapor."

Dena arrived behind them. "What's going on?"

"Go put on your skin suit," Ana said.

"Bite me, Old Man. You're not the boss of me. Why the alarm?"

"An unknown gas is venting into that compartment. It might be toxic. We're figuring it out. We don't need your help."

"You never do," Dena sighed. "What were you doing?"

"Just inspecting those two containers that we stole. This one has some vapor in it."

"What about the other one?" Dena asked.

"We'll get to it," Scruggs said. "But it's nothing to worry about."

"Thanks for the reassurance, kiddo," Dena said.

"Children," Ana said, "we have a situation here. We don't have time for this."

Dena flicked a dismissive wave. Scruggs returned it. Dena stomped off forward.

"Pilot, can you confirm that's all I see?"

"Cold water. That's what I see."

"If we all put our helmets on, we can lock the central access hatch . . ."

"And isolate this part of the ship," Ana said. "I'll do it." He pulled himself up the central corridor.

Gavin, Lee, and Scruggs waited till Ana reported the hatch closed, then reentered the space. Fog billowed out and condensed on their suits. Suit and ship sensors agreed that it was just water, so Gavin resumed cutting. After a half hour, a metal circle popped out.

"Give me that big water bottle from my tool kit," Gavin said.

Lee handed it to him. He sprayed the edge of the hole with the water, which steamed, ran, then froze.

"Nice smooth edge now. Scruggs, you're up."

Scruggs ducked and pointed a flashlight into the hole. Fog roiled the inside. She bent over, put her hands through, and pulled herself halfway in. Gavin's eyes flicked down at her behind as he nodded with positive appraisal. He looked up to see Ana and Lee watching him. Ana smiled, while Lee frowned.

"Scruggs," Gavin said, "What do you see?"

"Just fog. There's plenty of space in here. Help push me in."

The three lifted her and guided her legs in as she climbed into the container. She disappeared into the dark. More fog rolled out.

"Ice everywhere—and boxes," Scruggs said. "A bunch of ice-covered cardboard boxes."

"It's supposed to be pump parts," Gavin said.

"Do you ship pumps in blocks of ice?"

"Not normally."

Dena's voice came from behind them. "Did you get in?"

"Scruggs is in there now," Ana said. He didn't turn around. "Private, what do they say?"

"Can't read it. I'm going to open one," Scruggs said.

"That might not be the safest—"

"The stuff inside is frozen," Scruggs said. "I just have to pry one loose—whoops."

A steaming white slab flew out and thwacked the floor, causing them to back away.

"Emperor's balls," Ana said.

"Paterfather Zeus, save us," Lee said.

Scruggs's head stuck out through the hole. "There're boxes and boxes of these in here."

"What in the name of dead Emperors is it?" Gavin said.

"Tuna. It's a tuna," Dena said, ducking her head around Gavin. "Looks like we stole a container of frozen fish."

CHAPTER FOURTEEN

"What are we going to do with a container full of frozen fish?" Lee asked.

"Vary our diet quite a bit," Ana said. "Lots of nutrition in a fish. Protein. Micronutrients."

Ana, Lee, and Gavin stared down at the slab of fish.

Scruggs leaned on the edge of the hole in the container. "It's not packed full in here, but there are dozens of these boxes. They must have been frozen solid, then stacked in here. There's no cooling unit."

"Outside will take care of that for us," Gavin said.

"Long as they stay in space, what about when we land, Engineer?" Lee asked.

Gavin grimaced. "Fried fish, anybody?"

"I can cook fish, especially these tuna," Dena said from behind the group in the corridor. "Is it just tuna, or are there different types in there?"

"How would I know? I don't do food supplies," Scruggs said.

"Private," Ana said, "look around in there. Check the boxes. See if they have different markings on them or pictures or something. Give us a count, if you can."

"Yes, Centurion." Scruggs's head disappeared.

Ana picked up the frozen slab and examined it. "It's not professionally done. Looks almost hand caught and cut. Not factory-made."

Dirk rang through the intercom. "What's going on back there? Was there a fire?"

"Centurion is giving us lectures on sustainable aquaculture," Gavin said.

"What?"

"The container is full of frozen fish. The smoke was water ice fog."

"Outstanding," Dirk said. "I've been keenly feeling my shortage of omega-three acids for a while. It will be good for variety in our diets."

"Am I the only one that thinks a cargo we can sell is better than a cargo we can eat?" Ana asked.

"For once, I'm with you there, Old Man," Gavin said. "We should check the other one." He turned to the hatch where Dena was lounging. "What have you got there, Ms. Sexy Pants?" he asked.

"You know I don't like that name," Dena said. She tossed a black cylinder with a rounded end and two lugs on the side up into the air and caught it one-handed. "Not sure. While you were running your fire drill over here, I went to the other container, like you suggested."

"You got in?" Lee asked.

She tossed the cylinder up again and caught it. "It was locked, but I'm good with locks. There are crates and crates of these in there. They're all the same, the ones that I opened. They've got these weird metal knobs on the side, and the top part spins." She clicked the rounded end a quarter turn clockwise. "I've never seen anything like it."

"Friend Dena," Ana said, wiping sweat from his face. "Friend Dena, I would very much appreciate if you handed that to me, very carefully, and didn't handle it anymore."

"Why? I'm the one who found it. Can't I keep it?"

"I'll get you another if you'd like. Please, please, hand that to me. Very slowly."

Dena stuck her tongue out. "Fine, Old Man, fine. Here." She tossed it with terrible aim, not quite reaching Ana. He dove forward and caught it before it hit the floor, rolled, and landed on his back with an oof, cradling the object over his chest.

"Little work needed on your acrobatics there, Centurion," Gavin said.

"Are you okay, Centurion?" Lee said. "Let me help you." She reached for him.

"BACK," Ana yelled. "Stay back." He lay still for a moment, gripped the end and the shaft, and spun the top part counter-clockwise. It clicked a quarter turn.

Ana let out his breath with a whoosh, then rolled on one side and lay for a moment. He had to roll and stagger to get up because he wouldn't let go of the object. Once he got up he stopped to control his breathing.

"Are you losing it, Old Man?" Gavin asked. "Trying new yoga moves, what?"

"Didn't want this to hit the deck. Or a wall or anything."

"But what is it?" Dena asked. "Can we sell it?"

"Can we sell it?" Ana said. "Oh, we can sell it, all right."

"Is it valuable?" Gavin asked.

"For the right person, absolutely priceless," Ana said. "They'll pay a fortune. We just have to find them."

"Good. About time we got a break here."

"Was there anything else in that container?" Ana asked. "Any tube-like things?"

"A couple of boxes of them, tubes and some square metal plates. But mostly these things. What is it?"

"Mortar shell," Ana said. "Imperial design. Extreme high explosive. RDX932—if I remember rightly. Accurate for a portable weapon and great range. Very light for its destructive power. Can be combined in a battery with electronics for remote fire. One of these"—Ana held up the shell—"a single one, could easily destroy this ship."

"Paterfather Zeus, save us," Lee whispered.

"Don't worry, they're safe to transport if they're not armed."

"Are they armed?"

"Ask Nature Girl here," Ana said. "When she clicked the nose over, that armed the fuse." He grinned at her. "Gotta say, never expected you to throw a live mortar shell at me."

***

The crew assembled in the lounge. They were in jump space, so Dirk turned the alarm volume up in case of an alert.

"Well, at least now we know why they were in such hot pursuit," Dirk said.

Gavin winced when two pieces of metal clanged. "Do you think it was stolen, Pilot?"

Dirk nodded. "It's pretty standard for Imperial intelligence to provide weapons—"

CLANG.

"To provide weapons for different groups in a conflict," Dirk said, "either to ensure that one side wins or just to make mischief—"

CLANG.

"Centurion," Dirk said. "Is that absolutely necessary?"

Ana and Scruggs looked up from the mortar they were assembling. "Is what necessary?"

"Building a working piece of artillery in my ship."

"It's not your ship anymore. It's our ship. And it's not artillery. It's a crew-served weapon. And we're not building, we're training."

"Training in a galley?"

"Training never stops. Ready for the bolt, Private."

Scruggs slammed a heavy metal bolt into a socket and used a wrench to tighten it. "Got it, Centurion."

"Where'd you get a wrench that fits?" Gavin asked.

"Standard Imperial measurements," Ana said. "Plus, each assembly had a full tool kit with it and a cleaning kit, some spare parts, and a full battery electronics assembly for remote firing. The full package."

"It is my ship," Dirk said.

"Is it?" Ana said. "It's kind of our ship now, since we all helped with the stealing of it."

"I told everyone it's not stolen, it's just—"

"Borrowed," Lee said. "We know, Pilot. But you said that weeks ago, and now we've definitely gone beyond the time limit your employers gave you, so we're kind of in a gray area now."

"No gray area," Gavin said. "Totally black area. Good deal, makes things easier."

"But what's it doing there? This was supposed to be pump parts?" Dena asked.

"Before I was interrupted," Dirk said. "I pointed out this is clearly an Imperial intelligence operation. The Empire provided this to somebody to use. If I had to guess, it's for Nationalist elements on some planet to stage a revolt against the Confederation."

"The Empire supports the Nationalists?" Dena asked. "I thought the Empire and the Union of Nations didn't get along."

"They don't," Dirk said. "And the Empire doesn't get along with the Confederation, either. Lots of minor border incidents. We were part of one, remember?"

"Your buddy, the tribune, saved us. He must love you a lot."

"I think he loves shooting at the Confeds even more. And you know the saying, 'The enemy of my enemy is my friend,' and the Nats don't like the Confeds, either. So, if you had some Nat group asking for weapons that they might use against the Confeds somewhere, why not help them?"

"Makes sense."

"But in either case, this has all the looks of an Imperial intelligence operation," Dirk said.

"Can't it just be some company or criminal, smuggling weapons?" Dena asked. "That wants money?"

"Glad to hear your expertise extends to politics," Scruggs said.

"It's better than yours, Baby Marine," Dena said. "At least I can read."

"I can read better than—"

"Private," Ana said, "not now. But it's a good question. How do we know this wasn't an unofficial venture?"

"Can you tell when these were made—and where?" Dirk asked.

"Actually, yes, there's a manufacturer's plate on them, and the rounds have a date of manufacture stenciled on them. Everything is less than two years old."

"If it was a private deal, that would all be gone," Dirk said. "Make it harder to back trace where it was bought. Or stolen. But if it's official, they want everybody to know it's the real goods."

"Well, either way, it's a win for us," Gavin said. "This we can sell, and it will make a great price."

"We can't sell these," Lee said.

"It will be hard, I agree," Gavin said. "But if we take our time, I know some people who know some people, and with a few introductions, I can probably find a broker to take them off our hands."

"I didn't mean it will be hard," Lee said. "I mean we shouldn't do it at all."

"What?" Gavin said.

"We can't sell them," Lee said. "We have to give them back."

The discussion ranged for another hour. Dena went and got a fish, thawed it in the microwave, then cut it up into sushi while the argument flared.

"We're privateers or corsairs or whatever you want to call us," Gavin said. "We don't give away stuff we've stolen. We sell it."

"We can sell the fish, not the weapons," Lee said. "The Empire, the Emperor, sent those weapons to somebody. It would be treason not to help them along."

"I didn't swear to help some Emperor," Gavin said.

"I did," Lee said.

"Not often I'm on her side," Ana said, "but I did, too."

"You're stealing stuff all the time. You're a criminal, a smuggler," Gavin said.

"But an Imperial smuggler," Ana said. "Sure, I need to do some shady things to survive. Everybody's entitled to a living. Some of the things I do aren't strictly legal, but nothing I've done will hurt the Empire."

"I thought you deserted," Gavin said.

Ana jerked his thumb at Dirk. "That was Navy over there. He deserted. I retired."

"You retired?" Lee asked. "Pension and everything?"

"I had a complete ceremony—flags, salutes, all of it." Ana stared at the bulkhead over Gavin's shoulder. "I'm proud of my service."

"How come you aren't sitting somewhere, raising daisies or cattle or grandkids, even?" Gavin said.

"Wasn't exactly my choice to retire," Ana said, turning to Scruggs. "Private?"

"Centurion?"

"Here's an important piece of advice. When you sign papers about financial things, make sure all the currencies are Imperial, not planetary."

"Understood, Centurion," Scruggs said.

"For the record, I don't owe the Empire anything," Gavin said. "Far from it. I vote we sell these mortars first chance."

"I'm with the engineer," Dena said.

"You're not really part of the crew," Scruggs said.

"Now she is," Gavin said. "She's helped in the past. Helped you and the centurion out before, remember? And we all agreed."

"Oh, now that you need my vote, you're being polite. I see how it is," Dena said.

"Least you didn't have to sleep with him," Lee said.

Dena smirked at Lee. "Not yet. You suggesting I try?"

Lee narrowed her eyes.

"I say that we give them back," Ana said. "We'll just dump it, and they can have 'em."

"I agree, give them back," Lee said.

"No," Gavin said.

"Nope," Dena said. "Sell 'em."

They all looked at Scruggs.

"Whatever the centurion says," Scruggs said.

"You don't have to just do everything he says."

"Pilot says I do. And Centurion taught me a lot of things. Useful things. I trust him. If he wants to give them back, then that's what I vote."

"Think of the money you're giving up," Gavin said. "Those are worth a lot."

"I don't need the money."

"Everybody needs money," Dena said.

"I'm here for the adventure," Scruggs said. "I don't care about the money."

Ana looked at her. "You don't care about money?"

"Want me to change my vote, Centurion?" Scruggs asked.

Ana shook his head.

"Fine," Scruggs said. "I say give it back. That's three to two for giving it back. Pilot?"

All attention focused on Dirk. He'd been sitting quietly, eating what was put in front of him. Dena had been carving chunks off the fish and wrapping them in a piece of flatbread with a red sauce.

"This is good, Friend Dena. Best sushi I've had on this ship."

"Only sushi you've had on this ship," Gavin said. "Skipper, what's the story? You going to tie it up or break us for giving it back?"

"Pilot, remember you serve the Emperor," Lee said.

"I did. The Emperor put me in jail, remember?" Dirk sucked another piece of fish up. "Is that ketchup?"

"That's the only sauce we had," Dena said. "Cases of it."

"Lasts forever. No special handling. Always put it in stores," Dirk said. "You can cover a food tray with it."

"What's the word, Skipper? Riches or poverty?" Gavin asked.

"You think you can sell this, Engineer?"

"I'm pretty sure I can find a guy who knows a guy," Gavin said.

"This far out? We're outside the Imperial borders," Ana said. "And I know you haven't been out here—at least that's what you told me. So, if you can find somebody, you've got to be part of some organization."

"My past is my own business, we all agreed," Gavin said. "I can sell these, Skipper, for good money."

"Pilot, you're an Imperial officer," Lee said. "And a noble."

"And I'm a long way from the Empire."

"You haven't resigned your commission," Lee said. "And it wasn't stripped from you."

"How do you know that?" Ana asked.

"The engineer is not the only one with friends," Lee said. "Once I knew who he was, I did a check."

"How did you—Praetorian family, got it," Ana said. "Very sharp, Navigator."

"This fish is very good," Dirk said. "Can we sell it?"

"There's a couple of places close by that will take it. Pay decent money."

"Can you deal with that heating issue?" Dirk asked. "Won't it melt to slush?"

Gavin bit his lip. "It will be difficult."

"No, it won't," Ana said. "I saw the design you showed to the navigator earlier. Extra power cables, a blower—it's brilliant."

They all looked at him. "What? I've never said that he isn't competent. Just that I don't like him. You can fix it, so it doesn't melt, right?"

"The Emperor's anus," Gavin said. "Yes. I can fix it."

Dirk looked around the table. Everybody stared back. He chewed another piece of fish and dry-swallowed it, which made him choke. Dena handed him a full glass of basic, and Dirk chugged it.

"Sell the fish. Keep some for us. Return the weapons, apologize. I'm going to my cabin."

CHAPTER FIFTEEN

"Transition," Lee said. "Ship just came out of Jump behind us."

"Is it them?" Dirk asked.

"Right vector, right size, right place."

"Good enough," Dirk said, punching the intercom. "They're here. Everybody ready?"

"We've been ready for two days, Navy," Ana said over the intercom. "If you count sleeping and eating as being ready. We're coming up."

"Sorry," Dirk said. "I just get all exuberant, you know."

Lee looked at him. "Exuberant?"

Dirk waved it off. "Let's double-check our course."

The crew crowded into the bridge. Ana and Scruggs took their regular consoles—Ana was de facto sensor operator, but half the time, he'd made Scruggs do it and offered suggestions.

Gavin hung around behind them in case engineering expertise was needed.

"Not too late to cut and run," Gavin said. "Just blast away to where they can't follow."

"Can't do that anymore," Lee said. "We would have had to run before they arrived. And we need fuel."

"If we head for the jump limit, can they catch us?" Dirk asked.

"Doesn't matter," Ana said. "We've already had that discussion. We're not running."

"Mark my words, this will go sideways," Gavin said.

"Ray of sunshine, aren't you?" Dena said.

"Adapt, improvise, and overcome," Ana said. "I'm not worried."

"You're the only one, then," Dirk said. "Lee?"

"Got a channel, Pilot. A handshake anyway. Go ahead."

"Pursuing vessel, this is Heavyweight Items. Captain the Duke Dirriken Friedel commanding. There has been some confusion with your cargo. Please contact us for transfer."

The response took thirty seconds, about double the necessary light speed delay, then a man appeared on the screen. "Heavyweight Items, this is Benita's Luck. I'll say there's some confusion. Cut your thrust and prepare to be boarded. We will fire on you if you do not comply."

"Benita's luck, we will not comply, and you can fire all you want at this range, and all you'll do is warm our paint up a bit, if you even hit. We've got something of yours, but we took it by accident. We're willing to return it to you, planet side.

No hard feelings."

The pause dragged. "You're just going to give it to us after you stole it from us? How stupid do you think we are?"

Dirk smiled to the crew. "Best not to answer that." He keyed his microphone. "First, you need to look me up. Dirriken Friedel. F-R-I-E-D-E-L. You'll find some news that relates to me. Second, remember that not everything you hear in the news is true. Sometimes, it suits the Emperor for certain things to be thought true when they're not. Third, the Empire is big, with lots of competing bureaucracies. We were given incorrect information or somebody else's information—we're not clear. The bottom line is, we weren't supposed to steal that particular container, and we know it. Know it now. That container was provided to you by a different department. We didn't know that at the time. Our concerns are different. We're going to drop your container on the planet, sail away, and you can pick it up. Problem solved. Everybody goes home happily."

The pause, even longer this time, drew attention to a woman's figure on the video link. "Duke Friedel, the guy who massacred all those people."

"I didn't, never mind. Sure. I'm a natural-born killer," Dirk said. "I kill people for breakfast."

"That would make you a cannibal. I can believe that, too."

"You should believe the news less. The trial may not have been what you expect."

"Are you saying that the trial was faked, you're an Imperial agent, and you didn't know your military attaché provided us with that container of special cargo and that you're going to give it back to us, no questions asked?"

"Didn't take them long to figure that out," Lee said.

"They're pretty smart for colonials," Dirk said. Everybody in the cabin glared at him. "What? They were colonies originally," he said.

"Everybody not born in the core," Ana said, "you core-worlds twit, is a colonist to you."

"Right, sorry." Dirk keyed the microphone. "I'm not going to confirm anything, but we're en route to that planet, we're going to dump that container there, fly out, and you can retrieve it. We want you to have it as much as you do."

The pause was just the round-trip delay this time. "Why not dump it in space?"

"We don't quite trust you," Dirk said. "You have those two lasers, and you did fire on us last time. We think it's safer for us if you have to drop into an atmosphere to pick it up. Gives us time to skedaddle."

"Skedaddle?" Lee said. "Who says that?"

"Okay," the woman said before the picture died.

Everyone waited for another minute, but that was the only message. Dirk looked at Lee and raised his eyebrows.

Lee tapped her console. "Benita's Luck. Here is our vector. Landing coordinates are highlighted. We'll leave your cargo there."

This reply took five times the round-trip time. "Okay. Benita's Luck standing by."

Dena tapped on the door. "Hey."

Everyone turned.

"That seemed too easy."

"That's 'cause it was, Nature Girl," Ana said. "That's 'cause it was."

***

After one of Dirk's patented landings, Heart's Desire sat on the top of a large, flat hill. The crew stepped off the ramp onto the ground.

"Why here, Navigator?" Dirk asked. "Kind of uninviting."

"This is the biggest, widest, flattest area for a hundred miles around," Lee said. "Very visible. And plenty of room for nervous pilots to land in."

"I feel a little exposed here," Dirk said. "And cold. Should have brought my helmet. And worn boots rather than ship slippers."

"Exposure is the point," Lee said. "Easy for Benita's Luck to scan from orbit, seeing that there are no threats. If I wanted to hide, I'd have picked that lake with the hot springs ten miles that way, just down the river, past a waterfall. Narrow canyon, easy to get under these rocks, and lots of hot springs to mess up thermals."

"I'll keep that in mind if I need to hide," Dirk said. "Let's get started."

They dropped the lower hatch and lowered the ramp.

"Is this what they call a butte?" Gavin asked, looking around. The top of the hill was bare rock, with head-high boulders randomly distributed across it. Wind whistled across the gray stone. They walked toward a nearby cliff. The cliff face wasn't vertical, but it was steep and covered with snow. It ran down a thousand feet to a river valley down below. The slopes were mostly bare, except for the occasional rock that had broken loose from the top of the mesa and rolled down. But the valleys were heavily forested, the river invisible behind a cover of birch trees.

"This is a mesa," Scruggs said. She and Ana had stopped to load up with small packs and belt pouches before exiting the ship. "Buttes are taller than they are wide. Mesas are wider than they are tall."

"You constantly surprise me, Private," Ana said. "With your variety of knowledge."

"What's in the packs?" Gavin asked.

"Centurion says I should be ready for anything, so I've got a hostile environment emergency pack here."

"Suck up," Dena muttered.

"What was that, Nature Girl?" Ana asked. "And I'm carrying one as well." Ana tapped a pouch on his belt.

"Sorry, Old Man, forgot your hearing is going. I'll talk louder from now on."

Ana smiled at Dena. "Yep, gotta watch us old folks going senile. My vision's going, too. Hope I don't mistake you for a killer tabbo some night in the dark and shoot you by accident." He looked up. "What's your plan, Engineer?"

"Now you want my plan?" Gavin said.

"You have the most cargo experience," Ana said. "Plus, that container of mortar rounds is up near the top, and we don't have a crane. How do we drop it?"

Gavin faced Dirk. "Skipper, we'll unhook the chains. Then I want you to lift the ship, then tilt. Once it's tilted right, we'll cut the magnets and just dump it here. They can figure out the rest."

"Just to confirm your brilliant plan, Engineer," Ana said, "your idea is to drop a container full of highly explosive shells onto a rock surface from ten meters up, and hope none of the fuses go off by accident? Have I got that right?"

"Centurion's right," Dirk said. "I can hold the ship there for a while. You can just winch it down."

Gavin looked up. "Maybe. I'll need to be on the ground, though, directing things."

"That can work," Dirk said. "Lee will be in the ship handling comms with me."

"Scruggs and I can handle the chains," Ana said. "We'll make somebody a great cargo-handling team at this rate."

"Glad to see you're learning a useful skill, Centurion," Dirk said.

"I know lots of useful skills, Navy," Ana said. "Anytime you want me to demonstrate, let me know. Just make sure the medical bag is close by."

"What do you want me to do?" Dena asked.

"Nothing," they all said at once.

"Thanks for the support," Dena said. "Glad you're unanimous on how useless I am."

"The truth hurts," Ana said.

A shadow flashed from behind a rock ahead of them, and he spun to face it. The crew glimpsed a small form dashing behind a rock near the cliff edge.

"What was that?" Gavin asked.

"Animal of some sort but small," Ana said. "Nothing to worry about. Let's get going. Except for you, Nature Girl."

"I might be useless in space," Dena said. "But I know my way around a planet. See those clouds over there?" She pointed.

The crew turned and looked.

"I do," Dirk said. "Is that a storm?"

"Big one. And by the wind direction, headed our way. If you don't want to be covered in snow, and freeze in the dark, best get this done quickly."

It didn't work. Dirk couldn't get the ship to sit right the first few times. The winds kept hitting it from the side, knocking him off course. Gavin and Dena yelled at him over the radio from the ground until he took them off the circuit.

"I can't adjust for the wind," Dirk said to Lee. "The controls are too sluggish, and I don't have enough hands to keep us tilted while dealing with the wind."

"Why don't I handle the tilt?" Lee said. "Slave some of the controls to my board. I'll tilt us up, then you bring us over."

"You think you can pilot a ship?" Dirk asked.

"I think I can tilt it sixty degrees," Lee said. "And you're not setting a high bar here, Pilot."

Dirk glared at her. "I thought you at least appreciated my efforts here."

"I just want to get rid of this and get out of here. I'll help."

"Fine," Dirk said. "Slaving helm controls. You get these thrusters here"—he pointed at Lee—"you're in charge of lift. Give us just enough juice to keep the tilt. I'll pivot us around and deal with the wind. Try it out."

Dirk lifted the ship and turned control of the tilt to Lee. Lee tilted the ship at sixty degrees, using just the lower thrusters. They blew all over the mesa, but the tilt stayed. Dirk compensated with the lateral thrusters, then they edged around at the right aspect.

"I don't know what you changed down there," Ana said over the radio after Dirk cut him back in. "But this is much better. Scruggs and I only need one hand to hold on, rather than two."

"It's a team effort. We're keeping this altitude. Magnets are off. Start lowering. Lee, cut Gavin back in."

"Lazy, entitled, Imperial anus," Gavin radioed.

"We can hear you now," Dirk said.

"What's up with cutting me off? Hey, you're lowering now."

"Here it comes," Dirk said. "Guide us."

"Ten meters, nine, eight, keep it up, Centurion. Scruggs, faster . . . keep it level . . . a bit faster, Scruggs . . . looks good."

A gust of wind hit them, and Heart's Desire slipped sideways.

"Watch it," Gavin said.

The ship pivoted as Dirk tried to compensate for the wind.

"Keep it straight," Gavin said, "three meters . . . two meters . . . Get ready to release . . ."

With the wind increasing, Dirk gave it more thrusters, and when he felt the container touch, he yelled, "On ground, release."

Scruggs pulled her release lever first, and her chain ran free. The end of the container thumped down.

Ana pulled, but his was stuck. He pulled harder. "Emperor's knobby elbows. This one's stuck—I'm trying."

The wind dropped, and Dirk overcompensated. The ship spun around the single chain. The ship's nose dropped, and the ground reared up in front of them. Ana pushed hard. The front of the container thumped on the ground, and the chain fell slack but didn't release. The ship's nose dove closer to the ground. Ana leaned forward and hammered the release lever till it snapped open. The chain ran free as the container stuck on the ground. Lee pushed the thrusters, and the ship pushed up, pivoting on the attached chain. The ship tilted even more and lifted.

Gavin and Dena turned and ran as the thrusters pulsed, and the blast wave knocked them to the ground.

Ana pitched forward and over the side, falling a good ten meters. He hit the ground before rolling once, twice, then lay still.

The ship skidded sideways as competing thrusters fought for dominance. Dirk let it skid toward the far side of the mesa, leveled out, then cut all the other thrusters except the vertical ones. The ship stabilized and landed with a thud.

"No problem," Dirk said. "Easy as an admiral's wife when he's away at a staff conference."

"Centurion," Scruggs said, "are you okay?"

"Just resting here a moment," Ana said. "Recovering from crazy pilot maneuvers."

"I got the container down, didn't I?" Dirk said. "Without an explosion?"

"Barely," Gavin said. "Dena and I are hiding behind a rock. Can we come out now?"

Lee's board bonged, and the noise repeated over the radio.

"What's that alert?" Ana asked.

"Apparently, I miscalculated the thrust available to Benita's Luck," Lee said. "They're much faster than I accounted for. They'll be here sooner than I expected."

"How much sooner?" Gavin asked.

A shadow passed over the landing site as Benita's Luck slid over them, dropping to hover about two hundred meters away, on the far edge of the butte.

"Too much," Lee said.

CHAPTER SIXTEEN

Benita's Luck, the converted National freighter, blew rock dust and stray bits of snow as it landed at the end of the mesa. When the dust subsided, the lower hatch had already been opened, and the ramp lowered. Four figures ran out and split into two groups of two. One group ran to the container and the figures there, the other headed to Heart's Desire. Dirk and Lee watched from the control room as Benita's Luck's turret trained on them.

"Comm call," Lee said, keying her radio. "Heavyweight Items here."

"Where's your duke?" the woman from before said.

"I'm right here," Dirk said. "As I said I would be. You were supposed to wait."

"You never said anything about that," she said. "So, here we are. That ship's ramp stays down, and the thrusters stay cold, or you get a taste of the laser."

"A taste of the laser? Can't you do better than that for a description?" Dirk said.

"This isn't a grammar class. Thrusters stay cold, ramp stays down, and we want to see you at the head of it."

"Very well, I'm leaving now."

"And those folks at the container better not show any weapons, or we'll shoot 'em down like dogs."

Dirk closed the radio channel. "Shoot them down like dogs? Loves her bad-video talk, doesn't she?" He keyed the radio again. "I'll tell them. At the ramp head in one minute." He unbuckled and stood. "Lee, you're in charge."

"Of what? Centurion's calling."

"Yes, Centurion?" Dirk said.

"No battle plan survives contact with the enemy," Ana said.

"Thank you for that meaningless platitude. You are truly a balm in our time of need."

Ana laughed over the channel. "Scruggs, you there?"

"Yes, Centurion," Scruggs said. "I'm strapped up top. Centurion, are you okay?"

"I think I broke my ankle. Or at least a bad sprain."

"Can you walk, Centurion?"

"Not well. But I can fight. Scruggs, they don't know that you're there. Get your boarding shotgun and hide at the top of the ramp. Don't be seen but monitor the radio. If somebody tries to board the ship take care of 'em. Knock 'em out if you can but use lethal force if they keep coming. Navy, are you armed?"

"Funny you should say that. Our friend said that you weren't to show any weapons, or she'd, and I quote, 'Shoot you down like dogs.' But I'm putting on a gun belt."

"Good. Will make them feel better when they take it from you. Everybody else, don't mention Scruggs. We'll just show them this container, and we'll be on our way."

"There's no way they are going to let us live," Gavin said.

"If we give them what they want, they don't gain anything by killing us," Ana said.

"Except the joy of killing Imperials," Gavin said.

"Some people might enjoy that. Emperor's anus. They would probably enjoy shooting some random Imperials and never being caught—but two problems. One, they don't want to mess up this flow of weapons, and two, well, we have his high and superciliousness grand Duke Dirriken Friedel with us. Who's going to shoot him?"

"I'm not a grand duke," Dirk said. "I'm just a regular duke."

"I notice," Ana said. "You're not arguing with the high and superciliousness. That was the more descriptive part."

Dirk arrived at the bottom of the ramp to be confronted by two men in gray skin suits, complete with closed helmets and gray coveralls but without ship patches. One had a shotgun at port arms, the other his hand on his holster.

"No weapons," the first man said. "Drop the gun belt."

"I am an Imperial officer," Dirk said. He sniffed like he had smelled something bad. "This is my sidearm. Officers always carry sidearms."

"Word is, you're not an officer anymore," the man said.

"The real word is, you are not the person in charge here, and I will not be dealing with you."

"I had a cousin in New Madrid. He's dead now."

"I had three pilots. They're dead, too. Take me to the lady I spoke with earlier."

"And if we don't?"

"You want what's in that container very much. And it's rigged to blow. If it blows up, your boss will be very unhappy. The explosion might damage both ships."

The two men looked at each other.

"Whatever," the first one said. "Come with me."

"Stay out of my ship," Dirk said to the other.

"Don't want to go in your stinking ship," he said. "I want to do our business and get out of here."

"Well, we can both agree on that," Dirk said, walking away.

He strode to the container on the far side of the mesa. The guard on his ship was at the bottom, cradling the shotgun, facing away but watching him, and the first man followed two paces to his rear. Dirk stepped on a patch of ice, then slipped and fell to one knee.

The guard behind him laughed. "Solid, Imperial."

Dirk retrieved himself and treaded lightly. The rising wind froze his face, and the sky turned a darker gray, and he was glad of his skin suit.

Ana, Gavin, and Dena were standing to the front of the container. Two figures faced them, one with a shotgun, as faceless as the first group, the other a helmetless, middle-aged woman who radiated the kind of breezy professionalism that Dirk associated with dentists.

"Dirk Friedel?" she asked.

"I am. Whom am I addressing?"

"I'm an officer in the Union of Nations fleet. You can call me Major D, for now." She looked closely at his face. "You look like the vids, at least."

"Major D, I must protest at this unwarranted interference in our affairs. These weapons are absolutely not necessary. This is a simple misunderstanding that gentlemen and gentlewomen of good breeding can resolve quickly."

"You sound like him, too," Major D said. "I'm not sure that I believe you're Dirk Friedel, but you could be." She glanced at the group. "You're all definitely Imperials. That's an Imperial registered ship, but you are being suspiciously helpful."

"Then, let's do this and be about our business," Dirk said. "We have what you want. We're giving it to you."

Major D punched a button on her collar, activating her radio. "What sort of movement on the ship? Okay . . . anybody coming out. Do you see anybody else?" She looked at Dirk. "Who else is on board your ship?"

"Just our navigator," Dirk said. "You have spoken to her before. The rest of us are here."

She nodded and listened to her radio again. "MD out. Right, open that container. If it's what we want, we're all on our way."

"Pleasure doing business with you," Dirk said. "Cargo master, open it up."

Nobody moved. Dirk stepped forward. "Gavin, that's you. You're the cargo master."

Gavin looked at the woman. "Um, Skipper, about opening it."

"Just open it for the lady."

"See, it's locked, and we never actually unlocked it—"

"I'll do it," Dena said. "Give me a minute." She stepped up to the container and fiddled with the punch button lock.

Major D looked unimpressed. "You don't have the lock code?"

"It's not supposed to be ours, remember?" Dirk said. "We didn't know what was in it."

"So you say," Major D said. "I think—"

Dena pulled the lever, and the door swung open. "There you go. And you're welcome."

She pulled one door wide.

Ana limped up, swung the other, and stepped in. The box nearest to the door was cut open. He fished in it and pulled out a mortar shell. "Here you go, ma'am. Six complete mortars, with targeting equipment, and five thousand mortar shells." He showed her the one in his hand.

"Mortar shells," Major D said.

"Yes," Ana said.

"A container of mortar shells?"

"Yes, ma'am."

"What in the name of ten thousand dead empresses am I going to do with a container of mortar shells?" Major D drew her revolver. "Where's our goods?"

"Can you see them?" Scruggs asked over the intercom.

"Yes," Lee said. "They're all in front of the container. Friend Dena is working with it."

"You still call her Friend Dena?"

"I do. No reason not to be polite."

"She's only on the ship because she's sleeping with the pilot."

"You are only here because you stowed away and tried to hijack us," Lee said.

"Yes, but I'm doing things now. Centurion keeps me busy."

"He does at that," Lee said. "I'll say that you—something's happening."

"What?"

"That woman drew her gun and is pointing it at Dirk. I'm checking the channel," Lee said, fiddling with her console. Yelling voices filled the air.

"The one outside is coming up," Scruggs said. "I'm going to keep him out."

A shotgun boomed, then another, then Scruggs yelled, and a shotgun boomed again. Lee cycled the cameras but couldn't see anything useful. A shotgun banged again, then the ramp engine whined.

Scruggs appeared in the control room. "He came in firing. He's out now."

A figure appeared on the outer monitors, running away from the ship. A laser flashed in front of the control room, fizzing all the cameras with static.

"Pilot," Lee yelled into the radio, "they're shooting at us. What should we do?"

Another boom came over the radio, then rushing wind, a thud, then Dirk's voice. "Get the ship out of here. Take it to that place that we talked about, the hiding place that you talked about."

"I can't fly the ship."

"You did before. Do it now. Get away, and meet us there," Dirk said.

"But—"

The screens fizzed again, and the ship rocked sideways.

"That was the laser," Scruggs said. "Get us out of here."

Lee took a deep breath, then fired all the thrusters at once, lifting the ship. Another laser blast fizzed below them. Then she pushed the engines to make the ship slide sideways. After rolling over along the mesa and over the edge, it tilted over and slid down the cliff.

"Yeahagge," Lee screamed as the river and trees below filled the monitor screens.

***

"Take the ship," Major D said over her radio. She drew her gun and pointed it at the crew.

"Relax, relax," Ana said. "No need for that."

"We don't want your stupid weapons," Major D said. "Where's our goods?"

Ana held the mortar round in his hand. "Who doesn't want more weapons? What sort of army doesn't want weapons?"

"Then, go inside," Major D said over her radio.

"Look," Ana said, "this is the container we borrowed, I mean, stole from—"

A shotgun boomed from the Heart's Desire, then another. The Nationalist guard dashed down the ramp and dove off the side into the dust before the ramp lifted.

"Behind the container," Dirk yelled, gesturing with his hands. He, Dena, and Gavin ran behind the door to shelter behind the container. Ana remained, holding his hands up.

Ana heard Dirk's unintelligible yelling. "Look," Ana said to Major D, "we can work this out—"

The laser fired in front of Heart's Desire with a hiss of ions, followed by the Heart's thrusters firing up. Ana ducked around the container door and ran behind the container. His ankle hurt, but adrenaline allowed him to run through it.

He pulled around the corner to see the group pulling themselves off the ground. "Go, go, we need to get away from that laser."

They all ran.

The container shielded them from the Nationalists at the start. The group raced over a pile of broken rocks. Dena jumped on top of one, then leaped off but slid on her butt when she landed. She cursed, rolled, climbed up, and ran. Dirk and Ana weaved around the pile to its left. Then the crack of a gun and a puff of rock chips in front made them swerve right.

Gavin was in the lead but jerked to a stop and fell on the rock. "Whoa, hold up, hold up."

The plateau ended in a three-meter sheer drop just in front of them. The flat top gave way to a rock cliff that dropped straight. An unbroken slope of snow ran down four hundred meters to valley. There, a stand of birch trees filled the bottom, and a river was just visible beyond them.

"Too steep," Gavin said.

His crewmates straggled to a halt near the edge.

"Long way down," Dirk said.

"Where'd the ship go?" Dena asked.

"A place Lee and I know. She'll stay there till things calm down," Dirk said, frowning. "I hope."

"Freeze," Major D said behind them.

The crew turned.

Major D was walking closer, a revolver in hand. The other three guards pointed a revolver and two shotguns at them. The crew raised their hands.

"I don't have much time," Major D said. "Give me my goods, or I'll start shooting you one at a time."

"Look," Gavin said. "We're confused. We just want—"

Boom. She shot Gavin in the arm. He yelped and dropped. The puff of blue dust signified a frangible round.

"No more lies," Major D said. "Next one is in the head, at close range. Even frangibles can kill at six inches. Where are our real goods? Not some stupid pile of mortar shells."

The crew remaining upright looked at each other. Ana lowered his hands, one still holding the mortar shell. "I'll tell you, but you have to stop pointing those guns at us. We're all nervous. Accidents happen when people are nervous."

Major D lowered her revolver and held up a hand to her crew. The weapons dropped. "Well?"

Ana cradled the mortar shell in his arm, clicked the fuse to live, tossed it underhanded up into a high arc. "Fire in the hole."

The shell arced up. The National crew yelled and dove for cover.

Ana bent down, grabbed a groaning Gavin, and yanked him along behind him. "Everybody over the edge." He hobbled forward and jumped as far as he could, clearing the edge and falling three meters to the slick snow. Dirk and Dena thumped beside him.

The mortar shell exploded with a giant boom behind them, and the crew slid down the snow-covered hill, speeding down in the valley.

CHAPTER SEVENTEEN

"Pull up, pull up," Scruggs yelled.

The Heart's Desire flew down the hill, and Lee's ragged corrections pushed them sideways.

"Trying," Lee said. She pulsed the power on different thrusters. "I'm not used to this."

"Trees," Scruggs said. Birch and pine trees filled the screens. "Trees are bad."

"Not as bad as rocks," Lee said.

She slammed the control stick left, and the thrusters responded by rolling the Heart's Desire onto its side, missing a boulder that had appeared. They clipped a small tree with a crack.

"There's a forest down there. We're going to hit it."

Lee slapped the screen and pulsed another set of thrusters. The tilted Heart's Desire climbed. Trees flowed below them. She tapped another button, and they flattened, then skimmed along the river valley at treetop height.

"We're okay, we're okay," Lee said. "We're flying, we're flying." She pivoted to follow the river, which was visible under the trees.

"What happened? Where are we going?" Scruggs asked, then laughed. "That was great fun!"

"Place I showed the pilot when we landed. About ten miles from here, right down river. He said go there." She puffed a thruster, and the Heart's Desire pivoted in a turn as the river curved below them, then laughed. "It was exciting, wasn't it?"

"What about the Nats? Can they see us?"

"If they get some altitude, yes, but they'll have to launch for that, and they probably won't do that till their crew is on board, so we have time."

The river swept steadily to the right, and they followed above.

"Why did the shooting start? Was that an explosion we heard?"

"I'm busy, we'll talk about it later," Lee said. She slapped another button.

"We're going in circles," Scruggs said.

"We'll circle around that butte, then slide down river about ten miles. There's a place there."

They flashed over a snowfield covered with rocks.

"Won't the Nats find us?"

"I couldn't see down into the canyon when we overflew, and there are hot springs all down this river that will mess up the thermals," Lee said. She rolled them slightly to turn left, then leveled out. "Besides, that's where Pilot Dirk told me to go."

"I hope they're okay," Scruggs said. "Centurion sounded hurt at the start."

"I heard shooting at the beginning. It didn't sound good."

"If they're hurt, we should go back and get them."

"No, we should do what the Pilot said. That's the proper course."

"We can't leave them behind," Scruggs said. "Not alone. Not if they're hurt."

Lee looked at her. "You wanted to be a Marine, didn't you?"

"What's that got to do with anything?"

"Sometimes, Marines get hurt. Sometimes, they die. Sometimes, you can't save everybody."

Scruggs was silent.

"Learn to deal with it," Lee said.

***

The four crew members careened down the slope. Dirk was faceup. He tried to stop by digging his heels in. They dug in, but he flipped over his feet and slammed face-first with a bone-jarring thud. He rolled sideways and grabbed at the hard ice crust but couldn't grasp it. He hammered his fist into it as he slid, managed to break it, and dug his arm in. He pivoted forward over his shoulder, wrenching it as he tumbled before sliding feetfirst on his back.

The Emperor's hairy testicles—that hurt, Dirk thought. A ship flashed by, obscuring his view of the sky, thruster plumes shooting out at every angle.

Good for you, Lee, Dirk thought. Wait for us at the lake.

A figure collided with his left side and sent him spinning again. It looked like Gavin by the color of the uniform. He saw Ana flash ahead of him. Dirk's spinning continued, but he oriented himself feetfirst again.

Dirk slowed as the slope flattened. He turned, Gavin slid by headfirst, and Ana was visible just ahead. Gavin was yelling, but Ana flapped like a bag of empty skin suits. All three of them slid to a stop just short of the forest. Dirk tried to sit up but then lay back down as fire stabbed his right shoulder. He rolled onto his left shoulder and pulled himself to his knees.

Gavin lay two meters to his left, cradling his right arm across his chest and cursing. Ana was just ahead of them, silent and unmoving.

Dirk rolled over and looked uphill. Dena was perhaps twenty meters upslope, sliding down. She lay, belly-down, with both hands above her head, holding a knife that cut in the snow and slowed her progress. She stopped right next to him.

"How are you, Pilot?"

"Shoulder's busted or sprained. Something. Can't use it. Where did you learn that?"

"What?"

"That knife thing you're doing."

"Self-arrest on a glacier?"

"Yeah."

"By sliding down a glacier. Same way anybody learns anything, practice and study. You mean you don't know how to do this?"

"I've never been on a glacier before."

"This wasn't a glacier, it was just snow. And I've never been on a cargo ship before, but nobody seems to care. Gavin, will you shut up?"

Gavin had been yelling, "This really hurts. Can somebody help me?"

"Later. You're not the priority."

"I'm screaming here, and I'm not the priority?"

"If you can talk, you're not bad. Centurion isn't moving at all. We need to look at him." Dena slid over to Ana and turned him over.

"I'll help you," Dirk said. He slid over to Gavin and helped him sit up.

"Hurts like a tabbo's tusk is jammed in there," Gavin said.

"You've been stabbed by a tabbo?" Dirk asked.

"It's an expression, Skipper," Gavin said.

"Dirk, I need you," Dena said.

Dirk gripped Gavin on his unwounded shoulder and crawled over to Dena, favoring his right side. Ana was on his back, blood covering his face. "What happened? Is he dead?"

"He's breathing, and he has a pulse," Dena said. She placed Dirk's hand on Ana's bloodied head. "Put your hand here and press hard. Don't let go till I tell you."

Dirk did as ordered. "What happened?"

"If I had to guess, he hit a rock. Head wound, and his pupils are different sizes. Concussion." She ran her hands up and down his arms and legs, then pressed into his chest and stomach.

"What are you doing?"

"Checking for other injuries, broken bones, that sort of thing."

"Huh."

"Something else you don't know how to do?"

"Never done it on a ship."

"Have med computers on a ship. Don't have one here. I want to find out if there's anything more wrong with him before we move him."

"We're not moving anywhere," Gavin said. "At least not me. I'm just going to sit here for a while."

A rifle cracked from the plateau, and a tree splintered four meters ahead of them.

"You sure of that, Engineer?" Dena asked.

***

The canyon tapered as the Heart's Desire raced above the river. The valley was flat and full of trees, with the river meandering along the bottom, but the cliffs pressed in from the sides.

"How do you know exactly where we go?" Scruggs asked.

"We go over a waterfall. That's my landmark. There'll be a lake at the bottom. There it is." Lee pointed at her screens.

The valley walls narrowed, and the river sped up as it churned to the waterfall. Water vapor obscured a lake.

"Go over the waterfall?" Scruggs asked.

"Over, yes. After the waterfall is a lake. That's where the hot springs start. Right after that, the canyon walls are nearly perpendicular. We just drop down and pull under a cliff next to a spring. Almost impossible to see us with scan unless they get directly above us."

"So, we'll just go over the waterfall and what, hang there?"

"No, silly, the thrusters keep us aloft."

"But don't we have to drop down?"

"I just cut the thrusters that are keeping us up, then we can drop down."

"And land on the bottom."

"Like I just said."

"Okay. But we're still moving fast forward. Don't you have to spin and stop us or something?"

Lee's eyes widened, and she slapped controls on her screen.

"You've done that before, haven't you?" Scruggs asked.

Lee didn't respond, so Scruggs tightened her safety belts and sat back.

Heart's Desire flew over the churning river and past the spray that marked the waterfalls. Lee slapped one screen, and the ship dropped.

Except for a clear patch where the waterfall hit, the lake was iced over. Lee slapped a side thruster to pivot the ship but forgot to shut down the rear thruster. Instead of spinning in place, the ship described a circling dive.

"Awesome," Scruggs whooped.

The Heart's Desire spiraled down and slammed into the ice. It jounced along, spinning around like a tire bouncing off a ground car. The shore loomed ahead on the screens, and Lee flipped through control screens and hit the ALL THRUSTER EMERGENCY STOP button.

The Heart's Desire rolled along the ice, spinning like a coin, rolling toward the shoreline. It slid onshore, scraped up a cloud of snow, knocked over two small trees, four bushes, then slammed into the canyon wall sideways. They sat there, then the landing strut gave way, and the ship dropped one meter to the left. The screen went white as the cliffside's snow cover rumbled down on top of them. The ship sagged more, then everything was deathly quiet.

"You know," Scruggs said. "Maybe Pilot Dirk's landings aren't so bad after all."

***

"I've got Ana," Dena said, grabbing his collar. "Run into the trees, about thirty feet, and get something between you and the ridge." She waded ahead, crawling.

Dirk stumbled back to Gavin, helped him up, and the two lumbered forward, both huffing. With every step, they sank in the snow up to their waists, falling more than half the time. Snow began to fall. Bullets cracked, but they didn't see where they went. Dena had disappeared into the woods when the two men reached the first trees. Dirk and Gavin leaned against a tree. Another bullet twanged, and splinters blew off a tree to their left, canceling their rest. They stomped along Dena's trail and found her fussing over the centurion another ten meters in.

"How is he?" Dirk asked.

"Heavy," Dena said. She was sweating. "But I don't like the look of his pupils."

"Snow sucks," Gavin said. "I hate weather. Should have stayed on the ship."

"I saw the ship sailing over us when we were about halfway down," Dena said. "Lee abandoned us."

"No, I told her to go to a hiding place, one we'd discussed earlier," Dirk said.

"How convenient," Dena said. "How long will she hide I wonder."

"It's not far," Dirk said. "Just down the river. Less than twenty kilometers. We can walk."

"Ten, twelve miles? We can walk? You've never walked in the snow, have you?"

"No."

Dena crossed her arms. "How long do you think it will take to get there?"

Dirk looked at the falling snow. "Couple of hours. A person can walk, what, four kilometers an hour?"

"In the snow?" Dena shook her head. "In deep snow like this, you might make a mile an hour, and it's going to be very tiring. I doubt we could make four miles a day."

"Well, I'll call her to come pick us up," Dirk said. He reached for his belt comm and realized it wasn't there. "My comm's gone." He patted his waist. "The whole utility belt and holster is gone. How did that happen?"

"Snow. It grabs things. Happens all the time in avalanches. People lose things. So, no calling our hiding ship. If she's really hiding and hasn't sailed away."

"Maybe we can call those Nats to come pick us up," Gavin said.

"We can't call anybody, if we don't have comms. Where's yours?" Dena said.

"Next to my console on the ship. But we've got suit radios."

"So do the Nats," Dirk said. "Hold on that for now. And will they even work?"

Gavin looked at the surrounding trees and the glimpses of cliffs through the snow. "If she was airborne, sure. But in these canyons, I don't know."

"We're as likely to get the Nats as her," Dirk said. "Even if it's difficult, I think we should walk."

"Do you know which direction?" Dena asked.

"Just down the river," Dirk said.

"Down the river or up the river? And which direction is which. I'm kind of turned around since we jumped."

"I'm not sure," Dirk admitted.

"Great planning, Pilot. We could end up wandering for days," Dena said. "Anybody have any food?"

Dirk and Gavin shook their heads.

"No eating, then," Dena said. "That's another problem."

"We can't just sit here and wait to starve," Gavin said.

"We're not going to sit here and starve," Dena said.

"Good," Dirk said.

Dena gestured at the snow falling. "With this weather, we'll freeze to death long before we starve."

CHAPTER EIGHTEEN

"Have you got a sermon planned, Tribune?" Subprefect Lionel asked.

Devin shook his head. "I will not be speaking at this service." He, the subprefect, and fifty of Pollux's crew marched across a dirt-packed field fronting a barbed wire fence. "I'm purely here to worship."

"The tribune is well known for his piety," Bosun McSanchez said from behind them. "I encourage the younger crew members to follow his moral example."

The subprefect sniggered along with the party.

"Could you stop trying to be funny, Bosun?" Devin asked.

"I have no idea what you're talking about, sir," the bosun said. "Wasn't being funny at all."

"I am as moral as the next man."

"Is that what you discussed with that young female intelligence officer over dinner?" Subprefect Lionel asked. "Morals?"

"It was purely a professional gathering," Devin said. "We exchanged our views on the current situation."

"Took a long time, then," Lionel said. "All that exchanging. Is that why Lieutenant Weeks didn't attend, and it was just you and Lieutenant Hernandez?"

"She said he was busy," Devin said.

"Good of her to shoulder the whole load, then, so to speak, sir?" Bosun McSanchez said. "Nice to see the junior officers throwing themselves into their duties."

The group sniggered again.

"Et tu, Bosun?" Devin asked. "You mock me as well?"

"Remember, thou art but a mortal man, Tribune."

Devin looked back at the bosun and nodded. "True. Thank you."

"Happy to oblige, sir."

They approached a barbed wire gate.

Lionel held up his hand. "Hold up, please, sir."

"What for? I—"

A dozen men and women jogged past them. The first six were in Marine uniform, carrying sidearms. The second six wore white skin suits and carried bundles of sticks tied together, with an ax in the middle. The Marines fanned out to the sides, and the six other gathered in front of the gate.

"Lictors? Really?" Devin said.

"We're in the provinces now. Best to remind people."

"They've got axes for the Empire's sake. What are they going to do with those in a fight?"

"Remind people the consequences of starting one," Lionel said.

The head Lictor shouted an announcement, drawing a crowd. The outside guards swung the gate open, and the group inside pressed forward until the Marines stopped them. A short man with a big smile, wavy hair, and a high embroidered collar stepped forward.

"Welcome, I am Elder Meeks. By your attendants, you are the Imperial Tribune."

"Devin, Lord Lyon," Devin said.

"Welcome, sir. Do you worship the one spirit, Tribune?"

"In a fashion," Devin said. "And many of my crew are believers. They wished to attend mass."

"They are welcome, as are you," Elder Meeks said. He looked at the Marines and their weapons. "We are Imperial citizens and follow the Imperial rules. Are you here in a professional capacity?"

"I represent the Pontifex Maximus, yes," Devin said. "But provided you start with a prayer for the Emperor and family, there will be no need for me to give an oration."

Meeks feigned a smile. "We are truly blessed."

"More than you know," Lionel said. "I've heard his sermons before. The way he talks, and with how hot it is out, everyone would be snoring inside two minutes."

"Thanks for your support, Subprefect," Devin said.

"What? I swore I'd follow you into battle, not church," Lionel said. "And frankly, I think the crew would prefer a good fight to a sermon."

A murmur of assent swept through the troops.

"I won't need to give a sermon," Devin said. "But I expect the Imperial taxes will be collected appropriately."

Elder Meeks blinked. "These people are refugees, Tribune. As am I. Frankly, we do not have much."

"The Pontifex Maximus makes the rules. I just enforce them, Elder."

"And you felt the need to enforce this personally?" Meeks said. "We are lucky to have such a dedicated servant of the Empire with us today."

Devin narrowed his eyes. "You will say the appropriate Imperial prayers, you will make a collection, and you will remit the Imperial tithe. The rest of the service belongs to you, but you will follow the regulations. Is that clear, Elder?"

"We serve the Emperor, Tribune," Meeks said. "I must go prepare. With your leave?"

Devin nodded, then allowed himself to be guided to an area in the center of the makeshift church. The people who had been sitting there had mostly vacated it for his party, and any who didn't move were encouraged by the Marines and armed sailors.

"All this way for a hundred credits?" Lionel asked. "And to irritate a harmless preacher?"

"I doubt we'll even get a hundred credits," Devin said. "But the Empire's laws will be followed."

"You could remit the tax."

"Bad precedent. I'll give it back. I'll give back double from my personal funds," Devin said. "After they hand in their share first. They have to remember who is the font of generosity. As you said, we're in the provinces, and we need to remind them who's boss." He estimated the crowd. "This isn't as bad as I thought it would be. Less than a thousand here?"

"Much less. After the Confeds and Nats announced their exclusion zone last month, most of their people scuttled back across their respective borders and didn't try to cross over to our space. Last thing they wanted was to be stuck inside the Empire when the shooting starts. Almost everybody here in the camp are Imperial citizens or have some sort of Imperial connections. If you have even half-decent documentation, we put you on the next ship to your home of record. These ones here are just waiting for transport."

"How long will this be here?"

"We get a few ships of people every week now. Before, it was some every day. Some will stay a few weeks, but it peaked in size a month ago. It's been getting smaller since."

"Somebody doing their job for a change."

"Internal Security, believe it or not," Lionel said.

"It would have to be them, wouldn't it?"

A gong clashed, and the crowd stood. Groups of men in dark robes marched down the central aisle.

Lionel leaned closer to Devin. "They've taken advantage of the opportunity. They question everybody who goes through here, asking about the systems they were in. Military installations, spaceports, transit, mines, that sort of thing. And they're buying clothes."

"Buying clothes? Because they admire the Confeds' taste in jean shorts?"

"Labels and styles. Clothes, shoes, transit passes, documents, comm equipment, household items, musical instruments. Anything people have with them from the Confederation."

Devin coughed as a passing priest censed each side of the aisle. "In case I need to take a train with a trumpet?"

"So their spies have nothing that says 'Empire' on it. We can sneak somebody onto, say, Hartford, and have them dressed in locally made clothes, carrying a guitar imported from the next planet over, with an up-to-date transit pass. They can move around the capital and sing in bars with no questions."

The crowd sat, and the two men followed.

"That's actually smart."

"It's sad when your enemies aren't stupid, isn't it? The show is starting. Wow, they've laid it out. What's that smoke?"

"Incense. And before you ask, the thing they're swinging is called a censer."

Devin and Lionel sat upright as the priest spoke. "Blessed be the Emperor, for he is the font of all that is right—"

An hour later, a sweaty and well-censered crew marched to the gate. The camp's inhabitants watched them with envy but didn't try to follow. Piscium was a desert world. At least, in the camp, they had shade and water.

Elder Meeks was waiting by the gate with a bag. "Your taxes, Tribune."

"Not mine but the Emperor's. Bosun?" Bosun McSanchez stepped forward and took the bag.

"I provided them in cash. I assume that is what you wanted," Meeks said.

"I did not. Bosun, give them a receipt."

"No need for that, Tribune," Meeks said. "I understand how these things are."

The bosun counted the money in the bag, then fiddled with his comm, and Meeks's comm beeped. Meeks examined it and nodded. "Thank you, Tribune. I think this concludes our business."

"Not quite," Devin said. He waved at the bosun, who produced a credit chip and handed it to Meeks. "For the refugees," Devin said.

Meeks slotted the chip in his comm and examined it. He raised his eyebrows. "This is most generous and will be very helpful, Tribune."

"I'm sure you will use it wisely. Good day, Elder." Devin and his group turned to walk out of the camp.

"Tribune, wait," Meeks called, running after them.

Devin turned. "Yes?"

"Your intelligence people were here earlier and asked us many questions."

"That is so," Devin said. "I'm told you were most helpful."

"They were very insistent, and . . . well, threatening."

"That happens from time to time."

"We answered truthfully, of course. I am an Elder, but a number of the questions were somewhat ambiguous, and, well, I wasn't disposed to help them too much. Because of their attitude, you see."

"It's your duty as an Imperial citizen to assist all the officers of the Empire."

"Oh, I did, Tribune, I did. I told them everything I knew. Just not all that I suspected."

"It's hot out here, Elder. What's your point?"

"There was a freighter at Winsome Station. Imperial registered, with a somewhat odd crew, who I spoke to at some length. Long enough to get a good look at them. One of them reminded me of someone I had seen on the vids recently. Someone with an Imperial warrant."

"An Imperial warrant? Which crimes? Who for?"

"Not an arrest warrant. Just a person of interest. I don't know a name, just that I'd seen them before. It was a small freighter. Almost a Free Trader. And there were five or six people on it. Men, women. One was a Jovian. I remember something—"

Devin looked as the bosun. "Bosun, bring—"

Lionel beat the bosun. He stepped forward, holding his comm up. "This ship here—Heart's Desire? Or the same model?"

"It wasn't named that, and I don't know much about ships, so I can't say. But one of the crew resembled that citizen I had seen warrants for."

Lionel flipped through his comm screen. "Here. This man. Did you see him?"

"That man? Well, maybe, I'm not sure."

Lionel paged through different pictures. "I have other pictures. What about this?"

"Not him, no," Meeks said.

"Try this picture."

Meeks shook his head. "Sorry."

Lionel looked at Devin, who frowned. "Thank you for your time, Elder."

"Do you have any other pictures, Tribune?" Meeks asked.

Lionel brought up a list and helped Meeks scroll through them.

"Wait," Meeks said. "What's this group?"

Devin looked at Lionel's comm. There were six pictures arranged like a lineup of mugshots on the screen. "That's all the people on the ship that we're looking for. Do you recognize anyone?"

"Absolutely. That's the person I saw. The one with the Imperial warrant."

Devin smiled and pointed at Dirk's picture. "Just to confirm, this person here that you recognized was Dirk Friedel, also known as the Butcher of New Madrid. That's who you saw."

"Who? Him? That man?"

Devin tapped the screen. "Yes, this man. Dirk Friedel."

"I never saw him, no. I mean, he might have been on that ship, but I didn't notice him."

"You didn't see him at all?"

"Didn't notice him. No, I mean her."

Devin and Lionel looked at each other, then back at Meeks. "What? Which her?"

"This one here." Meeks pointed at Scruggs. "The others called her Scruggs. I've seen her picture. There's an Imperial warrant out for her."

CHAPTER NINETEEN

"I think I'm going to die from heatstroke," Dirk said, wiping sweat from his brow. He and Gavin were taking turns dragging Ana through the snow. "Not freezing. Besides I'm wearing a skinsuit, if it will keep me warm in space, why not here?"

"Where's your helmet?" Dena asked.

"On the ship."

"Are you wearing insulted mag boots?

"Ship slippers."

"Lot of heat loss through your head. And wet feet can freeze while the rest of you is nice and toasty.

"Suit should be able to compensate, right?" Dirk said.

"Sure. As long as the batteries last. How much power you got left?"

Dirk tapped a stud on his arm. A light flashed orange on his arm.

"What's orange mean? Dena asked.

"Orange means go back to the sip for recharge. Okay. March or die."

"I'm warm now, for sure," Gavin said. "But I'm also lost."

"And all that sweat will freeze to ice and kill you that much sooner when you stop moving," Dena said. "Go slower but keep going."

"Go where?"

"We need to get to where we can see the river," Dena said. "Before this storm gets too strong."

"What's the point of seeing a stupid river?"

"Because if we can find the river, we're not lost," Dena said. "We can follow it upriver or down river, if the pilot can figure out which way to go. We don't have a compass, and there aren't navigation satellites here."

"That's a good point," Dirk said. "But I'm not sure about the river."

"You mentioned a lake?"

"Yes."

"With a waterfall? Where was the mist?"

"The mist?"

"The smoke, the fog, the mist. When there's a big waterfall, there's always a mist of water vapor around. Was it on the lake?"

Dirk stopped and closed his eyes. "There was a river that wound down a canyon, then a waterfall, with the lake below. The mist covered the lake."

"Which means the water was falling into the lake, not out of it. So, that means, from where we are, that the lake is down river from here."

"So, we just have to find downriver," Dirk said.

"Have to find the river first," Gavin said.

"It can't be that far away," Dena said. "We could see it from the cliff. There." She pointed through the trees.

"All I see is . . . nothing," Gavin said.

"That's the point," Dena said. "No trees on a river."

They dragged Ana through the woods to a bank over a flat, empty space.

"I don't know how much farther I can carry him," Dirk said. "He's a big guy."

"Gavin," Dena said, "do you still have your knives?"

"Yes."

"Give one to me. You two take a rest," Dena said.

Gavin handed over a knife without comment and sat next to Dirk. Dena went to a grove of springy bushes on the bank and sawed two two-meter-long stout branches, then trimmed them at either end. Next, she cut a half dozen shorter, thinner cross branches and returned.

"I need to see the centurion's belt," Dena said. "He carries a survival pack." She pawed at his waist, produced a box, and opened it. "Flint and steel, fifty feet of high strength twine, a mirror, water purification pills, a wire hand saw, bandages, and antiseptic cream. 'Outstanding,' as he would say." She hefted a small bottle. "And pain pills. Strong ones." She opened the bottle, shook two out, and handed one each to Dirk and Gavin. "You two, one each. And one every eight hours or so. It will help you move and reduce the swelling."

Gavin swallowed his pill. "What's all that other stuff for?"

"Watch," she said, lashing the two long poles together at a thirty-degree angle. Next, she tied four other poles across them till she had a narrow triangle of wood, with cross beams every twenty centimeters.

"What's that?"

"It's called a travois," Dena said. "Now, get his overalls off."

"He'll freeze," Dirk said.

"He's still got his skin suit, but we need to lash him in. Watch."

As the two men watched, she peeled off the top of his overalls, laid him on the frame, then strapped his coveralls over top of the frame. Dena had to move a cross beam, but when they were done, he was securely lashed down, pointed end near his head. Dena tied the remaining twine on each carry pole to make a loop and wrapped it around an eight-inch stick to be used as a pulling handle.

"Got it. Now we can drag him."

Dena's contraption rendered dragging Ana easier, even with Gavin and Dirk's damaged arms and shoulders.

"That's amazing," Gavin said. "Where did you learn that?"

"I'm Nature Girl, remember? No use on a spaceship."

"Plenty of use here," Dirk said.

"Aren't you glad that I'm not one of those space-trained engineers now?" Dena said.

"Yes. Yes, I am," Dirk said.

Dena used the wire saw to cut two sturdier poles, which were two meters long and six centimeters thick.

"We'll need these on the water," she said.

She walked over to the bank and climbed down to the river. It wasn't entirely frozen. Ice water gurgled through clear patches next to rocks at the bank.

Dena smacked the pole on the ice ahead of her. Some of it shattered or let her push down to water, but she found a path out to the main part of the ice.

"Bring him out here. Follow my tracks," she said. "The snow isn't as deep out here. He'll be easier to drag."

Dirk and Gavin slid Ana and his rig down the bank and onto the ice. On the ice, they could walk, even dragging Ana.

"This is way easier," Gavin said. "He just kind of glides on the ice, and I'm not falling every two steps."

"You two drag, I'll lead," Dena said.

She walked about four paces ahead of them and thwacked her stick on the ice every meter or so.

"I'll drag first," Dirk said. "Gavin, you follow."

"Bring your stick," Dena said. "You'll need it to get back on the ice if you fall through."

"Fall through?"

"Ice might not be frozen all the way through. That's why I'm hitting in front of me, to make sure the ice is thick enough to support us."

"Will that be a problem?" Dirk said. "Thin ice I mean?"

Dena's stick cracked ahead of her. This time, rather than bouncing up, it shattered the thin layer that covered an airhole and splashed up cold water.

Dena pulled the stick back. "Sometimes."

***

"Sushi?" Lee said, stepping up to Scruggs and handing her a plate. "I cut up one of those fish. It's pretty tasty."

"Thanks," Scruggs said. She had opened the air lock facing the lake. Initially, it had opened to a wall of white snow, but after a few moments of pushing, they saw the frozen lake. "Sun's down. It will be dark soon. I hope they're okay."

"Centurion will take care of them," Lee said. "He always has so much stuff on his belt—he has a survival kit, water purifier, first aid, that sort of thing. They'll be fine."

"Long, cold walk," Scruggs said. She took a piece of fish and popped it in her mouth. "Have you heard from them on the radio?"

Lee chewed and swallowed. "No, but with these cliffs, it might be a problem. Skin suit radio's aren't that strong, and they rely on line of sight. Do you like them?"

"What?"

"The sushi, you just swallowed it down."

"Didn't notice," Scruggs said, shivering. "Getting colder. We should go help them."

"No," Lee said. "I told the pilot I'd wait here, and that's what we'll do. He's probably on his way."

"It's too dark to see."

"At least one of the moons is rising, so they can see."

"We should help them."

"We should do what we told them we'd do. If we leave, we might miss them while we travel back upriver, plus we can't go anywhere that those Nats are—they're looking for us."

"Why did they start shooting? We were giving them what they wanted."

"I have no idea," Lee said. "I'll ask the pilot if he gets here."

"You mean, when he gets here," Scruggs said.

"Right, that's what I meant," Lee said, shivering. "When he gets here."

***

They had walked for two hours in the dark before Gavin fell into the river. He and Dirk shared the pulling, handing off every half hour. Dena was in better physical shape and could have pulled as well, but the men wanted her up front to chart the course and pay attention to the ice. The moons made travel easy. The woods were dark shadows on either side of a bright white river. The thin ice was closest to the bank, so they stayed in the center.

They were tired, so it was only natural that their attention wandered. Ana hadn't woken and didn't cry out, but he huffed, worrying them all.

Dena still tapped in front of her, but she had been less than vigilant about tapping to the sides, and the wind-scoured ice was clear enough of snow that Gavin had not been following exactly in her's and Dirk's footsteps.

Gavin took a step. The ice cracked underfoot, and he pitched into the water. "Huuuh, huuhh, huuh, huulp."

Dena spun around. "Hold the pole. Keep hold of the pole, don't go under."

"Huuuh," he said. "Holding."

Dirk propelled forward. "Hang on, I'm—"

"STOP," Dena yelled. "Just stop. Where there's one patch of thin ice, there are more. Get down." She dropped to her knees, then lay flat on the ice, sliding forward. "Spread your weight out."

Dirk complied and slid to Gavin.

"Slipping," Gavin gasped.

He leaned onto the pole. He'd fallen into a meter-wide hole in the ice, but his pole had caught the edges, so he'd only dropped to his waist. "Cold. Help."

Dena slithered over to him. His left arm gripped the pole. His damaged right flapped as he tried to grasp. Dena snagged it and pulled.

"YEAAAH," he yelled. "That hurts."

Dena towed him forward to the edge of the hole, still leaning on the pole. "I'm going to pull you. Roll up and over."

"Imperial anus, that hurts," Gavin yelled.

"Dirk, over here and help me pull. Stay low, slide around."

Dirk crawled around the hole, lay next to Dena, and they pulled Gavin up and out before rolling him next to them.

"My arm hurts," Gavin said.

"Never mind your arm. What about your legs? And your feet?"

"They feel numb."

"Gotta get his boots off and get a fire going," Dena said. "Can't walk on frozen feet. Grab that pole. We need to get to shore."

The river faced a rocky beach, and by tapping with the poles, Dirk and Dena found a path to the shore. They helped Gavin stagger onto the beach and sit on a rock, then returned and dragged Ana along behind them.

"We have to warm his feet up before frostbite sets in," Dena said.

"I never thought about that. What about Ana? Will he get frostbite?"

"He's dressed and dry. He might get hypothermia later, but that's not a problem for now. If we don't get Gavin's feet dried out, they'll freeze. Water conducts heat better than air, so we need to dry his feet and his boots out."

Dena pointed at the nearest tree. "Break off those dead twigs under that bough, smaller than your pinky finger. Get me as many of them as you can. Watch me." She climbed over the snow and snapped off twigs.

Dirk ducked under the tree and broke off handfuls of twigs. Dena collected larger sticks, then branches.

"Pile them there next to Gavin, and get more branches and snap them like I did," Dena said.

Gavin sat in the middle of a pile of rocks. "Cold."

Dena stomped around and located a fallen tree nearby. "Dirk, come here." He clambered through the deep snow. "Here's Ana's saw. See how it works." She demonstrated cutting through a branch. "Get me as many of those thicker two-, three-inch branches as you can, about four feet long, and bring them over. I'll snap some more smaller ones."

Dirk cut five branches and dragged them over. Dena dug the snow out from between three rocks until she saw dirt. Then she laid a cover of small sticks on the ground. She put the smallest twigs in a pile, piled thicker ones on top of them in a teepee. She then built and piled larger branches in a square criss-cross around them, like a small log cabin, with smaller sticks in the middle, and the smallest at the bottom.

Dirk dragged another branch over. Dena took the oldest, driest branch and shaved it with her knife. She made a fist-sized pile, collected it, and stuck it under the laid fire. Then she did it again but kept that pile behind a rock, sheltered from the wind.

Dirk came back with more branches.

"Good for now," Dena said. "Get Gavin's boots off and get him closer to where the fire will be."

Dirk obediently walked over to help Gavin.

Gavin was shivering even more, and his fingers were clumsy. Dirk had to help him pull his boots off.

"What next?" Dirk said.

Piling her shavings and stroking her flint and steel, she laughed. "This is funny."

"Funny? You find this funny?"

"Weird-funny. The two of you are doing what I tell you right away. No taunting, no Nature Girl cracks, no raised eyebrows or condescending remarks."

"You seem to know what you're doing," Dirk said. "So, best to let you lead."

"Really?" Dena asked.

"I've never been in the woods at night before," Gavin said. "I'm confused." He looked at his feet. "And a little scared. This is all new to me—and scary."

Dirk nodded. "Me, too."

"Well, now you know how I feel all the time dealing with you on the ship," Dena said. "Confused. Angry. Frightened."

"What happens now?"

"We light a fire."

"Just like that? You can just make a fire?"

"Yes. Just like that."

"Won't the Nats see it?" Dirk said.

"They might, but small fires in the woods are hard to find at night. I know that for a fact. And if we don't, his feet will freeze."

"It's a risk."

"I'm not actually asking for permission," Dena said. "That was just information."

She took the flint and struck it on the steel. Sparks flew from her hands and glowed on the wood shavings. After five or six strikes, the shavings caught and glowed a dull red. Dena blew on it till a small flame came out. She cupped it in her hand, blew on it, and carried it to the main fire. She pushed it under the pile, laid her head next to it, and blew more. The shavings burned easily and lit the smaller twigs, which lit the larger ones. In less than two minutes, a blaze crackled in front of her.

"Feet by the fire. Boots next to them," Dena said. "Don't put the boots too close, or they'll burn." She pointed. "Put Centurion there—it's flat and close enough. He'll get some heat."

Gavin almost stuck his feet in the fire and put his boots just behind his ankles. He leaned in and held his hands just above the flames.

"Should we take Ana out of the travblah?" Dirk asked.

"Travois, and no. He'll be fine there."

"Won't he get frostbitten?"

"Eventually, yes, but the wind isn't bad, and he isn't wet, so he's safer. It's only for a few hours, anyway. We moved faster than I thought. We're probably halfway to this lake, if it's where you said it is."

"It is," Dirk said. "I'm a pilot. I'm good at measuring distances. I think we're halfway there, too."

"And you can believe as much of that as you want," Ana said.

"Ana? You're awake? How do you feel?" Dirk said before he and Dena ran over to him.

"Like a tabbo stepped on my head. Where are we?" Ana asked.

"Maybe five miles downriver from our fight," Dena said. "Pilot told Lee to take the ship to a hiding place ten miles away. Are you all right?"

"I'm very, very sleepy. Concussion?"

"We think so," Dena said. "No other injuries that we could see."

"Outstanding," Ana said. "Who's in charge?"

Dirk and Dena looked at each other.

"I'm in charge," Dena said. "I'm organizing the hike."

"Thank the Emperor," Ana said. "Somebody useful."

"You don't think I'm useful?" Dirk said. "Or Gavin?"

"Navy, I'd love to watch you and the kid wander around in the woods till you were eaten by a rabbit or killed by a crow but only if I was doing it in front of a vid in a warm bed, with a drink next to me, not when it looks like I'm counting on you to get me out of here." Ana shifted. "I think I can stand."

"You're lying," Dena said. "I've seen concussions before."

"I am. But I should try."

"We've got a fire. An hour or two and Engineer's boots will be dry, and we can keep going. The river's clear of most snow, and small accidents notwithstanding the ice is thick enough for easy walking. It won't take more than a day to get to this lake, according to the pilot."

"Anybody else hurt?" Ana asked.

"Everybody but me has some problems. Speaking of which, I took some pills out of your belt. Strong pills. I gave the pilot and engineer one each. Sorry, but needs must."

"That's okay, Friend Dena," Ana said. "Needs must." He coughed. "If I'm going to be sitting here, I could use one of those. And some water."

"Then, you'll certainly sleep."

"Might be for the best. I have a splitting headache, and I can't really see."

"Blind?"

"Very, very blurry, double vision, and this talking is an effort."

"We're in a good place for now," Dena said.

She pulled out the pill bottle, shook a pill, then put it in his mouth.

"Some snow to wash it down," Ana said.

Dirk dripped a few fingers of snow into Ana's mouth, and he swallowed.

"Better," Ana said. "Given our previous situation, things have worked out better than I expected."

"I'm cold but not freezing," Dirk said. "I can walk for another day, and that contraption that we're carrying you in works."

"Engineer, how are you feeling?" Dena said.

Gavin hugged his arms across his chest and stretched his feet to the fire. "Better. I'm still cold, but my feet aren't numb anymore. Kind of tingling."

"That's the blood coming back." She felt his boots. "Just damp now, not wet. Another hour, and you'll be dry."

"How about we all have a short rest?" Dirk said. "Wait an hour, dry out the engineer's boots, let Ana get back to sleep. Then we go down to the river again. We'll make it to the ship tomorrow."

"Mmmmmmm," Ana said. "Need a sentry."

"I'll do it," Gavin said. "I'm too wired from the fall to sleep."

"Dena and I will grab a nap, then. Wake us in an hour. You sure you can keep awake?"

"Yes. The fire's warm, but I'm awake. And if I get bored, I'll just watch those fireflies."

"Fireflies?" Dena asked.

"Out there," Gavin said. "I've been staring into the woods. I see fireflies sometimes."

"There's no fireflies in a pine forest," Dena said. "Not in the winter."

Gavin pointed. "I see them over there sometimes. There's one now."

Dena and Dirk looked at where he pointed. Light glittered under the trees. Lots of lights, each in pairs.

"Those aren't fireflies," Dirk said. "That's animals. There's a pack of wolves in the trees."

CHAPTER TWENTY

"We need to go back for them," Scruggs said.

"No, we do not. We need to wait here," Lee said. "I told the pilot that we'd be here."

They were standing at the opened air lock, and their breath steamed in the twilight. Between bashing the snow out and dumping a few piles in the air lock, they had got the side hatch open. "Plus that Nat ship is still out there. They'll shoot us out of the sky."

"Centurion says that lasers don't work well in atmosphere."

"They don't have to work well, they just have to work at all. One shot from even a low-power laser hits something important while we're lifting, and we'll crash. And he said that when we were running away from them. If we go hunt for the rest of the crew, we have to stay here—or close to here—and that means they get good shots at us from the ground. If they decide to lift and chase us around, what happens then? What happens to us if they get close?"

"What if they wait as long as we do?"

"There's no reason for them to do that. They got their goods—at least they should have. I don't know what went wrong, but they should leave."

"What if they look for us?"

"Only an idiot would hide here," Lee said.

"Wait, what?"

"What we'd normally do—if we had a pilot onboard when we lifted—was head to orbit or to the jump limit. Not dirtside. They won't think to look for us here. They'll be looking up. I bet that they are loading that stupid container right now, and as soon as they get it chained, they'll blast to orbit and start scanning up there. They won't be looking for us here. Staying here would be stupid. But we're well hidden from visuals, and if they have sensors, all they'll have is infrared, and they're so many of those springs." Lee pointed at steaming water that spewed out of the canyon wall two hundred meters downstream. "I saw those all over the place. We wait here till we know they're gone."

"How will we know they leave?"

"Normally, we would use our own sensors. Telescope or radar or our own infrared sensors."

"Normally?"

"Telescope is covered in snow, and it's not really a search thing. I don't want to use the radar—they can track us by the emissions and our own infrared . . ."

"Is on Engineer's broken list?" Scruggs said.

"It's a big list."

"Then how do we know how long to wait?"

"We should see them, or hear them, for sure. And once we hear them lift, we can maybe get back on the radio. Short range, at least."

"So, we need to stay outside to listen for them."

Lee hugged her shoulders. "Yep. Out here in the cold, in the snow. You take first watch. I'm going to have a nap. Wake me in a half shift."

It was an hour before Scruggs banged on Lee's cabin door. "Navigator, wake up."

Lee opened the door, rubbing sleep from her face. Scruggs grabbed her arm and towed her down the corridor. Since the ship was on its landing legs, the cabin's walls were down, and Lee had swiveled her accel couch into a bunk.

"Listen before it goes," Scruggs said.

Lee shivered as the cold air from the air lock hit her. "You know that, if you keep the doors closed, the warm air stays inside and the cold air stays out, don't you?"

"Listen," Scruggs said.

A rumbling growl came through the outer hatch.

"That's a ship's main drive," Lee said. "They're trying to cover some distance, or they're trying to lift to orbit."

"Which one?"

"Doesn't matter. They'll be long gone in a few minutes, either across the landscape or up high. Either way, once that sound ends, we can try the suit radios."

"How long do we wait?"

"Wait until we can't hear them at all, then ten minutes more, and Sister Scruggs?"

"Yes?"

"Do you mind waiting out here while I go put on my boots? My feet are really cold."

***

"They're not wolves," Dena said, standing by the fire.

"They sound like wolves," Dirk said.

"No, wolves growl or howl. These guys are barking," she said.

"Will they eat us?"

"Yes, they'll come leaping over the fire and tear your throat out with two-foot-long tusks and then they'll use eight-inch giant incisors to rip our face off and swallow it in one gulp," Dena said.

"Really?"

"No, not really, you idiots. I caught a glimpse of them. They're small, maybe twenty pounds each. Too small to have foot-long tusks. And they're scared of the fire—almost all animals are scared of fire. They won't approach us here or while we're up and moving. They'll follow us, and if one of us falls down in the snow and looks weak, they might swarm that person and try to cut a tendon. Then they'll all dive in."

"We're safe here?" Dirk asked.

"Afraid of some little dogs, Pilot?"

"I hate the woods."

Dena smiled. "I love the woods. For now, we're safe. But no sleeping, and we need the fire."

"How long will the fire last?"

"Long enough for Gavin to dry out, then we'll hike to the ship."

"Won't they follow us?" Gavin said.

"Yes."

"Won't we need protection?"

"Yes."

Dirk edged closer to the fire. "So, what do we do? Does anyone still have their revolver?"

Dena and Gavin shook their heads. "What can we do, then?" Dirk asked. "How do we keep them away?"

Dena closed her eyes. "Spacers. Dirk?"

"Yes?"

"Strip naked and give me your underwear."

It took a lot of hopping and cursing for Dirk to disrobe, get his underwear off, and get his skin suit back on.

"My feet are cold," he said to Dena.

She was shaving a branch into a smooth Y-shape. "Told you to stand on your skin suit."

"I didn't want to get it wet."

"It's waterproof, remember?"

"Doesn't feel that way."

"Don't be a big baby. How does this look?" She held up her carving.

"Like that slingshot thing you used before," Dirk said.

"Exactly."

She picked Dirk's underwear off the ground and cut it into strips, careful to select the elastic waistbands.

"You're going to defend us with a piece of wood and shredded clothes?" Gavin asked.

"Adapt, improvise, overcome. Isn't that what Centurion would say?"

"He'd sneer at us first," Gavin said. "And make disparaging remarks. The wood is the frame, and the elastic will let you fire rocks?"

"Rocks or whatever I can get," she said. "I'll find some and then fire a few shots at the dogs to scare them off. How are your feet?"

"Warm and toasty. And my boots are dry. I'm ready to walk," Gavin said.

"Well, we can—"

Lights flashed in the sky, and the roar of an engine echoed down the canyon.

"Is that what I think it is?" Dena asked.

"If you think it's a starship's main drive, then yes, it is." Dirk shaded his eyes. "Climbing away from us, too. They'll be orbital in minutes."

"Okay, dump all the wood on the fire to give us a last bit of heat, scare the dogs away, then let's get going," Dena said. "We leave in ten minutes."

She dug around the edge of the river for more smooth rocks.

"Who put you in charge?" Gavin asked.

"What put me in charge," Dena said. "Knowledge. Fire, travois, slingshot, anti-drowning poles. River crossing."

Gavin pulled his boots on. "True. Okay, let's go, Skipperette."

"Skipperette?" Dirk asked.

"Feminine form of leader," Gavin agreed. "She's in charge."

"So, I've been demoted?" Dirk asked. "I'm not the skipper anymore?"

Gavin slapped his shoulder. "We're sort of a pirate ship, right? If we are, we can change the skipper anytime, if circumstances warrant. I think circumstances warrant."

Dena pocketed two dozen round rocks and led them back onto the ice. She led, tapping the ice, and Gavin pulled Ana's sled. Dirk followed with the other pole, checking their rear from time to time. He tried calling the ship on the suit radio, but got no answers.

"Cliffs, I guess," Dirk said. "I'll try every half hour or so." He looked down. "It's a different color, the ice. It was white before. Now it's blue."

"More light." Dena pointed. "That other moon has risen. More light means more colors. Last night was just enough to see grays. Low light means no colors."

"Didn't know that," Dirk said. "Or didn't think about it."

"You don't know much about planets, do you?" Dena asked. "Or the woods."

"Other than where I was born and went to school, no. But it was nothing like this, and I was in the city."

He slipped on the snow, dropped to one knee, cursed, and pulled himself back up.

A group of six animal forms flicked to their rear. They were black, furry, with four feet and a tail. They barked and stood about forty-five centimeters high.

"Not so scary now that we can see them," Dirk said.

Gavin took a break from pulling Ana. "They're definitely dogs. How did dogs get here? They surely didn't evolve here."

"Probably strays from ships," Dena said. "Used to happen to us all the time, on Rockhaul. Dogs got off ships, bred with the local hounds, and presto, packs of stray dogs."

"What do they eat?"

"What ever else stowed away on ships. Rats. Birds. Squirrels. Small wood animals. Birds. Each other," Dena said.

"Dogs eat each other?"

"We'd eat each other if things got desperate," Dena said. "Heard of it happening in the winter."

"That's disgusting," Gavin said.

"Don't worry, Engineer," Dena said. "I won't eat you."

"Thank the Emperor."

"You're too scrawny," Dena said. "And too tough. Too much muscle." She grabbed Dirk's good arm and squeezed it. "Now this one, he's fat and juicy. We'd eat him first. Cooked over the fire, he'd be nice and tasty."

Dirk stepped back. "You're full of surprises, Dena."

"It's nice knowing what to do for a change," she said.

"Those dogs are catching up," Gavin said.

The pack had trotted closer.

"Even small, they can hurt us," Dirk said.

Dena stopped, aimed her slingshot into the gloom, and fired a rock. A dog yelped, and the whole group retreated.

"Don't worry, Pilot, I'll protect you from the little dogs," she said. "Saddle up, need to get moving."

Gavin picked up the sled and got moving, and Dirk trudged behind.

Gavin puffed along. "Not as bad as last night, pulling here."

Dena tapped out their route. Thump. Lift. Step. Step. Thump. "Less snow on this part of the river. Ice is easy to drag on."

"Feels easier," Gavin said. "Say, Skipperette, how come you had to use Dirk's underwear for your slingshot? If you just needed something elastic, couldn't you have used your own?"

Dena looked over her shoulder and winked.

"Emperor's anus," Dirk said.

The four crew members made good time. After two hours, the sun rose, the sky was clear, and the wind had died down. The storm had blown past.

They almost skated down the ice. Dirk and Gavin passed Ana off every half hour, and Dena took a turn or two to give them a longer break.

The dog pack followed along in the trees. Every hour or so, Dena would call a halt and ease close to the bank where they roamed. She fired a few shots, missing more often than she hit.

Dirk popped a handful of snow in his mouth. "Tenacious group." He swallowed. "I'm thirsty."

"Better to heat that first or drink river water," Dena said. "Your body uses too much energy to melt it."

"I'd do that, if we had a pot of water on a fire," Dirk said. "Or even a fire."

"Or even a pot," Gavin said.

"We're the biggest potential meal they've seen in a long time," Dena said. "And even if they don't eat us, where food people go, food follows. That's how wolfs became dogs, following groups of people."

"Sounds like you like dogs better than people," Gavin said.

"Better than some people, for sure," Dena said.

"Present company excepted, of course," Dirk said.

"Not really," Dena said. "How's the centurion?"

"Asleep, that pill knocked him out. Do we have any more of those? My arm is starting to hurt again."

"Mine, too," Gavin said.

"I think we should be careful how we use those," Dena said.

Dirk held out his hand. Dena shook her head, pulled out the pill bottle, and tossed it to Dirk. He swallowed one and threw it to Gavin. Gavin took one and pocketed it.

Dena held out her hand. "You done?"

"I can carry it," Gavin said.

"You said I was in charge, remember?"

"Of hiking, not pills."

Dena shrugged. "Suit yourself. Since you're all hopped up, how do you feel about hauling centurion up a cliff?"

"Why up a cliff?" Gavin said. "Can't we just stay on the river?"

"Hear that?" Dena cupped her ear.

"Yes, a rumble—is that the waterfall? We're almost there." Gavin grinned.

"I think so," Dena said.

"Well, let's move along, then." Gavin grabbed Ana's travois and pulled, but Dena didn't move.

"What, don't you want to get back to the ship?" Gavin asked.

"I do," Dena said. "What's your plan for doing that?"

"Same as yours. Follow this river till we get there."

"Got it," Dena said. "Follow this river till it hits . . ."

"A waterfall," Dirk said. "Right, we have to get off the river and hike around the waterfall." He surveyed the banks on either side. "They're already getting higher. That waterfall was in a canyon. We have to get into the trees. Easiest to do it here, too."

"We can do that. Only a couple of miles, right?" Gavin said. "It will be work, but we just have to avoid the dogs."

"And the weather," Dena said.

"What weather?" Dirk said. "It's clear and sunny."

Dena pointed behind him. He turned. Dark clouds were rolling in from upriver. As they faced the storm, the wind rose and whipped their clothes.

"That's another storm. And it'll be here soon. Less than an hour."

***

"How about hiking up the river to meet them?" Scruggs said. "Now that the Nats are gone?"

"We don't even know if they're there," Lee said. "We haven't heard from them on the radio yet."

"But you said that we couldn't hear them because of the canyons."

"Probably not," Lee said. "All right, how about this. If you get higher up, they might be able to hear your radio. How about you climb up there next to that waterfall. If they're coming from upriver, then they'll be coming that way. Think you can make it up that hill over there?" Lee pointed to a scree of broken rocks next to the falls.

"I can do it," Scruggs said. "I can climb up onto that hill on the right, and I'll be above this lake and up above the river as well. Let me get a pack and a holster and some food and water, and I'll go."

"You're that worried about them?"

"Centurion might need my help."

"What about the rest of them? Pilot and the others."

"Oh, them, too."

"Even Dena?"

"She can freeze."

"You're just mad because she beat you up."

"She didn't. I beat her up."

"Does your nose still hurt?"

Scruggs touched her nose.

"We need to stick together. That's the only reason why we're not all in jail or dead. Talk to Dena. She might teach you something."

Scruggs crossed her arms and glared at Lee. "Fine."

"Better get moving," Lee said.

"Why?"

"Look over there." Lee pointed. "Those clouds are nearly black. Storm coming in."

"I'll go now," Scruggs said. "I can get up and there before the storm hits."

An hour later, she had hiked across the lake, keeping close to the shore. The ice seemed firm enough to her, and she thought she was over shallow water. She walked as close to the waterfall as she dared, then went into the trees and climbed, which slowed her down. In places, the snow was deep, and she struggled through. In others, she could climb along bare patches of rock. After slipping off an ice-covered boulder for the second time, she stayed on the snow. Another hour saw her climb to the level of the waterfall. The upper river was hemmed in by five- to ten-meter cliffs. The slope eased as she edged away from the river, so she continued climbing diagonally away. She stopped for her breath. Snow whipped down the river and over the falls, blowing from atop the hill above her, decreasing her visibility.

"Not good, Scruggs. Be careful out here," she said. "Just got the weather to worry about."

She flopped down for a rest and was drinking water from her bottle when the howls started.

CHAPTER TWENTY-ONE

"I thought you said they weren't wolves," Gavin said.

"They're not," Dena said. "Dogs howl, too. Some dogs."

They stumbled through the woods. The good news was they could see the river chasm to their left as they climbed, so they wouldn't get lost. The bad news was the snow had become denser, offering more difficult navigation.

"So, we got the extra special space crew eating mutts," Gavin said.

They were plowing uphill through the snow. The falls crashed in the distance, and they had exited the riverbed onto the banks early enough that they could walk up a hill, rather than climb up a cliff. Ana's travois was slowing them. The snow was lighter and softer, but he sank more.

"We can't be far," Dirk said. "Once we're over the top here, it's all downhill to the ship."

"Downhill is just as bad," Dena said. "There will still be snow."

"Why do dogs howl, anyway?" Gavin asked. "What's the point?"

"You really want to know?"

"Yes."

"They're calling friends. That's a signal for the rest of the pack to get down here and chase us."

"How truly good," Dirk said. "How many of those rocks do you have?"

Dena ran her hands through her pockets. "Not enough."

The next hour was torture for the four crew members. The snow increased and so did the slope. The dogs howled in the gloom.

Dirk and Dena were hauling Ana up a snowbank, and Gavin pushed from below. They stopped to rest.

"I'm sweating like a pig," Gavin said. "I need to rest." He sat.

"If you don't keep walking, you'll be freezing like one soon," Dena said.

"There are frozen pigs?"

"Yes, they're dinner for dog packs," Dena said.

Gavin sprang up and tugged on Ana's travois. "He's heavy. Can we leave him behind and come back with the others?"

"Look, you two ship-bred, naval numbskulls. First, what will the others do?" Dena said. "They don't know anything more about carrying him than we do. Second, if we leave him in the dark, we'll never find him again. And third, the dogs will eat him. I'm not leaving him to be eaten by dogs. If he needs eating, I'll organize it myself."

Dirk and Gavin looked at each other. "Wow," Gavin said.

"Wow, what?" Dena asked.

"You sound exactly like the centurion does when he's giving orders," Dirk said. "Command voice, three options, declarative statement at the end."

"Even started with an insult denigrating the Navy," Gavin said.

"It's like you're channeling his spirit while he's sleeping," Dirk said.

"Spooky," Gavin said.

"Okay, little Centurion," Dirk said. "Off we go."

"To the Imperial hells with you," Dena said. But she smiled. "We can't haul him up the slopes anymore. It's too steep. We'll zigzag and haul him across the slope. Walk farther, but it will be easier."

Two hours later, they were lost. "Did we do too many zigs or too many zags?" Gavin asked.

"Which one is a zig and which one is a zag?" Dirk asked. "Left or right."

"Right is a zig, left is a zag," Dena said.

"Really? Why?"

"Shut up, Navy. We've just gone farther to one side, probably the right."

"Did she just call you Navy? That's even more Centurion-like," Gavin said.

"It will pass. We went too far to the right?"

"Yes."

"And you know that how?"

"Because I'm not swimming. If we went too far to the left, we would have fallen in the river. And we've been going uphill the whole time. We must be near the top," Dena said.

"I can't see the top," Gavin said.

"Really?" Dena said. "Gosh, Mr. Engineer, which is the problem, do you think? The dense forest or the driving snow? Watch out!"

She whipped her slingshot from a belt pocket and snapped a shot at a dog in the trees. It missed, and the dog bounded back. Dena turned a full circle, fumbling in her pocket. She looked at Dirk. "Duck."

He dropped, and a rock zinged over his head. A dog yelped in the gloom.

"They're getting bolder," Dena said.

"Seems more of them, too," Dirk said. "Let's keep going."

"Like we have any choice," Gavin said, shouldering Ana's travois.

"You can always stay and be dog meat," Dena said, helping drag it.

The trees thinned out, yielding increased visibility. But the wind increased, blotting their vision for minutes at a time.

They stopped at a last clump of trees to rest.

Dena pulled out her rocks and counted. "I've got four left."

"It looks like it goes down over there." Dirk pointed through the driving snow.

"Can't go back that way. The dogs are circling." Gavin pointed at shadows moving behind them.

"We should be near the ridge top," Dena said. "We've been climbing for nearly four hours. We need to start down—it's dark with this storm, but it's afternoon now, and we need to be off this hill before it gets even darker."

"Wait, if we're up on a hilltop over that lake, shouldn't we hear the ship?" Gavin said.

"Hear it singing happy birthday?"

"The suit radios. Does anybody have their radio on?"

Dirk fumbled with his collar controls. "Heart's Desire, Heart's Desire, this is Pilot."

The radio hissed, then crackled.

Scruggs's voice came through. "—you. Repeat fgruuup."

Gavin pointed. "We're not at the top yet over there, that clearing. We should hear better."

Dirk grabbed Ana's travois and pulled forward. The snow pushed at his back, and his feet sank, as they usually did, but then the snow supported his weight, and he walked on top. Ana slid along like he was on rails.

Gavin stomped his foot. "Is this ice?"

"Wind pack," Dena said. "We're at the top of the hill. The wind compresses the snow. Makes it dense enough to walk on."

"This is even better than the ice," Gavin said. "We don't sink, and it's not as slippery."

"Dogs," Dena said.

She spun and fired two quick shots. This time, the yelp was accompanied by a growl audible over the wind.

Gavin turned into the wind to look, and the wind blasted his face with ice particles.

He ducked and turned back. "We're not going back that way in this weather."

Dirk reached the top of the hill—or what could be the top of the hill. The blowing snow and dropping sun made it seem like they were in a gray soup that extended endlessly in all directions.

He dropped the travois as Gavin and Dena came up to him. "Stay close to each other," Dena said. "It will be easy to get separated, and this storm will fill in our tracks, so we won't be able to back track the way we came."

Gavin stopped and stomped on the snow. "This sounds hollow."

"Snow isn't hollow," Dena said, also stomping. "It does sound weird."

"Heart's Desire, Heart's Desire. This is Pilot, come in," Dirk said.

Scruggs answered instantly. "Pilot, you're alive. Is the centurion okay?"

"He's hurt," Dirk said. "We think a concussion. We need to get him to the ship. He needs better drugs."

"The medic is waiting at the ship. She can look at him right away. Where are you?"

"We think we're at the top of the ridge next to the waterfall."

"I've climbed up to almost the top of the ridge from the lake side. If you're correct about where you are, we can get down in an hour."

Dena and Gavin listened. "And tell her the rest of us are fine, too, Pilot," Dena said, "and thanks for her asking."

"The rest of us are okay. Where's the ship?"

"You can't see it?"

"No, I—dogs!" Dirk said.

Gavin and Dena turned.

The dogs had snuck in on Dirk's side. Three of them ran forward and pounced. Dena's slingshot hit one and missed another. Both ran away. One more jumped up on Ana's travois and snarled at them. Gavin lunged at him, but the dog growled and snapped. He focused on Gavin and ignored the centurion.

"Were those dogs?" Scruggs asked. "Are you surrounded by dogs? I see dogs."

"Yes, they are—wait, where are you, Scruggs?" Dirk said. "Can you see us?"

"Kind of. You're maybe ten meters upslope of me. I can see you through the snow drifts. You're right on top of a snow cliff."

"I don't see you, and I don't see a cliff," Dirk said. "If I go—whooooah."

Dirk's foot stepped out into nothingness. He fell forward, then threw himself sideways and thumped his arms into the snow. His hands scrabbled for purchase, and his legs dangled in the air. He had fallen over an invisible cliff in the murk.

"You just stepped over the edge, the edge of that snow cliff," Scruggs said over the radio. "But you can drop down, maybe three meters, and you'll fall on snow."

"I'm not dropping on anything," Dirk said. "Somebody help."

Gavin swung at the dog. The dog was less than a meter long and weighed ten kilograms or so. It snapped at him every time he swung his arms near. "Busy. This one is mad. And his friends are coming."

Dog shapes loomed out of the dusk.

Dena crawled over, grabbed Dirk by his arms, and hauled him upward. He came up and rolled onto his back. He rolled again away from the edge and sat up. "Stupid snow cliffs."

Dena crawled forward and looked over. "It's not a snow cliff. It's a cornice."

"In the name of the Emperor's hairy testicles, what's a cornice?" Dirk asked.

The ground . . . sagged.

The crew dropped several inches. Everybody froze, even the dogs, one of them whimpering.

"A pile of unstable snow that's wind-loaded on the top of a cliff," Dena said. "Snow builds up till it sticks out over the edge of the cliff."

"What's under this cornice?" Dirk asked.

"Nothing," Dena said.

The snow cracked open three meters behind them, and the four crew, the travois, and the nearest dog dropped in an avalanche down into the valley.

CHAPTER TWENTY-TWO

Dirk dropped into a white cloud. His vision blanked, and a grinding filled his ears. He couldn't see anything, but a whiteness shot through with sparks of light. Snow filled his mouth, and he spat it out. Stay on top, or you'll suffocate, he thought. His ear felt like he was tumbling, but he couldn't see anything to confirm. He kicked his feet, like he was swimming. Cold air splashed his face, and he spat again, then snow pushed into his nose, and he closed his mouth. A brown thing snapped by and stung his arm, but he kept moving. He kicked more and windmilled his hands in front of his chest. Bright lights appeared in his vision, and his right arm windmilled in empty air. He kicked some more, then he could hear the sloshing sound replacing the grinding like falling water. Air blasted his face again, and he sneezed snow. He gasped for breath but inhaled snow and tried to cough it out, but it wouldn't move. Snow plugged his nose and mouth, and his vision dimmed.

The tumbling and rolling stopped, and he slid, then stopped. It was dark. He couldn't breathe, his face frozen. His right leg and arm were stuck, but he could kick and grope left. He paddled his left arm in front of him, and the dark lightened to a soft white. Another kick and a push, and his face was partially uncovered. His hand reached his mouth, and he wiped the snow from it, but he still couldn't breathe. His fingers grabbed in his mouth as he yanked the plug of snow free. He wheezed in and out, in and out, and wiped the snow from his face. One nostril cleared, then the next. He kicked his right leg, and it gave way as he kicked again. Both legs could kick, and he rolled to his side.

He was laying sideways in the snow. Light flooded his face, and he could breathe. Another roll, and he lay on his back. The gray clouds loomed far above, and snow fell on his face.

"Skipper," Gavin said.

"Over here." Dirk sat up.

Gavin was ten meters away, sitting up. Dena was facedown between them. Her legs kicked, but her face stayed in the snow. Dirk rolled up and crawled over to her. He didn't sink at all. The snow was like ice. "Help me with her."

Dirk scraped the snow away from the side of her face. It was heavy and starting to freeze, but he pulled chunks away. She kept squirming and kicking and screaming.

Gavin joined and pulled snow off her. "This is too slow, Skipper. Heave her out." He grabbed one arm, and Dirk grabbed the other side. They pulled, and she popped out and flapped back on to Gavin.

She spat out snow and screamed for a second, then calmed. "I'm all right. I'm all right. I'm okay."

"You're good, it's good," Dirk said. "Breathe. Can you breathe."

"Yes, yes," Dena said.

"Are you hurt?" Dirk asked.

"No, no, just . . . I'm fine. I'm okay."

"Gavin?"

"I'm okay, Skipper. Just shaken up."

A voice echoed from behind them. The hill above them was empty of snow. Rocks, trees, and dirt showed through a white film. Scruggs hopped down at the edge of the avalanche, yelling and climbing down.

"Where's Centurion?" Dirk asked. "Where's Ana?" He stood and surveyed their landing.

They had slid all the way down from the top of the hill, maybe fifty meters above. The three of them were standing in a pile of broken snow that had stopped on the benchlands next to the lake. The storm had paused, and clouds of snow settled at the edge. A single uprooted tree lay ten meters away.

"Centurion? Centurion?" Dirk yelled.

Gavin looked at the piles of broken snow. "We'll never find him under this."

"How do we even look?" Dena said. "If we can't see him, he could be anywhere."

Dirk cupped his hands over his mouth. "Centurion, Centurion, where are you?"

Ana spoke from behind the tree. "I'm over here, Navy, and I'm confused. What in the name of the Emperor's twin testicles happened? Where are we? What did you do?" The dog whined from behind the tree. "And why is a dog sitting on my chest?"

***

The three of them collected Ana from behind the tree. His travois was sitting on top of the avalanche debris like they had set him down there to leave for a drink. The wolf—or dog or coyote—looked stunned. It limped off Ana and slunk back a few feet.

"It happens like that sometimes," Dena said. "The snow lifts him, and the tumbling or whatever just sets people on top."

"He's lucky," Dirk said. "What about that dog?"

"Looks pretty cowed now," Gavin said. "Centurion is lucky that dog didn't bite his face off."

"We're all lucky," Dena said. "We should all be dead or badly injured. Avalanches bang you around a lot. On Rockhaul, most of the people who died in avalanches were beaten against trees or suffocated."

"This snow's not deep enough to suffocate," Gavin said.

"It is if you're facedown, as I well know."

Gavin shivered. "Bad way to die."

"And thank you, both of you," Dena said. "I'd be dead if you weren't here."

"You'd have done the same for us," Dirk said.

"I might have checked if you owed me money first," Dena said.

"No, you wouldn't," Dirk said. "You'd have helped us, even if you were hurt."

Dena brushed snow off her arms, then wiped her hands. "You're right. I would have. Both of you. I don't like either of you, but you're crew."

They looked at each other and started to giggle, then chuckle, then laughed for a few minutes. They were still giggling when Scruggs arrived, forging across the snow.

"That was incredible. That was amazing. You just piled down there like you were on some sort of fair ride. I'm so jealous."

Everyone was silent.

"But what I want to know," Scruggs said, "is how you did it."

"Did what?" Dirk asked.

"How did you figure out how to trigger that avalanche?"

Scruggs looked confused as the three laughed again.

***

They reached the ship within ten minutes.

Scruggs radioed ahead.

Lee had turned on all the lights, collected a med kit, and ran to meet them. "Who's hurt?"

"Centurion is the worst," Dirk said.

"I'm fine," Ana said. "Just help me out of this contraption."

Gavin unbuckled him and helped him stand.

"See?" Ana said. "I'm fine. Just need a nap." He stepped forward, pitched onto his face in the snow, and retched yellow fluid.

"Help me get him in the med robot," Lee said. "What's that dog doing here?"

The killer wild dog had followed them across to the ship. It sat in the snow about ten meters away, staring at them.

"Ignore it," Dirk said. "He hasn't bothered us since the avalanche. I'll help you with the centurion, then I want to sit."

"And after that, some food," Gavin said.

All five carried Ana to the med robot and plugged him in. The robot diagnosed cranial swelling, concussion, and minor frostbite. Lee typed, "Approval," and the machine shot him up with anti-inflammatories, more drugs to stop the brain swelling, a sedative, and a glucose solution to feed him. The machine said to leave him asleep for at least a shift.

She checked over the others. Except for Scruggs, they all had bruises, so they got pain killer shots. Dirk's shoulder and Gavin's arms were diagnosed as a severe sprain and bruises.

"Eat, and sleep for a full shift," Lee said.

"We have to get out of here," Dirk said. "Off this planet."

"And go where?" Lee asked. "Somewhere we can sell a load of frozen fish? We can wait a shift to figure it out. At least eat first."

Everyone sat in the lounge and ate. Dirk and Dena nodded off halfway. Lee and Scruggs shooed them to their rooms, and when they came back, Gavin was asleep on the table. They guided him back to his room as well. Then they came back to clean up.

"Do we need to take a watch?" Scruggs said.

"I'm not sure what we can watch for," Lee said. "That Nat ship is gone, and even if it comes back, there's no way we'd see it in this storm. But I'm not tired, so why don't you sleep for a half shift? Then I'll take a turn."

"I can use it. That avalanche was awesome. I wish I'd rode that down. I'm so jealous."

Lee shook her head. "You're a crazy kid."

"Adventure awaits," Scruggs said.

"Await it in your bunk, I'll watch." Scruggs headed off. Lee picked up the trays of half-eaten food, intending to throw them in the recycler, then had a thought. She climbed down the center corridor to the air lock, opened the inner and the outer door, and stepped out onto the snow. The stray dog had bedded down next to the ship. Lee walked two meters to it. It hopped up and growled at her. She set one of the trays down and backed to the ship. The dog sniffed, then trotted to investigate the tray. After an initial poke, it gulped down all the food, then looked at Lee. It wagged its tail once, then again. Lee backed up to the air lock, leaving the second tray outside the door. Then she stepped inside the air lock and latched the outer door open. She went to the far side of the air lock, left the third tray, then stepped through to the ship and closed the inner door.

She shivered as she walked up to the control room. Sitting at her console in the bridge, she brought up the various cameras. The ones outside the air lock weren't working, but she caught one inside on the screen. She saw motion just outside the door, where the dog was eating from the other tray. Then a furry black head appeared over the door's coaming and sniffed. It disappeared, then the dog leaped into the lock. It sniffed around for a moment, located the third tray, and wolfed it down. Then it toured the air lock's internal perimeter, curled up, and lay in the corner.

"Welcome, little crew member," Lee said.

CHAPTER TWENTY-THREE

"You just leave the extra tray out there, and he'll eat the food," Lee said.

Scruggs had done her half shift, had awoken Lee, and they ate in the lounge. Lee was showing the dog in the air lock on her console.

"Does he bite?"

"I'm sure he does. But right now, he's just hungry. If we feed him, he'll be our friend. Come with me."

Scruggs, as usual, had eaten everything on her tray, so Lee took what remained on hers and walked to the air lock. When she opened the inner door, the dog jumped up and dashed to the exit but stopped at the outer door. Lee put down the tray and stepped back inside. Scruggs peeked around to see. The dog marched forward and scarfed up the food.

"He doesn't seem very scary," Scruggs said. "Pilot made it sound like he was a giant man-eating wolf."

"Maybe he was the smallest?"

"What do we do now? They're all still asleep."

"The usual, maintenance, fuel, and cleaning."

"More pumping for me," Scruggs said.

She spent the next two hours dragging connecting hoses from the water-cracking plant to the lake. The lake was within range of their longest hose, but the ice was a problem.

The two women deployed a heated drill.

"Good thing Engineer bought this," Lee said.

The battery powered drill charged from the ship's power and let them cut a hole wide enough to drop a hose in the lake. Once in, the ship's pump pulled water into the cracking plant and filled the tanks.

"It's colder than before," Scruggs said. "But storm's gone, and the sun is out. How can it be colder when the sun is out?"

"I've read that happens," Lee said. "It warms up when it gets cloudy and snows. Now that it's clear out, the land outgasses heat, or something."

Lee held out a piece of emergency ration bar to the dog. "Rocky's shivering. He wasn't doing that before."

"Rocky?"

"Gotta call him something."

She had brought two pockets of ration bars with her and dropped pieces around them while they worked.

Rocky the Dog had followed them from the ship and investigated anything she dropped. Since it was always food, he paid close attention to what they were doing.

"Come here, boy," Lee said, extending a half bar in her hand. The dog squirmed up, retreated, lunged forward, grabbed the bar, and dashed away. He chewed it down while they finished up.

"This is as good as it gets, and I'm freezing," Scruggs said. "Back to the ship."

The two women walked along a path beaten in the snow. Rocky followed about ten feet behind.

Midway, Scruggs checked a hose fitting, and Lee fed Rocky another half bar. "He's still shivering," Lee said.

"He's skinny. I can't see how he survived in this cold weather."

"They probably have a den somewhere that they all used to huddle together in. Keep each other warm."

"What will happen to him?"

"Dogs are pack animals. Without his pack, he'll probably die, freeze to death, or starve. He can't hunt by himself."

Scruggs winced. "That's sad. Can we keep him?"

"We can't make him. If he wants to be kept, we can help."

They opened the door and climbed into the air lock, which was full of snow.

"Centurion won't be happy the air lock is full of snow. Or water when this melts."

"Centurion will be out cold for another shift, maybe two, so it doesn't matter right now."

"It's freezing. We can't leave the door open."

"Let's try something," Lee said. She put piles of food on the floor and stood in the corner. "You go inside."

Rocky fell for their trick, hopping in and eating the food. He didn't see Lee till she had shut the door. When the door clanged, he snarled and growled and backed into a corner.

"Whoa," Scruggs said from the inner door. "Easy, boy, easy."

The dog snarled more and backed away. Lee set the heating for the air lock to blow warm ship air, then edged along the other wall. Rocky growled but didn't lunge.

Lee faced the dog, then backed through the inner air lock. "Leave it open. Rocky, you stay here. It's warm. You can stay here. Good boy."

The dog's ears were pinned back, but it didn't growl. He backed up until his butt was against the hot air vent and glared at them.

"Right, leave him here," Lee said. "He'll either adapt, or he won't. Leave the inner door open."

She and Scruggs returned, split up. Scruggs had a full list of cleaning duties to follow, and Lee figured out which systems were in reach and checked courses, without selecting any in the computer. She didn't know where they were going next.

It was a solid two shifts before the six of them reconvened in the lounge.

"This tray tastes particularly vile," Gavin said. He spat a green mouthful onto the tray. "Even with how hungry I am after that hike. I see why Scruggs puts that hot sauce on it."

"I don't know what you're complaining about. The trays aren't bad," Scruggs said. "But the hot sauce makes them better."

"My stomach hates you," Gavin said.

"My ears hate you," Scruggs said. "What's that stupid music you're playing?"

"Old Earth country."

"Should have stayed on Old Earth."

Gavin finished his pile of red mush. "These fake apples are okay. The rest isn't very good." He went to throw the food into the recycler, but Lee held up her hand. "Don't throw that away. We give it to Rocky."

"Rocky?" Gavin asked. "Who's Rocky?"

Dirk ran into the lounge, yelling, "One of those wolves got in here. It's in the air lock. All teeth and claws. I need to get my gun."

"That's Rocky," Scruggs yelled as he passed. "Our dog. We adopted him."

Gavin said. "What dog? You have a dog?"

"We have a dog," Lee said. "And he more adopted us than we adopted him. He lives in the air lock for now."

"I thought they were wolves."

"They're dogs."

"They attacked us."

"Must not have been much of an attack. This one is twenty pounds."

Dirk returned, fumbling shells into his gun.

"Pilot," Lee said, "you're not shooting my dog."

"It's a wolf, a dangerous wolf," Dirk said.

"It's a skinny dog. Put that away." Lee got up to block the passage to the air lock. "You're not shooting our dog."

"Your dog," Dirk said.

"Our dog," Lee said. She walked back to the air lock and peered inside. "There, there, little guy, it's okay. Don't worry about the mean man."

Dirk raised an eyebrow. "Is that Lee talking? Is she sick?"

"She really likes that dog," Scruggs said.

"What dog?" Dena said, arriving from her cabin. "Where?"

"Lee has adopted one of the wolves that tried to kill us," Gavin said.

"They're not wolves. They're dogs. And they were just very hungry. Did you feed it?"

"Lee did," Scruggs said. "Fed him little bits off trays and lured him into the air lock, and now he beds down there next to the air vent."

"That can work," Dena said. "Dogs are good companions. They've got a better sense of smell than people, and they can hear threats before we see them. They're fast, too, and they kill rats and such that would eat our food."

"We don't have a rat problem on this ship," Gavin said.

"You don't have a rat problem yet," Dena said. "One thing I do know about spacers, they end up with weird animals living with them. One ship brought a plague of lizards to us."

"A plague of lizards?"

"For a season. They all died next winter, but until then it was annoying. What's for dinner?"

"Trays, trays, and more trays. And they taste just as bad as they did before our adventure."

Lee came in. "Everyone, this is Rocky." She leaned down, held out a piece of food, cooed, then Rocky came in.

"He's skinnier than he looked out in the woods," Dena said. "Probably hungry."

"All I saw was teeth," Gavin said. "Hello, new shipmate."

"Hello, doggy," Dirk said, extending his hand. Rocky snarled and snapped at him.

"He doesn't like you," Lee said.

"Why?"

"Probably knows you were going to shoot him," Gavin said.

"He can't know that," Dirk said.

"Dogs are smart," Gavin said. "They understand commands, they know their name. You should watch out. He likes the rest of us."

Rocky sniffed Scruggs, Dena, and Gavin and suffered to be petted by Lee, but he kept a wary eye on Dirk.

"Well, greetings to our canine companion not-withstanding, I want some food," Dena said.

"Tray or tray?" Gavin asked.

"Too bad we don't have a cook on board," Dena said, opening a cupboard and checking out the tray selection.

"But we do. Pilot said he wanted to be a cook," Scruggs said.

The crew looked at Dirk.

He cocked his head. "Haven't practiced in years."

"Well, we have an entire container load of fish you could work on," Gavin said.

"You know," Dirk said. "That's a good idea. Let me go check that out."

The group engaged in desultory conversation while Dirk went to the container. Minutes later, he was back with an entire fish.

"I can do this. I'll cut the head and tail off, fillet it. I need a knife, but I've got some oil and spices. We just need to defrost this."

The crew kept their hunger in check as Dirk went to his quarters and returned with a set of knives.

"What happened with the changeover?" Lee said. "We were watching and listening. That lady went over to see you, and everything was fine. Then everything went bat-feces crazy. They fired the laser, and that shotgun guy tried to get on the ship. Scruggs shot him. You told us to run on the radio, then that explosion."

Dirk slammed a cleaver to the fish's head. "We have no clue. Everything was tense, but they seemed willing. Then when we showed them our container of weapons, they went Empire-damned crazy. Accused us of stealing things from them, or hijacking things or something." He chopped the tail and held it up. "Will the mutt eat frozen fish?"

"His name is Rocky," Lee said. "And I think so."

"Dogs eat anything," Dena said. "Any meat thing. Put it in the microwave to defrost it, and he'll eat it."

Dirk threw the head and tail on a tray and pushed them into the microwave. "They just started shooting. Shot Gavin in the arm, shot at us. Centurion got us out of there by throwing that mortar round down, and we jumped over the cliff."

"Is that where you were hurt?"

"All except Dena. She knew how to jump, and slide down a hill." Dirk sliced the fish lengthwise. "She knows her way around mountains."

"And lakes and streams and rivers," Gavin said, recounting all the things Dena had done, the travois, the first aid, the fire and the way-finding. "I'm not going to complain again about her not knowing about how to run a ship. Without her, I'd be dead. I'd have gotten lost and froze to death, even with all that stuff around here."

"Dena?" Scruggs asked. She pointed. "This Dena."

"This Dena," Dirk said. "From now on, she's our wilderness specialist. When we're in the woods, what she says goes."

"What who says goes?" Ana asked. He had climbed into the lounge. He sniffed. "Somebody is cooking fish?" Then he saw Rocky. "Is that the dog that was sitting on my chest when I woke up?"

"Same one," Lee said, leaning down to pet him. His ears rolled back, but he submitted. "He's our dog now. His name is Rocky. Pilot, how about that fish?"

Dirk juggled the hot tray and slid it over. Lee put it on the floor, and Rocky slid over and ate.

Lee rubbed his shoulder, his tail wagging the entire time. "I tempted him on board with food."

Dena leaned over and extended her hand. Rocky sniffed it, wagged once, and continued to eat. "He's friendly enough, now that he's not starving."

Dirk leaned down to pet him. Rocky's ears flattened, and he growled at Dirk and lunged. Dirk pulled his hand back.

Ana laughed. "I like that dog. He's a good judge of character. So, now we have a pet. How'd we get here? My memory is fuzzy after going over the cliff."

"You hit your head on a rock or the ice," Dena said. "We tied you up on a travois and dragged you."

"Travois? A wooden sledge thing?" Ana asked.

Dena explained all that had happened to him.

"This must have been all you," Ana said. "The fire, the river. No way Navy or the Punk would have figured this out."

"We could have figured it out," Dirk said. He rubbed a slice of fish with some salt and spices, then put it in the microwave.

"No, you couldn't have," Ana said. "Take away your console, and you're both useless. Dena, thanks for taking care of me. I owe you."

"Dena's our outdoor specialist now," Gavin said.

"I have some skills in that area myself," Ana said. "But this goes to prove, if we want to survive as a group, we need to share our skills around. Which brings up another topic. What in the name of the Emperor's balls happened back there? Why did those Nats go up in flames when we gave them their stuff? What did I miss?"

"Cold and misery," Gavin said.

"Animal attacks and killer snow," Dirk said.

"Explosions and crashing," Lee said.

Ana looked at them, then at Scruggs, who smiled.

"It was so much fun, Centurion! Flying, diving, a crash, spinning, and an avalanche. An adventure."

Ana kept his eyes on her. "I'm sorry I slept through it, Private. Would you like to do it again sometime?"

"Yes, please, Centurion," Scruggs said. "It was great fun."

The microwave dinged. Dirk removed the tray of steaming fish and parceled it out.

"Ignoring our miraculous escape," Ana said. "What happened? Why did they go nuts on us? We were giving them what they wanted." He skewered a piece of fish on his fork and tasted it. "This is outstanding." He spat a small bone out. "Except for the bones."

"Did they want to kill us to hide the evidence?" Gavin asked.

"If you're fighting a war, and somebody gives you weapons, you want them to keep coming. You don't kill the people providing them. You want more. Besides, they should have done it after they got everything from us, not in the middle of the transaction. Neater that way."

"They just snapped when they saw the mortars," Dena said. "I was watching them. They were very tense but focused. When you showed them the mortars, they got scared."

"Scared?"

"They expected something else, and they got scared and angry. Where did you learn to cook, Pilot?"

Dirk chewed and swallowed. "Took a class when I was younger for a year." He picked a bone off his piece before eating it. "Hard to get good fish. They are usually too bony."

"I thought you Navy types went to that academy right away?" Ana asked.

"Most do. I dropped out after a year and took cooking classes before I went back."

"Let me see if I understand this," Ana said. "After going through all the trouble of getting into one of the most exclusive and expensive schools in the Human Imperium, your way of rebelling against your oh-so-famous and rich family was to quit and learn to microwave fish?"

Dirk looked down. "It sounds silly now."

"It still sounds silly," Gavin said. "Worse than silly. But this fish tastes great."

"Thanks very much," Dirk said. "But it doesn't help us understand what went wrong there."

"Maybe they're nuts," Gavin said.

"Or not thinking clearly," Lee said.

Scruggs swallowed and scooped up the remaining chunk on her tray. "Or maybe they just wanted some of this delicious fish."

Dirk put down his fork and so did Ana, then everyone else.

Scruggs stuffed the final piece in her mouth and darted her eyes around as she ate in the silence. She gulped the piece and swallowed it whole. She wheezed for a second, drank a gulp of basic, and looked at the crew. "What did I say?"

***

They emptied three boxes before finding something. Gavin and Ana dug through each box and looked at how it was packed, emptied the packaging, and stirred it around. Each fish was examined closely. The other boxes were packed flat, but the third one bulged on top.

"They didn't even try to hide it," Ana said. He sliced the box open and pulled out the top fish. "Looks bloated. Navy? Got your cleaver?"

Dirk chopped the head off, and they found four message chips stuffed into the stomach. Gavin warmed them in his hand and put the first one in the nearest console on the wall. Screens flickered as he paged through the documents on it.

"Well?" Dirk asked. "What is it?"

"Starship plans. More than one. Deck plans, specifications. Ranges. Orders, too, looks like."

"What kind of starships?" Dirk said. "And what type of ranges?"

Gavin flipped through the screens, displaying different ships. "Warship type starships. And weapon ranges and countermeasures."

"For which ships?" Dirk asked.

"This is a Confed corvette." Gavin pointed at his screen. "Easy enough to figure out. They're so old, lots of navies have them. And this"—he paged through some screens—"looks like one of their auxiliary cruisers, the converted freighters." He continued flipping through screens. "Not sure what this is."

"That's one of the National assault carriers," Ana said. "They've only got two, and that's the Retribution. You can tell by the large cargo hatches."

The crew regarded Ana in silence. He stared right back. "I was onboard once."

"A tour?" Dirk asked.

"Yes. Sure. A tour," Ana said.

"Were you carrying a weapon during your tour?" Dirk asked.

"Maybe," Ana said.

"Recognize any others?" Dirk asked Gavin.

"This one. Some sort of frigate," Gavin said.

"Whose?" Ana asked.

"That's an Imperial frigate," Scruggs said. "You can tell by the weapons mount. In fact"—she leaned in, swiping screens—"these are all Imperial ships. Warships. Brand new ones."

"Imperial warships," Gavin said. "This is secret documentation on Imperial ships."

CHAPTER TWENTY-FOUR

"Centurion, we can't give the Nats' Imperial secrets," Scruggs said.

"Of course we can," Ana said. "There's a complete list of contact points and backup listed in that file. We just fly to the right place, show the right recognition signals, and they come to see us. It doesn't seem that hard. It seems well within even Navy's limited piloting skills. Give me that pick thing."

He and Scruggs were on the lake, retrieving the water hose preparatory to takeoff. They had all looked at the secret dossiers found in the fish and had argued but never reached a conclusion. Dirk had insisted they get ready to lift while they thought about it.

The hose had frozen solid in the ice overnight. They decided to drill new holes around the base, chip it out, and drag it back to the heated ship, where they could melt the ice off it.

Scruggs handed him the pick. "I mean, we shouldn't give those secrets away. Those are secret Imperial documents. If we give them to the Nats, they'll have an advantage in a war. Knowing ranges and performance of weapons will give them a huge advantage."

"Changed your mind? You're a loyal Imperial subject now, aren't you, Ms. Smuggler?" Ana said.

"Smuggling and treason aren't the same," Scruggs said. "The only people in danger if we're smuggling is us. Not an Empire of people."

Ana swung the pick and chipped a small hole in the ice. "There. Now position that core drill here."

They manhandled the drill over Ana's pilot hole and started it up.

"I don't see how this will work, Centurion," Scruggs said.

"We're just going to drill a bunch of big holes in a circle around that pipe," Ana said. "If we make them overlap, we can cut it free."

"Why not just saw the ice?" Scruggs asked.

"Do you see a saw around here, Private?" Ana said.

"No, Centurion, just the drill. We'll adapt."

"Outstanding," Ana said. "You do listen to me." He swung the pick at the next starting point.

"Centurion, let me do that, please," Scruggs said.

"Think I can't handle it, Private?" Ana swung again.

Scruggs took a deep breath. "I mean, in your condition, you shouldn't be exercising that hard. Something might happen."

Ana stopped and held the pick in his hand. "I don't have any conditions,

Private."

Scruggs blushed and hung her head. "I looked up your pills. After our last fight. And Dena told me about the other ones that you take, that she found in your pockets when you were being chased. I looked those up, too."

"Big invasion of privacy there, Private," Ana said. "A betrayal. Not like you. How would you like it if I snooped into your private life?"

"You told me once that your private life was only private when it didn't endanger others. Having a squad mate that's not . . . what did you call it . . . fit for duty was a problem. Are you fit for duty, Centurion?"

Ana leaned on the pick. "You judging my fitness, Private?"

"No, I'm asking you to judge it and tell me." Scruggs put her hand out. "Pick?"

Ana held the pick and examined it, then slid it back to her. "Only because it's a good learning experience for you, then."

"Yes, I've always wanted to learn how to swing a pick on ice," Scruggs said. "I'll put it on my resume. Think I'll get contracts, Centurion?"

The drill bonged, and they fussed with it. It had extracted a six-inch ice core down to the water. They pulled the core up, discarded it on the ice, repositioned the drill on the next hole, and started it again.

"I'm sorry I wasn't there to help you, Centurion," Scruggs said.

"Where? In the woods?"

"Yes."

"You were where you were told to be. Doing your job. I was doing mine. You have to trust your crew mates to do theirs."

"But I don't," Scruggs said.

"Don't what?"

"Trust them. Not all of them."

"You mean Dena?"

"I don't like her. I don't trust her."

"She saved me. Saved the group. What's not to trust?"

"I'm just, just . . ."

"Young, stupid, and jealous. That girl has a few things to teach you. I'm not the only one you can learn from. I'm not the only one you should learn from."

Scruggs continued cracking the pick into the ice. The ice chips made for an easy starting point for the drill.

"How long?" Scruggs asked.

"How long what?"

"You know what I mean, Centurion. Will you have a heart attack?"

"Probably at some point. That's not the problem. I'm not going to die from a heart attack."

"The cancer? I thought those other pills, the red ones—"

"Suppress it, yes. You're too close. The holes don't have to overlap. Just be close enough we can smash the ice away."

"I think it's better if they overlap, Centurion. Then we only have to drill once."

"Are you challenging my extensive experience, Private?"

"Your experience in drilling holes in ice, Centurion? Do you do this often?"

"Talking back to me? You're starting to sound like Navy and that punk, Gavin. I knew they'd be a bad influence."

"Or it could be that I'm just getting older. How long?"

"A few months after I stop taking them. I might do that soon, make it easier on everybody."

"Don't do that, Centurion."

"It's my choice, Private. You have nothing to say about it."

The drill bonged again, and they dumped the core and moved it. They had cleared a quarter of the pipe so far.

"You promised. You have an obligation."

"I didn't promise anybody anything about my life," Ana said.

"You said you'd teach me things. If I followed orders and did what you said. You promised to teach me how to use long-range sensors."

"We don't have long-range sensors on that rust bucket. We hardly have a functioning telescope."

"Not my problem," Scruggs said. "If you didn't have sensors, you shouldn't have promised. But you did, so you owe me. I want my training. You can't die. It would be dishonorable."

"Do you really think I'll fall for that kind of obvious manipulation, Private?"

"Yes," Scruggs said. She resumed chipping another pilot hole. "You are very easy to manipulate. I just need to know the right buttons to press."

Ana narrowed his eyes. "You're way smarter than you look and not nearly as naive as you sound."

"Oh, I'm naive in a lot of ways," Scruggs said. "I know that. But one thing I do know is guilt. Lots of guilt in my family, and I know how to use it."

"Want to talk about your family, do you?"

"Nope. We're talking about you. You can't die or kill yourself or whatever. You promised to help me learn things. I'm holding you to that promise."

Ana held out his hand. "I'll do the last pilot hole."

Scruggs shook her head. "Bad things can happen to you."

Ana reached into his pocket and produced a pill bottle. He held it where Scruggs could see it. "Nitroglycerin. See?" He popped one pill out, swallowed it, then held out his hand. "I can work hard now. My turn."

Scruggs handed him the pick. "How many of those pills do you have, Centurion?"

"We need more money," Ana said.

"I didn't ask—"

"I know where you're going. I've got a month's worth left. Longer if I cut the doses. The pain pills, I only need sometimes, and any sort of pain pill will do. The nitroglycerin ones are expensive, but I can cope. The anti-cancer ones, those cost money. Real money."

"Is that why, when we found you at that station . . ."

"Being a customs inspector is an easy job if you take bribes. Big ones. It kept me in cash."

"I thought you had a pension."

"I do. From Pallas. A good one. Or it was when I joined up."

The drill bonged again. They slid it to its new starting point. "Once more, and I think we're done," Ana said. "We'll be able to chip the hose out after this one."

"I can do it now," Scruggs said. "Give me the pick." She chipped away at the ice around the hose. "When you joined up? What does that mean?"

"Check the exchange rate someday, Private. Compare Pallas credits to Imperial ones. I need Imperial credits."

"How many credits do you need, for, say a five-year supply of all your pills?"

Ana named an impressive sum.

"That's a lot, Centurion," Scruggs said.

"Living is expensive, Private," Ana said. "Dying, on the other hand, can be quite affordable."

The drill raced. The hose popped loose and floated in the smashed hole. The two of them pushed the drill away and dragged the hose end up onto the ice.

"Just get all this back into the lock and let it sit for an hour, and we should be able to stow it," Ana said.

"I know where we can get credits like that, Centurion," Scruggs said, dragging the hose along the ice.

"You do, huh? Where? Rob a bank? Or maybe take on a special Imperial courier?"

"Nothing that hard, Centurion. I know who will give us that money, no bother."

"And who would that be, Private?"

"The Nats. They'll pay for Imperial secrets. And we have lots of those now."

***

"This is the main cross valve between the tanks," Gavin said. He pointed to the largest valve in the pipe locker. "It's supposed to be remotely controlled from the bridge or the engineering console, but I removed the actuator a while back and reused it elsewhere."

He and Dena stood just inside of the air lock's open door. After Dena had proved her forest ranger extraordinaire expertise, everyone had agreed she could be trusted to at least stand a regular watch, provided she was trained.

Gavin walked the ship with her, showing relevant systems.

Dena pointed. "Right, what's that thing, the thing that looks like a metal bar?"

"That? It's a bar made of metal."

Dena stuck out her tongue. "Thank you so much, oh wonderful engineering guru. What's it used for, then?"

"It's a cheater pipe." Gavin demonstrated by sliding it between the handles and twisting. "Use it as a lever on a stuck valve."

"Do the valves get stuck often?"

"They're robust, but any sort of big jar or shake can make them stick."

"Like every time Dirk makes one of his patented landings?"

"Why do you think I took out the actuator? It kept burning out, trying to open and close jammed valves." He spun it fully closed. "The manual shut-offs for the water intake for the cracking system are outside. We can go out there, and I can show you where they are."

"I hate the cold, and I've had enough of it recently."

"Your skin suit will help."

"Or we can stay in here where it's warm, and we can talk about it."

"Let's go to engineering, and I'll show you the atmo vent systems," Gavin said.

"Lead on," Dena said. She stuck her head into the air lock. "You coming, Rocky?"

Rocky the Dog lay on an old blanket that Lee had found somewhere. He had dragged it up to the hot air vent and piled it up into a bed. His tail thumped twice, then he straggled up, stretched, and hopped after them. He jumped out of the air lock and watched while they closed the door.

"Keep the heat up in there," Gavin said. "They'll need to melt the snow off those hoses before stashing them in the racks. Once they're done recovering them, we can lift off."

Dena spun the temperature dial to hot. "Lift off to where?"

"Isn't that the question."

"Are those files worth money, do you think?"

"Quite a bit of money," Gavin said. He walked down the central corridor. "To the right people, they'd be worth a lot of money."

"I'll bet you could find the right people," Dena said. "You seem like the type."

Gavin stopped at the hatch below the lounge. "What's that supposed to mean?"

"Don't act so innocent," Dena said. "I've watched you, and I've seen what you've done elsewhere. You were some sort of thief. You know you how to get rid of stolen things or how to buy them. When we're in a bar, you get these looks from people."

Gavin spun the hatch open. "I don't know what you're talking about. I'm just a second-rate engineer trying to keep this maintainer's nightmare flying."

"I don't believe it," Dena said. "If that was the truth, you'd be on a regular route. Instead, you're here, on the SS Duplicity, and even a close orbit around an Imperial dog sanctuary sends you into fits in case one of the dogs gets your scent.

The Empire's looking for you, and you don't want to be found." Dena looked back at their furry companion. "No insult intended, Rocky."

Rocky wagged his tail.

"Everybody here has secrets," Gavin said.

"How much? How much can you get?"

"I'll tell you this much for free. That's a pretty hot item. It would be very, very hard to find a buyer."

"Which means that they're worth a fortune," Dena said. "How much? Enough to fix everything here and give us some decent cash. Enough to fix everything on this ship?"

Gavin tapped the monitors as they passed the foyer that connected to the first group of six containers. "The containers are numbered A1 through F1. You number clockwise, starting from the top, going to port." He turned the screen off. "Enough to buy another ship, maybe two, if it's real," Gavin said. "But I'm not sure I want to give away the Empire's secrets to our enemies."

"Our enemies? You're the one who hates the Empire the most."

"I don't hate the Empire. I—"

"Love them?"

"They . . . were involved in the death of my family." One monitor showed a single yellow light. Gavin tapped it twice, and it turned to green. "That temperature sensor is loose. Getting involved in this will not bring my family back."

"Are you afraid of them?" Dena asked.

"Aren't you?" Gavin asked. "They're big, powerful, and can crush you like a bug. The only thing that keeps them from hunting us down right now and killing all of us, you included, Nature Girl, is that we're not really on their radar."

"What about super-duper traitor Dirk there—they're looking for him."

"Not very hard," Gavin said. "It's a puzzle. But the skipper wasn't convicted of treason, it was incompetence. They're easier with incompetence."

"They'd rather have loyal, incompetent officers than competent ones that might be a bit shady?"

"If they fired all the incompetent officers, the Imperial Army would be empty, and the Navy would be half empty, from what I've seen," Gavin said.

They arrived at engineering and another hatch. Gavin spun it open, and Rocky nosed up and jumped through to investigate. "For something that was trying to eat us earlier, he's amazingly friendly."

"We feed him," Dena said. "Dogs are like that. They love anybody that feeds them, takes care of them."

"You just have to wear a collar, do what we say."

"Sounds like you and the Empire. Even if they beat you from time to time, you still put up with them. You never bite back."

"You have no idea what it's like to be on your own without allies," Gavin said.

"You mean like right now. Light years from my planet, which I can't go back to anyway, with a bunch of people who think I'm useless and disposable?"

"We don't think that anymore," Gavin said. "I'll admit, you showed us. We'd all be dead if you hadn't taken care of us out in the woods." He stepped through to engineering.

"Yeah, but what have I done for you lately?" Dena said. "Memories are short. Cash is forever."

"You have trust issues."

"How much are those plans worth, Gavin? How much would the Nats give us for those blueprints?"

"A lot," Gavin said.

"Enough to fix this ship and keep us going for a while?"

Gavin powered up the engineering console. "Enough to buy an entire new ship."

***

Dena's cabin entry bonged. "It's open."

Scruggs stood there with Rocky.

"Hey, Rocky, hey boy," Dena said. Rocky wagged his tail. "Baby Marine," Dena said.

"Don't call me that—never mind. Call me what you want," Scruggs said.

"That's what you are."

"Sure. You only do it to mess with me, so I don't care. I don't care what you think."

"Good to know," Dena said.

Rocky, tired of not being the center of attention, jumped up on her bunk, and curled up next to her.

"Rocky likes you," Scruggs said.

"I like him. He can tell. I don't like you."

"Thank you."

"What?"

"Thanks for helping Centurion and the others."

"No thanks needed."

"It was . . . kind of you."

Dena laughed and petted Rocky. "No, it wasn't. We were lost in the woods. Needed to stay together to get back here. It was best to stay with them."

"Gavin and Pilot told me about your hike. They were all hurt. They held you back. You could have been here in a few hours, said they were killed."

"I didn't know where to go."

"As soon as Dirk told you, you could have left them in the snow. They wouldn't have caught up. They would have frozen in the snow or drowned in the river or gotten hurt by those dogs. You were never lost. You knew where you were. You could have made it to the ship by yourself."

"And who'd fly it, then?"

"Lee. To the next planet. And with no pilot or engineer, she would have sold it. She's so honest she'd give you your share. You'd be on your own with a ton of money. That's what you wanted, right? That's why you left that dump of a planet."

"One of the reasons," Dena said. "What's your point?"

"Why didn't you leave them?"

"Dirk and I had been—"

Scruggs giggled. "I know you well enough to tell that wouldn't have held you back at all."

Rocky nuzzled her, demanding more petting. She complied and played with his ears. "They treated me right. Made me a member of the crew."

"They said you were useless, made fun of you."

"They make fun of everybody. But they expected me to pull my weight. Wasn't their fault that I'm not useful on a ship, only other places."

"You are. You were. Useful. You're part of the crew now."

"And you're here to give me a hug."

"No, I want to ask you a favor. Crew to crew."

Dena looked at Scruggs for a moment. "What type of favor?"

"I want you to teach me some things. I can help you out, show you some ship things. I had a technical education. Math, science, things like that. I can help you with that stuff. Centurion said I should learn things from you, and he's right."

"You always do what Centurion says, don't you?" Dena asked.

"For now," Scruggs said. "The things I want to learn, he knows a lot more about them than I do. I don't even know enough to make good decisions on some things yet. But that will change eventually."

"So he said learn from me. We're on this crew together, that's fair. I need help with some of this electrical stuff. Electronics. Computers. I can read, but some of the concepts—"

"I can help with that," Scruggs said. "I want you to show me some other things."

"Sure. Next forested planet we're at, I'll set you up."

"That's not exactly what I had in mind." Scruggs petted Rocky, who rolled over and presented his belly. "There is a different topic I want advice on."

CHAPTER TWENTY-FIVE

"My board shows green, Pilot," Lee said.

The control room was crowded. Dirk in the pilot's chair, Lee next to him with a navigation screen up, Ana behind them, looking at a sensor screen, Scruggs mirroring it.

"Engineering?" Dirk said.

"Full load of hydrogen, oxygen, and plain old water, Skipper," Gavin said over the intercom. "Atmo is at one hundred percent capacity, and temperature, humidity, and pressure are within norms. We did a hundred percent replacement with planetary air as well."

"Good," Dirk said. "Internals."

Dena commed, "I'm good, I guess. What do I say?"

"What's on your screens."

"Gavin mirrored some of the cargo and maintenance screens on my cabin's console."

"Are the external hatches closed?" Dirk said.

"They say they are."

"Internal air lock doors closed?"

"Yep."

"Are all the internal hatches closed as well?"

"Yes, I checked."

"I know you checked," Dirk said. "But what does your screen say?"

"The lights are all green."

"So, you say, 'Internal and external hatches green, air locks green, and valves green.'"

"The engineer can see all that—"

"But he might be busy. Practice saying it."

Dena groaned. "This space stuff is more boring than I thought." Her voice ramped up an octave. "Internals reports all hatches and valves green. God save the Empire!"

"The Empire," Dirk, Ana, and Lee responded automatically, then looked embarrassed.

"Comms?" Dirk asked.

"Board is green, Pilot," Scruggs said.

"Sensors?"

"Really, Navy, you want a sensor report?" Ana asked.

"Yes."

"Fine. We're in a hole in the ice surrounded by trees and big rocks. My telescope shows snow. My infrared says it's cold. Nothing on radar except rocks fifty feet away. Can't see more because the cliffs block everything, and my radar receiver isn't receiving any threats. But that's because it's broken, and the engineer hasn't fixed it yet."

"Parts," Gavin said. "I need parts. Or money for parts."

"And somewhere to spend the money," Ana said.

"You could have just said, 'board is green,'" Lee said.

"Bite my green Imperial behind," Ana said. "Fine. Sensors says board is green. Sensors out."

The ship was silent.

After a minute, Lee flicked her screen. "Course is ready, Pilot."

Dirk tapped through his screens but didn't engage the thrusters or the main drive.

The ship was silent again.

Scruggs switched the intercom to all stations. "Sell them. I vote to sell those plans. Who's with me?"

"Private, we can't do that," Ana said. "We're loyal Imperial citizens. We can't help our enemies."

"Then, we starve. Starve here. No, first we freeze, then we starve. The Empire's given you nothing but grief, Centurion. Sell the plans."

"I vote no," Ana said. "So should you."

"I vote yes," Scruggs said.

"This is a surprise," Dirk said. "Scruggs disagreeing with the centurion."

Dena's voice came over the intercom. "I vote sell. We need the money. We deserve the money. We went through a lot of trouble for those plans."

"The Empire—" Ana said.

"Where was the Empire when your toes were freezing off? Not here," Dena said. "It was me who got you through this, and Scruggs, who helped carry you back. And Lee here, who fixed you up. Where's your Empire, then, huh? If it was up to the Empire, you'd be dead. You owe Scruggs and I. You owe Lee."

"Don't drag me into this," Lee said. "I'm just doing my job."

"Sell or not? Should we sell those plans?" Dena asked.

"I . . . I abstain," Lee said. "I'll go with what the group decides."

"You're a Praetorian," Ana said. "Sworn to the Emperor."

"If the Emperor tells me to not sell those plans, that's what I'll do. But the Emperor isn't here right now," Lee said. "So, I'll go with the group."

"Two for, one against, one abstention," Dena said. "Gavin? Sell or not?"

"We can't take the chance. It's too dangerous. No."

"Another surprise," Dirk said. "Gavin counseling prudence."

"Two for, two against," Scruggs said. "Lee isn't voting. Pilot, up to you."

Dirk hesitated.

"It's the wrong thing to do, Navy," Ana said. "You're an officer."

"Was an officer," Scruggs said. "They don't want you anymore. They put you in jail."

"It's too dangerous, Skipper," Gavin said. "They'll hunt us like dogs."

"We've already got Dirk's old buddy, the Imperial—what's his name?— Tribune and destroyer owner trying to find us and blast us to pieces," Dena said. "How can it get worse?"

"It can always get worse," Ana said.

"Doesn't have to. Enough money, and we can go farther out. Beyond the verge. Shuttle goods there. We just need a better ship. One with everything working."

"And what happens when we run out of money there?" Ana said.

"Exactly what happens to us right now, except farther in the future," Dena said. "Lee, have you got a course for the contact planet? What's it called?"

"Saragas IV. Two jumps, and we're there," Lee said.

"We don't even have to refuel. We have enough to get there, right? Engineer, can we do two jumps without refueling?"

"Yeah. We can do two. But then we're stuck at that planet with not much fuel and not much money."

"What's the better idea? Sell a container load of frozen fish somewhere?"

"It was supposed to be wine—"

"It isn't. Dirk, it's up to you. Where are we going?"

Dirk tapped his screen and cycled all the thrusters. "Navigator, give me a course for Saragas IV."

***

"No, Scruggs has to deliver the plans," Dena said. "None of you four can leave the ship."

The Heart's Desire had made record time to Saragas IV. One jump to an empty system, a few hours' calculations and fuel checks, then the second jump.

Lee had dropped them as close as she dared to the planet, and they'd endured another one of Dirk's screaming landings to the starport outside of town.

Saragas IV was flat, with shallow seas and far too much carbon dioxide for people to breathe. It was comfortably warm, had extensive plant life—mostly large ferns, some of which were actually edible—and was devoid of animals, except fish in the oceans.

The crew hadn't actually argued during the trip, but they had been short with each other and kept to themselves.

"Scruggs? What are you talking about?" Dirk said.

"Lee is a Jovian Praetorian. There's no way that anybody will believe that she is some sort of spy or mixed up in spying against the Empire. She doesn't even believe it herself."

Lee muttered something indistinct and hung her head.

"You, your gracious Imperial Dukeness"—Dena pointed at Dirk—"you are too famous, and you're supposed to be in jail. It will just complicate things. We can bring you in later, maybe. Ana here is so obviously an old soldier that they'd be suspicious. I'm clearly a hick. Nobody will believe that I have Imperial secrets."

"And they'll believe Scruggs has them?" Dirk asked. "Does she look like a super-spy?"

"Engineer, they'll believe he's shady," Ana said. "He looks the part. Anyone seeing him walk by puts their hand on their wallet."

"Thanks for the character reference, Old Man," Gavin said.

"He's right," Dirk said. "In terms of who looks most like a spy or a thief, it's you."

"Probably because you are one," Dena said.

Gavin glared. "Fine, I'll make the first contact."

"Not by yourself," Dena said. "You need somebody with you."

"They might not trust me if I bring somebody."

"We don't trust you unless you bring somebody. Scruggs voted for this. You didn't, and you were pretty vocal about it. I don't want you messing things up accidentally-on-purpose."

"Private Scruggs is not suitable for this sort of operation," Ana said.

"She is now. She and I talked, and I showed her a few things."

"She's a great soldier," Ana said, "but she's not . . . sophisticated enough for this type of thing."

"Why not, Centurion?" Scruggs said from behind. "I've dressed up for it." She stepped into the lounge and twirled around. "What do you think?"

She'd dumped her normal coveralls and replaced them with a light red sundress, knee-high cowboy boots, and a cowboy hat. She wandered up to Gavin and leaned into him, sticking herself to his side from hip to shoulder. Then she put her arms around him and kissed him on the cheek. "Hi, handsome. Have any secrets you want to sell to me?"

CHAPTER TWENTY-SIX

"Tribune, we have a situation on that freighter you asked us to stop," the Pollux's comm officer said.

"Of course we do." Devin, Lord Lyon, rubbed his hands. "What have you found? What are they smuggling? Weapons? Stolen goods? Illegal narcotics?"

"I'm still getting the details, sir. But they're calling for medical assistance."

"Dispatch the doctor," Devin ordered. "They must have resisted. And send another squad. We'll show them what it's like to oppose the Emperor's laws." Devin got up and paced around.

Subprefect Lionel walked onto the bridge. "Tribune."

"Subprefect. My instincts were correct. That freighter is up to no good."

"Your instincts, sir?"

"Just look at that ship. Old. Scarred. The drives look like they're a hundred years old. It hasn't been painted since the Emperor's investiture—really, it hasn't been painted since his father's investiture. That's exactly the type of ship that rebels or smugglers or pirates use."

"Looks like just an old junky freighter captain trying to make a living," Lionel said.

"I know these things. That's why I'm the tribune, and you're not."

"I thought it had more to do with you being heir to several planets, and your sister being the Empress?"

"Trifles. Where is that Marine carrier? If we discover something, we may need to call for reinforcement."

"They're out at the gas giants, doing some sort of training on that rocky moon."

"Training? It's a frozen ball of ice. What training do they do there?"

"Brigadier Santana said they were going to drop third company onto the planet to dig holes and live in them for a month, while practicing getting frostbite."

"Practice getting frostbite? He said that?"

"I'm paraphrasing, but he said something about toughening the troops up and gaining experience in 'maneuvering in hostile environments.'"

"Do they need toughening up?"

"He said they volunteered. They had a contest to figure out which company would go."

"And that third company lost?"

"No, they won. Marines like being miserable. It makes them happy for some reason."

Devin looked at the screen. "I'm glad I joined the Navy."

"Me, too, Tribune."

"Sir," the comm officer said. "Doctor is online."

"Doctor," the tribune said, "How is your medical issue?"

"Dental," the doctor said over the comm.

"Pardon?"

"Dental emergency. Impacted wisdom teeth. They want me to operate. Take about two hours. Do I have permission, Tribune?"

The bridge was silent. Each crew member found a console display that fascinated them.

Devin pursed his lips. "I must have misunderstood. This wasn't a battle injury?"

"Battle? No, sir. No battle. This is a family ship. Mom, Dad, three kids, and an uncle. They've been very welcoming. Gave me tea."

"Gave you tea?"

"English Breakfast. With real milk. They have a goat."

"A goat?"

"Angora goat. The fur is very soft. I've been petting it."

"I sent a team to search for contraband, and you're all wasting time petting some dirty sheep?"

"Goat, sir. Totally different type of animal. He's very clean. About the operation, Tribune?"

"On the . . . uncle?"

"Yep. Tribune. The uncle has the tooth problem. He's been waiting till they get to a rim planet where things are cheaper. But they figure I can do it for no charge."

"They want you to be a dentist? For free?"

"Could I, Tribune? My staff and I get very little work as it is. And it would be good for the younger nurses and med techs to practice in a real surgical setting. Good experience for them. Good training."

"But what about"—Devin looked at Lionel, who was looking at a sensor screen—"what about the smuggling and the stolen goods?"

"I don't think any of that is here, Tribune. Their containers are empty. Mostly empty. Wait."

The channel was silent.

The doctor came back. "The sergeant here says one container of slippers. They scanned it and opened some random boxes, but that's it. Just slippers."

"I sent a Pollux class warship chasing after a freighter with a load of slippers?" Devin said.

"Not true," Lionel said. "It wasn't just slippers, it was also a crew with poor oral hygiene."

The doctor spoke. "Tribune? Do I have permission?"

"To fix their teeth?"

"Yes, please, Tribune."

Devin sat in his bridge chair, then got back up. "Fine. Doctor. Do your work." He stopped as his office door swung open.

"Tribune," Lionel said, "should we seek out some other potential troublemakers? Search some other vessels in the system."

Devin paused at his door. "Do as you like, Subprefect."

"We'll need you to . . ."

"I know. Execute. Execute." Devin sighed. "And execute."

Six hours later, Devin sat in his office and looked at his screen. "Skylancer class passenger ship."

"Indeed," Lionel said from his seat in front of the desk. "Brand new. Maiden voyage."

"Must cost a fortune for a ticket."

"Two fortunes. Only very rich people or very important people on it."

"How many fugitives?"

"Three confirmed Imperial warrants so far. One crate of some sort of narcotics. And one of radioactives."

"Radioactives? How were they hiding that?"

"They weren't. Captain said they've never been boarded before."

"Weapons-grade?"

"Pretty much."

"What was it listed as on the manifest?"

Lionel scrolled down his list. "Metal, uranium, enriched."

"You've got to be kidding me."

"Nope. You need special licenses to transport it, but the captain says they had them. Except they didn't. They're fake."

"We should arrest the captain," Devin said.

"He says he doesn't know what a uranium transport license looks like. Do you?"

"I certainly would recognize it when I saw it."

"So, Tribune"—Lionel leaned forward—"who issues these licenses? The Navy? Ministry of energy? Director of Trade and Commerce?"

"Well, I would think, that it comes . . ."

"You have no idea."

"None." Devin shrugged. "You looked it up, of course?"

"Ministry of Agriculture."

"What?"

"They used to be in charge of mines. One of their remits is to prevent cross contamination between worlds. Radiation was listed as contamination."

"I should ask to be on the agriculture committee in the senate."

"You couldn't afford the bribes," Lionel said.

"I'm fabulously wealthy."

"And these big companies don't like being messed with. They'll outspend you. But that's not why I'm here."

"The fugitives."

"One in particular. The one with that special warrant. He's outside."

"Outside? Now?"

"Tribune"—Lionel took a breath—"we can't hide this one. When he realized we were running everyone's ID, he announced himself, said his real name in front of forty people. He assumed we were looking for him, so he surrendered so that his people won't get involved."

Devin got up and paced around the room. "Send him in."

"Should I send for Imin or the bosun?"

"No, I'll be fine by myself. Just send him in."

The subprefect got up and walked out. The door shut behind him, and the room was silent before a balding middle-aged man with a pot belly entered.

"Senator," Devin said.

"For the Emperor's sake, Devin," the man said. "We're cousins. Call me Marcus."

"Second cousins, once removed. It wouldn't be proper."

"You always were a priggish killjoy, weren't you? I blame your father. Have anything to drink?" Devin gestured at the sideboard, and Marcus walked over and dug through the bottles. "How did you find me?"

"Pure luck," Devin said. "Our last inspection turned up nothing except some dental work, and on the way back, we decided to board you on a whim."

"Dental work? You're a mobile hospital now, are you? Hardly proper work for a man of your stature, wouldn't you say?"

"And treason is?"

"Who says it's treason?"

"The Emperor. His signature on your death warrant."

Marcus pulled a bottle from a high shelf. "He never said any such thing." He pulled the cork with his teeth, spat it on the sideboard, and took a slug. "Read the warrant. Ah. This is good stuff. Must be a hundred years old." He poured a huge glass and gulped it down.

"Be careful with that. It hits hard."

"Harder the better. Next while, next short while is not going to be fun for me."

"What did you mean by 'he didn't?'" Devin asked.

Marcus collapsed into Devin's favorite armchair in the corner. "Read the warrant, like I said."

Devin pulled up the warrant on his comm. He flipped through a few pages. "It seems in order."

"Not signed by the Emperor," Marcus said.

"Well, he doesn't sign everything personally, but he should be aware . . . Isn't this his secretary?"

"Was. He's Imperial Chancellor now. He can act in the Emperor's name. And in my case, he did."

"Did you do these things?" Devin asked. "Plot to overthrow the throne?"

"Do I look like some sort of criminal?"

"Absolutely," Devin said. He went to his cabinet and poured himself a small glass. "You're known as the most grasping, greedy, venal governor in the history of the senate. You'll shake down a Varrien rug merchant, steal a baby's socks. You are the worst example of an entitled aristocratic thief. And a complete hound. You should be in jail a dozen times over, and I'm amazed that some woman's husband hasn't stabbed you to death with a fork for the things you say to their wives at dinner. You're greasy, slimy, and a complete embarrassment to the senatorial class."

Marcus took another swig. "Okay, agreed. But other than that, I'm a good guy, right?"

"Have you been listening to me at all?" Devin asked.

"Treason, cousin. What do you think about that?"

Devin sipped and grimaced. "I am surprised to see that on the warrant."

"You don't know what it's like back there, Devin. Internal Security is all over the place. The Chancellor is in on it. If you cross them in anything, or don't pay a bribe. Next thing you know, there's a warrant out on you."

"But the Emperor, my sister . . ."

"Are being unduly influenced by those weasels. When they're even on Capitol to take charge. If you speak up against those security people, well, you see what happens."

"This could just be you trying to save your skin, lying to me about this."

Marcus gulped the rest of his glass. "Could be. But ask yourself this—you know what a lazy weasel I am. Why would I mess up a perfectly good embezzlement and influence peddling scheme? I like money. That's why I steal it. But treason?"

Devin was silent.

Marcus got up for another drink. "Listen, cousin, I've got boxes of money hidden in my luggage over there. It's yours if you let me go."

"You know I can't do that," Devin said.

"True. You're a self-centered prig, but you've never been accused of being greedy." Marcus sat back in the chair. "Nice office here, large."

"Yes," Devin said.

"Why am I still breathing? We passed a half dozen air locks on the way here."

"There are some peculiarities on this warrant."

Marcus snorted. "You have to do it personally, don't you?"

"Or watch," Devin said.

"And you're such a kiss-up that you'll follow all the rules. Tell you what, I'll make it easy on you. My people over there, old retainers. Do you have anything on them?"

"Nothing in particular, but in the circumstances . . ."

"In the circumstances, how about you send them on their way with my money—or some of it—and I'll make this easy for you?"

"Marcus, how could you possibly make it easy for me?" Devin asked.

"You still have your family's sword?"

"Yes."

"Here? Right here on this ship, right now?"

"Yes."

"I always envied you that sword. It was the best example I've ever seen. When I was a boy, your father would come over to talk to Uncle, and he'd let me touch it. I loved that sword." Marcus took another drink and looked around. "Lots of room here."

"I can send for it," Devin said.

"Do that. I'll want some privacy."

"I can do that, too."

"My people, they get away? No problems?"

Devin walked to his desk and touched a button.

"Tribune?" the comm officer said.

"Suspend the search on that liner. Recall our troops. Undock as soon as they are aboard."

"Tribune, they haven't finished checking all the passengers yet, and we've collected those people who were with the special prisoner, but we haven't—"

"Let them go. All of them. Bring the troops back."

"Recalling the troops now, Tribune," the comm officer said.

Devin clicked the button off. "Marcus. Any messages?"

"Already sent, when I found out it was your ship. I knew how this would end."

"I didn't," Devin said.

"You're the only one in the entire Empire who doesn't know how this is going to end," Marcus said. He threw the cross-chest salute. "The Empire."

"The Empire," Devin agreed, stepped outside of his office and waited for the door to close.

Lionel, the bosun, his steward, and two Marines stood outside his door.

The bosun coughed. "I had Imin bring your gladius, sir. I had a feeling you might need it."

His steward extended his sword, then saluted. "The Emperor."

Devin took it and spun it in his hand, then returned the salute. "The Emper— The Empire." He turned to open his door.

CHAPTER TWENTY-SEVEN

Ana and Dena walked thirty paces behind Scruggs and Gavin. After arriving at Saragas IV, a loud, intense discussion ensued. Gavin and Scruggs became the 'A' team, and Dena and Ana were set up as the 'B' team.

If they were noticed, Gavin would claim they were just shipmates who were watching his back for what they thought was a standard sale of stolen goods. Scruggs linked her arm with his and leaned into him at every pace. She stumbled on her heels but made it seem like she was holding Gavin.

"How did you get her to do that?" Ana asked. "It was you, wasn't it? She didn't figure this out by herself."

"We practiced," Dena said. "I got her to watch vids. We traded clothes. She never traded clothes with her sisters."

"Did you?"

"My sisters stole my good clothes from me and kept them," Dena said. "Painful, but I will admit, you learn what looks good on people."

"You learned to buy clothes that looked good on you?"

"No, I learned to buy clothes that would look horrible on my sisters, so when they stole them and wore them, they looked ugly. Then I would wear my backup set, and the boys would chase me."

"That's pretty mean and petty," Ana said.

"Thanks."

"Wasn't supposed to be a compliment."

"Sounded like one."

"You were a pretty mean sister."

"They started it. Where are we going?"

"Not sure," Ana said. "The only thing we got was an address and a unit number. We were told to go there, find somewhere private, and wait."

They walked through different buildings—a shopping concourse, rows of apartments, and offices. The buildings connected via enclosed walkways to keep the tainted atmosphere out. All were unremarkable concrete and glass construction. The air locks at the entrances and exits were unusual, open as people walked through. Even with that, many people carried a filter mask and an emergency air bottle.

"Speaking of what looks good on people," Dena said. "Those clothes are not a good look for those women."

She gestured at a group of women wearing plain brown dresses with white aprons and caps. The dresses were long-sleeved and went all the way to the ankle.

Only the women's hands and faces remained uncovered.

"Some religious thing," Ana said. "Common here, I think."

"Not very stylish."

"Not meant to be. That looks like the place," Ana said. "The kids are going inside."

"You call them the kids? What do you call me?"

Ana slowed down. "The infant? Femme fatale?"

Scruggs and Gavin had walked into the foyer of another nondescript glass building, checked their comms, and consulted the tenants list next to the elevators. Ana steered them into a cafe facing it. He put his back to the wall and sat Dena across from him. "Late for dinner? Order us some drinks. I'll watch what's going on."

Dena waved a waiter over and got them a local specialty tea. "I can be a femme fatale. You try the tea. It's made out of some sort of ground plant."

Ana took a sip and scrunched his face. "Tastes like warm urine. Good choice."

"Do you always have to be so sarcastic?" Dena asked. "How am I supposed to know what some local concoction tastes like?"

Ana smiled at her.

Dena rocked backward. "Don't do that."

"What?"

"Smile. It's like your face exploded. It creeps me out."

Ana grinned wider. "I'll do it more often, then. No, this was a good choice. I can see everything happening in this lobby from here. Perfect field of view. My back's to the wall, so nobody can sneak up on me. I've got this drink in front of me that I'll never touch, so I won't be expected to order more or to leave. This is a perfect spot to watch from."

"I didn't choose here deliberately."

"Yes. You did. Good choice, like I said."

"Thanks, Centurion," Dena said. "Sometimes, you're not so bad."

"You picked here so that you could check your hair in the glass behind me."

Dena put her hand to her head. "I did. How did you know that?"

"Lots of shallow and vain people do that. People like you."

"And he's back. I missed the old geezer. Fine, what do you see?"

"Gavin and Scruggs just went up the elevator. Three Union of Nations spies are sitting at the table next to the entrance. One of them just left to go up and follow our two."

"Union of Nation spies? But we're not in Nat territory."

"This is a free port. Imperial ships can call here and trade and not look like total idiots. So can National ships."

"How do you know they were spies?"

"They watched everybody walking into and out of the building, and they talked to each other when they saw Gavin and Scruggs. And Gavin gave his description in the email, so they'll know what he looks like."

"Did they see us?"

"Not at all. They were too focused on Gavin, totally missed us. And as long as you keep talking, I can keep looking over your shoulder and watch them. From a distance it looks like I'm talking to you."

"What do I do now?"

"Say something vapid and shallow. Check your hair. Admire your good looks in the mirror."

"You're an Imperial turd sometimes, Centurion."

"It's always better to call things as they are."

"I saved your life, you know. Back on that iceberg of a planet."

"I know, that's why I wanted you along. You think well on your feet and don't freeze up when the unexpected happens."

"Thanks."

"And you have such a strong sense of self-preservation, I can count on you to try to save yourself, so I just have to follow along behind you. He's looking this way. Laugh or giggle."

Dena snickered and touched the centurion's arm, digging her nails in till they drew blood. "You sanctimonious Imperial turd. I saved all of you. I brought all three of you back in out of the cold."

Ana looked at his bleeding arm. "Because you thought it through. You could have saved yourself, but if you did that and left us behind, you'd have died on that planet. You needed a pilot and an engineer."

"I saved your life out of self-interest?"

Ana smiled again. "I appreciate that. Makes you easy to work with. I understand you. Motion. One's moving."

Dena stretched and caught sight of movement in the mirror. "I see one leaving."

"Probably to report to somebody else. The other's still there, staring at the far door."

"They can't be spies," Dena said. "Electric-blue shirts—one is wearing a bright orange shirt. They stand out. Everybody will remember them."

"They'll remember the shirts," Ana said. "But that's all. You saw that one walk away, the one with the blue shirt. What else was he wearing? What color was his hair? How did he walk?"

"I . . . I don't know."

"He changes that shirt, and he disappears, nothing else stands out. Keep talking."

"About what?"

"Your favorite topic, maybe. Yourself."

"So, I'm a narcissistic, self-indulgent party girl who only looks out for myself."

"I don't think you're self-indulgent," Ana said. "As for the rest, if the skin suit fits, wear it. But I understand your motivations, that makes you easy to work with."

"So, you've got me pegged. What about the others?"

"Navy just wants to not go back to jail. He's not even sure why he was in jail in the first place. He's not thinking clearly yet. Scruggs wants adventure. You're out to get as far away from that dead-end planet you were born on as possible. And good job so far. You've made excellent progress. The navigator, I'm not sure of, but she's embarrassed about something. Some weird Jovian thing, she broke some strange rule. The only one I don't understand is the engineer."

"He's running away from something."

"But what or who? He gets on and off the ship with no problems, and he's talented enough to get a berth somewhere else. Why's he here?"

"I don't know. Do you trust him?"

"As much as I trust everybody."

"You know, Centurion," Dena said. "You didn't explain yourself in that discussion, did you?"

"I did not. Not going to, either. Whoops. Showtime."

"What's up?"

"Police. Local police. Two uniforms just came in the front door."

"I can't—"

"Next to the plant."

Dena tilted to the right. "I still can't see them. Where are they going?"

"Right to that Nat spy's table."

***

The elevator flicked open, and Gavin and Scruggs stepped out, then stopped and surveyed the foyer in front of them.

"A library," Gavin said. "We're going to trade secrets in a library."

Two women in long dresses and aprons sat behind a counter ahead of them. A sign above them welcomed them to the Church of the Word Memorial Library.

To their right were dozens of head-high bookshelves in rows containing real paper books. On the left, people sat in clusters of chairs, reading. Low bookcases separated the clusters. At the rear, behind the women, a wooden staircase ran up to a mezzanine running around above the readers.

Scruggs pointed up. "In the name of the Emperor's greasy nose hair, what's that up there?"

The library was four stories, with open balconies surrounding a central interior courtyard. Stairs went from floor to floor on each side. A sculpture hung from the roof, filling the central space. Crates and boxes of books ascended and descended on ropes hung from the ceiling. Books spun in a spiral around a central bar that hung from the rooftop. Lines of ropes pulled and pushed the maze in a spinning, climbing and falling circle that was mesmerizing in its complexity. Piles of books flowed up to the ceiling, then spun back down.

Gavin pointed to a plaque next to a bank of humming electric motors. "It's

180

called 'knowledge in motion.' Says it's a 'representation of humanity's search for the stars through the transfer of knowledge.'"

"Looks more like what happens when mediocre talent meets government funding," Scruggs said.

"You're normally this catty."

"Must be the boots. They make me feel . . . powerful."

"And the hat."

"Hat makes me feel daring. And the dress makes me feel sexy." She looked at Gavin. "You should try it."

"I don't look good in dresses. Makes my calves look fat."

"I meant the hat, but whatever you want. It's a small ship. We should try to keep out of each other's private business."

"I'm going to ignore that," Gavin said. "Scruggs, everyone is looking at us." A number of the readers were watching them, and the two women behind the counter were outright staring. "Why is everyone watching us?"

"Skin suits," Scruggs said. "We're the only ones wearing skin suits. They probably don't get any spacers in here. That's why your contact picked this place. We stand out."

"Your dress makes you stand out."

"You don't like it."

"It's great. Very sexy. But we can't sneak around with everybody looking at us."

"We don't have to," Scruggs said. "They're already here, probably. One of these people watching us. But with everybody looking at us, we can't tell who's who."

"What do we do? They said find a private place by a window and wait there and that they would find us." His hand strayed to his knife. "They'll be able to get close before we figure out who they are. I might need my knife."

Scruggs leaned into his neck and whispered. "Do you draw your knife with your right hand or your left?"

"I'm right handed."

She slid to his left so the women couldn't see him. She padded through his fingers till she found one with a ring. "I need this." She slid it off his hand and placed it on her finger.

"That's an engineer's school graduation ring."

She took his hand and led him forward. "Doesn't matter. Any ring will do. I'll stay on your left. This way, I won't block you if you need your knives. But let me try something first. Let me do the talking. Just agree with what I say."

They walked hand in hand to the counter between a row of plinths with mini busts of men's heads on them.

Gavin's boots clacked on the polished wood floor.

"Who are they?" Gavin asked, looking at the sculptures.

"Probably patrons who contributed money."

"Some of those are glass. That one's metal." He pointed at an elaborate one near the end. "That looks like stone."

"The more you donate, the better a display you get. Stone face probably gave the most money."

"You know a lot about libraries."

"Spent a lot of time in them when I was younger."

They reached the counter.

"Remember, follow my lead."

A woman of Scruggs's age sat behind a sign that read, "Mrs. Davis." The elder woman's sign read, "Mrs. Stevens."

Mrs. Stevens examined Scruggs. "How may we help you spacers?"

Scruggs smiled. "Peace and the blessing of the one be with you, sisters."

The two women exchanged glances, then Mrs. Stevens said, "And also with you, sister."

"Is it not a glorious day to be one with our Savior? Truly, the most high showers us with blessings."

"Indeed." The two women looked at her clothes. "Showers us." They traded glances again.

"Could I prevail upon the two of you for some guidance of a spiritual fashion?"

"Spiritual?" the younger woman said. "Really?" The elder elbowed her, then faced Scruggs. "What is vexing you, child?"

"My husband and I have recently arrived, as you can tell from our garments. We were walking among your buildings, and I was overcome with a desire to give thanks to our Creator. When traveling, we cannot always find a divine service that meets our schedule. I often came to the church library for quiet succor between the weekly services. They are private and quiet. I ask you this. Is there perhaps a quiet place, perhaps upstairs, where he and I may pray for some time?"

Scruggs beamed at them.

The women exchanged glances. "You want to go somewhere private and pray?" Mrs. Stevens, the elder said.

"Yes, please," Scruggs said.

"Pray?" Mrs. Davis, the younger, said. "Dressed like that?"

Scruggs glowered. "My husband has dressed me like this. Should I deny him?" Scruggs leaned into Gavin's chest. "Challenge him? Is he not master in our union?"

"But, but . . ." Mrs. Davis said.

"We are doing God's work." Scruggs glanced around. People were watching them but returned to their books when her gaze swept over them. She leaned forward to the women and whispered, "He has sometimes . . . a difficulty praying . . . finding the right mood. I help in any way I can. The clothes, the privacy, the . . . risk," Scruggs murmured. "It's embarrassing, I know, but you are a married woman. You understand young men, and their . . . needs?"

Mrs. Stevens laughed. "I see, sister. Yes, I see. How long will this praying take, sister?"

"As long as he desires. But usually only a few minutes is sufficient. More than sufficient."

"My husband often prayed for that long as well, when we were younger. He had a similar problem in the . . . duration of his praying." Stevens sighed. "Now he hardly prays at all. There's a quiet corner on the next floor. Go up the staircase, turn right, then left. There's an alcove down that aisle. It has a window with an excellent view and some chairs. It's quiet. Private. Nobody goes there."

"But Milda, we can't," Mrs. Davis said. "I mean, can we?"

"There is no sin in a marriage bed, sister," Scruggs said. "Is that not so?"

Mrs. Davis nodded once. Then nodded again.

"And which would be the greater sin, to disobey my husband, or . . . ?"

Mrs. Stevens smiled. "A woman should always follow her husband's desires. Take your time. We do not close for two hours."

"Blessings upon you," Scruggs said and tugged Gavin away.

She could still hear them talking.

"But Milda, are they . . . ?"

"Girl, you're always complaining about that yourself. Get a dress like that and meet Steve at the door when he comes home from work. Better yet, get that hat."

"Wear the hat and the dress when he comes home?"

"No. Just the hat."

CHAPTER TWENTY-EIGHT

Gavin slouched up the stairs, Scruggs clinging to his side. "Do those women really think we're going to go have sex in a corner of a library?" Gavin asked.

"They sure do."

"But out in public?"

"One of the main fantasies of religious people is exhibitionism, others watching them. It's about three, four times as common with really devout people as with non-members."

"That statistic has got to be made up."

"For these restrictive sects, no. I have personal experience."

"You do?" Gavin asked. Scruggs ignored him. "But why are they like that?"

"Don't know. Maybe because they're so tightly wound, all that pressure just builds up till they explode. That's why I asked the older woman. Chances are, she knew somebody like this, or one of the other woman told her. Given how weird some of them are about sex, I was thinking of asking her if she could come and watch."

"Scruggs!"

"It's just to make it sound realistic."

Gavin shook his head. "How old are you again?"

"It's just a thought."

Gavin reached the top and glanced around. Nobody was within earshot. "What's wrong with you. This is totally out of character. Normally you blush when we talk about you not having any boyfriends. Now you're planning a threesome on a library table."

Scruggs grinned. "Dena was super helpful. She told me to treat the clothes like a costume, act a part like I was in a play. Don't think like yourself. So, that's what I'm doing. I feel different. It's fun, pretending to be somebody else for a change. It's like when I used to get dressed for dance recitals. I was somebody else while I danced. A different person. Bigger, more confident, more attractive."

"You dance?" Gavin asked.

Scruggs ran a finger down his face. "Someday, I'll dance for you. I'll turn your bones to water." She smiled, grabbed his hand, and led him around the corner.

Gavin skidded behind. "The Emperors hairy armpits, what have we done? We've created a monster."

Scruggs turned right, walked around the balcony, then turned left into a narrow aisle. It ran back between two bookshelves, then opened up to a small sitting area with a couch facing a window.

"Mrs. Stevens treated us well," Scruggs said, dropping onto the couch. "There's plenty of room for the happy couple here." She patted the seat next to her. "Have a seat."

"I'll stay standing," Gavin said.

"You scared of me now?"

"Now? Yes. Very much so," Gavin said.

"Huh." Scruggs adjusted her hat. "That's kind of cool. I kinda like people being scared of me."

"You can fight, and now I know that you can—"

CRASH.

Something glass had broken in the lobby. Scruggs jumped, and Gavin pulled his knife. "What was that?"

A man appeared between the bookshelves. He was overweight, balding, wore an electric-blue shirt, beige shorts, sandals, and carried a stack of heavy books. The top one was The Big Book of Model Railroading.

"Howdy, strangers," he said.

"Who are you? What do you want?" Gavin asked.

"To give you some money, if you have more items of the quality that you sent to our email address."

Gavin looked him up and down. "You're a spy?"

"Spies are supposed to be invisible," the man said. "And looking like this in a library, I'm the next best thing to invisible, yes. But you two are the proverbial tabbos in a glass factory. Can't be anything but spacers. I know you have a knife under that sleeve. I saw you fiddling with it earlier." He pulled his shirt tail up. "I've got a gun, so don't bother pulling it."

He stepped past them and looked out the window. He raised one hand, three fingers extended, then turned back to them. "Just need to keep the backup teams from panicking."

"Or just pretend you have backup when you're actually here alone," Gavin said. He took his hand off his knife but kept his arms ready.

"That was one of my backups. Smashed his tea mug on the floor. Everybody looked at him, and I was able to sneak in here. Right now, everybody thinks it's just the two of you in here." He looked at Scruggs. "What did you say to Milda? She's been sniggering since you talked to her. And Gabriella called her husband, and now she's blushing like a schoolgirl."

"We're just doing God's work is all," Scruggs said.

"God's work? Is that what it's called?" He shook his head. "Never mind. To business. Call me Art."

"That's your name?"

"Nope. But call me that anyway. You match the description given by somebody who sent a document to an email address, and you're in the place you're supposed to be, so you want to speak to me. Tell me what I need to know."

"That's pretty vague."

"We work that way, as you know. Otherwise, you wouldn't have known that email address." Art tapped his lips. "Mister, do I know you? You look familiar."

"You don't know me," Gavin said.

"You sure?"

"I'm sure all Imperials look alike to you

"No, they don't. I only know a few Imperials. You're not one of them. I've seen you somewhere else."

"I could be a vid star."

"Don't flatter yourself. I said you were familiar, not attractive," Art said. "And you're way out of your league with this hottie here. Next time, find her a better-looking partner."

Scruggs grinned. "He thinks I'm hot."

"I'm going to have a long talk with Dena about this," Gavin said.

"You don't think I'm hot?"

"I don't think of you that way. You're like a sister to me."

"A hot sister?" Scruggs asked.

"A very, very long talk with Dena," Gavin said. He turned to Art. "Can we get on with it?"

"It's your show," Art said. "And I'm ready. You're the one arguing with hot stuff here."

"I just want to make sure—"

"That I'm not Imperial counter-intelligence, perhaps? Getting you out here to arrest you. I could be, you know."

Scruggs stepped away from the two men and took a ready pose that centurion had taught her. Gavin put his hand back on his knife arm.

"And you, young lady, are more than a pretty face. Going to give me a thrashing, are you? Imperial trained, as well, from the looks of it—I recognize the style. And you both have faint accents that you should have gotten rid of. But no need to worry. I'm not from the Empire. Now you need to prove who you are."

"No need," said Gavin. "You know who we are. You want what we're selling."

"We don't need what you're selling," Art said. "We got it from another source."

"Don't be an Imperial turd. If you didn't want it, you wouldn't be here. You might have some of it, not all of it. You're waiting for the rest of it."

Art cocked his head. "What do you mean?"

"We're at least the second group that showed you a sample and gave you that list," Gavin said. "Another group offered to sell it to you. I'll bet they're overdue in contacting you."

Art nodded. "I'm listening."

"We're a . . . rival group. We acquired that information ourselves, before your other friends could get it."

"If there's an original group, perhaps I should wait for them."

"You won't be hearing from them. We got the whole package. They don't have it anymore. We've got it now."

"What do you want?" Art asked.

"Money," Scruggs said. "Lots and lots of money. More than the others."

"Double crossing us, are you?"

"Not even a single cross," Scruggs said. "We've never talked to you before, and we didn't make any deals with you, not till now." Scruggs dropped her defense pose. "We've got what you want, and we want twice as much money as your friends."

"We won't pay," Art said.

Scruggs pointed at Gavin. "My friend here has a chip with the engineering schematics for a Pollux class destroyer. He's an engineer himself, and he says they are legitimate and that it's also something you can check other ways. With it is a list of the other items we have. More schematics. Reactor and drive performance. And most importantly, weapon ranges and hit probabilities. An entire Imperial test procedure for all the weapons on those destroyers."

Art grinned. "Definitely not just a pretty face. Who's in charge here, engineer guy? You or her?"

"We work together, and we have some other friends helping us out," Gavin said. "You're not the only ones with a backup team. Here's another taste." He handed the man a data chip. Art slotted it into a comm he had pulled from his belt and examined it. "It looks reasonable to me, but I'm not an expert."

"Check the list of items in the next packet."

Art glanced at the list. "Anybody can make a list. I need to verify it."

"We're willing to meet a ship close to Imperial space, one of yours. With experts on board. You can check five percent of the documents. If you like them, then you give us our cash, and we send you the rest."

"Why not do it here?"

"Because you've got people all on the ground here, and the local government is too friendly to you."

"This is a free port, not a Union of Nations world."

"Still too friendly. We want to meet near Imperial space."

"That won't work."

"Not a core world," Gavin said. "A planet with an Imperial presence and ships but not an actual Imperial world. Papillon."

Art shrugged. "Could work. Not my decision. How do we get in touch with you?"

"You don't. There's rendezvous coordinates there, and a date. You've got enough time to send a message and get a ship jumped there and a day to spare. Long enough to get there, not long enough to plan a trap. Take it or leave it."

"What if we leave it?"

"We can be in the Confederation in three jumps from here."

"And once you jump in, you'll never leave. I'll talk to some people. Maybe they'll be there, maybe they won't."

"Your choice," Gavin said. "But if you don't make it, our next stop is a Confederation border station."

"Not my decision," Art said.

CLANG.

Metal clanged on metal below.

"What's that?" Gavin said.

"Your friend have another mug of tea?" Scruggs asked.

"Nope." The three stepped forward to the balcony and peered down. Six uniformed police stood in the library's foyer. Two stood by the door. One was talking to the two women at the counter. One picked up a statue she had somehow knocked over.

And two marched up the stairs, heading for the second floor, where the group waited.

CHAPTER TWENTY-NINE

The two uniformed police cornered the Nat spy at the table in front of Ana and Dena. The spy, a man, remained seated, and everybody lowered their voices, but an argument was clearly happening. One police officer pointed at the elevators across the lobby where Gavin and Scruggs had disappeared. The man at the table shook his head. The officer crossed his arms. The spy shook his head again. The officer reached for his belt holster. The spy put his hands up in a placating manner but kept talking. The other officer picked a chunky comm off his belt and spoke into it.

Dena had pulled her comm out. "My signal's blocked."

"They just closed down the network," Ana said. "Something's happening."

"Well, what can we—Emperor's testicles."

Six uniformed police emerged from a connecting corridor. They stopped by the entrance, conferred with the other officers, then ran across the foyer to the other building. Once they had all disappeared through the door, Ana stood. "Let's go. Follow my lead."

He and Dena got up and walked to the door.

A waiter intercepted them. "Strangers, are you leaving us?"

"None of your business," Ana said, shouldering by.

"Stop, you can't just leave," the waiter said.

"Try and stop me," Ana said.

"Help, thieves," the waiter said. "Officer, stop them. They haven't paid."

The police stopped talking to each other. One stepped in front of Ana. "Halt. You have to pay."

"Don't make me hurt you, little man," Ana said.

The officer stepped back and drew his revolver. "Hands up."

Ana didn't stop. "Just step aside. I'm not interested in getting arrested today."

"Larry," the other cop said, "we don't have time for this. Just make them pay and get out of here."

"Pay?" Ana rounded on Dena. "You didn't pay."

"Why would I pay?"

"We're supposed to pay when we sit," Ana said. "You picked the stupid place."

"I don't pay with a man. Men pay for me."

"Of all the stupid, self-centered, idiot things you've done, girl, this is the stupidest," Ana said. "Almost getting us arrested. What would your mother say?"

Dena's mouth dropped. "What—"

Ana side-eyed the police, then back to Dena. He winked and slid back a step.

Dena glowered. "My mother? What's my mother got to do with this?"

"Just that you're a natural-born idiot, just like your mother."

"You don't know my mother," Dena said. "You've never—"

"Oh, I know her, all right," Ana said, stepping back. "Her royal fatness? I know her, all right."

"Don't talk about her that way," Dena yelled. "She's not fat. And she was right, you are a worthless deadbeat."

"Not fat? She's so fat you have to take two trains and bus to get on her good side." Ana stepped between the two bemused policemen.

"You shut up, or I'll—"

Ana reached out and grabbed the police by the head and smacked their heads together. They reeled for a moment, then collapsed. Ana bent down and relieved them of their revolvers and comms. As he did this, the remaining spy rolled off his chair and dashed away.

"Ana, he's running," Dena said.

"Let him go," Ana said. He examined the comms. "Need a code. No time. Come on."

He dashed across the foyer and into the other building. Dena followed. Ana paused to toss the comms into a trash can.

They crashed through the building. Two people stood, gawking at the elevator and talking. "We're with the police," Ana yelled. "Where did they go? What floor?"

"Six," one man said. "They went to the sixth."

"Thanks," Ana said. He dashed onto the stairs and pounded his way up the stairs. Dena raced behind.

Ana made it to the third-floor landing before he started gasping. At the fourth floor, he leaned against the wall and fumbled in his pocket for his pills.

"What is wrong with you?" Dena asked. "I saw those in the woods. That's pretty powerful stuff."

"Never get old," Ana said. "It doesn't end well." He dry-swallowed one pill and put the other in his mouth. "I'm fine now."

His breath kept coming in gasps, and he didn't move from the wall.

"You don't look fine. Don't they have to dissolve or something?" Dena said.

"No. We just need to get up there and warn them."

"Well, standing here won't do it. I'll go and let them know."

"Wait for me, I'll—"

"Just slow me down, you old geezer," Dena said. She sprang up the steps two at a time. "I'll tell you what happened."

Gasping, Ana said, "Getting old sucks."

***

190

Scruggs, Gavin, and Art stepped back from the balcony. "This is new," Art said. He put his stack of books on a shelf. "Normally, the locals leave us alone and just watch. Something has stirred them up."

Gavin had his hand on his knives. "Why did you call them in?"

"Idiot," Art said, edging up to the end of the shelves and peering around. "Why would I do that? If I wanted you arrested, I'd just have sent them to your ship, Heavyweight Items, as you call it." He smirked as Gavin reacted. "Of course, that's not its real name. Didn't think I knew that, did you? We've been watching you since you left. Your request came within minutes of landing, so we figured it was you. No, we want even incompetent spies to give us what they've got. I'll say this, though, this official presence has roused my interest. There's something about you that these people want. Makes it more likely you have the real goods." He pocketed the data chip Gavin had given him. "Tell you what, with all this extra commotion, I'm going to recommend that you get your meeting. If you make it out of here alive and free, there will be somebody at Papillon." He named a bar and a time. "You have just enough time to get there, if your Jump drive works. Be there." He picked a second chip out of his pocket. "Here's a down payment for what you gave me. We'll see you in a week, with the rest of your money. Safe travels." He straightened his blue shirt tails, reseated his glasses, and disappeared around the corner. Then his head poked back. "One word of advice, don't hurt the cops. Fisticuffs here is barely a misdemeanor. But anything with weapons, that's big time."

"Well, mission successful, sort of," Gavin said. "Now all we have to do is get out of here." He stuck his head around the corner, then ducked back. "Two of the cops, one with a shotgun, the other with a shock stick, are talking to Art."

He and Scruggs ducked farther into the alcove and waited. They could hear the three talking.

". . . my id. It's all in order, as you can see," Art said.

Another voice said, "It's in order. You can go. Just check in with the officer by the front door and tell them Blue Chrome says you can go."

"Blue Chrome? You guys been watching too many vids, sounds like."

"Tell me about it, citizen," the voice said. "The captain has. He got it from some old adventure book. Sorry to interrupt your reading."

Gavin pulled Scruggs into a corner and whispered, "Be quiet."

The officer's boots clacked on the floor. His footsteps walked and turned down their corridor.

Gavin looked around. "Mmmmurph—"

Scruggs leaned into Gavin, threw her arms around his neck, and kissed him. The boots clicked to a stop. Scruggs pulled Gavin closer and held on.

The boots clicked away and faded down the aisle. Scruggs held on and didn't move.

"I think they're gone," Gavin whispered.

"I think so, too," Scruggs said.

"Scruggs?"

"Yes?"

"You can stop kissing me now."

Scruggs dropped her arms. Her face turned red. "Sorry, sorry, Engineer."

"Since we've been locking lips, you should probably call me Gavin."

"I just got carried away, playing the part, like Dena said."

"You played it well."

"Sorry."

"Don't be sorry, it was nice," Gavin said. "We've got the code phrase. Let's get out of here." He grabbed her arm and dragged her down the corridor to the balcony. "We'll just slide down and do that Blue Chrome thing." He rounded the edge onto the mezzanine around the lobby and almost hit the two police waiting there.

"You two finished?" the first one asked. "We didn't want to interrupt. Turn around and put your hands behind your back. You're under arrest."

"We didn't do anything," Scruggs said.

"You're coming with us," the first policeman said. He waggled his shock stick. His nametag said "Budawan." "Got some people want to talk to you."

Gavin drifted left and put his arm on the railing. He glanced below and saw two other police guarding the door and Art's shirt exiting to the corridor. "We're just in here, borrowing some books," Gavin said. "We're big bibliophiles." He slouched against the railing and gave Scruggs a push to the right. Scruggs took the hint and stepped right, forcing the police to look back and forth between them.

"Oh, you are, are you?" the second cop said, cradling his shotgun. His nametag said "Ptarn." "Well, thanks for admitting it. Now, normally we don't care what kind of freakish acts you deviants like doing, but this is a family library, and we don't put up with that type of behavior."

"Freakish acts?" Gavin said.

"Deviant behavior?" Scruggs said.

Budawan turned to his partner. "I'm a bit confused myself."

"What type of behavior?" Scruggs asked. "Borrowing books? It's a library?"

"We don't need any of you bibliophile types here," Ptarn said.

"What's wrong with bibliophiles?" Scruggs asked.

Gavin raised his eyebrows. "It means people who like books. That's why we're in a library. We like books."

Ptarn looked at Budawan. Budawan nodded. "Bibliophile. Means they like books."

"I didn't know that," Ptarn said. "I thought it meant something else."

"What did you think it meant?"

"Never mind," Ptarn said.

"Well, if it helps any," Scruggs said, "I'll have you know that I'm a noted thespian, and I'm often seen masticating in public."

Ptarn scowled at her. "In public. That's just the type of thing that we're trying to prevent."

Gavin laughed. "Masticating. In public."

Scruggs was giggling as well. "With a noted thespian."

Budawan tried holding a straight face but snickered.

"Sir," Ptarn said, "this isn't funny."

"Yes it is," Gavin said.

"Definitely," Scruggs said.

Budawan snorted.

Gavin stepped forward and slapped his shoulder. "Let it all out, buddy."

Budawan bawled with laughter, and Scruggs and Gavin joined in. Gavin bent over, slapping his thighs. Budawan leaned into the railing.

Gavin laughed and slapped Budawan's back, then grabbed his belt with his left arm and his shoulder with his right, and pivoted him over the railing. Budawan's laugh turned to a scream, and he fell a story onto a table loaded with books, computers, and three plant pots.

Ptarn racked his shotgun and pointed it at his head. "Move, and you're dead."

Gavin raised his hands. "Easy. Easy."

"Easy, I'll—"

BAM.

Scruggs clouted his head with a book, and he dropped to the floor. The shotgun clattered onto the tiles.

"Art said no weapons," Gavin said.

Scruggs held up her book. "Think they're going to put us in jail for unsanctioned use of The Big Book of Model Railroading?"

"Guess not. Let's drop."

Gavin ran along the balcony, turned the corner to the stair landing, and ran headfirst into a shock stick-carrying guard. The guard staggered and swayed in place, but Gavin bounced back and dropped to a knee.

Scruggs ran up to him, set her legs, and clouted the guard with the book.

"Eat model trains, dirtbag," she yelled.

Gavin looked down and saw the other guard at the bottom aiming a shotgun up the stairs. "Gun!" He dropped flat, pulling Scruggs down. The shotgun boomed over his head. He rolled back around the corner.

Scruggs grabbed him and dragged him away from the stairs. "Other way."

They turned and raced the other direction around the mezzanine. They ran to the opposite side where another stairway led up. They sprinted up, then continued around to the other side to the next stairs.

"Eat model trains?" Gavin said, running up the stairs. "That's the best you got?"

"BBMR for the win," Scruggs said.

They reached the top and circled the open foyer, but the stairs ended.

"Where are they? What's going on?" Gavin asked.

Scruggs leaned over the rail, then climbed up and stood on it to peer down.

"Two of them, running up. They'll be on this floor in a minute."

"We're stuck up here," Gavin said. "No way out. See any exits?"

Scruggs pointed to an emergency exit behind a chair in the far corner. "Follow me." She hopped down from the rail headed to the corner, Gavin right behind her.

Two police ran up the last set of stairs to their right as they raced for the corner.

The emergency exit came into view as they reached the last of the bookshelves on the level. She ran at it, hit the crash bar full tilt with her shoulder, and bounced back off the door. It was locked.

Gavin thumped into her, and they crashed over a low table in front of the door. They pulled themselves up. The two pursuers had stepped into the walkway between bookshelves and were approaching from the other side. The bookshelves on that side lined the wall and the rail.

Gavin grabbed Scruggs's hand and ran down the nearest aisle, then stopped at the rail. "Whoops. Nothing but air here."

Scruggs ran back to the aisle and threw a book down the corridor, then ducked back.

"They're behind us. BBMR gave us a few moments, but we're stuck. They'll be here in a second." She hopped up and balanced on the rail. "Get up here. We can walk around to the stairs on the rail. They'll have to dodge back and forth in the inner corridor."

"BBMR?" Gavin said.

"Big book of Model Railroading, get up here."

Gavin hopped up behind her and teetered on the rail. The foyer opened below them, stretching four stories to the plinth-studded lobby. "If we fall from here, we would skewer on one of those statues."

"They're stone. You'll probably just smash your skull."

"That's better?"

"Don't fall, then. Follow me." Scruggs edged along the railing. She and Gavin made good time around the railing and were halfway to the stairs when a uniformed figure stuck their head out two aisles in front of them and aimed a shotgun.

"Peekaboo," the policeman said.

Scruggs pivoted on her feet and helped turn Gavin around. "Other way, go, go."

Gavin walked back the way they had come and then another head poked out in front.

"Take it easy, strangers," the policewoman said. "Climb down here, and you won't get hurt."

"If we don't?" Scruggs said.

The figure in front racked a shotgun and pointed it at them. "Long way down."

CHAPTER THIRTY

Dena turned the corner from the stairs and looked down the corridor. The door down the hall emitted a stream of people. She marched ahead and pushed through the confusion. A man in a blue shirt walked past her, giving her the usual head-to-toe she received from men. Then he slowed and gave her another look.

Dena ignored him and walked by but paused. His clicking feet on the floor had stopped. She whirled around. The man was standing two steps behind her.

"Can I help you?" Dena asked.

"The police are checking IDs of people inside. We're happy with what your friends are offering. Somebody will meet you at the rendezvous if you can make it. There will be money." He walked away. "The password to get in and out is 'Blue Chrome.' Good luck." He paused again, then said, "You and the other girl are wearing the same style of clothes. That's a giveaway." He headed down the hall.

Dena pursed her lips, adjusted the dress she wore over her skin suit, and stepped up to the door. Just as the man said, a police officer was checking people's IDs.

"Nobody allowed in, miss," the doorman said.

Dena leaned over. "Blue Chrome sent me."

"To come back in?"

"Yes," Dena said. "I'm waiting to identify somebody if they catch them."

"Wait here," the officer said. "I'll have to check—"

A yelling figure crashed onto a loaded table near the stairs, spraying broken plant pots and dirt everywhere.

A shotgun boomed, and Dena saw a policeman crouch on the stairs as another rolled past him. People were screaming, and Dena saw Gavin and Scruggs running along the second-floor balcony. Then the two police on the stairs stood and gave chase.

The crowd stampeded out the front door. The desk officer was knocked down and didn't get back up from the crush. Dena was pushed to one side and into a statue. It crashed to the floor, but the crowd didn't slow.

She glanced up. Scruggs and Gavin raced up to the top floor. The police pounded after them. The two in the foyer were struggling to control the crowd.

Dena picked herself up, tripped over the statue's broken head, and fell again. She climbed up, kicked the head, and cursed as her toes hit solid rock.

"Stupid, stupid," she yelled.

She looked up. Gavin and Scruggs had climbed up onto the rail and were circling the foyer on an upper ledge. They made it about halfway to the stairs when a figure popped out in front of them. They reversed course but then got caught halfway between two separate shotguns.

Dena stepped sideways for a better view. The elaborate hanging centerpiece of books swung gently as its motor yanked it in and out. Dena looked up at her crewmates and looked at the motor set in the wall, then back up.

She skittered over to her destroyed statue and grabbed the disembodied stone head. She lugged it over to the side where the motor that pulled the ropes and moved the statue was reeling it in.

After lifting the stone above her head, she smashed it down on the motor. Sparks flew. She smashed it again, the motor sputtered, and a blue flame appeared. She smashed a third time, knocking it off the wall.

The effect was immediate. The spring-loaded ropes leading to the sculpture loosened and spun backward. With no motor to stop it, the piles of books at each level spun backward and dropped to the ground level. They fanned out as their speed increased, like a skater throwing her arms out as she spun. The books spun at the end of their tethers, like rocks on a string.

"Scruggs, Gavin," Dena yelled.

The two looked down at her.

"Grab the books and jump," Dena yelled.

Gavin didn't wait but just leaped out and grabbed the first box of books that flew by. Scruggs followed a beat later. They hung on as the piles of books spiraled down around the center axle, dropping lower with every rotation.

The first of the descending spinning books hit the walls and bookshelves on the first floor. Higher up, stretched ropes broke and slammed boxes into shelves, spilling the books onto the floor and over the rails. Piles of descending books smashed into bookshelves. On the far side of the ground floor, three hits in rapid succession struck a shelf, and the shelf overbalanced and crashed into the next one, which dominoed into the others. The almighty crash blanketed all other noise.

The remaining officer appeared, pointing his shotgun at Dena. She dropped the stone head and put her hands up.

Another bookshelf crashed. His mouth moved, but she couldn't make it out.

"What? I can't hear you," Dena said.

"I said, put your—"

Gavin caught him with a kick in the head with his heels as he spun down to ground level, then plowed into the floor. The shotgun clattered to the floor, the policeman only a moment behind it.

Scruggs followed two seconds later, but she judged the landing better, let go of her rope, hit, rolled once, and came upright.

"You two okay?" Dena asked.

Gavin climbed up and surveyed the room. Almost all the bookshelves on the ground floor were down.

The "Knowledge in Motion" sculpture was wrecked. On the higher floors, bookshelves had been knocked over by flying debris.

"I'm fine," he said. "Little beaten up."

Scruggs snapped up and giggled. "That was glorious! So much fun."

Dena and Gavin looked at her. Scruggs grinned again and giggled even more. "Adventure awaits."

Ana walked into the lobby behind them. He was sweating and looked flushed, but his voice was level.

"What in the name of the Emperor's hairy earwax happened here?"

"I destroyed a library, Centurion," Scruggs said.

Ana looked around and pursed his lips. "That, you did." He turned to Gavin. "Did you talk to the guy?"

"We're all set," Gavin said. "Have a rendezvous."

"Let's get back to the ship and drop," Ana said.

"Nobody is going anywhere," a new voice said.

They all turned. The officer that Gavin had knocked over on his descent stood. He was bleeding from a cut to his cheek, and his left arm was hanging loose, but he cradled a shotgun in his right arm. "All of you get down on the ground or by the Empress's rosy—"

Another shelf crashed above. A shower of books fell from an upper floor. They smashed down around the policeman. He dropped to the ground, the shotgun clattering next to him.

Scruggs stepped over, scooped up the shotgun, and checked him. "He's knocked out." She leaned down and picked up the book that had hit him. "Look, another copy of The Big Book of Model Railroading." She hefted it. "I wonder if they'll let me keep it?"

CHAPTER THIRTY-ONE

"Ten credits on this one," Dirk said, handing Lee the credit chip.

"We're rich," Lee said. "Pilot, imagine all the places we can go with that much money."

She took the chip, slotted it into her comm, and transferred the money to their starport account.

"Sarcasm doesn't become you," Dirk said.

"What we've become is poor. Does that become us? Where did all our money go?"

"Silk and alligators, mostly. Some luxuries, like fuel and food."

"We're not very good smugglers," Lee said.

"There seems to be a knack for it," Dirk said. "Which we don't have." He held up another chip. "I think this one has three credits on it."

"Hardly worth it," Lee said.

"It gives me a feeling of completion, cleaning all these out," Dirk said.

"Give it to me. Speaking of cleaning, who's doing the heads now."

"I thought Scruggs—"

"Is tired of being the only person who does cleaning. You were wrong. There wasn't three credits on this chip."

"More?"

"Less, two credits, fifteen."

"That will get us a coffee."

"Not on this planet, too expensive. They sell some sort of herbal tea for that."

"What type of herbs?"

"They make some sort of industrial pine nut oil. There's a local tree that they pull seeds off of, mix 'em with a solvent, and crush them. Then they take the remaining food waste, sticks and old leaves that are left, and brew tea with them."

"They sell tea made of industrial byproducts? Who drinks that?"

"We have a case in the locker. Scruggs quite likes it."

Dirk slotted another chip into his comm and peered at the amount. "That girl has no sense of taste. Maybe it's a problem with her sense of smell."

"That's probably why she's been doing the cleaning with so few complaints. But she's said that's going to stop."

"She's the junior crew member. She needs to do the cleaning. You should explain that to her."

"Crew issues are the captain's prerogative."

"Really?"

"Yes. Says so in the manual for merchant skippers."

"It does?" He handed her the last chip. "Jackpot. Two hundred credits on this one."

"Wealth beyond imagining." Lee put the chip in her comm. "You haven't read the manual, have you?"

"I didn't know that we had any manuals. Are any of them useful?"

"There's one called 'How To Make A Million In Low-Risk Smuggling Jobs.' You should check it out."

"Really?"

"No." Lee pulled the last chip out of her comm. "Not really. Hi, Rocky."

The little black dog entered the control room, hopped up onto Lee's lap, and licked her face. She cooed at him.

"How'd he do during the flight here?"

"He sleeps either with me or Scruggs, depending on who's off shift. Dena rigged a harness for him, and we can strap him in on our bunks if we're maneuvering. He doesn't seem to mind."

"Where does he, you know, do his business?"

"Air lock. I put a tray in the corner. He's smart, figured it out."

"Does it smell?"

"No worse than you do when you forget to use your ship perfume on off days." She held up the last chip. "Anymore?"

"Not that I found," Dirk said. "How much do we have?"

Lee tapped her comm. "I just paid our fuel bill. That took our ready cash. So, they won't lock us down. Plenty of water, H, and O. We have plenty of food trays. Our landing fees are paid, but we can't afford starport power or any services. Nothing dangerous is broken, according to the engineer. Well, nothing really, really dangerous."

"So, we have fuel, water, food, life support, and a dirty ship. 'Outstanding,' as the centurion would say."

Lee looked at Dirk, who tapped screens. "Nothing back from the crew. We'll just wait till they tell us how things went."

"Things like espionage," Lee said.

"It's not that," Dirk said.

Lee looked at the screen. Her eyes misted.

Dirk coughed. "I'll talk to Scruggs. I'll use my moral authority to convince her to keep cleaning."

"Your moral authority?" Lee said. "You're an escaped convict."

"I was framed."

"You stole this ship."

"Borrowed, and we'll return it when we get a chance."

"We vandalized an office and stole data tapes."

"At the owners request. Or the operator's request."

"Then we stole containers right out of a yard."

"They're insured."

"We don't actually know that, do we?" Lee said. She hugged Rocky close, and he licked her face even more.

"Huh," Dirk said. "You know, that's true. We never did actually see any paperwork."

"Every single port we've been to we've gotten in some sort of brawl or battle. People get hurt, ships damaged, things stolen or set on fire, and now—"

Lee began to cry. Rocky whined a little and licked her face even more.

"Lee," Dirk said. He reached over to pat her shoulder. Rocky pushed his head out and growled at him. "I'm just trying. I just want—"

Rocky snarled and snapped his teeth.

Dirk yanked his hand back. "I just want to keep all my fingers. I'm sorry, Lee, I don't know how it came to this."

"We're useless as traders. And smugglers. And criminals."

"This should set us up—"

"As traitors. You swore an oath to defend the Empire, and now you're going to give secrets away to our enemies. I'm going to give away secrets. And you're okay with that."

Dirk dropped his hands on his lap. "Not really, I'm… it's complicated."

"Was it complicated before, when you were a rich duke?"

"No."

"So, now that we're poor, you've become a traitor. Is loyalty only for rich people?"

"I'm not rich. You're not rich. We're not rich," Dirk said. "Not anymore."

"I trusted you to do the right thing. To protect the Empire. And now you'll sell it out for a better class of tea?" Lee snuffled. "I'm a traitor. I'm a thief and a liar. I've given up everything I believe in."

"We're poor," Dirk said. He tapped his screen. "Things are always more complicated when you're poor."

The board in front of them lit up. Dirk had slaved one of the channels to the intercom. "Heads up, Heavyweight Items," Gavin's voice said. "Inbound hot. Drop as soon as we're on board. We're clear to our destination."

"Any problems?"

"Nothing worth mentioning," Gavin said.

Dirk tapped the screen. "Why do I not believe you?" he said.

Ana's voice broke in. "Because he's lying—that's why. There were problems. Police. Gunplay. Overdue library books. Get us out of here soonest."

Dirk thumped his head on the console. "Any good news?"

"Scruggs can run in heels," Gavin said. "And climb in them and all sorts of things."

"Can she fight in them?" Dirk asked. "Like Centurion taught her?"

"Very much so. In fact, I think she can do anything Centurion can, backward and in heels."

"She can?"

"She says she learned it in dance class."

"Outstanding," Dirk said. "I'm warming the systems up. Drop the chains as soon as you board. Once the air lock's shut, I'll drop and push us out. Engineer, you'll need to get to your console before we jump."

"Adventure awaits," Scruggs said.

Dirk closed his eyes. "I will not hit the kid. I will not hit the kid." He paged through his screen. "Lee, I need a course."

Lee kept sniffling but selected a course from some pre-loaded into her console.

"Buck up, Navigator. Your duke-pilot is on the job. I'll figure something out." He reached over to slap her shoulder.

Rocky's ears went back, and he growled at Dirk. Dirk pulled his hand back and looked at the crying navigator and the growling dog.

Dirk let out a breath. "Dog, you're probably the best judge of personality on this ship."

***

"I told you not to step there," Dena said as everybody gathered around the lounge table.

"There should not be piles of dog poop in the air lock," Ana said. "It's disgusting."

"He has to poop somewhere. That's where we showed him. It's not his fault that you can't tell the difference between a tray full of dog poop and a locker to stow your gear in."

"Lockers are on walls. He needs to do it somewhere else."

"Not when we're not under spin."

Lee sat. Rocky bounded up on her lap, and licked her face. "Don't listen to the mean man, Rocky," Lee said. "That's a fine place to poop. And if the mean man doesn't like it, I'll teach you to find his cabin."

Dirk slid a plate in front of each of them. "And speaking of poop," Ana said. "What's this now."

"Deep-fried fish," Dirk said.

"We've had fish for the last six meals," Lee said.

"And we'll have it for the next six. Or sixty, until we're done with that container, or we make a big score."

"I never thought I'd miss trays," Ana said.

"Trays cost money," Dirk said. "Fish are free. For us."

Scruggs came in, petted Rocky, picked up a tray, and ate, leaning against the wall. "Fish! Yay."

"Your optimism is . . ." Dirk said.

"Refreshing? Uplifting?" Scruggs said.

"Misplaced?" Ana said.

"I was going to say . . . never mind. How's the fish?"

"Great as always, Pilot."

Ana shook his head. "Private, your stomach is a marvel."

Scruggs beamed. "Thank you, Centurion. It's always nice to have a good meal." She grinned at Dirk.

Ana looked up at her. "Are you taller, Private?"

Scruggs stuck her leg out. "I'm wearing those boots that we got at Rockhaul. Dena convinced me that they show my legs off better."

"They do," Dena said. "It's a good look for her."

Rocky jumped off Lee's lap and barked.

Scruggs bent down and rubbed his forehead. "Do you want to go to the air lock, boy?"

Rocky's tail thumped, and Scruggs led him to the air lock.

Dena watched her go. "Once she got clothes that fit, she's actually a very pretty girl. And those boots work for her."

"I agree," Dirk said. "Makes her behind look sexy."

Everyone stopped eating and looked at him.

"What?" Dirk said. "I can't comment?"

"We're going to be traitors," Lee said. "Why not perverts as well?"

Dirk threw his hands up. "I mean, it looks very nice on her, but it's not like I'd ever, you know, do anything."

"Do what?" Scruggs said, coming back with Rocky.

"Just . . . do . . . stuff," Dirk said.

"Is this another job for me, Centurion?" Scruggs asked. "Is there something you need me to do, something to learn?"

Ana grinned. Everybody leaned back. "I told you to stop that," Dena said.

"Private, there's nothing I need you to do. But there are a few things you might want to learn."

"Always willing to learn something new, Centurion," Scruggs said.

"But not from me this time," Ana said. "I think Friend Dena will be a better teacher, in this case."

"Is that so. What do you want done? Some sort of job task."

"Not so much what . . ." Dena said. "A different use of the word. And it's not so much a task—more of a challenge. We'll talk about it later."

"Good idea," Dirk said. "We have more important things to discuss."

"Rebellion. Revolt. Treason," Lee said.

"Kind of agree with her," Ana said. "But too late to back out now. Onward to victory."

"Old man, we don't need your platitudes right now," Gavin said. "This is a for-real problem, not training troops."

"Train how you fight," Ana said. "And going in halfway will get us all way killed. What are we doing? How are we transferring these goods? And what are we transferring, anyway?"

Gavin explained the deal he'd worked out in the library and put the plans up on the console.

"Should we be looking at these?" Lee asked.

"No," Ana said. "We can get in a lot of trouble for looking at them."

"Oh, good, 'cause, even though we're selling Imperial secrets to the Nats, we wouldn't want to get in more trouble," Gavin said.

"We better make sure they're real," Dirk said. He paged through the plans. "If they're experts, they could check them and find something wrong. Things could go sideways in a hurry."

"Won't they say that they're fake regardless, just to cheat us out of our money?" Lee said.

"They could," Gavin said. "In fact, they probably will argue a little. But they don't want to scare us away."

"I'm scared enough now."

"The thing is," Dirk said, "they want real info. If these are totally fake, they'll kick us out. But if they're real or even close, they'll want more from where these came from. So, they'll pay top dollar for these and hope we bring more next time."

"There'll be a next time?" Lee asked. "They lied. Treason does prosper."

"Not if we get enough money," Scruggs said.

"These look real enough to me," Dirk said. "At least they look like plans I've seen before. I had access to plans during my . . . naval career."

"Former career," Ana said. "Find something you know and cross-check it. You said you were on some scout ships?"

"Yes," Dirk said.

"Well, the list is indexed," Ana said, tapping the console. "There. Max acceleration, max fuel capacity, max range for the weaponry. Did that match what you know?"

Dirk tapped a few settings and brought up details. "It matches what I remember from talking to the scouts. Looks accurate."

"Outstanding," Ana said. "So, these are real plans?"

"Seems like," Dirk said.

"There's a few questions, though," Scruggs said. She tapped the screen next to a number. "Look there, on this Pollux class frigate. It shows the new positron guns they're outfitting them with, rather than the older lasers."

"A posi-what?" Dena asked.

"It's a sub-atomic particle," Scruggs said. "Positron guns are experimental, but that range looks shorter than it should be. They should outrange the lasers. This shows them with only twenty percent of the laser's range."

"Why replace longer range weapons with shorter range ones?" Dena asked. "That's like replacing a rifle with a pistol."

"It works if your rifle is being replaced with ten pistols, though," Gavin said.

"Lasers disperse and scatter, and you can protect against them with sand. Sand's cheap. Positrons don't disperse as much—you can steer them magnetically, and they'll combine with electrons in the target and self-annihilate. That means that a less energetic positronic beam will produce more energy than a laser at the same power output, so positronic weapons will be more powerful than laser-based ones. And look here"—Gavin pointed to the blueprint—"they're in dual mounts rather than single, but the power couplings for the dual mount are smaller than the single mount laser couplings."

"That so?" Ana said. "So, shorter range versus more damage. I didn't know that. That read the same way to you, Navy?"

"It does," Dirk said. "That's what I was taught at the academy. But they were very much experimental then." He looked at Scruggs. "Are you sure they're positronic weapons?"

"Plans here show them installed." Scruggs pointed. "You can see the different-shaped turrets here, and the targeting radars are different-shaped than the lasers. No capacitors, either, they don't need them like the pulse lasers do. These are very detailed plans. Definitely the new positronic guns."

"Spend a lot of time reading deck plans of Imperial warships, do you, Private?" Ana asked.

Scruggs jerked her hand back. "I just—it's something I heard, that's all."

"Where did you hear that?" Ana asked.

"Just . . . somewhere, Centurion. Somewhere."

Dena smirked at Scruggs. "Does the little runaway girl know more about weapons than she should?"

"Indeed," Ana said. "Indeed, she does."

"Where did you learn that?" Dena said.

Scruggs was silent.

Ana laughed. "There's a mystery here. Navy there"—he pointed at Dirk—"he should know his way around starship weapons. He went to that fancy academy, after all. Me, I knew ground stuff. We use lasers and microwaves. The theory is the same, so I can follow the discussion, but I couldn't tell a set of starship plans from a circuit diagram for a microwave oven. But there's a mystery here, for sure."

"A mystery about why Scruggs knows so much about weapons that she could tell what type they were just by looking at the plans?" Dena asked.

"I should have said they're two mysteries here," Ana said. "One, how Scruggs knows what she knows." Ana pointed at Gavin. "And two, how does this punk kid know the regular size of power couplings in a Pollux class frigate?"

CHAPTER THIRTY-TWO

"I'm sorry, Tribune, but the blood won't come out," midshipman Calroy said, holding up a spray bottle of chemicals. "Even with the enzymes."

Devin, the Lord Lyon, looked up from behind his desk at the blood-stained armchair. "Never mind, you've done your best." He grimaced. "That was my favorite chair."

"Should I remove this chair, Tribune?" he asked.

"Just leave it for now. That will be all."

"Tribune," Calroy said, saluting across his chest, which Devin returned. Calroy didn't move.

"What is it, midshipman?"

"When will my punishment be finished sir?"

"You don't like cleaning?"

"No especially, no sir. It's beneath me."

Devin looked back at his screen. "We are Imperial officers. Nothing necessary is beneath us. Dismissed."

After he left, Devin rested his chin on his hand and stared at the spot until the door alarm bonged. "What?" he said to his intercom.

"Your ever loyal second in command craves audience with his Imperial muchness, Lord Lyon," Subprefect Lionel said.

Devin pressed a button, and the subprefect came in. Lionel sat in front of his desk and looked at the stained armchair against the wall. "Stains didn't come out, huh, Tribune?"

"No."

"They have this enzyme spray—"

"Tried it. Didn't work."

"Wasn't that your favorite chair?"

"It was."

"Pretty selfish of the senator, bleeding all over your best furniture. Good thing you made sure he won't do that again."

Devin leaned back and hung his head. "You cannot speak to me this way. I'm an Imperial Tribune. I can have you executed for any reason I want."

"You don't even need a reason, given your Imperium and all," Lionel said.

Devin rubbed his eyes. "Aren't you the least bit frightened of me? Shouldn't you be scared that I'll have you killed?"

"Will I get to use your sword?" Lionel asked. "Because the senator seemed to think—"

"To the Imperial hells with the senator," Devin said.

"Well, you certainly guaranteed that," Lionel said.

Devin gritted his teeth. "He was my cousin, and I killed him."

"Second cousin. And technically, you just gave him a sword."

"I'm the one who enforced the warrant."

"Maybe not do that next time?" Lionel asked.

"Be careful. That's treason."

"You've already threatened to kill me once so far in this conversation. What's a little treason? Besides, you only kill people if you're ordered to."

"That's not the point," Devin said.

"It kind of is exactly the point." Lionel leaned forward. "Tribune, anybody else would have killed me by now or killed some of the crew or the odd freighter captain and probably hacked a passing mungo bird to death on general principle. At least you're trying to enforce the actual laws, as opposed to the Imperial Chancellor's whims. Problem is you're confused. Which are which?"

"The Imperial Chancellor is the Emperor's deputy." Devin stared at the chair.

"Wonder if the Emperor knows his deputy is shaking down senators, then killing them and their families if they don't pay up."

"Surely, that's not the case?" Devin asked.

"Sounded like it with your cousin, Senator Marcus," Lionel said.

"He was just trying to save his worthless hide. He always was a bandit," Devin said.

"Might want to double-check that," Lionel said. "Ask somebody who might know. I wonder who might know that. Maybe an Empress? Don't you know one?"

"First excuse I get, I'm having you executed," Devin muttered.

"Ahhh, I'll bet you tell that to all your subordinates. The other nobles do, so we low-level peons are used to it."

"Why are you here? What's your report?"

"Good news and bad news."

"Start with the bad news."

"A new intelligence summary arrived. You'll have to look at it and confirm receipt."

"Summarize, please."

"Can't. It's sealed to you only. Big update, too, if the file size is anything to go by. Take you hours to go through."

"Wonderful. Good news?"

"Brigadier Santana has finished his drill and wants you to invite him to dinner. He says your cook is much better than his."

"He's right. That's good news. He's always entertaining. When is he available?"

"Tonight, he says."

"Tell Imin to set it up," Devin said. "Anything else?"

"Yes."

"Good or bad?"

"Not sure."

"What is it?"

"While we were gallivanting after passenger liners—"

"Tribunes do not gallivant," Devin said

"Traipsing? Meandering?" Lionel said. "Never mind. While we were gallivanting after passenger liners . . . A courier found Santana in the outer system. They transferred a member of Internal Security to his ship. He's bringing her with him. She has something she needs to brief you personally on."

"How's a briefing by a ranking Internal Security officer good news?"

"It's the woman who you met before, the one who likes you."

"Hernandez?"

"The same. Is this good news or bad news, Tribune?"

"By the Emperor's hairy nostrils, I don't know. I really don't know."

***

As a tribune appointed directly by the Emperor, Devin stood second only to sector governors, admirals of the fleet, and generals of the armies in order of precedence. As a royal duke, he ranked almost every noble in the Empire except the royal family, and possibly even one of them—if you counted rubbing spit goobers into the Empress's hair when she was five as 'ranking' her.

Either way, he didn't make a habit of meeting his guests at the dock. He waited in his dining room.

The door whished open, and the Marines stepped in and aside, then the subprefect escorted Hernandez and Santana into the room.

He looked at Hernandez's uniform. "You're a Lieutenant Colonel now? You were a lieutenant before. Are you a Lieutenant Colonel?"

"That's the uniform I'm wearing right now," Hernandez said.

"Which one is correct?"

"Do you care?"

"Not for a second." Santana followed her through the door. "Brigadier, welcome. How was your extreme weather training?"

Santana grinned. "Three of my troops had to be evacuated for frostbite. A whole squad had their water freeze and had to lick ice for hydration. A million credit long-range artillery system was destroyed when some idiot hit the aiming mechanism with a hammer. The cold made the metal so brittle it shattered like glass."

"I see. A huge success, then?"

"Completely. But I should have listened to that master sergeant. He told me not to try to hammer the aiming wheel."

"You were there? On the ground?"

208

"For the whole week. I got second-degree frostbite. My toes are black. Would you like to see them?"

"Perhaps after dinner," Devin said. "Imin, bring the first course, please, and then a bucket of warm water for the brigadier to soak his feet in. Or his brains. His choice."

The food appeared, and they talked of trivialities until dinner was done.

Lionel stood. "Tribune, with your permission, I have the watch."

"Senior officers don't take watches," Devin said.

"I'm covering for comm while she does some tutoring for the midshipmen."

"Uncover, I need you here."

"Tribune, unless you order me to stay, I'm leaving you behind to have secret conversations with your guests."

Devin looked at the plates Imin had placed in front of them. "But we're having bread pudding."

Lionel stood and waited. Devin waved his hand. "Fine. Go." Lionel gave the cross-chest salute. "The Empire," he said. Devin returned it.

Imin placed bowls in front of everybody. Santana tasted his. "This is amazing, Steward, the subprefect will be sorry he missed it."

"Oh, he won't miss it, sir," Imin said. "I saved some for him. And the Tribune always has us make a lot extra when he has a dinner party. He shares it out among the crew."

Santana gestured at his plate. "The crew eat like this?"

"Not all of them, sir," Imin said. "And not always. But there's a selection, a rotation. If it's your birthday or a service anniversary, you get something, or if you come on top of your division in drills or pass a test or a new baby or something like that. The bosun keeps track, and the tribune just makes me cook double or triple, and we all get something eventually."

"Outstanding," Santana said. "And this tastes wonderful."

"Thank you, sir. Tribune, if you're done with me?"

"We can get our drinks ourselves. Thank you, Imin," Devin said.

Imin exited, and they sat in silence, swallowing.

"No wonder your crew adores you, Tribune," Hernandez said. "If you feed them like this."

"A better crew than I deserve," Devin said.

"I agree," Hernandez said.

Devin frowned at her. "You're supposed to argue or something."

"I won't. It's sad."

"Sad?"

"You give them some cake occasionally, and in return, they risk their life on your whims."

"I don't risk them on a whim. I'm not whimsical."

"So, is a non-whim death any better?"

Devin scraped his bowl and didn't answer. Hernandez looked at Santana.

"Brigadier, do you bribe your men with food, too?"

"Food?" Santana said. "Of course not. They're Marines. They don't need to be bribed with food." He licked his spoon. "Weapons, we bribe them with guns."

"Guns? What do you mean?"

"Rather than give them food when they perform, we let them shoot something or blow something up. For your birthday, we let you throw grenades. Promotion, shoot off mortars. We had one beat the record on the obstacle course. We let them fire off our heavy artillery."

"He was an artillery specialist?"

"She. Nope. Combat logistics. Totally muffed the actual firing. Lost the tip of her finger in the recoil."

"That's horrible."

"She didn't think so. She framed the x-ray and put it on the wall of her squad room. That picture was so popular we had to make copies."

"You're both kind of crazy, you know that?"

"We serve the Emperor," Santana said. "Tribune, Internal Security has some sort of intelligence briefing for you. She said I should be here for it."

"Yes, Tribune," Hernandez said. "Did you read the intelligence briefing?"

"No," Devin said.

"Well, then you'll have seen—what?"

"I don't read them. They're all the same."

"Really? Can you enlighten me on their sameness?"

"Yes." Devin ticked things off on his fingers. "One. The Nats hate us and want to go to war with us. Two. The Confeds hate us and want to go to war with us. Three, they hate each other as well, and that's the only thing that is keeping them from going to war with us. Four, as soon as they see the chance of getting away with going to war with us or each other and winning, they'll do it. Five, let's not have that happen. Six, the independent planets don't like us, and don't want to join the Empire, no matter what external affairs says. Seven, most of our own planets in this sector don't like us either because we ignore them except at tax time. Eight, there are too many pirates. Nine, we don't have enough ships to patrol for the pirates. Ten, every one of these things gets worse every update." Devin regarded the table. "I think that covers it."

"Impressive, Tribune," Santana said. "But you didn't mention that we don't have enough Marines to deal with the revolts, either."

"I always stop at ten."

"Because you don't think Marines are important?"

"Because I don't want to take off my shoes," Devin said. "What's in the intelligence update, Colonel?"

"Well, it's . . . it's pretty much what you said, actually. Except that pirate activity in this sector is down over fifty percent and dropping since your ship has been . . . what's the word we used?"

"Lollygagging?"

"That's it. Since you've been lollygagging around, the pirates have fled."

"Why?" Devin asked. "We haven't caught that many."

Hernandez looked at her glass and raised her eyebrows.

"Sorry," Devin said. "Let me get you something." He stepped to the sideboard and poured drinks for them all. "Try this." He set them on the table. "It's related to bourbon."

Santana sipped and licked his lips a few times. "Related by marriage? Distantly related by marriage? 'Cause I wouldn't admit to being related to something like this."

"It takes some getting used to," Devin agreed. "Colonel, you were saying? My very presence strikes fear in the pirates."

"Yes," Hernandez said before sipping. "How did you know?"

"Know what? That I scare the pirates?"

"You do. Our intelligence indicates that literally dozens of pirates have fled the system—all—so they won't tangle with you."

"That can't be true. I have only the Pollux," Devin said. "It's one ship—well-drilled, I'll admit—and I think it's the best ship in the fleet, but others would disagree."

"Not the pirates, apparently. Once they got the word, they fled," Hernandez said.

"But why?" Devin asked.

"Money," Santana said.

"What?" Devin said.

Santana pushed his drink toward Devin. "I don't think I'll finish that. Tribune, can I have something a little less . . . sophisticated? With less bite? Like rocket fuel or gasoline?"

Devin got up and rummaged in the cabinet. "There's a bottle of cheap whiskey that Imin used to clean the floor with here."

"Half glass, no ice."

Devin poured and shoved it at him. "We were talking about money."

"You have it," Santana said.

"That's not a surprise."

"Lots of other people don't," Santana said.

"Stop being so obtuse."

"If you're the captain of a warship on anti-pirate patrol in Imperial space, what's the best way to make money?"

"Sell tourist excursions to view the Crab Nebula? Out with it," Devin said.

"Bribes. Take bribes," Santana said. "Let the pirates pay you off. They stay away from the big lines, anything owned by a core family. They can hunt Confed or Nat ships or small independents. They capture them, sell the contents, pay you off. Or even sell the contents direct to you, in some cases."

"That would never work," Devin said. "You'd need to have a whole ship's crew be corrupt and have some sort of shipyard to deal with the ships and crews."

"Your crew will risk death for you because you give them bread pudding," Santana said. "And also because you try to enforce the law. Imagine what would happen if you gave them a fortune in stolen goods. And really, you'd only need the officers in on it. Find a frontier planet with a tiny repair yard, a few of its own ships, and just take your cut. It could be done."

Devin was silent for a moment, then turned to Hernandez, who nodded.

"I don't believe it," Devin said.

"Okay," Santana said.

"Do you have proof?"

"No. Proof is hard to come by."

"No Imperial noble would lower themselves to this level."

"You know more nobles than I do, Tribune. You're better placed to judge," Santana said. He gulped his drink. "Much better. This is much more my style." He held up his glass. "May I have some more, Tribune?"

"Help yourself," Devin said. His gaze clouded, and he seemed to be looking inward.

Santana stood, grabbed the bottle, and poured himself another drink. He gestured to Hernandez, who pushed her old glass to him. He poured her one as well and sat.

"There must be some other explanation," Devin said.

"Surely," Santana agreed. "But I'm a simple fellow. I don't understand these things. Explain it to me."

"I don't take bribes. There hasn't been any attempt to bribe me."

"I hear that your cousin tried to give you a fortune to let him go. You didn't take it."

"It wasn't an offer, it was . . . a discussion. He was worried about his people."

"See, Colonel?" Santana raised his glass. "Tribune is so rich he doesn't even recognize a bribe when it's actually dropped in front of him. He thinks it's a discussion." Santana and Hernandez clinked glasses.

"I don't believe it," Devin said. He leaned forward and punched his comm.

"Bridge, Subprefect Lionel," Lionel said.

"Subprefect," Devin said. "Those pirate captains that we caught, did they try to bribe you? Bribe me?"

"Every single one of them, Prefect."

"Why didn't you tell me?"

"Tribune," Lionel said, "we don't tell you when they vomit on the deck, either, and you're probably just as interested in that as you are in bribes. Probably more interested. You get offended by a dirty ship."

"How much?"

"How much did they bribe? Don't know. They could say anything."

"Do they ever indicate that they're . . . involved with . . ."

"Other noble families? All the time. Last one said I'd regret stopping him because he knew people."

212

"What did you say?"

"That we knew people, too, and our people were way more dangerous than his."

"What did he say to that?"

"Bbbbbllllleeerrrgggge."

"What?"

"We opened the air lock at that point, and he blew out. Couldn't make out what he was saying."

Devin stared at the intercom. Finally, he said, "Thank you, Subprefect. Out." He stared at the others. "I will have to think on this. Can we talk on something else?"

"I could tell you how the plan you worked with us previously went," Hernandez said.

"Yes," Devin said. "Your intelligence mission with the Nats. Your drop off, boarding thing that we did with you. Where we put you and Weeks onto that ship. How did that work out?"

"Unmitigated disaster," Hernandez said. "Our intelligence got misdirected, then stolen. Our courier got into a fight, and pirates escaped with Imperial secrets. Weeks stayed to try to cut down the fallout. We had shooting, betrayal of agents, lots of noise, a general cluster."

Santana blinked. "Wow. Even the Marines don't admit to that huge a disaster without temporizing. Must have been epic for you to describe it that way."

"It was," Hernandez said.

"What were you trying to do, anyway?" Santana asked.

"Normally, that's on a need-to-know, but interestingly enough, now the two of you need to know."

"Know what?" Devin said. He swallowed the last of his drink and looked at the empty glass. Santana stood, grabbed the cheap whiskey, and poured him a drink. He also topped off Hernandez's glass.

"We were trying to get some intelligence out to some people so that they could act on it. It got intercepted, misrouted, all manner of things. But now it looks like we can salvage the situation. We can strike a blow for the Empire against both the Nats and the Confeds."

"And save your reputation at the same time, no doubt," Santana said.

"Isn't that the most important thing?" Hernandez said. "Regardless, we can do the Emperor's work and come out looking good in the process."

"Doing well by doing good."

"Precisely. But we need your and the tribune's help."

"Do we get to blow up some pirates?" Santana asked.

"Maybe."

"Then, I'm in," Santana said. "What do we need to do?"

"We need the tribune to help."

"What do you want?" Devin asked.

"Remember your friend, Dirk Friedel, you want to talk to?"

"I want to do more than talk to him," Devin said.

"And yet, you've had several opportunities that you haven't—"

"Haven't what?" Devin said. "I don't take well to innuendos. What do you want from me?"

"Would you like another conversation with your friend, Dirk?"

"Yes."

"We can tell you where he'll be in a few days."

"I would like that. We'll talk. Then I'll blow him up."

"Well"—Hernandez looked at her drink—"about that."

"What now?" Devin asked.

"There's a complication."

"What?"

"Not a what." Hernandez drained her drink. "A who."

CHAPTER THIRTY-THREE

"I never thought we'd be back here," Lee said.

"I never wanted to be back here," Ana said.

"I don't actually know how to land here," Dirk said.

The crew turned to Dirk. The Heart's Desire had finished jumping to the Papillon system and was on course for the planet. They had been laying out the final course.

"We landed here last time," Ana said. "On those pads." He sniffed. "What's that smell?"

"I was drunk when I landed," Dirk said. He also sniffed. "Sweat. Circulating fan must have failed again."

"You're always drunk when we land," Ana said. "So what. And why hasn't the engineer fixed those fans?"

"Because we don't have any spares. We can't afford them." Dirk tapped his screen. "I'm not anymore. Drunk, I mean. I don't drink when I land."

Ana and Lee looked at each other. Lee nodded. "I think it's true. Pilot doesn't stink of booze anymore when we're landing."

"You mean," Ana said, "it's just his personal stench that you have to deal with?"

"I don't stench," Dirk said. "I wash."

"It's more of a reek," Lee said.

"What's the difference? Reek versus stench?" Ana asked.

"Stench is overpowering," Lee said. "You can't tell what it is. But reek is more specific. With Pilot Dirk, it's mostly his feet that I smell. Moldy or fungus."

"True, he does remind me of rotting wood when I have to sit next to him."

"To Imperial Hades with you two," Dirk said. "You don't smell like flowers, either."

"I'm always clean," Ana said. "Other than when I'm exercising. And I use ship perfume twice a day on my non-water days."

"I use a floral scent," Lee said.

"Really?" Dirk asked. "You two think you smell better than me?"

Ana tapped his comm. "Nature Girl, you there?"

"Stop calling me that," Dena said. "What do you want?"

"What does Lee smell like?"

"Her perfume? Flowers."

"And me?"

"Something tangy. Masculine." Dena paused. "Citrus."

"What about the pilot? What does he smell like?"

"Booze, mostly, when he doesn't smell like feet."

"I do not smell like feet," Dirk said.

"Thank you, Nature Girl." Ana tapped another button. "Engineer?"

"What do you want, Old Man?" Gavin said.

"Everybody gets rude when they get tense," Ana said. "What does the pilot smell like?"

"Booze."

"Lately?"

"Well," Gavin said, "no, he doesn't smell of booze anymore."

"Anything else?"

"No, no booze."

"Ha," Dirk said. "See?"

"Of course, there's always that feet smell around him on off days, when he doesn't shower. But that doesn't count. It's a personal thing. Always there. Maybe his diet or something."

"We all eat the same food."

"Good point, Old Man."

"I told you not to call me that, Punk."

"You did, Old Man, you did."

Ana tapped his comm off. "It's official, Navy. By popular vote, you're the smelly kid in class."

Dirk played with his controls. "This is embarrassing."

"Smell does not make a person, Pilot," Lee said. "Paterfather Zeus has said that it is inner worth and skill, that shows the true person. With the upcoming landing, you have an opportunity to demonstrate your worth in Zeus's eyes."

An hour later, they were on the ground. Gavin popped the ramp in the hab section, then let it crash to the ground. He raced down, ignoring the dry dust and the heat, stepped off the ramp, dropped to his knees, and vomited profusely.

Scruggs followed him down and puked next to him. They sprawled on the ground, wiping their mouths, breathing hard. Dena stumbled down the ramp next and sat next to them, panting.

"That was the worst yet," Gavin said. "I barely made it here."

"Me, too, the worst," Scruggs said.

"I'll have you know, children, that I don't need to puke," Dena said.

"Really? That didn't bother you?"

"It did. I already puked all over my cabin. What's wrong with the pilot? These get worse and worse."

Ana strode down the ramp. "The pilot has stopped drinking," he said.

"Can we have a vote on that?" Gavin said. "All of us?"

Rocky the Dog trotted down the ramp. He sniffed the two women, licked Scruggs's face, then went over and peed against the landing strut.

"I just fixed that," Gavin said. "Don't let him do that. It'll get rusty."

"You mean metals hardened for deep-space transit will be destroyed by dog pee? Then, we need better struts."

"It's different. It's acid and stuff. Why do we still have that dog?"

"He's one of the few crew members who doesn't puke when we land," Lee said. "Right, boy?"

Rocky wagged his tail.

"He poops in the air lock," Gavin said.

"And Dena pukes in her cabin," Lee said. "Tow-may-tow, tow-mah-tow. Besides, he's a good watch dog. He'll bark when strangers and undesirable people come close."

Rocky turned to the ramp, barked, then showed his teeth and growled.

Dirk was coming down the ramp.

Ana laughed. "Can't argue with his evaluations of people, at least."

Dirk stopped and extended his hand. "Nice doggy."

Rocky growled again. Dirk stepped back. "Why does that dog hate me so much?"

"We all hate you right now," Dena said. "He's just better at getting his point across."

"Everyone, listen up," Ana said. "Gavin and I have talked about this, and we've got a plan."

"Shouldn't you have run that by me, Centurion?"

"Navy," Ana said, "we've talked about this before. In orbit, flying, whatever, you do your pilot thing. But we're on terra firma, so this is a security matter."

"So, why'd you talk to the engineer?"

"Because we're also selling stolen goods, and he's our most talented criminal."

"I'm not a criminal," Gavin said. "I'm a smuggler, if I'm anything."

"Isn't a smuggler just a type of criminal, Engineer?" Scruggs said.

"Not the time, youngster," Dirk said. "You two worked this out?"

"We did," Ana said. "And we both agree." He looked at the skeptical faces around them. "Surprised the heck out of me, too, but on some things, we think similarly. Engineer, you're up."

Gavin explained the plan. The spies knew him, so he was going as the main contact. Ana and Dena would be the backup team to help out with problems. . Gavin would bring the five percent of data that they had promised, and the Nat buyers would evaluate it. Gavin was going to ask for the money at that point, and they would transfer the rest of the data after they got the money by physical hand-off. Lee would stay on board. Since she was a Jovian she was too noticeable, and they didn't want to attract attention. More attention.

"Can't we just send them the data electronically?"

"In theory," Gavin said. "In practice, there is a huge volume of it. Starship plans aren't small. We would be a long while sending it, even at high speeds, so a physical transfer on a storage chip is better."

"Where am I in this?" Scruggs asked.

"Private," Ana said, "I need you here with a weapon. They know our ship. They'll be watching for it. You've proved that you can keep boarders off, so we'll keep you here."

"I'm staying with the pilot and navigator?"

"With the navigator. The pilot's coming with us."

Dirk crossed his arms. "I'm going to the hand off? Why?"

"Just to show your pretty face, Navy. Just to show your pretty face."

Gavin and Dirk cleared Papillon customs with the usual intense security and rigorous physical searches.

"They enjoy that far too much," Gavin said.

"Or you do," Dirk said. "Why did they choose here? Papillon, I mean. It's such a pain to get in, and the security's so tight."

"It's because of that, Skipper," Gavin said. "Means that nobody has a weapon."

"Those Confeds had weapons last time."

"Those guys with machine guns? Big bribe. And can't do it more than once. Remember, they don't want to kill us. They want to talk to us. They want this data."

"I need to figure out a way to get weapons past the customs people," Dirk said.

"Drop 'em somewhere outside of town on approach, and pick 'em up later," Gavin said.

"That's a great idea."

"Done it before. Just need a transponder that we can ping and ground transport."

"Outstanding. I'm surprised at you, Engineer."

"I contain multitudes."

Dirk raised an eyebrow.

"Fine. I have experience. Check this place out, Skipper." Gavin pointed at a restaurant.

"Lunch and dinner specials. Fresh vegetables. Homemade soup. Local wines. Looks marvelous."

"It does. Too bad we're not going there," Gavin said, pointing next door. "That's our place."

"Cheap beer," Dirk read. "Draft. Pitchers. Alcohol odd lots." He frowned. "What's an odd lot?"

"Best not to ask." Gavin pushed the door open, and they went inside.

They sat and ordered draft beers. Dirk said it was the worst beer in the galaxy. Gavin pointed out they hadn't been to the entire galaxy.

"I'll bet on it right now," Dirk said. "You pay ten now. I'll give you back fifty if we ever find worse." He sipped it and grimaced. "You didn't want Scruggs here. Why not?"

"Actually, I did want her here," Gavin said. "Centurion talked me out of it.

First, as a guard, she's great. She actually shoots people."

"I shoot people," Dirk said.

"Not really, and not without thinking. Centurion's trained her to fire without thinking. She sees a threat, she fires. You want to stop and talk about it?"

"True," Dirk said. "But that's not the real reason, is it?"

"What do you think, Skipper?" Gavin asked.

He put his mug to his mouth and surveyed the crowd. He didn't actually drink any beer.

"You want ex-Imperial officer shamed and exiled, Duke Dirriken Friedel, the Butcher of New Madrid here. They'll think that I'm the one who stole this data, and I'm selling it to damage the Empire."

"Gotta admit it makes a good story, doesn't it?"

Gavin waved a server over and ordered two different beers off her tray. She made Gavin pay in advance before dropping them on the table.

Gavin took a drink. "This beer stinks."

Dirk tried his. "Almost as bad as my reputation does."

Gavin nodded. "That's on you, Skipper."

"You didn't have to make it worse."

"Dena didn't have to drag our worthless butts through the woods. Lee and I didn't have to dig through swamp water to try to salvage our goods. Ana didn't have to get in a firefight with only his private parts and a mortar shell as weapons. Scruggs didn't have to shoot somebody climbing into the ship."

"We're all wanted people."

"Some of us are more wanted than others, Skipper," Gavin said. "Most of the time, it's the great Duke Friedel that people want to talk to, not some two-bit criminal Gavin Crewjacki."

"I don't think you're two-bit."

"Join the minority." Gavin looked at a man walking across the bar. "Showtime."

The nondescript man sat with them. His eyes and hair were brown, his skin suit gray, as were his coveralls. They had a red-and-blue logo that had no words on it. "Hello, friends. I'm going to order a beer so things look normal."

"You do that," Gavin said. "What's your name?"

"You can call me Art."

"That's what the last guy said."

"Yes."

"Fine, you're Art-2."

Art-2 ordered a beer from a passing waiter, and they sat in silence till the beer returned. Art-2 took a long pull of the beer. "Ahhh. This is the worst beer I've had in forever. That can just sit there." He put the mug down.

Gavin scanned him. "You guys surely have this bland blend in thing down well. I'm sitting across from you, and I can't describe you."

"Tradecraft," Art-2 said. "You should learn some before you make any big mistakes, get yourselves killed."

"We don't make mistakes," Gavin said.

"This guy"—Art-2 pointed at Dirk—"is Duke Dirriken Friedel, an escaped prisoner, one of the most wanted criminals in the Empire."

"Good thing we're not in the Empire, then," Dirk said. "Just a border planet."

"One with close ties to the Empire. I could denounce you right now to planetary security, and you'd be in a fix."

"And you wouldn't get your plans," Gavin said. "You do want the plans, don't you?"

"I had friends on New Madrid."

"Everybody had friends on New Madrid," Dirk said. "It must be the friendliest planet in the galaxy. So what."

"You didn't have to kill all those people."

"I didn't do it personally."

"Well, get them killed," Art-2 said.

"Kill me or deal with me. Your choice," Dirk said. He glanced at his comm. "Happy hour starts soon. You think this beer is bad? Imagine what the cheap stuff will taste like."

"You promised a sample to give to our engineers," Art-2 said.

Gavin slid a chip across the table. Art-2 clicked it into his comm. "That's being sent to people nearby, who understand such things. We'll sit and relax while they examine it. Oh, and we're broadcasting to them. They can hear us."

"Will this take long?" Dirk said.

"Have an appointment, your Grace? Have to meet with the Emperor and discuss the current border situation?"

"Bite my ducal buttocks," Dirk said. "You know what I mean."

"I'm not used to royalty," Art-2 said. "Did I commit some sort of social faux-pas?"

"It could take days to validate that information," Dirk said. "We'll be here forever."

"It won't take days. We're just comparing a very small part of what you gave us against a known quantity. You just don't know which part. See, we have a lot of these plans already. We're just going to compare them against what we have. If they match, we deal. If not, well, I'll have to look up the bounty on one Dirk Friedel." Art-2's comm bonged. "Well, that was quick. Let's see if we're still friends." He studied his screen.

Gavin's hands were below the table, but his right drifted to his knives.

Art-2 nodded. "Good news. We're almost best friends. We'll take the rest."

"We'll take the money first," Gavin said.

Art pulled a chip out of his pocket and gave it to Gavin. "We pay our bills. It's part of the bland, non-threatening thing we do. Here's payment for the second tranche."

"This is a regular bank account here," Gavin said.

"Good as cash here. And less noticeable. We're a trading company. You have a ship. We paid you for a load. Happens all the time. Thousands of transactions like that every day."

"That works," Gavin said. He slid another chip across the table. "Here's the coordinates for the hand-over. It's in far orbit. There's a lot of traffic there, so we can shuttle it across."

"You don't have the rest of the data with you?"

"No."

"Transmit it. We'll give you an address."

"It's too much to transmit. You know that," Gavin said.

"We do," Art-2 said. "Wasn't sure if you did. So, we just let you walk away and hope that you meet us where you say you will."

"Pretty much," Gavin said.

"Okay," Art-2 said. "See you there."

Gavin and Dirk exchanged glances. "That's it? Just see you there."

"Is there any reason not to trust you? You weren't planning a double cross, were you?"

"No."

"Well, then." Art-2 stood. "See you soon."

Dirk and Gavin stood.

"One thing, though," Art-2 said. He flipped his hand open to reveal a small revolver. "I've got this. The others here do as well."

"Why does everybody except us always have guns here?" Dirk said.

"We pay much, much better bribes," Art said. "First, there's a different meeting point on that chip. One looooong jump away. We'll see you there ASAP. And we want something else."

"What?" Gavin said.

"You"—he pointed at Gavin—"go to your ship, get the data, and meet us. You"—he pointed at Dirk—"Royal Duke Friedel. You're coming with us. To our ship. We'll chat about the court and your time playing croquet with the royal family while we wait for what we paid for." He smiled at them. "Won't that be fun?"

CHAPTER THIRTY-FOUR

Ana and Dena sat at the cafe on the main street across from Gavin and Dirk. Eateries lined the main street. The spaceport secured area debouched there, adjacent to a long distance monorail station and the central public transit hub. The spaceport was one of the biggest employers on the planet, its entertainment district bustling night and day.

"Get the special, Centurion," Dena said. "There's soup, a salad, and some sort of meat for a main."

"I don't eat 'some sort of meat,'" Ana said. "I like mine to have a name."

"Like Sue or Rashid? Or Honey Bumpkins."

"Like beef or pork or goose. No mystery meat."

"You eat goose? I love goose. The red meat, barbecued with a sauce."

"Yes, marinated in vinegar for a day and cooked for another," Ana said.

"Maybe we're more alike than you think."

"Now you're just being nasty. Somebody's joined Gavin and Dirk. He bought a beer."

"That's what you notice? The beer."

"He's completely nondescript. Pale, small, short hair, but not too short. If he put on a colorful cap or carried a yellow toolbox, we'd never identify him. He's a pro."

Dena adjusted her hair. "I can't see in the mirror this time."

The waiter arrived, and they both ordered the special. The soup and salad showed up at the same time. Ana ate as he kept watch across the road.

"Are you sure they won't notice us?" Dena asked.

"All these outdoor cafes, too many people." Ana notched his head sideways. "We're just one of at least ten people who have a direct view of that table. Our punk engineer picked the perfect table for being seen without the people watching having to identify themselves."

"This soup is even better than the last time," Dena said. "Well, we're lucky he picked there."

"It's more a stew but very good. Spicy." Ana slurped down the last bit and took big bites out of the sandwich in front of him. "And this is actual pork in here. Spicy, too. It wasn't luck, it was deliberate—the punk passed up four other tables with worse sightlines to pick that one. He's done an observed hand-off before."

"He did seem to know how to pick the tables."

"If only he wasn't so nervous."

"How can you tell?" Dena asked.

"I know him. He's just sipping his beer. Normally, he takes big swigs. He's being dainty. He should work on that."

"Same as you should work on your eating. When you're nervous, you eat fast."

Ana looked down at his nearly empty plate and the fragment of sandwich he held in his hand, then across at Dena's substantial meal. "Will you look at that. I'm still learning things, even at my age." He put the sandwich down. "Good observation. I knew I could count on you to keep your head."

"I'm inexperienced with the culture here, not stupid."

"Hard to tell the two apart," Ana said. "The new guy, he's got a chip in a reader now."

"Happy days," Dena said. She waved the waiter over, ordered two bitter coffees, and paid the whole bill. "And now, as the great senior centurion has taught me, we can linger as long as we want, talking over our coffees, or we can bolt right out, having already paid."

"It's nice to have a student that listens," Ana said.

"Scruggs isn't good enough for you?"

"She listens well, but she's very . . . straightforward in her thinking. She's brave, but sometimes oblivious. You're more oblique in your thinking."

"I'm not sure oblique is a compliment."

"How did you talk her into getting dressed up at that last place, anyway? I'd never have been able to convince her to do that."

"I know fashion, I know clothes, and I know what men want. I just helped her improve on some natural ability. You should try different clothes yourself." Dena gave his ironed ship suit a once-over. "I'll teach you about something called colors. You'll like it."

"Well, in my case, you can't teach an old dog new tricks."

"In your case, you're not a dog. You're just old."

"I'd be wounded, except it's true. Why'd you do it? Help her?"

Dena sipped her coffee and nearly spat it out. "Tastes like cleaning fluid. You said something once about teaching each other."

"Must have been one of my old-dog moments," Ana said. "Surprised you were listening."

"Most of what you say is low-grade maneuvering fuel, but occasionally, you get it right. If I'm going to survive, I have to learn from the others, get them to teach me things. And the only things I have to trade is teaching them things or sleeping with them. And that wouldn't work with Scruggs."

"Because she's so wholesome?"

"Because I tried to see if she was interested, and she wasn't. Didn't even know what I was suggesting."

"Must have confused her."

"More surprised, I think. She seems to understand a lot of things in a theoretical way but not really notice them when they're in front of her. Kind of like she's always seen the universe through a pane of glass."

"Some people are like that," Ana agreed. "Gavin is getting up and moving. About time."

"You were worried?"

"No, we've been here long enough. I'd have had to drink some of that lousy coffee."

Gavin, Dirk, and the new man walked down the pedestrian mall to a staircase that led to the plaza in front of the starport entrance.

Dirk and the man stepped into the entrance and disappeared from view. Dirk hadn't made any fuss about going away. Gavin hopped up and sat on an ornamental planter, swinging his knees like a sightseer without a care in the world.

Ana took Dena's arm and swung her around the opposite side behind Gavin. "Stop and fix your shoe right there." Dena came up to the planter and leaned a leg on the top and played with the buckles on her shoes.

Ana crossed his arms, glared at Dena, and turned so that his back was to Gavin. There wasn't anybody else within earshot. "Status, Engineer?" he said, loud enough to be heard over his shoulder.

Gavin didn't turn back to them but answered in a low voice. "I'm heading back to the ship. Dirk is going with our contact. We've got an orbital rendezvous, but not in this system, and they want to keep Dirk with them till the hand-over."

"If it was up to me, they could keep Navy forever, but this could be a bit of a problem," Ana said. "Should we intervene?"

"And do what? Run after him and have a stern conversation? We don't have any weapons. They're armed. One of them is, at least."

"Do you have to flash yourself like that?" Ana said.

Dena had put an extra bend into her leg lift, and a group of young men had responded positively with whistles from across the plaza. "Not that I care, but we're supposed to blend in here."

"You and Gavin keep talking," Dena said, bending farther. "Trust me, nobody is paying you and him any attention at all right now."

Ana scowled and glared at the boys. "Engineer, you were there. I wasn't. Suggestions?"

"Return to the ship," Gavin said. "I'll go ahead, beat you there, in case we're being tailed. We've got enough fuel to lift, and I've got some more credits from them. We'll load up, and we can make this rendezvous easily. Follow in a bit. Free Trades."

"Free Trades," Ana agreed. Dena put her foot back down and straightened up. "You enjoyed that, didn't you?"

"I surely did," Dena said. "And they did, and you would have if you'd been paying attention, admit it."

"In my younger days, yes. And you're right—it worked." He took her arm and walked her into the starport. "We'll go browse a store or two, then catch up with the engineer."

They entered, shopped, cleared the customs formalities, and took the monorail back to their ship. It didn't go directly but dumped them at a satellite terminal, where they had to take a shuttle bus. Because of a delay in the schedule, they caught up with Gavin again.

At their docking bay, they climbed off the bus, and walked around. Each landing pad was surrounded by a large Earth berm to contain any explosions, so they had to zigzag through the crooked access tunnels leading through the berm to the pad.

"I'll fire up the engines as soon as we get on board. I think Lee can jump us to orbit without a problem and set up the jump, but we'll need Dirk if we have to land."

"Getting to orbit is straightforward," Ana said, shoving a chain-link door open. "Computer can do it if need be. Just fire the engines and point up. Docking might be a problem, but they can dock to us if necessary. What's the chances of this being a trap, where they blow us up and steal the plans?"

"Same discussion as before," Gavin said. He stepped around a drain in the middle of the tunnel. "They want more of these plans, so we're the goose, and the plans are the golden eggs, like in that old story. They don't want to kill us."

The three of them exited the last turn of the corridor and walked onto the pad.

The large, clean, empty pad.

All turned to look at the number painted on the wall.

"Docking bay ninety-four," Ana said. "That's where we landed."

"Where'd they go?" Dena said.

"Don't know," Gavin said, keying his comm. "They're not answering."

"You were right, Engineer," Ana said. "I don't often say that, but this time, you were correct."

"About what?"

"That old story. The goose. The golden eggs."

"What are you blathering about, Old Man?"

"We're the goose. Don't you remember? Once they got the golden eggs, what happened to the goose?"

"What?"

"They killed it," Ana said.

***

Scruggs had been cleaning the heads again when she felt the ship lift. She put the cleaning tools away and headed for the control room. "Last time I'm doing that." She strapped herself into her chair. "I didn't see the others. Where is everybody? And why isn't Pilot Dirk here?"

Lee concentrated on her screens. "I have to lift us off to orbit and wait."

"Wait for what?"

"They didn't say," Lee said. "Just lift to orbit and wait."

"Okay. Now, how are we going to do this? Who's responsible now?"

"What do you mean? I'm not responsible. Are you saying I'm responsible?"

"Well, you have to shoulder some of the blame," Scruggs said. "You do take advantage of the situation, after all."

"I'm not taking advantage of the situation. I'm doing my best. How can you say otherwise? This wasn't my idea."

"I agree it wasn't your idea. It was mostly the others, especially the centurion, but you went along," Scruggs said. "And I've done a lot of the heavy work. But Engineer has done some as well."

Lee looked at Scruggs. "Only under protest."

"I didn't hear you protesting," Scruggs said. "You just waited for everybody to agree, and you went along."

"I couldn't. I shouldn't say anything."

"Why not?" Scruggs asked. "It's your ship, too, after all. Or part of it. You should do your share as well."

"I can't do it, I just can't," Lee said. "That's why I lifted the ship. I couldn't be a spy. I stood by before and let people do dishonorable things, but this time, it's too much."

"Be a spy?" Scruggs said.

"Yes. I left them there. I'm not going to help them sell those plans to the Empire. I stood by and let others do dishonorable things before, and I didn't intervene. This time I will. We're going to stay in orbit till those National spies leave. I can't be a party to betraying the Empire."

"Betray the Empire? Stay in orbit? Is that what we are talking about?" Scruggs said.

"That's what I was talking about," Lee said. "Lifting without the others. What did you mean?"

"I mean I wouldn't be cleaning the toilets anymore," Scruggs said. "Where's the others? What have you done?"

CHAPTER THIRTY-FIVE

"I'm working on it, Centurion, but the navigator has gone nuts," Scruggs said. She had retreated back to the lounge and called the others.

"Why did she take the ship?" Ana asked.

"She said she won't be party to betraying the Empire again," Scruggs said.

"Again? What did she mean again?"

"I don't know, exactly. She said her family has been kicked out of the Jovians, sent away. I'm not exactly clear why or what that means, something about a betrayal. She wasn't particularly rational."

"Can she hear you?" Ana asked.

"No, Centurion, I closed the bridge hatch, and the intercom is off."

"Private, we're stuck here," Ana said. "The pilot is on the Nat's ship as surety for our exchange."

"They took the pilot?" Scruggs asked. "Is he going to be okay?"

"He is for now, but I won't guarantee anything if we're not there to give them that data. The engineer has the remainder of the data on Heart's Desire. If we don't make that rendezvous, the Nats will be upset. They'll do something to the Pilot."

"Understood, Centurion."

"Get in there and talk some sense into her."

"Will do, Centurion." Scruggs headed for the locker where the weapons were kept.

"Reason with her."

"Yes, Centurion." Scruggs yanked the handle on the weapons locker. It held fast.

"Convince her."

"Yes."

"And if that doesn't work"—Ana lowered his voice—"you might need to knock her out and take control, Private. Can you do that, Private?"

"I think so. Well, I suppose." Scruggs climbed down to the cabin level and went into her cabin.

"You suppose? This is no time for supposing. Can you knock her out or not?"

"Oh, I can, Centurion, I can."

"Well, then. Do it if necessary."

"Of course, Centurion, of course. Just one thing."

"We don't have much time, Private."

"It's important, Centurion."

"We're stuck on the ground without a ship, the pilot's been kidnapped, we're carrying secret Imperial plans that could get us executed, and our navigator has gone crazy and stolen our only means of transportation. What's so important right now?"

Scruggs opened her personal locker and pulled out a boarding shotgun. She located a box of shells and fed them into the magazine. "I'm sort of a ground mercenary, Centurion. I don't know much other than fighting and some sensor work. If I knock the navigator out, who will fly the ship?"

The centurion's cursing went on so long Scruggs wrote them down. They might come in handy someday.

Scruggs was playing with Rocky in the lounge when Lee came back. "You throttled back the gravity," Scruggs said.

"I slowed our accel to almost nothing," Lee said. "But we're still moving. I don't like to be in total zero G all the time. Even light gravity helps a lot."

Scruggs lobbed a blue object over Rocky's head. He jumped up and caught it, then bounced over to drop it in front of her for another throw.

"He doesn't seem to mind the low gravity," Lee said.

"I looked up how to train a dog for variable gravity. They said play games with him as much as possible, so he'll associate low gravity with fun, and that, as long as they get practice, they'll learn to adapt." She lobbed the ball in a different direction, and Rocky raced after it.

"Where'd you get the ball?"

"It's a piece of rubber hose with some old socks wrapped on it. That was in the book, too. They said the smellier, the better."

"You gave up a pair of your socks?"

"They're Pilot's. He'll never know."

"Bit of a rebel, aren't you?"

"Well, I haven't hijacked any spaceships recently," Scruggs said. "Unlike some. You ready to talk about that?"

"I'm not going back," Lee said.

Scruggs faked the ball left, then threw right. Rocky fell for the fake. He stopped and darted his head around while he tried to locate the ball. When he saw it, he raced over and clomped it into his mouth.

"I saved your life," Scruggs said. "You call me sister. Can you at least tell me what's going on, why you did this?"

"They'll all be safe down there," Lee said. "I just have to wait them out. I know that Gavin left most of the data up here. They can get a hotel or something, just wait there. I'm on a four-day looping course. After four days, I'll cycle back and pick them up. They'll be fine. They can all drink beer for a couple and ogle the local women."

"Dena's with them."

"Local men, then. Don't try to stop me."

"Centurion says I should knock you out," Scruggs said.

She tossed the ball again, and Rocky snatched it. He veered away from Scruggs and dropped the ball in front of Lee. He crouched in a play bow, with the ball between him and Lee, his tail wagging.

"Good boy," Lee said. She grabbed the ball and threw it. Rocky chased after it. "Are you going to knock me out?"

Scruggs stood and stretched. "Think I could do it?"

"Maybe," Lee said. "Should I get my shotgun?"

"Would you shoot me?" Scruggs asked.

Lee threw Rocky's ball again. "Probably not. Would you hit me? Beat me up?"

"Let's say I did," Scruggs said. "Then, what? I can't fly a ship."

"So, I'm safe from you," Lee said. "I didn't think of that. Wouldn't have noticed if you hadn't pointed it out. Whose side are you on?"

"Our side," Scruggs said. "All of us."

"I don't think that exists."

Scruggs grabbed at the ball in Rocky's mouth as he raced by, and they played tug of war for a moment. "It does. Our side is the most important one."

"The Empire is the most important one," Lee said.

"We haven't been on the Empire's side since this mess started. We're sort of on the Empire's side and sort of not. But either way, the Empire's a long way away."

"I support the Empire. I'm a loyal servant of the Empire."

"Even after they kicked you out? Exiled you?" Scruggs asked.

"What are you talking about? I'm on—"

"That Rumspringa thing, that traveling and meeting men you mentioned before. I don't really believe you. I think you've been sent away to learn something or other. Sit, Rocky, sit."

Rocky had gotten aggressive with tugging the ball. He settled down and wagged his tail.

"Drop," Scruggs said. Rocky dropped the ball and crouched to chase it again. "Good boy, Rocky, good boy." She threw the ball and faced Lee. "I think the Empire exiled you, kicked you out, derated you, whatever. You're not on the run. I don't think anybody is looking for you, but you can't go back. You avoid all the other Jovians. Centurion and Gavin both commented that you should be seeking them out, but you're avoiding them. You stay on the ship a lot and just do your work. You spout off about loyalty to the Empire, but you didn't really do it. You didn't vote against selling these secrets to start with until you had this attack of conscience. Why'd you do it?"

"It's just—I mean, I don't want to talk about it," Lee said.

"Okay. It's not my thing. But what about the pilot?"

"What about the pilot?"

"They're going to kill him, Centurion says. He's on that Nat ship, waiting for the data. If they don't get it, they're going to toss him out an air lock."

Lee stood. "The pilot is on the ship? How? Why?"

"Don't know. But he's there. And if you don't turn this ship around, it's like you're killing him. You, personally." Scruggs scooped up Rocky's ball and threw it. Rocky dashed away. "So, where's your precious Empire now, when your friends are going to die?"

***

"So, you're Duke Friedel," Art-2 said.

Dirk had followed the Nat spies back to their ship. He'd made no attempt to escape, and they hadn't asked him any questions until they were seated in accel pods in their ship's lounge.

"I'm just Dirk now. I imagine my father has disinherited me at this point."

"Not the last time I checked. So, what should I call you, Duke?"

"Call me crazy if you want. What do you want with me?"

Art-2 kept the revolver on Dirk. "Are you going to cause me any trouble?"

"Why would I do that?" Dirk said. "We brought these plans to you. Met at your chosen meeting points. Gave you the samples you wanted. You didn't even need that gun to get me here. You just could have asked."

"If we asked you nicely you'd have come along?" Art-2 asked.

"We've done everything you've asked so far," Dirk said before he licked his lips. "Can I have some basic, please?"

"All this spy stuff making you thirsty?"

"No, you keep your ship drier than ours. Could you turn the humidity up?"

"I'll talk to the engineer and see what she says."

"Just talk to the pilot. Life support is run from the control room. At least, it is on freighters, and this looks suspiciously like a standard freighter. Don't you Nat people have better spy ships?"

"Sorry, we don't have the budget you Imperials have." The main engines fired, and they were pushed into their chairs. Dirk and Art-2 stayed silent for the next few minutes. Art-2 kept the pistol in his hand, even though the effort clearly hurt. Once they were clear of the planet, the drives cut out, and the pilot announced zero G for twenty minutes while they coasted.

Art-2 holstered his pistol and unbuckled from the accel couch. "On our way. Can I trust you not to try anything?"

"No, you can't," Dirk said. "First chance I get, I'm hijacking the ship, tying all of you up, driving us to the rendezvous, transferring the data you want, then flying away and leaving you with it. Because that's what I want." Dirk swung onto the ladder. "But first, some basic."

Art-2 followed him, and they sat in the lounge. Dirk pulled a glass of basic and pulled one for Art-2 without asking.

"Bottoms up," Dirk said.

"I don't like basic," Art-2 said, pushing the cup into its holder.

"Well, on your budget, you should be used to it," Dirk said. He drained half the glass. "Yours tastes different. Sweeter. Less citrus."

"Tell us about the plans," Art-2 said.

"What's to tell?"

"Where did you get them?"

"From a lady. A senior Imperial aristocrat."

"A pretty lady?"

"Very," Dirk said.

"So, this pretty lady just hands out state secrets to every handsome man she meets?"

"I sent her a comm after my . . . departure from Imperial space. Her husband isn't the father of her children. They're about to inherit the Barony. It's a big deal. If they're not his kids, there will be yelling. Noise. Might be a small war."

"And how do you know that the kids aren't his?"

Dirk drank his basic and raised his eyebrows.

Art-2's eyes widened. "You? Both of them?"

"All of them. Three. You'd think we would have learned the first time," Dirk said. "But I've always been a slow learner."

"But with genetic scans . . ."

"Genetic scans only matter if they're performed. If the kids don't join the Navy or the government, they'll never get scanned properly."

"Right, you stole these plans from a former lover. How did she get them?"

"They own a shipyard. It makes ships."

"Imperial warships?"

"No, ice cream-mining ships. Of course warships."

"Which shipyard? Where is it?"

"No idea."

"You have no idea which shipyard?"

"I know what it's called. I don't know where it is. I've never been."

"That's hard to believe."

"Do I look like the type of guy who spends his time at shipyards?" Dirk asked.

"Gotta admit, no," Art-2 said. "But this is hard to take. Are you telling the truth?"

"The truth?" Dirk shook his head. "Of course not. The real truth is that I stole a ship with a bunch of other criminals, and we stole a container of packaged fish as payoff for vandalizing an office in an insurance scam, and when we tried to get rid of the fish, we got attacked and stranded on some frozen planet and stalked by wolves. But instead of dying, we adopted one of the wolves, named him Rocky, forged across the ice, fixed our ship, discovered the secret plans by accident, then flew here to sell them to you, and here we are. Oh, and the wolf is living in our air lock now. How's that sound? Is that a better story?"

Art-2 laughed. "You're pretty creative. You should write fiction."

"Fiction has to make sense," Dirk said. "Reality can do what it wants. How long till the rendezvous so you can get your plans, and we can get our money?"

"We have to go into Jump," Art-2 said. "I've got a room for you. We'll lock you into your room for your own protection."

"My own protection?" Dirk asked. "What are you protecting me against?"

"Some of us had friends on New Madrid. 'Had' being the operative word."

"Oh, sorry," Dirk said.

"Sorry? That's it—never mind. That's what we expected."

The ship's address system bonged three times, and Art-2 tapped his collar to turn on his suit radio. He listened for a moment.

"There's a complication."

"What's that?"

"Your ship seems to be speeding away to the jump limit."

"That's where it should be going, right?"

Art-2 drew his revolver again. "In the opposite direction, away from the rendezvous."

CHAPTER THIRTY-SIX

Lee slumped in her seat in the lounge. Rocky was sitting on the floor, panting. Scruggs clambered back up from the cabin deck.

"Finest Amiens Brandy, Centurion says." Scruggs collected two basic glasses and poured a shot in each. "Bottoms up." She gasped as she drank it. "If that's the finest brandy, I'd hate to drink the cheapest stuff."

"Stick with us. I'm sure you'll get the opportunity to drink worse." Lee downed her glass without a change in expression. "It's actually pretty good."

"Well, Sister Lee," Scruggs said, "time's a-wasting. You going to kill your friend, your pilot, your commander, or are you going to turn around and save him?"

"We're not in the Navy. He's not my commander."

"You act like it."

Lee poured another round of drinks and downed it again. "Do you know how you get into Praetorian units? Or Praetorian schools?"

"I would assume you have to be Jovian."

"Pretty much. That's the basic requirement. You have to pledge loyalty to the Emperor personally. You have to promise to serve for twenty-five years. But that just gets you into the program, so to speak. Then you have to pick a school. I got into navigation."

"And Medicine," Scruggs said. "You're a doctor, right?"

"Three-quarters of the way there," Lee said. "Two years of navigation, three years of medicine."

"That's amazing. You're amazing. I've heard those schools are impossible to get into. They only take the best of the best of the best. The tests are supposed to be incredibly hard."

"The tests are almost impossible. Easy, Rocky," Lee said. Rocky had jumped on her lap and licked her face. "Extremely demanding, high stress, and there's a lot of them. Do you know how I passed?"

"You're awesome, and your natural brilliance shines through?"

"I cheated," Lee said.

Scruggs sat still for a moment, then poured her another drink. "Well, that's in the past. Whatever you did or didn't do on some old tests, you know your stuff. You've fixed up I don't know how many of us for how many injuries. And you navigated us here—look how far we've traveled. And you even flew the ship for a while during that stupid hand-over. You can be a pilot, too."

"Piloting is about reactions and quick decisions. Pilots have to decide quickly with incomplete information. Navigation is different. You have to take your time, make sure you do all the math. Same with most medical things. You can usually pause and collect more information. Different type of activities."

"That's nice, but you're good at both of them. We're glad you're here. We don't care about any cheating. So you cheated on a test. Big deal. This is the real world, and our real friend is going to die unless you get over this Empire thing."

"That's the hard part," Lee said. "I cheated."

"You said that. What does that have to do with Dirk dying?"

"Everybody cheated. All the others. Everybody in my class. They cheated or bribed somebody or something like that. It was expected. This whole Jovian 'guardian of the Empire's honor' is all a lie. All of it. The Empire is founded on lies."

Lee slugged her drink. "Can I have more brandy?"

"So, if you lied and cheated like the rest of them, how come they threw you out?" Scruggs asked.

"I told," Lee said. "I turned myself in. I turned the others in my class in. I had a crisis of confidence. I made a public declaration."

"What happened?"

"To the others? Nothing. To me? They threw me out. Got the psychologist to say I wasn't 'psychologically ready' for the Praetorian guard. Kicked me out. The only person who was on my side was my priest. He concocted this Rumspringa thing to get me out of there. Gave me an acceptable reason to leave. Everyone agreed to this polite fiction about me going out for life experience, when, instead, it's lifelong exile. I can't go back."

"So, what's the problem?" Scruggs asked. "Cool. You hate the Empire. Or at least the Praetorians. They hate you back. Let's get the pilot, trade these plans, and be on our way."

"But I don't want to believe that the Empire was like this. This whole time, I believed that, if I just worked hard, and stayed out of trouble, eventually, they'd fix things. Punish those others. Not just me."

"Let me see if I understand this," Scruggs said. "You believe the Empire isn't corrupt, that it's just misunderstood or something, that what you suffered from is just, and if you just wait long enough, justice will prevail?"

"Sort of."

"And in the meantime, your pilot friend is going to die," Scruggs said.

"Yes."

Scruggs got up. "Okay." She walked away.

"Okay? That's it?"

Scruggs stopped at the ladder. "That's it. You're my friend. I'm not going to hurt you. Either you're a duplicitous, cheating scumbag who tarnished the good name of the Empire and deserve what you get or you're a misunderstood patriot who tried to live up to the old ways or honor and justice, but the Empire is too corrupt to accept that and unjustly exiled you."

"I never thought about it that way."

Scruggs shrugged. "Sometimes, you need somebody else to explain your own life to you. I did. Didn't enjoy it."

"Want to talk about that?"

"Nope. I will say one thing, though."

"What?"

"Whether you're a misunderstood patriot in a corrupt system or the world's worst scumbag cheater, both of those mean that you can go rescue the pilot."

CHAPTER THIRTY-SEVEN

"I'm going to shoot her," Ana said. He spun the air lock door open and stepped inside.

"We need a navigator, don't we?" Dena asked, stepping in beside him.

"We need a lot of things," Ana said. "To get out of here, for starters. How much did this shuttle cost, Engineer?"

"Best not to ask," Gavin said. "Short answer is, almost everything that we had. All the money we got so far from the Nats."

"I didn't realize how much shuttles cost," Dena said.

"The engineer is just a particularly bad negotiator," Ana said.

"Or maybe it's that the centurion didn't remember to bring his helmet, gloves, and boots with him when he left the ship," Gavin said. "And you, Nature Girl, didn't have a skin suit with you. Buying all the pieces for you two set us back almost as much as the shuttle rental."

"You don't need that on a planet," Ana said.

"Well, we're not on a planet now," Gavin said. "We're in an air lock, waiting to hop over. Dena, are you ready?"

"I don't know. What do I do?"

"Stand still," Ana said. He ran his hands over her skin suit, checking connections, valves, and seams. "Now lean over and spread your legs," Ana said.

"Shouldn't you give me a kiss first or at least buy me a drink?" Dena said.

"Spread your legs so I can check your suit seams," Ana said. "The last thing you want is to have a leak there. And what's even more fun, because you don't do this all that often is that, as soon as I'm done, the engineer will be groping you as well."

"What if I find this . . . intrusive?" Dena said.

"I won't do it if you don't want," Ana said. "I'm not the one who will be getting a vacuum burn if these crummy suits pop. Ever had a vacuum burn, girl?"

"No, what's it like?"

"Skin doesn't like cold or heat. A vacuum burn feels exactly the same to you, as if we dragged a red-hot poker over your crotch and left it there till the skin bubbled. You up for that?"

Dena bent over and stretched. "Both of you check. Twice."

Ana did a quick, professional check of all her seams, and Gavin did the same. Gavin double-checked Ana, then Ana reached for him.

"Turn around." Gavin pivoted, and Ana patted him. His hands stopped at a boot. "Engineer, there's a problem here. This isn't quite set."

"They don't fit," Gavin said. "Not quite. It's not critical. The air I'll lose is minor, so it's not a concern."

"It's going to hurt like a herd of tabbos jumping on your ankle when the air leaks," Ana said. "Wait, these aren't your boots."

"They're the ones we bought. They didn't have the right sizes. These fit me, mostly. I tried them on Dena. They don't work on her at all. Mine are better quality and adjustable, so she's got mine, and I'll make do with these."

Ana regarded him for a moment. "You sure?"

"It's just for the jump over there, Centurion," Gavin said.

"We'll take it out of Lee's hide," Ana said. The lights in the air lock flashed. Dena just looked around, but Ana and Gavin pushed comm buttons on their collars.

"What?" Ana said.

"Which one are you again?" the shuttle pilot said. "The old grumpy one, or the smiling sleazy one?"

"Kiss my Imperial buttocks," Ana said.

"The old grumpy one. Got it. We're almost at zero-zero to your ship."

"Any problems?"

"It's right on the course your crew person said. They told me that I had to rendezvous with them, which I prefer, to be honest. You freighter people are notoriously bad at docking."

"The freighter people thank you," Gavin said.

"When the light flashes green," the pilot continued, "pop the outer hatch and be on your way. They'll be about twenty meters directly in front of you. An easy jump, and you'll be there."

"The girl's not outside very often, we'll need a tether and a jet pack in case," Gavin said.

"You didn't ask for one before," the voice said. "It's not part of the standard package, so if you want one—"

"This is the grumpy old guy," Ana said. "If you tell me, after all the cash we've shoved your way, that we have to pay extra for a tether, I'll come back in, grab the emergency fire ax, break into the bridge, slice your belly open, pull your entrails out, drag them down the corridor to the air lock hatch and into the lock, tie them off on the girl, then push her out to the far ship, trusting that your intestines will be long enough to haul her back with if she doesn't make it. And if we're short, I'll just keep pulling intestines out till I have enough distance. What do you say to that?"

Everyone waited, then the pilot said, "Lucky you. Today only, as a special deal, we provide tethers and jet packs, included in our regular package."

A light flashed on a locker, and the door popped open. Inside were tethers and jet packs. Ana handed them out and helped Dena put hers on. He and Gavin clipped to her.

"That was a pretty specific threat, Centurion," Gavin said. "Could you really use intestines as a tether?"

"Of course not," Ana said.

"Not strong enough?" Gavin asked.

"Plenty strong," Ana said. "Just not long enough. A person has maybe ten meters of intestines when you pull them out. We'd need two people's worth. We have to go double the distance."

"How do you know how long intestines are?" Dena said.

"Measured it out once," Ana said.

"Measured it out? On somebody who was dead?"

"Dead?" Ana said. "When we were done, sure. Lights."

The air lock light had flashed green. Gavin spun the wheel, and they left the air lock.

Dena didn't need as much help outside as Gavin and Ana gave her. But the two men were privately very worried about the suit. She'd never had to deal with a leak, and they didn't know how she'd react. Ana hadn't downplayed the pain— vacuum burns weren't dangerous, but they hurt, and some people panicked on their first one. He and Gavin had trained by being outside and having to take off a glove or boot under controlled conditions and feeling the pain. Dena hadn't, and right then was not the time to experiment.

They pushed off together and flew across the intervening space. Ana and Gavin spun to land feetfirst and held Dena between them. Once the mag locked on, they clomped to the air lock and let themselves in. Ana exchanged a few more insults with the shuttle pilot, but he stayed until they were inside.

"Dead people don't become regular customers," the pilot said.

They crowded the air lock but got in and pulled off their helmets. Ana didn't bother to remove boots, just spun the air lock and stepped out.

"Where are you, freak?" he yelled. "We need to have words."

"We're in the lounge," Scruggs yelled.

"Coming," Gavin said, climbing down to the lounge.

Dena followed.

Ana smoldered and racked his helmet and equipment. Then he followed them down the ladder.

"Where is that stupid freak? I'm going to beat her senseless," Ana said. He got off the ladder and turned.

Scruggs was there, standing next to the table. She had a boarding shotgun, and it was pointed at the three arrivals.

"About that," Scruggs said. "We need to have a quick talk before we go on."

CHAPTER THIRTY-EIGHT

"Not another hijacking," Ana said. "Your last one didn't go very well."

"I've been practicing," Scruggs said. "I'll do better this time."

"Are you going to shoot me, Private?" Ana asked. He folded his arms and narrowed his eyes but didn't step farther into the lounge.

"If I have to," Scruggs said. "But first. We need to talk about Lee stealing the ship before we do anything. Heel, Rocky."

Rocky was lounging in the corner, and he had got up when the others arrived.

"I don't want to talk. I want to hit somebody. Like her. And I don't believe you'll shoot me."

BLAM.

Scruggs aimed and fired the shotgun in one smooth motion. The frangible round whipped between Ana and Gavin. Gavin and Dena dove to one side and held their arms up. Rocky barked. Ana didn't move, even as the dust billowed. When the dust cleared, he touched his ear, and his fingers came back bloodied. A splinter had cut him.

"I guess I was mistaken," Ana said.

"You were. I wanted to show you that I'm serious," Scruggs said.

"No need to apologize, Private," Ana said.

"I didn't," Scruggs said.

Ana pursed his lips. "No, you didn't, did you? Well, you have my attention. What do you want to say to me before I pummel the freak?"

"First, stop calling her freak. She's a member of this crew."

"Stealing this ship kind of disqualifies her from that."

"The pilot stole it once. I tried to hijack it before. We've all stolen things. Are we crew members?"

"You didn't run away when the going got tough."

"Neither did she. She hid the ship when we got blown up. She waited till we were safe, and all there."

"She didn't come and look for us. Left us to die."

"Staying where we were supposed to be was the best decision. We all agreed. I agreed. I stayed with her. And you weren't helping at the time. You were out cold. The rest of the crew carried you."

"I didn't exactly volunteer to be put in that position," Ana said.

"None of us did."

"Why did she take off and strand us there?"

"She was in a bad position here. Some things in her past bothered her. We fixed it."

"Where is she?"

"In her cabin. I told her to wait there."

"So, she's afraid of me?" Ana asked.

"Centurion, you can be kind of scary. I'm afraid of you. We all are sometimes. But you see reason. Mostly."

"Let's hear your reasons, then."

"She didn't want to sell the plans to the Nats. Or the Confeds. Whoever. She panicked. But we talked about it. The Empire hadn't treated her well, and she needed time to sort through that. She's fine now."

"That's it? She's fine now? And we just forget this happened? That she ran away?"

"What's important is that she came back."

"You mean you made her come back," Ana said.

"Nope. She did it by herself. We talked, and she turned the ship around." Scruggs moved the shotgun. "We came back. We need to move on and rescue the pilot."

"You expect me to just forgive and forget? After pointing a weapon at me?"

"People point weapons at you all the time, Centurion. Really, it's just a way to get your attention."

Gavin laughed. "She's kind of got you there, Centurion."

Ana scowled at Gavin. "What if she'd hit me with that shot."

"Didn't you teach her how to shoot it? That would make it your fault, right?"

Ana turned back to Scruggs. "We just move on, then?"

"Yes."

"Not gonna happen, Private. Now, just step aside—"

BLAM.

That time, Ana cringed and reached for his other ear. His hand came away bloody.

Rocky barked again, then whimpered and ran up into the air lock.

"Two shots, two ears, Centurion," Scruggs said. "Next one goes in your chest."

"I've been patient up to now, Private," Ana said. "But we need to get this freak off the ship and go get the pilot."

"She's not leaving."

"We can't trust her."

"I vouch for her."

"And that's enough?"

"Better be. Otherwise, you'll have to come through me first," Scruggs said.

Ana squared his shoulders. "You think you can take me, Private?"

"Yes," Scruggs said, stepping back and pointing the gun up slightly. "I've been watching you. You've been teaching me. That shoulder movement was a cover so you could move your feet—now you're braced to jump forw—"

"She's right. You changed your stance."

"Not now, Engineer," Ana said. "Private, I can still take you."

"Only if I hesitate or if you surprise me," Scruggs said. "That's why I'm holding the gun the way I am. I've got my finger on the trigger, and I've stepped back. If you jump like you normally do, you'll try to slap the barrel down and to the side. I've got it high enough that, even if you manage to slap it, I'll still range on you when you push down, and I'm far enough away I can get off a shot."

Ana flexed for a moment. "You feel this much about the navigator?"

"Yes. She made a mistake, but we've all done that. We'll forgive her and move on."

Ana scowled at everyone. "Why did she do it?"

"It's a secret," Scruggs said. "We don't need to share it."

"I really need to know," Ana said.

"I keep your secrets, Centurion, and I can keep hers," Scruggs said.

Dena called from her spot by the wall. "Centurion has secrets? What ones?"

"Not now," Ana said. "What's your play here, Private."

"You promise not to shoot her or kill her or harm her. Just forget this happened. We'll move on and get the pilot, and just forget this happened." She flicked her eyes at Dena and Gavin. "Same goes for you two?"

"Not our fight," Gavin said. He held up his hands. "But you don't have to convince me."

Dena clapped. "This is better than any vid I've ever seen. I want to see how it ends."

Ana looked at her. "You want to see how it ends?"

"Sure. Especially if you get a little shrapnel. I don't want you dead, but you are a cantankerous old geezer. Getting shot a little might make you more agreeable, at least for a while. Go for it, Baby Marine."

"There you have it," Scruggs said. "Forget about Lee's problems. Or . . ."

"Or?" Ana asked.

"I pull the trigger," Scruggs said. "I'd rather not, but right now, we need a navigator more than a centurion."

"Huh," Ana said.

"Decide soon," Scruggs said. "I can't hold my trigger finger forever. And if I have to stop, I need the threat removed."

Ana looked at her for a moment, then nodded. "Okay. I agree. No comebacks."

"You have to be polite to her as well, Centurion. No insults, nothing like that."

"I will. I promise."

"Okay," Scruggs said. She pulled the shotgun up. "Everybody to their stations. We need to get to the jump limit. I'll rack this, brief the navigator. Then let's go get the pilot." She filed out of the lounge.

Dena looked around. "That's it? He says he promises, and you all just take that. What if he's lying?"

"He's a creepy, old, violent psychopath sometimes," Gavin said. "But he is honest. And I've never heard him break his word."

"I'll take that as a compliment," Ana said.

"That you never break your word?" Dena said.

"No, the violent psychopath. That's a good reputation to have. I'll go and warm up the sensors." Ana reached up and fiddled with his ears. "First time I've ever had parts of both ears blown off. Did you see that? What she did with the shotgun?"

"She seemed pretty crazy for a minute," Dena said. "Almost blowing your head off."

"Almost, but she didn't do it. What control. She got both ears and didn't touch my body at all. In a crowded room with a cheap shotgun. Outstanding shot."

"Did you think she was really going to shoot you?"

"Absolutely. If I'd gone for her, she'd have blown a hole in my guts. Outstanding." Ana wiped his eyes.

"Centurion," Dena said. "Are you crying?"

"Of course not." He wiped his eyes again. "She would have killed me. Shot me like a bug." He wiped his eyes again, then smiled. "I don't think I've ever been so proud in my life. I best get to my board." He headed up to the control room.

Dena turned to Gavin after he left. "I don't know how to take that."

"Take it as you now have two crazy psychotic killers on board, rather than one. But these crazed killers are your crazed killers, so sleep easy," Gavin said.

"What about Lee? Why did she run away?"

"You can ask her if you want. Or Scruggs."

"Scruggs isn't the only one with a shotgun. I'm not going to ask now. Maybe later. Can we trust her?"

"As much as you can trust the rest of us. As much as we can trust you."

"I saved you in the woods."

"And you nearly got us killed way back when, on Rockhaul."

"That didn't work out the way I expected."

"Things rarely do. Lee's decided who she's with now. Us. So have you."

"What do we do now?"

Gavin dusted some bullet residue off his skin suit. "I'm going to warm up engineering. We go get the skipper and trade some secret info for cash. You do what you like." Gavin climbed down the ladder.

Dena surveyed the lounge.

Rocky the Dog poked his nose in from the air lock, then trotted over. He looked up and wagged his tail when Dena looked at him.

"Adventure awaits, Rocky. Adventure awaits," she said and went and buckled in at the console in the lounge.

CHAPTER THIRTY-NINE

"Sandra Caroline Ruger-Gascoigne—she goes by Scruggs," Hernandez said.

"Ruger? As in Ruger Industries? The shipyards?" Subprefect Lionel said. He and Hernandez were sitting in the tribune's office, looking at pictures of the Heart's Desire crew taken outside their ship at Winsome Station that Hernandez had brought out in the latest intelligence files. Scruggs was prominent in the middle.

"The same," Hernandez said.

"She can't be the daughter," Devin said. "The daughter died years ago, some sort of industrial accident."

"Weapons test that went wrong," Hernandez said. "She's his niece."

"Let me guess," Devin said. "His favorite niece?"

"His favorite niece, his only niece and, other than the sister, Scruggs's mother, his closest living relative." She tapped her screen. "Word on the street is that she's in his will, gets everything when he dies."

"By everything you mean controlling interest in Ruger Industries?" Devin asked.

"What's she going to do with that? Controlling interest, I mean?"

"Sell it for a tabbo's feces pile of money," Hernandez said. "Or exercise control if she wants. It's an actual majority position."

"I've never heard of her," Devin said.

"The family kept a low profile. They go by Gascoigne, her parents. Father's name. He was a shuttle pilot, then went into academia. He's a professor now. Met the mother at some sort of Gala celebrating a launch. Sort of retired to one of those religious cluster worlds."

"Don't tell me they're those Church of the Word people."

"They're not, but they live with them. Father is quite a nice, thoughtful fellow, we're told. Mother was a semi-professional dancer. Quite the scandal when they got married."

"Is the family involved in the business?" Devin asked.

"The mother is very . . . spiritual. Crystals, incense type. Doesn't like violence. Or money."

"Flake," Lionel said.

"The father is a real academic. Teaches classes. Publishes papers. Jump drive theory, mostly. His hobby is . . ." Hernandez's mouth worked. "Can't pronounce it." She flipped her tablet around it and showed it to Lionel.

"Bou-gain-vil-le-a," he said. "What is it?"

"Type of flower," Hernandez said. "He has a garden full of them. Raises them and enters them in competitions."

The three looked at each other.

"Fine," Devin said. "Her dad's a florist, and her mother's a hippie. What's she doing with a bunch of galactic lowlifes? And why is this our problem?"

"The parents think she was kidnapped. They put out an alert for her."

"We're not the police. We don't go running after schoolgirls who get into trouble."

"We do if the schoolgirls are the heir to a fortune, and especially if her favorite uncle, who dotes on her, made a habit of discussing the latest changes he made to ships he was building."

"What type of ships does he build."

"Warships. Lots of warships. Imperial warships."

"What type of warships? Important ones? New ones? Secret ones?" Devin said.

"You tell me," Hernandez said.

"How would I know?"

"Cause he built this ship. The Pollux," Hernandez said. "Scruggs even got a tour, just before it launched." She tapped the wall. "Feels pretty new and important to me."

***

"So, Duke, you need to stay in your room," Art-2 said. "Just for the duration of the jump."

Dirk held up his hand, which was handcuffed to the bed in what was 'his' cabin. "Can't really go anywhere right now."

"Sorry about that," Art-2 said. "But stay here for now."

"Food?"

"Two meals a day. Packs."

"Not even hot food? No trays?" Dirk said.

"Nope."

"What if I need to use the bathroom?" Dirk said. "Can I do that?"

Art-2 unlocked the cuffs. "These can stay off, as long as you don't leave your room. But you have to be escorted to the bathroom. Think you can put up with this?"

Dirk rubbed his wrists. "I want this to work, remember. I'm not going to cause problems. What do I call you? I can't keep calling you Art-2."

"Yes, you can," Art-2 said. "This is for your own safety. The other crew are more suspicious of you than I am. Your ship is acting oddly. They were heading away and then they reversed course and met a shuttle in orbit. Now they're full steam for the jump limit. Any idea why they left the planet?"

"Why don't you ask them?" Dirk said.

"Not a good idea to get involved at this point," Art-2 said, stepping into the hall. "Fresher is down here. Follow me. We'll ask them at Sidecar, but for now, we don't want anybody to see the two ships together here. Or communicating."

"What's a sidecar?" Dirk asked, stopping in front of a door.

"Rocky system. Halfway to several stops on the main trade routes. We jump there, float, they meet us, and we swap info for money, then we head separate ways. You go back to the Empire or Papillon or whatever. We're two jumps from National space."

"If my spatial recognition is correct, we're also perhaps two jumps from Confed space. Aren't you worried about meeting a Confed ship? Or one seeing you trade things with a stolen Imperial ship."

"Stolen? Your ship isn't stolen," Art said. "We ran you at Saragas four, when we had that library incident. Your ship isn't listed as stolen."

"You probably didn't get the latest Imperial warrants."

"We pay good money for the latest info about Imperial warrants, and we courier it around. The Union of Nations isn't as big as the Empire, but we're efficient. We wouldn't necessarily do anything about a stolen Imperial ship, but we would know. That's useful info for us. You going in or not?" Art-2 indicated the fresher.

Dirk slid inside and took care of business. When he was done, he rubbed ship perfume on and stepped outside.

Art-2 sniffed. "I see you've decided you're even days for the showers."

"Old habits," Dirk said. "You sure my ship isn't stolen?"

"I don't know if it's stolen, and I don't care if it's stolen, but it's not listed as wanted, not in any database we have."

"Interesting," Dirk said. They walked down the corridor to his room. "Any chance of letting me out more often?"

"Nope. It's only a few days. You'll live."

"What about gym time? Or the lounge?" Dirk asked.

A new voice answered from behind him. "Come down to the gym. We'll spot you some exercises. Talk about old times together."

Dirk turned and saw a brown-haired man in a generic skin suit. His nametag said 'Jacks.'

"I know you?" Dirk asked.

"We served together," Jacks said. "On New Madrid."

"I don't think so," Dirk said. "I remember everybody from there."

"Oh, not on the same side," Jacks said. "But at the same time. Nice to finally meet the butcher."

Art-2 pushed past Dirk and got in Jacks's face. "Jacks, you know the rules. Back to your cabin. Now."

Jacks grinned at Dirk. "I'll see you around. We can talk about old times. About all those people you killed on New Madrid."

Art-2 stayed between the two till Jacks disappeared down the corridor. "We have to clear the corridors when you're out of your cabin," he said.

"So, your people don't know who I am?"

"We all know who you are," Art-2 said. "That's the problem. Some of us had friends at New Madrid. They're not happy with you. I'm not happy with you. I need you to get to Sidecar and do the exchange. So, you're staying in your room." Art-2 pushed the entrance button to open Dirk's door. "But if you don't stay in your room, you might accidentally-on-purpose fall out an air lock. Get it?" Art-2 propelled Dirk inside. "Enjoy your trip."

***

"So, we have to rescue the girl from her kidnappers," Devin said. "And they're taking her to this Sidecar system."

"That's what our agents tell us, Tribune, yes."

Devin looked at Lionel. "Subprefect?"

"Two jumps. We can be there in a few days. Course is laid in."

Devin punched his intercom. "Helm?"

"Tribune?"

"Execute, execute," Devin said.

"Right away, sir," the helm officer said. "Sir, I need one more."

"One more?" Devin grimaced. "Execute. And here's a spare execute just in case. Execute."

"Understood, Tribune," the helm officer said. Alarms rang as the Pollux changed aspect and accelerated.

"You didn't give any orders," Hernandez said.

"No," Devin agreed.

"But how, I mean . . ."

"They do what they like," Devin said. "Subprefect taught them that. I'm just along for the ride."

"But you're the Emperor's appointed captain, a Tribune."

"Matters a lot less than you'd think," Devin said. "Let's look at this video again. Show us that girl."

Hernandez cued the video, and they watched as Scruggs exited the Heart's Desire with several crew members. The pictures were clear but didn't play sounds. "As you can see here, she's being held hostage by the crew."

Lionel leaned forward and pointed. "Is she wearing a sidearm?"

"Of course not. They wouldn't give a sidearm to a prisoner."

A loader arrived with what looked like boxes of supplies and consumables for the ship, then piled it on the deck. Scruggs walked over to it. Three men arrived from another entrance and walked toward the pile. One carried a shock stick. Scruggs pulled a revolver and pointed it at the arriving group, who stopped.

"Sure looks like it's real," Lionel said.

"It's fake," Hernandez said. "It must be. They may have given it to her to make her feel less stressed. Make her feel more in control of her environment."

On the video, the men's leader made a rude gesture and advanced. Scruggs pointed the revolver at the floor and fired. Dust ballooned where the frangible round impacted the deck. Scruggs raised the gun and pointed it at the lead man's chest. He and his two friends held up their hands and backed away, then disappeared down the corridor.

"Nothing like a loaded weapon to reduce your stress, is there, Tribune?" Lionel said. "Makes you feel in control of your environment."

"Indeed," Devin said. "You said we're supposed to bring her back."

"Among other things."

"Well, when we're done here, there will be a kidnapping to deal with," Devin said. "Problem is, looks like we'll be the kidnappers."

CHAPTER FORTY

"Coming out of Jump," Lee said. The crew was in the control room, entering the Sidecar system.

"Scanning," Scruggs said.

"Pow, pow, pew, pew," Dena said. With Dirk away, she had been given his seat. She was pointing at things on her screen and making noises.

"What in the name of the Emperor's greasy big toe are you doing?" Ana asked from the sensor seat.

"Pretending to blow things up," Dena said. "This is cool. I see why Dirk likes it. Sitting here. All these screens. Spaceshippy things are fun."

"Spaceshippy?" Ana asked.

"Don't touch anything," Lee said.

"What will happen if I do?"

"You could mess up our aspect, misfire the thrusters, send us into a spin, waste fuel, drive us off course, crash into an asteroid."

"In other words," Dena said, "Nothing that can't or doesn't happen when Dirk is driving."

"But I don't smack Navy on the back of the head when he messes up, like I will with you," Ana said.

"Why not?" Dena asked. "Might make his piloting better."

Ana cocked his head. "You've kind of got something there. Maybe I should alter my approach. Navigator, bring us in."

Lee looked at Ana. "Talking to me now?"

"Only if necessary," Ana said. "And as little as possible."

"So, you hate me now?" Lee asked.

"Navigator, you're assuming that I stopped hating you before. Let's just say I want to keep things professional."

"You're not angry?"

"In the legion we shot deserters. But I promised no comebacks. I keep my promises. You're in no danger from me."

"Good to know," Lee said.

"Don't be so pleased. Space is dangerous," Ana said. "Things happen. Training accidents. Maintenance issues. Might come a time when you need to ask me for help. We'll have a different conversation then."

"You don't like any of us, do you?" Lee asked. "None of the crew."

"I like that pup," Ana said. "Rocky the whippet. He's smart. He doesn't get spacesick, stays out of my way, and he'll bite Navy if he gets a chance. I like that.

Where is he, anyway?"

"He naps on my bunk," Lee said. "I strap him in if we're going in or out of jump. How do you know what breed he is?"

"Had one when I was younger," Ana said. "Great dogs, whippets."

"Problem," Scruggs said. "Beacons. Centurion, multiple beacons. Lots of ships here. Five. Six."

"That's unexpected," Ana said.

"Not really," Gavin said over the intercom.

Everybody waited, but he didn't say anything else.

"Going to enlighten us, Punk?" Ana said.

"Of course, Old Man," Gavin said. "This is a trading entrepôt."

"Entrepôt? Is that another name for home of criminal-smuggling scum?" Ana asked.

"Yes," Gavin said.

The crew waited for further instruction.

"Engineer," Ana said.

"Yes, Centurion?"

Ana gritted his teeth. "Go on, please. Why are all these ships here."

"Perfect spot to swap cargo," Gavin said. "Let's say I've got a load of . . . frozen fish. And I want to swap it for a load of mortar bullets."

"Shells," Scruggs said. "They're called shells. Not bullets."

"Listen to you, Baby Marine," Dena said. "All proper names and all."

Scruggs stood, leaned forward, and stuck her face into Dena's space. "Stop calling me that."

"Make me."

Scruggs reached down and stuffed a finger into Dena's stomach. Dena exhaled with an oof. Scruggs grasped the cross-chest seat restraints and yanked the buckle as tight as she could, then sat back down. "Go on, Engineer," Scruggs said. "You meet in the dark. I assume you just swap containers?"

"Right," Gavin said. "You leave one port with twelve containers, you arrive at another with twelve. If you do your documentation right, you're cleared out with your old cargo. You can now deliver your shipment of 'fish' to your buyer."

Dena gasped as she tried to inhale.

Gavin continued. "Unless customs physically inspects the container, you'll pass. Even better, you head to the next place and put the container in storage. Somebody comes out and clears the storage out. What's that noise?"

Dena was trying to yell, but all that came out was "Whoop whoop." She scrabbled at her belt.

"Dena's just excited to be learning something new," Scruggs said. She reached forward and unbuckled Dena's belt. Dena choked a breath in.

"Well," Gavin said, "there's more to it than that, but the big thing is the authorities can't connect you with the other ship—there's no record of you being in the same place at the same time."

"But won't people notice that your trip takes longer that it should?" Scruggs asked.

"Maybe if they watch closely. But if you're careful, in a system like this, the jump limit is so small, you only add a day or two, and that's within the margin of error of most small freighters."

"And that's why we're here," Ana said. "We're going to swap a chip for Navy and some ready cash."

Dena let out a long, loud, exhale.

"There's that noise again," Gavin said.

"That's just the children playing," Ana said. "Can we ignore those other ships?"

"Yes. Lee should have the rendezvous coordinates. The other ships will see us head for an orbit to meet up with somebody. They'll figure we're smuggling like them."

"Why orbit?" Lee asked. "Why not meet in the dark?"

"Fuel. There's a lot of ice rocks here. If you're short of fuel, you can catch some. The moons of that gas giant are icy as well."

"We're not short of fuel."

"Everybody else is. We'll stand out if we don't drive in. They all do it."

"Been here before?" Ana asked.

"You know I have, Centurion, and you know I'm not going to talk about it."

"Are we all agreed, then?" Ana asked. "Head into orbit. Wait for that other ship to maneuver to meet us?" He waited till he collected enough muttered yeses. "Then we'll meet them in the air lock. Engineer, they'll expect you there. I'll be ready with a weapon. Navigator up front here. Scruggs, you're on sensors. Just watch the other ships. See if you see anything."

"Got it, Centurion," Scruggs said. "Can Dena help?"

Lee and Ana turned to face her, both looking confused.

"Huh?" Gavin said over the intercom. "Did she just ask Dena to help?"

"Yes," Scruggs said. "She should learn more ship side skills."

"You two get along now? Didn't you have a fist fight recently?" Gavin asked.

"She knows things I don't," Scruggs said. "She taught me some stuff about clothes. I'll return the favor. As long as she stops calling me Baby Marine."

"Well, Nature Girl, looks like you have a fan," Ana said.

"Centurion," Dena said, "how would you know, since you've never had one?" She glared at Scruggs. "Don't pull my belt."

"Don't call me Baby Marine, Nature Girl." Scruggs glared back. The two didn't break eye contact but then started giggling and didn't stop.

"What's going on up there?" Gavin asked.

"I'm not sure, Engineer," Ana said. He looked at the two giggling women. "But if I had to make a guess, I'd say 'adventure awaits.'"

***

250

"Run the board for me, tactical," Devin, the Lord Lyon said from the command chair.

The Pollux was at Battle Stations for ship-to-ship combat. Subprefect Lionel was at the tactical station. Every other station was manned, all airtight hatches were sealed, and their guest, Hernandez, was seated next to the communications console.

"Eight targets," Lionel said. "Heavyweight Items, the freighter with Ms. Ruger-Gascoigne onboard, has just cleared the jump limit and is heading in system. They are on a course that will see them orbit that moon, here"—He highlighted the largest moon of that gas giant—"as is that unidentified National fast freighter. Both could orbit and rendezvous. Primary is so small, and that gas giant is far out, so they can be in and out in a few hours."

"Are you sure it's a National freighter?" Devin asked.

"Tribune, we're not. It's National-built and recent, but it could be registered anywhere. Could even be registered in the Empire."

"But that's not the way to bet, is it?" Devin said.

"No, Tribune, it's not. There's a pair of Imperial freighters over here, orbiting this moon." Lionel pointed. "We put a telescope on them. They're transferring containers."

"That's four," Devin said.

"Two other ships, one National, one Confederation. We're calling them pirates. Both armed, both heading in from the jump limit. One matches a description that we got from an Imperial freighter that jumped away from a suspicious pursuer a few months back. Drive plume is the same, with ninety-eight percent consistency. The other is going just a little too fast for a regular freighter, so we figure they upgraded the engines. They look to be meeting up as well."

"Why would they do that? Those two don't get along."

"If they're pirates, they want to trade goods," Hernandez said. "If they've stolen from their own ships, they can't sell anything they picked up locally. They trade it to the foreigners, who take it far away, no questions asked."

"Any chance they're warships?" Devin asked.

"None," Lionel said. "We've got good imagery of both. Up-gunned freighters, that's all. And not freighters built to be converted to auxiliaries, either. Just regular ones."

"That's six. The other two?" Devin asked.

"Well, now," Lionel said, "those two are interesting." He highlighted two widely separated dots on the screen. "Neither have their beacons turned on. I'll bet that those other ships don't even know they're there. We can see them on passive sensors. Both are outside of the jump limit and staying there."

"Could we catch them?"

"Not from here, no. We might be able to swing around eventually, but they'd see us coming from a long way away, and they could escape any time they want."

"What are they?"

"This one here is a Confederation courier, according to the computer. This one here, we're not as certain, but it looks like it's a National corvette."

"Both warships? Are they supporting their respective consorts?"

Lionel looked at Hernandez and then looked back at Devin. "I don't know, could be."

"A couple other points, Tribune," Hernandez said. "They can see our beacon, and they can see that we're a big ship, but they're far away enough that they can't tell exactly what type of ship we are."

"They don't know we're a warship?"

"Not unless they put active sensors on us, and we'll know when they do that."

"We can jam them, Tribune," Lionel said, "but then everybody in system will know we're a warship. All these ships will go nuts."

"Not yet. Recommendations?"

"Slow and easy slide in system. Standard freighter acceleration. Aim for an orbit around everybody's favorite gas giant, and try to get there just after those two pirates are in orbit. We'll get a good look at everybody, passive scans will tell us what's going on, and if we're careful, we'll all be close enough to get a shot at everybody in system."

"What about the out-system watchers?"

"Let 'em watch."

***

"Understood," Lee said over the comm. She keyed off the comm and hit the intercom. "They say they'll meet us in orbit. They say Pilot is fine."

"Saying he's fine doesn't mean anything," Ana said. "We need proof of life. We need to hear from him. Make sure he's not dead."

"Just a question," Dena said. "If he's dead, does that mean the swap is off, or does that mean that we're just going to carry on regardless?"

"I'm sure he's fine," Lee said.

"I just want to know if we care if he's dead or not?" Dena asked.

"Not now," Lee said.

"That's kind of what I thought," Dena said. "Boy, we're turning into real mercenaries, aren't we?"

"It doesn't matter if he's dead," Ana said.

"Okay, it doesn't matter," Dena said. "But do we care?"

"Shut up, Nature Girl," Ana said. "Engineer, get that data chip ready. I'm going to oil a shotgun. Private, why don't you show your new best girlfriend that scan thing you do? Then meet me in the airlock with a shotgun." Ana got up and left the control room.

"Watch this," Scruggs said. "We pick one of the ships with a beacon." She highlighted the ship Dirk was in. "Read the beacon. See this? Says what type of ship it's supposed to be, what model."

"Okay," Dena said. "But they're probably lying, right?"

"Oh, of course they are," Scruggs said. "But let's find out how much they're lying. We look up the specs here." Scruggs brought up another screen. "Note down the length. Now, put the telescope on them, find the drive plume . . ."

Scruggs walked Dena through measuring the target ship's length via the telescope, then how to use the nav computer to determine what the length should be given in the course aspect.

"Centurion helped me build the program," Scruggs said, typing numbers. "It takes into account our viewing angle. And you see, two hundred forty-nine is what we're seeing, and the specs say two hundred fifty-three, so close enough."

"What if we measure wrong? Or if it's way off?"

"We check by hitting them with the radar," Scruggs said. "A directional pulse. Now that we know where they are, do a scan." She tapped buttons. "And it comes back two hundred fifty-one, so even closer."

"Won't they be upset about us hitting them with radar?" Dena asked.

"If they have a detector on, sure, maybe, or maybe they won't care. And we're meeting up with them, so why not? I don't do it for warships."

"That's pretty cool—you know that the beacon is at least close to their size."

"Right. Okay, you try."

Ana's voice came over the intercom. "Private, did you just ping the Nats?"

"Yes, Centurion."

"They noticed. They say don't do it anymore."

"Sorry, Centurion."

"Don't be. I hate 'em, and I'm happy to yank their chain. But they're bringing the pilot up to talk to us, so I want to hear that first."

"Understood, Centurion. Should we stop?"

"Of course not. Track those other ships."

"Got it, Centurion," Scruggs said. She clicked off the intercom. "Okay, you do this one over here . . . start by pulling the beacon. I'm going to suit up in case there are problems, and meet the centurion in the lock. You get ready with the radar."

CHAPTER FORTY-ONE

Dirk's intercom bonged. "Yes?"

"Up and at 'em, Your Dukeness. Your friends haven't forgotten you. They want to talk," Art-2 said. The door slid open, and he was there.

Dirk stood. "Thank the Emperor. I'm so bored that I was reading the ship maintenance schedules."

For the last few days prior, he'd had two bathroom breaks a day to deal with his protein pack meals, as much computer and video time as he wanted, and no comm or access to the rest of the ship.

"Our ship manuals?" Art-2 said.

"Yes. Did you know that hatch hinges should be greased with graphite quarterly, and that all the valves in the heads should be removed once a year and inspected for calcium deposits?"

"Missed that in my briefing," Art-2 said.

"Can't say that I'm impressed with a man who will put up with squeaky hatch hinges," Dirk said.

"Can't say that I care much," Art-2 said. "We're going to the bridge." He led Dirk to the central corridor to the ladder to the bridge. Dirk followed him and waited as Art-2 mounted the ladder. "Don't you want me to go first?"

"Why?"

"Aren't you afraid that I'll do something?"

"Like what?"

"Try to escape?"

"We're in deep space. Where would you escape to?"

"I could try to sabotage the ship."

"This ship? The one you're on? Full of the air you need to breathe? One thing I've learned by reading the record of your trial is that you are pretty unlikely to sacrifice yourself for the greater good."

"You don't know anything about me," Dirk said. "That's not the way that it was."

"Tell the rest of the universe. They probably care more than me." Art-2 pulled himself forward against the weak gravity until they reached the lounge. He pointed to a console on the wall. "Sit there." He leaned over and tapped a button on the screen. "We're back, Heavyweight Items. Here's your boy."

"Dirk here," Dirk said.

"Navy, sounds like you," Ana said immediately. Heart's Desire must have been close. "But it's hard to be sure. You could be an impostor."

"Centurion, when I'm back, I'm going to take that stupid stick you practice with and beat you over the head with it. Then I'm going to stuff it somewhere that you won't like very much and run a thousand volts through it. And after your eyes pop out, I'm going to polish them and hang them on your uniform like decorations."

"That's him," Ana said. "Have you been tortured?"

"No," Dirk said.

"You sure?" Ana said. "Not even a little bit?"

"I'd know if I was tortured, Centurion."

"Hey, kidnapper guy, you there?"

Art-2 stepped up. "I'm here."

"Did you torture him?"

"He told you no."

"You sure you don't want to? Just some fingernails yanked by pliers? Smack his face a few times? You still have time."

Art-2 muted the channel. "Is he for real?"

"Yes," Dirk said. "Unfortunately."

"Quite a crew you have there," Art-2 said.

"You have no idea," Dirk said.

Art-2 flicked the channel back on. "Well, he's alive. You ready to do the exchange?"

"Soon as you drop into your orbit, we'll be right here. Uh, you might have to dock with us."

"Why?" Art-2 asked.

"You've got our pilot, remember? Our current pilot is . . . experimenting."

Art-2 looked at Dirk. "You're the only pilot on board?"

"We're a lean operation," Dirk said.

Art-2 shook his head. "Understood, Heavyweight Items. We're hitting orbit in two minutes. Never mind docking. We'll brake till you catch up. Be in your air lock with the goods. We'll come over with the money and pick up the chips. Once we've examined it, if we like what we get, you get your captain back."

"Well, you could keep him a bit longer—what's that? You sure, private? Heavyweight Items out," Ana said.

"What was that about?" Art-2 said.

"He's training one of the crew in sensors. She probably screwed up something."

"I'm taking you back to your room," Art-2 said. "Suit up for EVA and be ready. But keep your door locked. The rest of the crew isn't as well disposed to you as I am."

***

"Turn that alarm off," Devin said. The bonging in the bridge stopped. "Who scanned us? The Confeds or the Nats?"

Lionel looked at his screen. "Neither. Your friend Dirk."

"He's in a freighter. How did he scan us?"

"Tracked our beacon, then pointed a radar at us. Good technique, actually."

"Did they know it's us?" Devin asked.

"Not precisely. But they know we're not who we're pretending to be. We need to do something."

"You confident about those pirates, Subprefect?"

"Totally. We can take them no problem."

"Helm, set a course flank speed for—"

"Tribune," Hernandez said, "do you recall your intelligence briefing I gave you last night?"

"Do not interrupt me on my own bridge—" Devin said. "I, I, Emperor's stinking armpits. Helm."

"Tribune?" the helmsman said.

"Set a course for the closest pirate. Thirty percent of maximum speed."

"Course laid in, nearest pirate, fl—say again all after course, sir?"

"Do not exceed thirty percent output on the drives. Not under any circumstances."

"Understood. Course ready."

"Execute," Devin said. An alarm bonged, and the gravity shifted as the Pollux accelerated.

"Well," Lionel said, "thirty percent speed. It's always good to go . . . sauntering in to bring justice to the Emperor's enemies."

Devin stared ahead.

"Tribune," Lionel said, "may I have a word in private?"

Devin glared at Hernandez, who smirked. "No. You may not. Maintain course and speed." He shook his head. "This is all my fault."

"Tribune?" Lionel said.

"I know Dirk. Even with everything else, he was a career naval officer. A professional. I'll bet he's got a crack crew monitoring everything we do. He's probably recruited a team of experts who are watching our every move."

***

"Let go of my hair," Lee yelled, "or I'll smack you out an air lock."

"Then stop ignoring me," Dena said, tugging again. "That other ship is fake." She had been yelling at Lee to stop closing the National ship and run out of the system. "That one out there that I scanned? It's twice as big as it should be."

"You're not a sensor operator. You're just some kid who's following steps in a book."

"And you're not a real navigator, are you? I figured it out. You never actually graduated from those schools, did you, before they kicked you out for cheating?

You're just faking it."

"I am not faking it. And how did you know? Did Scruggs tell you?"

"The cameras record the common areas, remember? I just looked up your conversation when we came back. I know all about your past now. You don't have a navigator's certificate or a medic's one."

"I went to school for years."

"But you didn't finish."

"I exposed a cheating ring."

"Or did you just fail out, and you hide it with some stupid story?"

Lee tapped her screen. "We need to rescue the pilot."

"We need to get out of here," Dena snapped.

Her screen bonged. She let go of Lee's hair and tapped on the display.

"You sure that ship's fake?" Lee asked. "You think you're that good a sensor op?"

"I'm as good a sensor person as you are a pilot," Dena said.

Lee tapped a button. "Brace. High G maneuvers in five seconds." She turned to Dena. "Any complaints."

"Nope. But look at this screen." Dena pointed. "Does that mean what I think it means?"

"That freighter that you scanned just tripled its speed. It's a warship, and it's coming in system. We need to go now."

Lee silenced the alarm, then tapped the engines to full output.

***

Gavin and Ana snatched the grab bars inside the air lock and hung on. Lee's sudden course changes slammed them into the wall, but their death grip kept them from bouncing around. The color drained out of Gavin's face as he punched his chin radio. "Navigator. Stop. That's too much thrust. Way too much. We'll break something."

"They're coming for us. The Imperials. We need to save the pilot," Lee said.

"We can't save the pilot if we snap in half," Gavin yelled. "Cut our acceleration."

Ana's face paled. "I didn't know that this ship could go this fast."

"Me neither," Gavin said.

"It's been a long while since I've had this type of accel," Ana said.

"Yeah? How long?" Gavin asked.

Sweat trickled down Ana's brow, and his breath came in gasps. "Too long."

***

"Imperial mansug grub," Dena said. The acceleration had pinned her in her seat, and she was having trouble talking.

257

"What?" Lee said.

She had both hands gripping the control screen's edges, holding herself steady.

"Problaks talking. Dark."

"Sorry." Lee punched a button, and the acceleration stopped. "Just turned off all the safeties."

"My vision is blurring," Dena said.

"Happens if you're not used to this," Lee said. She slapped another button, and the Heart's Desire pitched up.

"What's going on?"

"Just setting up for the retro," Lee said. "Hang on."

***

"You don't look so good, Centurion," Gavin said.

"That crazy Praetorian, I'll kill her," Ana said. "I can't keep up with this. Why do we need this acceleration?"

The accel stopped, and the ship spun. "She's going to run a retro," Ana said.

The ship finished its one hundred eighty pivot, and the engines reengaged.

"Engineer. Gavin, I think . . ."

"What is it, Old Man?" Gavin asked.

"I'm going to—"

Ana's eyes rolled up, his grip released, and he slipped, flailing off the grab bar and slammed into the hatch.

"Emperor's hairy . . . Lee? Dena?" Gavin slammed his chin down to cycle through radio channels. "Scruggs?"

"Yes, Engineer? What's with all the maneuvering? I thought we were on a simple approach."

"Don't know. Control isn't answering. Centurion just passed out. The accel got him."

"Understood. I'm on my way."

Gavin positioned himself with his back pressing into the wall and released the grab bar. The thrust kept him pinned him there, but he slid sideways to the hatch. Once there, he groaned and reached up to Ana. Pulling as hard as he could, he pinned Ana's head against a wall and checked his breathing. He saw the hatch wheel spin, and the hatch rocked but didn't open.

His radio crackled.

"Engineer," Scruggs said, "I can't open the hatch against the accel."

"Understood." Gavin keyed his radio channels. "Lee? Dena?" He cycled through a few others. "Lee? Control?" He came back to Scruggs's personal channel. "Scruggs, they're not answering me."

"Me neither. How's the centurion?"

"He passed out. He's pale."

"He can't take the Gs?"

"That shouldn't be it. He had to be under this much stress before. It must be something else."

"It is something else," Scruggs said. "The accel just made it worse. He needs his pills."

"Pain pills? Now?"

"He has other pills. Check his right outer skin suit pocket."

Gavin reached for the pocket. He yanked on the zipper but could only pull it a few centimeters against the acceleration. "I can feel a bottle, but I can't reach it."

"Flat bottle, with a pop top," Scruggs said over the radio. "Pop the top if you can and pull out a pill."

"There's no way he can swallow like this," Gavin said.

"They dissolve in his mouth."

Gavin braced himself against the bulkhead, stretched, then reached into Ana's pocket. He palmed the pill bottle, then maneuvered it close to the centurion's mouth but couldn't release his other hand.

"Scruggs, it won't work. I've only got one hand. I can't take a pill out."

"Get it over his mouth, pop the top, and shake one in, then. They'll dissolve, and he'll be fine."

Gavin positioned the pill bottle over Ana's mouth and used his thumb to pop the top off. "Okay, I'm going to shake some pills in there."

"Good, just one," Scruggs said.

Gavin shook the bottle. Nothing happened. He shook harder. Nothing happened again. He used his whole arm and banged the pill bottle on Ana's chin, and four pills popped out, bounced off Ana's nose, over his lip, and into his mouth.

Scruggs's voice shot through the radio. "Did you do it?"

"Yes."

"How's he look?"

"Fine. For now."

"Fine? What do you mean?"

"There's a bit of a problem," Gavin said.

Then the engines cut. Gavin floated up, caught himself on a grab bar, and reached for Ana.

The hatch door swung open, and Scruggs came in. "Let me check him." She checked his breathing. "His pulse is super fast. What did you do?"

Lee came over the intercom. "Anybody there?"

Gavin stood and punched the intercom. "Lee. Emperor's balls. Why didn't you answer? What's going on?"

"There's a warship out there. Just appeared. It's chasing those two ships on the far side of the gas giant. We need to pick up the pilot, so I decided to pick up the pace. We're set for a zero-zero with those Nat people. Let's get the pilot and get out of here."

"The pilot and our money," Scruggs said. "But Centurion doesn't look good."

"We'll talk about this later," Gavin said. "When will those Nats be coming aboard?"

A clang echoed through the air lock. Gavin looked out the view port and saw a skin-suited figure hammering on the side of the ship.

"Should be here right now. Um. Is everything ready down there?"

***

"Did you see that turn over for that zero-zero approach?" Devin said. "That's piloting. Whoever that pilot is, he must be from one of the best Imperial training programs."

"Or she must be," Hernandez said.

"Of course, of course. But that was a manual eyeball flip. They shimmied but corrected. And ended up zero-zero, what? Twenty meters away. Think you could do that, Helm?" Devin asked.

"I'd need some practice, I admit Tribune," the helmsman said. "Can I try?"

"No," Lionel and Devin said together.

"Sir," the weapons officer said, "in range of the first target in less than a minute. I have a firing solution."

"Um, hold there," Devin said. "Let me know when we are within one-third range."

"Sir? One-third range?" the weapons officer said.

"One quarter," Hernandez said. "Make it one quarter. No more."

"One quarter, then," Devin said. "One-quarter range."

The weapons officer opened his mouth to speak, then closed it. He looked at the subprefect. Lionel looked at the tribune, then at Hernandez, then back at the tribune. "You want us to take the range, divide by four, and only shoot when we're that close?"

"Yes," Devin said.

Lionel got out of his chair. "Tribune, I'll help him calculate that."

"Thank you, Subprefect," Devin said. "Once you have your range, you may fire at will. I want that pirate destroyed."

"Of course, Tribune," Lionel said.

Hernandez coughed. Everybody looked at her. She raised an eyebrow at Devin.

Devin's lips compressed in a tight line. "Subprefect. Make sure your first two shots miss."

"Tribune?"

"Don't hit him till the third shot. Aim close but don't hit."

"Understood, Tribune," Lionel said. "Targeting for a miss."

CHAPTER FORTY-TWO

Dirk had just finished checking his skin suit, donning gloves, boots, and readying his helmet when the alarm bonged. "Free fall, free fall." He grabbed a grab bar in his cabin and continued his check. The boots, gloves, and helmet weren't his, so he double-checked. Then he looked around his cabin and frowned. Out of boredom, he punched the door button.

It had been locked for the last few days, but this time, it opened. He looked at the open door, checked his helmet was clipped to his belt, and pulled himself out and along the hall. Seconds later, he was in the lounge. He snapped open the food cupboard, pulled two trays out, and loaded them up in the microwave. Sixty seconds later, he pulled the first tray out and scarfed it down. He didn't even sit.

The second tray went just as fast, but this time, he noticed it felt cold. "Not long enough, Dirk." He went back to the cupboard and searched. He selected one tray labeled "Soups" and another with mashed superpotatoes and applesauce. He punched the microwave for one minute, then punched it again. He thought about it, then punched it a third time.

He slipped into the seat and pushed his feet through the straps. Then waited. The lounge was empty and tight. Two benches and a table, microwave on the opposite wall, looking out on a ladder with two hatches for the bow and stern corridors.

A figure came up the ladder. It was the brown-haired man he had met earlier.

"Well, if it isn't Duke Friedel. And all alone. Shirleen? How long is Art going to be?"

"Don't know. Get up to the control room and see," a woman said from below.

"I don't think so," the brown-haired man said. He stood and stared at Dirk. "I definitely don't think so."

A slim black-haired woman in a skin suit pulled herself up the ladder. "Jacks, get yourself to the control room and get ready for the—who's this?"

"His royal excellency Dirk Friedel," Jacks said.

"Actually, I'm not a royal duke," Dirk said. "That title is reserved for—"

"Shut up," Jacks said. "I don't care about that name. I care about the other name. The Butcher of New Madrid."

"So, you're the Butcher of New Madrid," Shirleen said. She examined Dirk. "I thought you would be taller."

"I get that a lot," Dirk said. "Sorry to disappoint."

Shirleen pulled a revolver from her belt and pointed it at Dirk. "I'm not disappointed. Do I look disappointed? How do I look?" she asked Dirk.

"You look angry," Dirk said.

"I am. I am. Shooting's too good for you."

"Wait, Shirl." Jacks popped a stubby knife out of his belt. "This isn't a butcher knife, but it's good enough for a butcher," Jacks said and laughed. "That's kind of poetry."

Shirleen lowered the gun but didn't holster it. "That's a much better idea. And who doesn't like poetic justice?"

Dirk grabbed his gloves from the table and slipped them on. "Somewhat poetic, yes. Look, there's no need for violence here, don't you agree? Jacks, is it? And miss, how do you feel about attacking a prisoner?"

"Feels pretty good, actually," Shirleen said. "My roommate from bootcamp was at New Madrid. Biggest part they found of her fit in a handbag. That was your doing. I figure it's only fair that we cut you into the same-sized pieces as she was. Go at it, Jacks."

"I'll be quick," Jacks said.

"So I don't feel a thing?" Dirk said. He stood and backed away from the table.

"You'll feel a lot," Jacks said. "But we need to get you carved up and pushed out that air lock before Art gets back. He's a bit squeamish sometimes, but if we give him a fait-accompli, he'll just accept it and move on."

"My crew won't trade if I'm dead."

"I heard your crew didn't care much one way or the other and just checked in on you as an afterthought. But Art's over there right now, picking up what we need, so we won't have to test that theory."

The top microwave bonged, then the bottom one. "Excuse me for one moment," Dirk said. "My lunch is ready. Just let me get it. You people haven't been very good about getting me fed."

"We don't have time for this," Shirleen said.

"Even the condemned get a final meal," Dirk said.

Without waiting for permission, he reached up and popped the tray out of the top oven and then the bottom. He grabbed one tray in each hand and turned to them.

"My friends didn't," Jacks said, raising the knife.

Dirk threw the tray at him.

Jacks stuck his knife hand up and batted it away. It was only an aluminum tray, and it banged off to the side, clattering down the wall. But the food—the hot, boiling, overcooked food—kept coming. Jacks got a face full of boiling soup, screamed, dropped the knife, and grabbed his face with both hands.

Shirleen brought up her revolver and fired. Dirk wasn't quick enough and took a frangible round to his left arm. He yelled and banged back into the oven but flung the tray from his right hand at her face.

Instead of soup, Shirleen got a face full of hot mashed potatoes. She yelled and stepped back but kept her grip on her revolver. She fired at Dirk and missed.

He bounced off the wall and drove forward in the low gravity. His left arm hung by his side, but he was able to push with his right. Shirleen kept firing blindly, and bullets poofed off the deck and wall. Then Dirk hit her and grabbed her firing arm. They wrestled and rolled. She fired again and again, then the revolver clicked dry.

"Emperor's testicles," she yelled, rubbing potatoes off her face.

Dirk set his mag boots and latched onto the floor. With his feet as levers, he propelled her down the central corridor and slammed the hatch behind her. Jacks was sitting in the corner, cursing in a monotone.

"Sorry," Dirk said. His arm hurt, but the frangibles hadn't punctured his suit. He grabbed Jacks and pulled him up to the next level, found him a fresher, and shoved him in it. Then he leaned in and turned the shower on cold. "Get under there," Dirk said. "As much cold water as you can. Sorry."

Dirk pulled himself back into the central corridor and up to the air lock level. He climbed inside, pulled his helmet off his belt, and snapped it on. He made sure the internal hatch was locked and punched the Emergency Evac button. The outer vent dropped, and the atmo blasted clear. He spun the outer lock open and stepped out. The Heart's Desire was hanging twenty meters away. He set his feet, aimed for the far air lock, and pushed.

***

"Number one, fire," Lionel said. The weapons officer tapped a screen, and red lights flashed on various screens.

"Miss," the weapons officer said.

"If I wasn't a gunner, I wouldn't be here," Lionel chanted. "I've left my home and all I hold dear. Out in the dark, there's nothing to fear. Number two, fire."

"Miss," the weapons officer said again.

"If I wasn't a gunner . . ."

Hernandez looked at Devin. "Tribune?"

"Counting cadence for firing salutes," Devin said. "Keeps the timing the same. If those warships are monitoring our shots, they'll think we need a recharge cycle."

"-nothing to fear. Number three, fire."

"Hit. Explosion," the weapons officer said. The bridge was silent while he tapped his screens. "Target has suffered a reactor explosion. Completely destroyed."

"Set course for the second target," Devin said.

"One-quarter speed and miss twice?" Lionel asked.

"Yes," Devin said.

Lionel tapped his screen. "If I wasn't a gunner . . ."

***

Gavin and Scruggs maneuvered Ana's dead weight through the air lock hatch and into the ship. They laid him gently on the floor next to the air lock. Gavin paused to spin the lock closed. The air lock light flashed green, then red.

"Whoever is out there is coming in," Gavin said. "They must have been waiting."

"What do we do with Centurion?" Scruggs said. "He looks bad."

Lee came over the intercom. "That warship is chasing somebody else, but they can switch to us anytime. Hurry it up."

"Hurrying," Gavin said. "Take him down a level."

He and Scruggs carried Ana down the access way and strapped him into a couch in the lounge. They scampered back up to the air lock. The air lock door was just spinning open as they faced it.

Art-2 stepped through the door, brandishing a shotgun.

Gavin reached for his knife, then realized his heavy gloves covered it. Scruggs slapped for her holster, but she wasn't wearing it, either. They traded glances.

Art-2 held the shotgun loosely, pointing at them with one hand, using the other to flip his helmet off.

"You're that engineer fellow," Art-2 said.

"Right," Gavin agreed.

"And you're the pretty young girl who wrecked an entire library," Art-2 said.

"I didn't wreck the library. Well, not the entire library."

"You knocked over like forty shelves, spilled thousands of books on the floor, damaged a dozen busts of donors, knocked out the staff, and completely destroyed their signature sculpture."

"Oh," Scruggs said. "Sorry."

"Sorry? That's what I should tell them? Sorry."

Scruggs turned and fished in the locker behind her. She pulled out a book and gave it to Art-2. "I feel guilty about the whole thing. Please give them this."

Art-2 took the book in his free hand and examined it. "The Big Book of Model Railroading?"

"I took it without checking it out," Scruggs said. "I feel sick about that."

"You caused thousands of credits of damage, mostly destroyed a public building, and hurt a half dozen police, and you're worried that you didn't properly borrow a library book?"

"Taking the book without checking it out is stealing. My parents told me never to steal anything."

"Did they mention anything about smashing four-story sculptures?" Art-2 asked.

"Not specifically," Scruggs said. "I'll ask the next time I see them."

Art-2 hefted the book in one hand and the shotgun in the other. Scruggs and Gavin tensed.

"Did you know your air lock is full of frozen dog poo?"

"It's the latest thing," Gavin said. "What's with the shotgun?"

"Here," Art-2 said, pushing the shotgun into Gavin's hands, "you left this in your air lock. Vacuum is bad for firearms. I've got your money. Where's my chips?"

***

"Tribune," the communication tech said. "That second pirate ship is hailing us. They're saying they want to surrender."

"Are they really?" Devin said. "First question, who do they think they're surrendering to, and second, are we sure they're pirates? Subprefect?"

"In reverse order," Lionel said. "They are definitely pirates. They match the imagery of a ship that chased and fired on a group of freights six months ago in the Barslighton system. One freighter got away, two didn't. Nothing heard of the other two, overdue and presumed lost. Crew never reappeared."

"Comm, tag that ship 'Pirate-2.' Note their surrender attempt in the log. Carry on, Subprefect."

Lionel tapped his screen. "And I believe they know who we are. Which ship, why we're here, and who is commanding."

"How do you make that assumption?" Devin asked.

"We've been moving between nearby systems on anti-pirate patrol and your . . . private issues for months. Word gets around. We're the only frigate in this sector, and you've been mentioned personally on a couple of news items. They can extrapolate."

"Good supposition," Devin said.

"Also, they headed the message 'To Tribune the Lord Lyon, officer commanding Frigate ISS Pollux," Lionel said. "That's a hint, too."

Devin scowled. "You could have led with that."

"More fun this way," Lionel said. "But it is a little suspicious that they are that confident in their identification—"

Hernandez interrupted. "Subprefect, will those ships outside the jump limit know who we are?"

"The warships?" Lionel said. "By now? Absolutely. Their passive systems will have a good look at us, since we're not jamming. They'll know class and size, and if they have a decent warbook, a good idea of specs."

"They told them." Hernandez turned to Devin. "The Nats or the Confeds or both. They sent a directional message in and told them."

"Good to know," Devin said. "Helm, continue course and speed. Weapons, hold until within one-quarter range. Then fire."

The bridge went back to work, and the crew busied themselves on their duties. Hernandez looked puzzled. "What's going on?"

"We're going to destroy them," Devin said.

"But they've surrendered."

"Offered to surrender," Devin said. "Not the same thing. They offer, we accept. Except we didn't. And we're not going to."

"But they . . . international conventions . . ."

"They're not a nation," Devin said. "Just a group of vicious criminals who got caught. Imperial law is quite clear on pirates. Executed at once. Captain's discretion. No need for a trial."

"But," Hernandez said, "you're the captain. You have discretion."

"Yes, but nobody has ever called me discrete," Devin said.

"Coming into one-quarter range, Tribune," the weapons officer said.

"I'll do this myself," Devin said. "If I wanted to be a gunner . . . ?" He looked at the subprefect.

"If I wasn't a gunner."

"Right," Devin agreed. "Ready, weapons? Good. If I wasn't a gunner, I wouldn't be here. I've left my home and all I held dear. Out in the dark, there's nothing to fear. Number one, fire."

CHAPTER FORTY-THREE

"One case, money," Art-2 said. He had collected a case from the air lock and stepped into the Heart's Desire foyer. "Here's a receipt. Sign here."

"What?" Gavin said. "Sign?"

"Yes. How do you spell your name?"

"We're desperate criminals helping you steal plans from an enemy government, and you want us to fill out paperwork?" Gavin asked.

"There's no need for you to fill out paperwork," Art-2 said.

"Good," Gavin said.

"I don't do it that way anymore. My contacts always screwed it up. Caused no end of problems to sort it out. I fill it out now. You just have to sign."

"I don't believe this," Gavin said. "We are not signing anything."

"You know that, somewhere, somehow, this money is coming from a government. Government equals paperwork. You want the money, I need signatures. That duke guy called you Gavin. G-A-V-I-N." Art-2 tapped his screen. "Last name?"

"Crewjacki," Gavin said.

"Maybe it would have been smarter to give him a fake name, Engineer," Scruggs said.

"It is a fake name," Gavin said. "Wait." He turned to Art-2. "Do we get our money if it's a fake name. Do we—is? Is it? I mean it isn't. It's a real name. That's me. Gavin Crewjacki."

"Don't care if it's real or not, as long as the paperwork gets filled out," Art-2 said. "Drewjacki?"

"Crewjacki."

"D-R."

"No. C-R-E-W."

"Got it," Art-2 said. "You next, miss."

"Surreal," Scruggs said.

"That a first name or last, Ms. Surreal?"

"Scruggs, call me Scruggs," Scruggs said. "I meant this was surreal."

"I can spell that." Art-2 tapped a few screens. "Okay, you two, thumb here and here and here."

"This is ridiculous," Gavin said, thumbing the pad. "We haven't even checked the money. Wait, let's check the money."

Art-2 pointed at the case on the floor.

Gavin flipped it open. "What's this? Silver?"

"Platinum," Art-2 said. "Ten percent platinum. Gives you some ready cash. Rest is Confederation credits, as our agreement specifies."

"We didn't sign any agreement," Gavin said.

Art-2 reversed his pad. "Your thumb here says otherwise."

"Oh," Gavin said. "I didn't realize we agreed on Confed credits."

"You can always invoke the arbitration clause," Art-2 said. "Of course, you'll have to travel to Vega. That's where the arbitration is settled. And request the appointment of three arbitrators. Now, you'll have to provide and pay for one of the arbitrators yourself, one will be—"

"Never mind," Scruggs said. She took the pad and thumbed it. "We'll take it. If there's a problem, we'll fix it next time."

"If there is a next time," Gavin said.

"We'd like there to be. If you have more where this came from, we want it. We pay well, considering what we're getting. Speaking of." Art-2 held his hand out.

Gavin reached into his pocket and pulled out four chips.

"Four?" Art-2 asked.

"Lots of data."

"Well, I always say this, but this time, I mean it. Pleasure doing business with you."

"What about our pilot?"

"I left him in our lounge. Just in case of problems. He can come now."

"You never were going to 'validate' those plans, were you?" Gavin asked.

Art-2 shook his head. "We don't know how. We sent the first ones to some experts. They were happy with what you sent and asked for more. We figure some of these will be fake but enough good stuff there to make it worthwhile. And if it's not real, we'll come looking for you. Your captain, as soon as I'm back across, I'll release him."

Scruggs nodded. "I'll come with you."

A bang cracked, and they looked into the open air lock and out through the view port.

"Would that be your captain?" Art-2 asked.

"Looks like," Scruggs said.

"Weird. I left him locked in a cabin. Well, he's here."

"Let him in," Gavin said.

He closed the lock, and they waited thirty seconds while Dirk cycled in. Dirk opened the lock and stepped into the foyer. They all crowded back as he removed his helmet.

"You okay, Skipper?" Gavin asked.

"Fine. Just fine."

Scruggs hugged him in his suit. "We were all worried about you."

"That the truth?" Dirk asked.

"Nope," Gavin said. "Well. Some of us were. Well. One. Scruggs was."

"Nice to be missed. Did we get the money?"

Gavin hefted the case. "Right here."

"Well, Mr. Art the second. Our business here is concluded, then. Soon as you're out that lock, we're moving."

"How'd you get out?" Art-2 asked.

"You forgot to lock the staterooms this time," Dirk said.

"That's possible, I guess," Art-2 said. "Did you run into any of the crew?"

"Two of them. Jacks and Shirleen."

"Did you kill them?"

"Of course not," Dirk said. "When I left, Shirleen was going to engineering, and Jacks was taking a shower."

"What happened? Did they break into your room? Did they try to kill you?"

"You left the door open, so I went up to the lounge."

"And they found you in the lounge?"

"Yes."

"What happened?"

"Nothing much," Dirk said, blinking. "I fed them lunch, is all."

***

"Tribune, the two Imperial ships swapping containers have killed their drives and said they are standing by for inspection," the comm officer said.

"Good," Devin said.

"They are requesting to know how long till they are inspected, Tribune," the comm officer said.

"Find out how long their life support will last and then add a day and tell them that," Lionel said. "Let's see how they like that." He smiled at Hernandez. "See Lieutin—Colonel . . . Hernandez. See, as they said on Old Earth, sometimes you 'have to kill people pour encouragez les autres.'"

"That wasn't about pirates, that was about admirals," Hernandez said. "And aren't you a kind of admiral? Shouldn't it apply to you more than them?"

"I like her," Lionel muttered. "I hope she stays."

"What was that, Subprefect?" Devin asked.

"I'd like to stay put, Tribune, but we need to pursue those other ships," Lionel said. "Course, sir?"

"Suggestions?"

Lionel looked at the plot. "At thirty percent thrust, we can catch either the Heart's Desire, Ms. Ruger-Gascoigne's ship, or the National freighter they met. They've split and are heading on diverging courses, so we have to pick one." He played with the screen. "At thirty, we'll just catch the freighter."

"Well, I can't destroy Ruger-Gascoigne's ship," Devin said.

"And that other freighter has to get away, Tribune," Hernandez said. "And the two watchers have to see it. See at least one of these ships get away after being closely pursued."

"The Emperor's armpit," Devin said. "Follow the National freighter and target it."

"Two misses and a hit?" Lionel asked.

"No," Devin said. He settled into his chair. "Time the intersection to hit just at the jump limit. Miss with every shot." He glared around the silent bridge

Lionel sidled up to Devin. "What about Dirk?"

"He gets away, this time."

"This time?"

"This intelligence operation won't last forever. Once we're done here, we can go hunting again. I have other ways of finding him."

Lionel gave the crossed-chest salute. "The Emper—"—he paused—"the Empire."

Devin returned the salute but didn't say anything. He took a deep breath and then did it again. "The Empire."

***

"Welcome back, Pilot," Lee said. "Glad to have you back. Can we go?"

"Good to be back," Dirk said, stepping into the control room. "Let's get out of here before that warship catches us."

"Did you get the money?" Dena asked.

"You're in my seat."

"I've been using it. Didn't miss you at all. Lee did the driving. I'm doing sensors with Scruggs. Centurion handles comms when Lee's busy. And Gavin's in engineering." She pursed her lips. "And Rocky barks at strangers. What do you do here again?"

"Move," Dirk said. "Somebody has to drive while Lee figures out our jump. Lee, where's that warship?"

"It's chasing the National freighter. Chasing it slowly."

"Jump to where?" Dena said. "Where are we going? And you didn't answer about the money."

Dirk glanced at Lee's screen. "How about Papillon? It's close. It does repairs. We have some money to spend. It's not an Imperial planet."

"Every time we've been there, we've gotten shot or kidnapped or beaten up," Scruggs said.

"We need to get used to that. I think it's going to happen a lot."

"The Empire! God save the Empire! God save the Emperor! And the Empress!" Ana yelled before singing a marching song.

"What in the Emperor's name?" Dirk said.

Ana appeared behind them. "Pilotyou'rebackwelcomehomedidyougetthemoneyareyouokayletsgetoutofherebef orethatImperialshipchasesus."

"The Emperor's ear hairs," Dirk said.

"Sorry," Gavin said from behind them. "I was just checking him out, and he woke up, yelled, and began running around. He's gone berserk."

"Is he okay?" Dirk asked. "What happened?"

"Lee's maneuvering was too much for him," Gavin said. "He passed out in the air lock. He looked like death, then Scruggs had me give him some pills."

"I feel great!" Ana said. "You know what I need! I need pushups. Everybody do them with me." He stepped out of the control room, got down in the corridor, strapped his feet, and did pushups. "One, two, three—"

"What were those pills?" Dirk asked.

"Nitroglycerin," Scruggs said.

"For heart problems?" Dirk asked.

"Don't know. And some other stuff. How many did you give him, Engineer?"

"I tried to just give him one, but we were under thrust, so I gave him four."

Ana had reached sixty and showed no signs of stopping.

"What else is there in there?" Dirk asked.

"I've got the bottle, I took it," Gavin said. He pulled a pill bottle out of his pants. "Adrenaline."

"Not fatal, then," Dirk said. "It will wear off with no ill effects, won't it, Lee?"

"Ninety-eight, ninety-nine, one hundred," Ana said from the corridor. "And another hundred for the Emperor! One, two—"

"Yes," Lee said, "in a few hours or so."

Ana kept counting behind them.

"Maybe," she said.

Dirk took over the board to monitor the ship while Lee set up the jump. Gavin went to the engine room to "fix what the Praetorian broke." Dena went to count the money. Scruggs went to watch her. Ana went to the gym and said he was going to lift one hundred thousand pounds, one hundred pounds at a time.

"He won't hurt himself, will he, Medic?" Dirk asked Lee.

"Not badly. Well, not very badly. I've got the jump to Papillon dialed in."

Dirk hit the intercom. "Listen up, everyone. Those Nats told me that our ship isn't registered as stolen any more. We can go back to Papillon and get some repairs."

"And some decent food," Dena said.

"And some spare parts," Gavin said.

"And dog treats," Scruggs said.

"And better nav charts," Lee said.

"And Scruggs can return her library book," Gavin said.

"Huh?" Dirk said.

"Never mind."

"Hey, Navy," Ana said. "Is that warship still chasing us?"

Dirk looked at Lee, who shook her head. "It's ignoring us. Destroyed those two pirate-like ships, and it's chasing the National freighter to the jump limit but away from us."

"How come it didn't catch it and blow it up? It's a warship, right?"

"Aren't you doing weights?" Gavin asked.

"One-handed curls. On my way to my 100K. Seriously, why aren't we dead. They should have had enough speed to catch all of us. Or at least destroy all of us."

"They had to get close to fire, Centurion," Lee said. "I watched the battle. They got in close before they fired. Must be those new positron weapons. They were close. They missed a couple, but one hit was all it took to destroy a ship."

"How close?" Ana asked. "As close as those plans we took."

Lee tapped on a screen and showed it to Dirk. Dirk shook his head. "Almost bang on the range we saw in the plans."

"You told us that was too short," Ana said.

"I did," Dirk said.

"Seemed short to me," Gavin said.

"And to me," Scruggs said.

"We'll come back to you two and your surprising insights," Ana said. "But for right now, what I heard is there's a warship in system going suspiciously slow, with crappy weapons."

"That seems to be the case," Dirk said.

"And we're getting away?" Ana asked.

"Yes," Lee said. "Jump limit shortly."

"Let's get out of here and keep quiet about this," Gavin said.

"Nope," Ana said. "Let's get out of here and tell everybody about this. The speed, the range, all of it. We're supposed to tell everybody about this."

"What are you talking about, Centurion?" Gavin asked.

"That ship is acting exactly as those plans say it should. And we know something's wrong. But only cause we've seen that type of ship—or that exact ship—is it your friend the tribune, Navy?"

"It could be," Lee said. "Same type of ship, it looks like, and there can't be that many out here."

"So, they're faking it. Matching the plans. Cause somebody wanted those plans to seem to be correct, so somebody else will think Imperial ships are shorter ranged and slower than they really are. Any idea who that somebody might be, Navy?"

"That's a lot of somebodies," Dirk said.

"It is," Ana said.

"What do we do now?" Lee asked.

"Play our part. Go to Papillon. Spend the money. Talk about what we saw. Return a library book. And try to stay out of the way of whatever fleets are showing up to take advantage of that fake intelligence. There's a war coming."

An alarm bonged in the background.

"Is that the jump limit?" Ana asked.

"Yes," Lee said.

"Jump," Ana said.

☐

GET A FREE EBOOK

Thanks for reading. I hope you enjoyed it. Word-of-mouth reviews are critical to independent authors. Please consider leaving a review on Amazon or Goodreads or wherever you purchased this book.

If you'd like to be notified of future releases, please join my mailing list. I send a few updates a year, and if you subscribe you get a free ebook copy of Sigma Draconis IV, a short novella in the Jake Stewart universe. You can also follow me on Amazon, or follow me on BookBub.

Join my mailing list here:
https://BookHip.com/JTHTJK

Andrew Moriarty

ABOUT THE AUTHOR

Andrew Moriarty has been reading science fiction his whole life, and he always wondered about the stories he read. How did they ever pay the mortgage for that spaceship? Why doesn't it ever need to be refueled? What would happen if it broke, but the parts were backordered for weeks? And why doesn't anybody ever have to charge sales tax? Despairing on finding the answers to these questions, he decided to write a book about how spaceships would function in the real world. Ships need fuel, fuel costs money, and the accountants run everything.

He was born in Canada, and has lived in Toronto, Vancouver, Los Angeles, Germany, Park City, and Maastricht. Previously he worked as a telephone newspaper subscriptions salesman, a pizza delivery driver, a wedding disc jockey, and a technology trainer. Unfortunately, he also spent a great deal of time in the IT industry, designing networks and configuring routers and switches. Along the way, he picked up an ex-spy with a predilection for French Champagne, and a whippet with a murderous possessiveness for tennis balls. They live together in Brooklyn.

Please buy his books. Tennis balls are expensive.

BOOKS BY ANDREW MORIARTY

Adventures of a Jump Space Accountant

1. Trans Galactic Insurance

2. Orbital Claims Adjustor

3. Third Moon Chemicals

4. A Corporate Coup

5. The Jump Ship.

6 The Military Advisor (Forthcoming)

Decline and Fall of the Galactic Empire

Imperial Deserter

Imperial Smuggler

Imperial Mercenary. (Forthcoming)